Dark Horse

Also by Gregg Hurwitz

Dark Horse

GREGG HURWITZ

MICHAEL  JOSEPH

MICHAEL JOSEPH

UK | USA | Canada | Ireland | Australia
India | New Zealand | South Africa

Michael Joseph is part of the Penguin Random House group of companies
whose addresses can be found at global.penguinrandomhouse.com

First published in the United States of America by Minotaur Books,
an imprint of St Martin's Publishing Group, 2022
First published in Great Britain by Michael Joseph 2022
001

Copyright © Gregg Hurwitz, 2022

Set in 13.5/16pt Garamond MT Std
Typeset by Jouve (UK), Milton Keynes
Printed and bound in Great Britain by Clays Ltd, Elcograf S.p.A.

The authorized representative in the EEA is Penguin Random House Ireland,
Morrison Chambers, 32 Nassau Street, Dublin D02 YH68

A CIP catalogue record for this book is available from the British Library

HARDBACK ISBN: 978–0–241–40287–0
TRADE PAPERBACK ISBN: 978–0–241–40288–7

www.greenpenguin.co.uk

For Laeta Kalogridis, Billy Ray, and Shawn Ryan

The trio I'd want next to me
to go to war,
lead a charge,
or bury a body

and perhaps

The trio with whom
I have already done all three

When the devil wants to dance with you, you better say never.
— Immortal Technique

One hears only those questions for which one is able to find answers.
— Nietzsche

1. A World That Contained Men Like Him

Some men speak of angels and devils.

Some talk about their emotions or unbidden urges.

Aragón Urrea knew it as a battle between two parts of himself in the dead center of his soul.

Standing now at the edge of the spit-polished dance floor watching his daughter pinball between clusters of friends in her burnt-orange *quinceañera* dress, he understood that he could not be as bad as his reputation suggested because she came from him. Anjelina's hair fell across one eye. Her skin, smooth as satin. Tejano cheeks like her mother's, broad and defined. The impossible sweetness of her gaze.

A pair of rhinestone-studded high heels swung at her side, looped around her index finger, her head swaying to the band's cover of the Stones. *Wild, wild horses couldn't drag me awaaay.* He'd offered Mick Jagger ten million dollars to fly down here to no-fuck-where South Texas and sing it himself, but Mick Jagger didn't need ten million dollars or the reputational damage.

Aragón watched his girl glide across the maple hardwood, her hips and shoulders moving separately and yet in sync, an orbit of muscle and grace. As if music was a language that spoke through her body when she danced.

He turned his gaze to the boys and men watching her. As they sensed his stare, they quickly moved their focus elsewhere.

Anjelina's purity – her inner light – brought a familiar ache to his chest. That the world did not deserve her. That it would hurt her as it was designed to hurt all beautiful young women. And that even if he summoned the whole of the power and menace at his disposal to preserve her innocence, he would eventually fail, because innocence was destined for spoiling.

The one perfect thing he'd ever had a hand in creating, and now he was haunted by her very existence – her vulnerability in a world that contained men like him. The curse of every father who loved beyond logic, beyond reason.

Tonight was her eighteenth birthday. And yet she'd recut and altered her *quinceañera* dress, not wanting to waste money on something new, on something that would put her even more fully in the spotlight. She didn't want to appear garish in front of the other girls from Eden, this expanse of unincorporated land upstream from Brownsville on the north bank of the yellow-brown sludge of the Rio Grande.

Aragón had refrigerator-size blocks of shrink-wrapped cash stacked in various structures around his compound, so many that he had to pay teams of men to rotate them so they wouldn't rot or wind up chewed to a pulp by rats. And yet Anjelina preferred to alter a three-year-old gown so as not to show anyone up, even wearing a shawl draped over her shoulders and hanging down her front side to dress down further. He'd offered her Mexico City, New York, or Paris for the venue, and she'd chosen the community center right here at home. Tissue-paper decorations and a buffet served up by Arnulfo and Hortensia, the rickety couple who owned the local taquería and needed the business.

Aragón sat at the most prominent table with his aunt, who'd been both mother and father to him since poverty had killed his parents shortly after his birth in a Hidalgo County regional hospital – *Mamá* from an undiagnosed bladder infection, *Papá* from a knife in the kidney when he'd tried to stop a fight behind a Whataburger in Corpus Christi.

The band was in inadvertent uniform – alligator-belly boots, sapphire cowboy shirts, bedazzled vests, true-blue jeans and, of course, giant oval belt buckles featuring buckin' broncos or Indian-chief heads or bullshit family crests cranked out at the mall gift shop in McAllen.

With the faintest flare of a hand, Aragón conveyed his wishes across the dance floor. At the tiny movement, the lead singer stopped in mid-chorus, the music severed with guillotine finality. The singer mopped his forehead with a hanky, nodded to his compatriots, and the band struck up a Norteño number. The notes of the wheezing accordion nourished Aragón's very genes.

At the musical detour, Anjelina stopped dancing with her friends to set her arms akimbo and frown at her father with mock frustration. Then she broke into that life-affirming smile, impossibly symmetrical, impossibly wide, the smile of her mother, Belicia, who should be here at Aragón's side rather than languishing in her bedroom.

Anjelina flipped her high heels aside, and the men clapped and cheered and the women trilled and she was twirling and gliding, her lush brown curls washing across her eyes, gold locket bouncing just beneath her sparkle-dusted collarbones. A number of boys surrounded her and clapped, but none dared ask her to dance, not with Aragón under the same roof overseeing the festivities with stern paternalism and an aquiline profile worthy of a coin. And certainly not with his men stationed around the perimeter, hands crossed at their belt buckles, jackets bulging at the hips. The young men held their ground respectfully, waiting in hope for her to choose her partner for the waltz.

Slumped bonelessly in a chair at the periphery, the Esposito boy watched from beneath his mother's wing. Twelve years old with ankle-foot orthotics bowing out his sneakers on either side. His arms, wrapped in elbow-prophylactic braces, were splayed wide as if anticipating a hug. Last year Aragón had had him flown to the Cerebral Palsy Clinic at Cook Children's in Fort Worth so he could be neuroimaged and fitted with carbon-fiber prosthetics.

Anjelina slowed, calves fluttering in place, hips swaying, her movements tasteful if not chaste. Her focus swiveled to take in her options. The young men encircling her were pea-cocking, showing off their best moves, their best faces, their eyes shiny and eager.

But she looked right through them all to Nico Esposito. Then she drifted to the boy's table, the crowd parting. When she crouched in front of him, his distorted face lit up with joy. She took his hands and helped him to his feet.

Walking backward gingerly, she encouraged him onto the dance floor. He waddled nervously on his orthotics. She was six years older and a head taller, and yet Nico found a solidity to his ruined spine, rising to the moment because her atten-tion demanded it. The braces held his arms aloft, a natural strong frame for the box step, the Velcro straps rasping against Anjelina's dress until she adjusted for even that.

She held him firmly to aid his balance, creating the illusion that he was leading, and all of a sudden he was moving in her arms and she in his and he was beaming, freed for the moment from the prison of his body. The other young men overcame their envy and clapped along, whooping and pat-ting Nico on the back as Anjelina swept him within the throng of bodies. He was sweating, a sheen across his face, and yet his sloppy grin was unencumbered. They moved faster, faster, courting disaster right through the crescendo, and yet impossibly they finished the waltz, eliciting a hail-storm of cheers.

Leading Nico back to his mother, Anjelina eased him

down into his chair and crouched before him. Even across the dance floor, Aragón could read her lips: *Thank you for the dance,* guapo.

Nico's dark eyes glowed, his face flushed from the miracle he'd just played a part in.

Aragón realized that his own cheeks were wet. And yet he was unashamed. Like them all, he was blessed to breathe the same air as his daughter, to admire her and know that some part of her was his and some part of him hers.

La Tía reached across the table and took Aragón's hand. Her palm was dry, the skin papery. Arthritis gnarled her knuckles, but still she wore big turquoise rings on all her fingers. Over prominent wrinkles she'd applied foundation, blush, eye shadow, lipstick. Neither age nor ailment could dampen the spirit of a Mexican matriarch.

'My boy,' she said. 'Now you give your toast. Speak to your daughter.'

Aragón stepped forward, and the hundred-plus bodies in the community center took note. The boys in their cheap church clothes and the men in their polyester two-tone suits and the women flashing shawls of primary colors. All that beautiful brown skin and the scent of cologne in the air and everyone hanging on his next movement.

Facing his daughter across the dance floor, Aragón held out a hand, and his body man, Eduardo Gómez, materialized out of thin air to place a flute of Cristal in his palm.

Aragón began his toast. 'Today you turn eighteen.' He paused, caught off guard by the emotion graveling his deep voice. 'You become an adult in the eyes of the law. For me and your *mamá* – who wishes with all her heart that she could be here – this is wondrous. And yet also bittersweet.'

'I'm sorry, Papá.' Anjelina's eyes were moist, her slender fingers at her gold locket.

'You apologize too much,' he said. 'You must unlearn this now to be a woman.' He turned to the crowd, catching a glimpse of himself in the big window's reflection. Broad shoulders, undiminished by age. Big, bold features. Ugly-handsome and virile, like Carlos Fuentes or Charles Bronson. 'Our children grow up and our hearts hurt for it, but they must grow up.' He swung the flute back toward his daughter, the perfumed liquid catching the light, fizzing and straw-colored. 'They tell us it goes by so swiftly. Blink and they're grown. But the thing is . . .'

He felt the gravel gathering in his voice and paused once more to compose himself.

'It didn't go by fast for me. I didn't miss a single moment. Not when you were one breath old and I held you to my chest. Those first steps on the front lawn of the church, how you wobbled and fell and got back up again. Three years old in panties and sandals and not a stitch more, clanging pots and pans on the floor of the kitchen. Your first tooth falling out. I remember listening at the door of your piano lesson while you tortured yourself over the fingering for "Here Comes the Sun." Picking you up from cross-country prac-tice when you were all braces and a messy ponytail and that awful music you'd sing into your deodorant stick on the drive – who was it?'

Anjelina was hugging herself around her stomach, crying and smiling. 'Ed Sheeran.'

'Yes. Yes. Sheeran. And that bad haircut you got before your confirmation. Your first dance. That time you crashed your car –' He crossed himself. 'Our trip to Zihuatanejo during Semana Santa and the fight we had over that string bikini –'

'It wasn't a *string* bikini, Papá!'

'You're right. More like dental floss.'

Laughter washed through the room.

'Feeding you ice chips when your wisdom teeth came out. How you cried yourself to sleep the night we had to put Lulu down. And now your eighteenth –' He stopped, his eyes moistening. Cleared his throat. And again. The room waited for him. He lifted his gaze to her once more. 'I didn't miss a second of you.'

Heat in his chest. His throat. There was heartbreak in every rite of passage, in every living moment if careful attention were paid. Not a shattering or crumbling of the heart but a cracking open to accommodate *more*. More feeling, more understanding, more room for the cruelty of time without which there could be no beauty, no meaning. It was so much greater than anything he could convey here amid the cheap birthday decorations and fake wood paneling and the scent of cilantro and table wine. She had saved him. She had breathed life into him. She had civilized him, turned him into a human.

The community center was silent. The squeak of a shoe on the dance floor. Someone coughed. La Tía held a crumpled tissue at the ready. Could the emotion of this moment squeeze a tear from even her?

Aragón cleared his throat. Hoisted the flute. '*Hija de mi alma.* To you. The best person I know.'

The hall thundered with applause, as much from relief as anything else. He sipped, set his glass down, and the band struck up a lively western number. Anjelina wiped at her face and held her arms wide for him to cross the dance floor and meet her in an embrace. He paused to admire her. There was an impossible hugeness to her dark eyes that brought him back to when she was two, seven, thirteen. Maybe that's all aging was, an ability to see the past in the present, to comprehend the totality of a living soul all at once. Maybe that's what love was, too.

As he started for her, Eduardo grasped his biceps gently. As Aragón's right-hand man, he was permitted a casual proximity that Aragón's other men wouldn't dare attempt. 'The business we discussed, *Patrón*,' he said quietly. 'It requires you. We have him waiting in the next room.'

Aragón hesitated and regarded his daughter once more through the press of bodies. One of her girlfriends – Teresa, the chesty one – tugged at her hand, reeling her toward the dance floor.

Eduardo released Aragón's arm and tilted his head to the door behind them.

Aragón gestured to his daughter. *Be right back.*

Before she could respond, she was swept into the dance-floor mix.

He followed Eduardo out, his other men coalescing at his back. He had not nearly as many enemies as he once had, but that left plenty still.

Even at ten at night, the South Texas humidity hit him in the face like a tar mop. They'd taken Chucho Ochoa to the administrative office building next door. This was helpful. For what was to come, adjoining walls were not preferable.

As they pushed into the lobby, Eduardo hummed to himself off-key, another of the tics that had earned him the nickname 'Special Ed'. He wore cover-up to hide the acne scars pitting both cheeks, a particular the others noticed but didn't dare acknowledge. He had a tattoo of a gun at his appendix and upper groin, so when he let his guayabera flutter open, it looked like he had a weapon tucked into his belt. Right now the ink was redundant, a Glock 21 with a gleaming hard-chromed slide set in place over the tattoo like a saw filling out its outline on a workshop pegboard.

On one side of the lobby, Chucho slumped in a vinyl

chair as if he'd been soft-served into it. Chipped nails from working the sorghum fields, jeans with dirt stains at the knees, sun damage ripening his middle-aged face into that of a septuagenarian. A homely man with a hawk nose, folds of skin gathered like fabric around the eyes. His face quivered, on the verge of crying, and his hand jogged back and forth in his lap in something just shy of a tremor.

On the opposite side of the lobby, as far from Chucho as the room allowed, sat Silvia Vélez and her nineteen-year-old daughter, Celina. A pretty girl, shiny dark straight hair, full in the face and chest and hips. She was curled into her mother's side, feet drawn beneath her, her face pressed to the ledge of her mother's bosom. Her shirt was pulled up to reveal a strip of smooth flesh at the waist. There was a bruise around her right eye. Silvia looked as weary as Aragón had ever seen her, eyes sunken as if trying to retreat into her skull. She'd been working hard in Eden for the past five years, sending money back to her husband in Reynosa.

Like the hundred or so bodies next door, they were Aragón's people. All the residents of Eden were his people. They flourished in the light of his grace and withered in its absence.

Aragón's number three, Enrique Pérez, stood at the back of the room, hidden in shadow, thumbs looped through the wide leather belt along with the holster of his overcompensatory *Dirty Harry* S&W .44 Magnum. To augment his height, he wore lifts in his cowboy boots that pushed him to five-seven. A distended beer belly stretched his polo shirt, dimpled by his belt buckle. A bristling mustache sought to add gravitas to his sweet, soft face. He went by 'Kiki', which, on top of his partnership with Eduardo, had saddled him with the inevitable sobriquet 'Special K.'

Kiki held his head tilted back as always, either in an

assumed air of righteousness or to smooth out the rolls of his chin. '*Patrón*,' he said.

Aragón strode across the open floor between the parallel rows of hideous chairs. They were cheaply cushioned beneath cracked teal vinyl, connected armrest to armrest, suited to a hospital or a DMV. His men spread out through the room, positioning along the walls.

Chucho slid himself forward, elbows finding his knees, his eyes rising only far enough to take in the tips of Aragón's boots. Even at this small movement, Celina gave a little cry and burrowed further into her mother, her childish affect so at odds with her womanly body. Nineteen was such a confusing age for girls. Confusing for them and for men lacking restraint.

'I'm sorry, Don Urrea,' Chucho said, his voice soft with humility. 'I couldn't help myself.'

'Couldn't help yourself.' Aragón paced over, breathing down on Chucho's head until he lifted his gaze. 'You want to give her that power? You want to let a nineteen-year-old girl reduce you? A husband? A father? A son? Reduce you to a savage?'

'I'm sorry, Don Urrea. I'd worked a long day. She was walking along the roadside wearing a tight dress. Very revealing.'

'I am saving for new clothes for her,' Silvia snarled, patting her daughter's head. 'It was not a revealing dress. It was too small.'

'Please, Doña Vélez,' Aragón said. 'Allow me.'

Silvia silenced.

He turned back to Chucho. 'Did Celina ask for your attention?'

'It was impossible not to give it.'

'Impossible.' Aragón tried the word on, found it not to his liking. 'Did she resist you?'

Chucho folded his hands, stared down at them. 'Sometimes girls like a man to be in charge.'

Across the lobby Celina sniffled and covered her exposed ear with the flat of her palm.

'But she did not, and she told you,' Aragón said. 'Women should never be dominated. If you want a woman, you must earn her.'

'You're right, Don Urrea. I am ashamed.'

Aragón's chest filled with a cold-burning rage, a flame inside a block of ice.

'*Shame*,' he said. 'Men get to have this kind of shame. Do you know what a woman has? *Fear*. Fear that a man like you will come along, pry her open, and shove yourself inside her. That you'll blacken her eye, take from her what she doesn't want to give. That she'll have to remember the stink of you for the rest of her life. That she'll see you in the darkness of every room she enters before she turns on the light. That she'll need to fight you out of the memories of her muscles on her wedding night. That she'll go to her grave having learned that she can be reduced to a thing because some men' – and here he paused to give oxygen to his disdain – 'cannot help themselves.'

As Aragón spoke, Chucho deflated in his chair, shoulders bowing, arms curling inward.

'And,' Aragón said, 'she has shame, too. Not your shame. Your shame is a luxury. *Her* shame is a stain you put on her soul.'

'I'm sorry.' Chucho's words came warped from sobs. 'I'm sorry, Don Urrea.'

'Do you remember Juan Manuel Marín?'

Chucho broke now, his head drooping, the bumps of the vertebrae thrusting up at the base of his neck like knuckles. He shook and drooled a bit onto his knee. 'Please, Don Urrea. Please, no.'

'Do you remember him?'

Unable to muster words, Chucho nodded.

Everyone in Eden remembered. A few years ago, Marín had visited a similar violation upon a school friend of Anjelina's. By sunrise the next day, he'd found himself tied naked to a street sign in Matamoros, the south-of-the-border town from which the girl's family hailed. She had sixteen cousins still there, ten of them male and capable with hacksaws.

'You have two choices,' Aragón told the top of Chucho's head. 'You can greet the sun tomorrow morning in Reynosa. Or we will take all ten of your digits at the first knuckle.'

A wail escaped Chucho. It did not sound human.

'You will be allowed stitches.'

'Please,' Chucho sobbed. He reached for Aragón's hand, but Aragón held it limp until he let go. 'Please. How will I work? My family?'

'I will take care of Daniela and your sons. They will not want for basics.'

'No,' Chucho said. '*No no no.*'

'Not answering evil is the greatest evil of all,' Aragón said. 'I will not let you ensnare me in your sin. Choose.'

'Don Urrea, I beg of you —'

'*Choose!*'

Chucho jerked back, hair spilled across his eyes, chest heaving. He stared at Aragón, but Aragón gave nothing up. He was a wall of stone.

Chucho shook his head like a child, stifled a sob.

And then — slowly, slowly — held out his hands, proffering his trembling fingers.

Kiki reached in his back pocket, removed a pair of pruning shears, and handed them to Special Ed.

Urrea turned to Silvia and Celina. '*Señoritas,*' he said. 'You may remain or not, as you desire.'

Celina pried herself from her mother and rushed out, hand clamped over her mouth. Silvia straightened in her chair. 'I will watch every last second.'

'Then I will leave you in the care of my men, Doña Vélez.'

Chucho slid out of his chair, puddled on the tile, and curled into a loose fetal position. Advancing on him, Eduardo flicked the catch on the shears, and the spring-loaded blades scissored open with a sound like a plucked wire.

Aragón exited, closing the door firmly behind him.

The wind scraped between the buildings, drowning out the sound of Chucho's wail. An actual tumbleweed jounced along the corridor like an escapee from a Gary Cooper movie. Aragón paused to watch it journey out beyond the lights into the eternal dirt. He could taste grit in the humid air. This blessed godforsaken land.

He swung open the door to the dance hall and halted at the threshold. His breath froze in his chest. It was immediately apparent that something horrible had happened. The guests stood immobile on the dance floor, the band silent, instruments lowered. A napkin swirled above the dais, caught on a current from . . . what? There: The big window shattered, the rear door shuddering in its frame as if it had been slammed open. A trio of overturned chairs and the buffet table knocked askew.

'What happened?' Aragón's voice seemed to come from far away. For the first time since his childhood, he heard panic in it.

The guests stared at him wide-eyed, a statue garden. La Tía's makeup was streaked in neat channels down both cheeks, her expression glazed. Through the maw of the window, the wind howled and howled.

Aragón wheeled to take in the room. Everything was wrong. '*What happened?*'

Standing by the rear door, Arnulfo held a red handkerchief to his mouth. No, not red. Not originally. He lowered the cloth, his bottom lip split straight through, a flap hanging loose. As he spoke, blood misted over his cheap server's shirt.

'They took her,' he said, the words blurred through the wreckage of his face. 'They took our Anjelina.'

2. Supervillain Lair

No one noticed the battered cargo van at first.

Tinted windshield, no rear windows, just a slow-rolling creepmobile coasting into the parking lot. All that was missing was FREE CANDY spray-painted on the side in dripping letters.

Mexican day laborers lined the curb of the Home Depot, propping up the cracked stucco with their shoulder blades, fingers pinched around smoldering cigarette butts. Flannel shirts and jeans – always jeans – to protect them from prickly brush or splintering roof shingles or whatever a day of off-the-books work might bring.

June gloom had finally cooked off, the 6:00 A.M. Los Angeles sun spiking over the horizon like a spear through the eye. The air smelled of gas-station coffee and hot garbage wafting from the row of dumpsters.

When the van grumbled up before them, the men flicked away their cigarettes and perked up, assuming postures of swagger or humility. *Pick me, pick me.*

No movement behind the tinted windshield.

Exhaust leaking from the rattling tailpipe.

Finally the driver's door opened.

An Original S.W.A.T. boot stepped down onto the baking asphalt. The gringo attached to it had a quiet energy and a stillness that made the world around him – the half dozen workers stirring in their steel-toe Rhinos, the balled-up fast-food wrappers wagging in the gutter, the commuters lurching endlessly by on Van Nuys Boulevard – seem to flutter with nervous energy. He wasn't particularly tall or muscular.

Just an ordinary guy, not too handsome.

The Mexicans hooked thumbs through belt loops, drew back their shoulders, tilted their chins high with pride. *Pick me, pick me.*

The gringo approached the most amply proportioned worker, who had peeled himself off the wall. 'Do you speak English?'

The worker nodded, his double chin tripling. 'I do.'

'What's your day rate?'

The worker tugged at his droopy mustache. 'One hundred per day, my friend. That is for eight hours. Then twenty an hour beyond that. If you want more of us, I will handle the money.'

The gringo nodded.

The others turned their dark eyes to him. The youngest had a shiny scar on his forearm, likely from a tattoo's being removed with a knife. The man beside him wore jeans with patches at the knees that had been restitched so many times the surrounding denim had turned threadbare. He smiled kindly, showing off a front tooth chipped down to a nub.

The fat worker said to his peers, '*Nos está ofreciendo ochenta al día para diez horas.*'

The men looked down at the sidewalk. Cheekbones raw from malnutrition. Fake gold crosses glittering at their chests. They nodded, resigned. They were in no position to negotiate.

The kid with the forearm scar lifted his gaze to the gringo. '*Gracias, señor,*' he said. And then he forced out a bit of broken English. 'We . . . work hard for you.'

The gringo looked past the fat worker to address the others, switching to seamless Spanish. '*You five are hired. You will be treated fairly. I'll come back here at midnight to pick you up. I will pay you each one thousand dollars for six hours of work.*'

16

The men stiffened and looked among themselves. Except for the big guy, who glared at the gringo.

The gringo ignored him. Started back toward his van. Paused with his back still turned. '*Do not trust your friend here anymore. He is trying to steal your wages.*'

The gringo climbed into his van. And drove off.

At 11:59 P.M. the van returned to Home Depot.

The five workers hummed with excitement. They had not wanted to believe it was true, this magical offer.

There was nervousness as well.

What kind of work was worth one thousand dollars a day?

Scraping by in the broke neighborhoods of Los Angeles, they'd had plenty of brushes with perversion and vice. Back home in Sinaloa, they had endured worse.

They were scared, but they were willing.

They had mouths to feed in Culiacán. And *polleros* who demanded additional payment for bringing them here, who knew where their wives and daughters slept.

But the gringo had been honest with them. He had laid bare the truth of Gordo's deception. That meant he could be trusted. Didn't it?

The gringo emerged from the cargo van and opened the back.

Benches lined either side.

The men were familiar with claustrophobic transportation. The old joke: Why did Santa Anna take just six thousand troops to the Alamo? *Because he only had one Chevy.*

The workers climbed in.

The doors swung shut behind them.

There was a barrier between them and the front cabin.

They couldn't see where they were going.

As the van pulled out, they jogged on their seats like inmates on a prison bus. Heading to God knew where.

They rumbled across train tracks and then banked around in a wide curve, maybe onto a freeway. They did not know if they would be traveling ten minutes or ten hours. If they paid close attention, they might have realized that they were being driven in a massive loop. And then another. And then another.

One hour and seventeen minutes later, the van bumped over a curb and descended abruptly.

It parked.

The men heard the driver's door open and then close. Footsteps moving away. Now moving back.

The van's rear doors yawned open.

The gringo stared in at them. *'Come with me. Quickly.'*

They walked through a concrete subterranean garage. The lights had been turned off. It was very dark.

They ascended a brief flight of stairs.

There was a sign to the side of the door, but it had been covered with a square of cardboard.

They stepped into the building. It was dead-of-night silent. A lobby of some sort lay ahead, but the gringo immediately steered them down a rear hallway to a service elevator. Its doors rested ajar, waiting.

They boarded and rode up. The floor indicators were taped over. None of the men spoke. The gringo did not either. They might have ridden ten floors or thirty.

When the elevator stopped, they walked down a carpeted hallway to a door. The number on the door had been covered with cardboard as well.

The gringo unlocked the door.

The space inside was not visible. Construction tarp had

been hung on either side of the doorway, describing a narrow path from the entry through the interior. Additional sheeting draped the top of their labyrinth route, forming a low ceiling. The men huddled together and followed the gringo as if progressing into a coal mine. They walked farther down the makeshift corridor than seemed to make sense, the space unfolding and unfolding. Were they in a multilevel warehouse? A storage facility? A supervillain lair?

They reached an open space.

A series of huge windows composed a wall.

But they couldn't see through the glass; a few feet beyond the building, more tarp had been suspended presumably in midair, blocking the view in its entirety. A closer look revealed that the windows had been prepped. Drywall crowbarred away from the frames. Sashes, springs, and stops revealed. Panes ready to be lifted out. Several oscillating saws rested on plastic sheeting as well as hammers and chisels, calking guns and flashing tape, levels and drills, gloves of various sizes, and jugs of water and yellow Gatorade.

The gringo whipped a tarp off a mound to the side, revealing a stack of enormous replacement windowpanes. They looked identical to the ones that were to be removed.

'*The new windowpanes are too heavy for me to lift alone.*' The gringo stripped off his outer shirt, revealing a gray V-necked T-shirt. '*But I will work at your side until they are in place. I'll ask you to be as quiet as possible. I can handle the finish work myself.*'

The men could not distinguish the difference between regular glass and bullet-resistant polycarbonate thermoplastic resin. Just as they could not know that the neighbor who lived immediately downstairs was away for his August vacation. Or that they were not the first secret midnight shift of workers to be brought to this location to perform a highly specific task.

In teams of two, they toiled. Bruises, sweat, an occasional grunt, the crack of a knee.

The kid with the forearm scar – Rogelio – noticed scorch marks seared into the concrete floor. Growing up in Sinaloa, he knew what the aftermath of an explosion looked like. He waited for the gringo to pause for water and then asked him, '*What happened here?*'

The gringo took a swig, wiped his mouth with his forearm, and then looked into Rogelio as if scanning his very thoughts.

The gringo's eyes held a story he did not seem eager to tell.

3. Not the Best of Circumstances

Six Months Earlier . . .

Evan Smoak is midair and plummeting.

The overpressure from the detonation inside his penthouse was sufficient to blast him straight off his balcony into thin air.

Pebbles of bullet-resistant glass shower around him, gleaming bits catching the sunset gold.

The breath of the explosion blisters his neck.

After his last mission, an airborne incendiary device had flown autonomously to his bedroom window and detonated, reacquainting him with Newton's Second Law of Motion. A longer story, not one worth recounting now with the pavement waiting to introduce his spleen to his uvula.

He has eliminated all the threats beyond this blast. There is no one after him, no one left to neutralize. All he has to do to be free and clear is not die in the coming seconds, a possibility that seems increasingly unlikely.

Fortunately, the Lexan windows and discreet armor sunscreens provided sufficient buffer from the blast for his bones to remain inside his skin.

He'd had just enough time to rip the BASE-jumping parachute from its hiding place in the succulent planter on the balcony before he was swept off the twenty-first floor into thin air.

But he decides not to count his blessings just yet.

For one, he's only managed to get his left arm through the parachute strap; the other strap flutters tauntingly before him.

Two: He is rotating, the world a washing-machine whirl around him.

Three: This is not a reasonable BASE-jumping height.

He spends a precious quarter second on math. He has already fallen beneath the lip of his balcony. Twenty floors at a luxurious sixteen feet per gives him 320 feet, or approximately one hundred meters.

For a BASE jump, thirty meters is suicidal.

Sixty meters is idiotic.

Under the best of circumstances, one hundred meters is optimistic.

This is not the best of circumstances.

Neglecting air resistance, he'll hit the ground at forty-five meters per second or nearly one hundred miles an hour, a survivable impact if he lands on a haystack or a deep snowdrift, neither of which is very likely off Wilshire Boulevard.

Which means he has less than six seconds to figure something out.

Every inch, every instant, is life-or-death.

He'd packed the parachute with no slider around the lines, which means it should deploy with air-bag-like speed. That is, if he can even himself out, get the backpack properly positioned, and pull the rip cord.

The building's façade blurs by.

Was that the seventeenth floor?

No, the fifteenth.

Flattening out to add more drag, he threads his free arm through the flapping strap. No time to cinch, but he feels the vinyl bands seat against his shoulders.

Ground rush quickening.

He reaches for the rip cord, misses.

Ninth floor.

Eighth.

The rushing air roars in his ears, forces water from his eyes.

He grabs again, the steel handle tapping across his fingertips, dancing in and out of his fist.

The sidewalk looming.

His hand closes around the rip cord.

Fifth floor.

Too late?

Metal against his palm. Clench, yank.

Fooomp.

His shoulders are ripped upward. He feels the right dislocate, tendons screaming. His body is torn in two directions, his torso snatched to heaven, his legs sucked to hell. It's like being caught between the warring jaws of a great white and a pterodactyl.

He has precious little time to register the fresh hell of sensations before the sidewalk flies up and bounces against him, or him against it.

He hears a bone crack. The area around his patella goes numb. He is mostly sure his face is still attached to his skull.

The pavement holds the daytime sun; it leeches into his cheek.

A lesson branded into the base of his brain flickers to awareness: Pain only wins when you fight it. When you tense up around it, you put your muscles into spasm, lock it into your cells. If you let it in all the way, let it wash through, you show it that it doesn't own you.

He lets it in. Relaxes so his body is nothing more than soft flesh poured over his bones, melting into the pavement, softening, softening, softening. The pain thunders through him, a barbed-wire express train.

He says, 'Ouch.'

Or at least the vowels.

Across the street a white guy with ratty dreads and a crocheted rasta-cap is leaning against his VW Beetle, a vape pen suspended before the perfect O of his stunned mouth. A breeze riffles Evan's hair, bringing with it the skunky scent of weed.

Too late he tries to shed the shoulder straps.

Before he can, the wind fills the canopy, jerking Evan off his chalk-outline sprawl. It drags him six feet across pavement and bowling-balls him into a parking meter. He hears a rib crack.

He says, 'Ouch.'

The white Rastafarian jogs over. His eyes are rimmed red, as are his nostrils. He seems to be in shock, trembling like a Chihuahua. He looks down at Evan. 'Brah,' he says. And then, with more feeling, 'Brah.'

Evan finds a knee, the knuckles of one fist pressed to the concrete like a superhero landing from a great height. He rises, every last vertebra complaining.

Twenty-one stories up, a secondary explosion blows out another mist of bullet-resistant glass. Fire belches from the penthouse orifices.

The rastadude stares up. His mouth still has not closed. 'How'd the fire start?' he asks in a hushed voice.

With a groan, Evan shrugs out of the backpack straps, lets the wind drag the parachute away across Wilshire.

He says, 'Really, really small.'

4. Protection from Your Protection

The van arrived back at Home Depot with the rising dawn. To the east, pale blues and lavenders suffused the clouds where mountain met sky. Los Angeles is most alluring as it bookends the day. A city with a million secrets to keep and a million promises to break, so much deceit and ugliness hidden beneath that violet splendor.

There Gordo stood, alone in front of the stucco wall as if he'd never left. It was like a police lineup once the innocent suspects cleared out. He glared at the approaching van as it coasted to a stop just past him.

The gringo got out and swung open the rear doors.

As the workers emerged, he handed out rubber-banded rolls of hundred-dollar bills and thanked them for their work. They nodded and smiled, showing off questionable dentistry and a kind of gratitude that no school can teach.

As the others drifted off, Rogelio paused and scratched at the shiny patch scarring his forearm. '*The explosion,*' he said. '*It targeted the gas line?*'

The gringo studied him. '*Why do you think that?*'

Rogelio said, '*The dress factory I worked at in Culiacán as a boy met the same fate. The owner was a courteous man.*' He lifted the cross pendant and pressed it to his lips – respect for the departed. '*But at some point you can only pay so much protection. And who do you turn to when you need protection from your protection?*'

'*That's a fine question.*'

Over by the building, Gordo started bickering with the other workers, but the gringo paid them no mind.

'*This work we did for you . . .*' Rogelio scratched at his scar some more, his eyes lowered. He held the roll of money at his hip; he still hadn't put it into his pocket. '*I'd like to know that it isn't bad work. That it won't hurt anyone. That we didn't help you if . . .*'

'*If what?*'

'*If you are a bad man.*' Rogelio wet his lips. '*Are you a bad man or a good man?*'

'*I suppose both.*'

'*What is it you do?*'

'*I help people who are desperate. Who have nowhere else to turn. Who are powerless.*'

'*Do* you *have power?*'

The gringo thought about it. '*I don't know if I have it. But when I am trying to help others, sometimes it finds me.*'

Only now did Rogelio pocket the cash. But he remained where he was, staring down at the toe of his boot, which he ground into the asphalt as if crushing a bug. Weighing something.

The gringo waited patiently, and finally Rogelio spoke. '*I know someone who needs help like this. He is desperate. He has nowhere else to turn. But he is not powerless, my friend. Far, far from it.*'

The gringo looked at the sunrise, the light turning his face bronze. '*Is he a bad man or a good man?*'

'*He is both. Like you.*'

'*What he needs help with – his cause. Is it just?*'

'*It is the most just cause I have ever known.*'

The gringo looked at Rogelio. Rogelio looked back at him.

The gringo thought about how hard the kid had toiled. How he'd refused to pocket the money until he'd confirmed that the work he'd done wasn't dirty.

The gringo said, '1-855-2-NOWHERE.'

As he walked away, Rogelio called after him. '*What's that?*'

The gringo paused at the driver's door. '*When your friend calls, he will find out.*'

5. Unsafe Asset

Seven thousand empty square feet.

Well, not *entirely* empty.

The open floorplan of Evan's penthouse in the Castle Heights Residential Tower made the sparseness seem even more sparse.

The workout stations, training mats, and furniture of the great room had been incinerated in the blast, but the freshly restored fireplace rose like a tree from the middle of the poured-concrete plain. A few pillars had made their way back into existence, along with a steel staircase that spiraled up to a partially rehabbed loft with empty bookshelves that still smelled of sawdust and wood glue.

The kitchen had come along the furthest: gunmetal-gray countertops, brushed-nickel fixtures, and a broad center island at which Evan ate his meals alone. Bluish plastic wrap colored the face of the unused oven and limned the edge of the dishwasher. About half of the mirrored subway tiles composing the backsplash had been laid in place, trailing off like an abandoned Lego project.

Last week's work had seen the return of his glass vodka freezer room, though its shelves had yet to be fully replenished. And the week before had brought the restoration of the living wall, a vertical garden that thrust up from the floor. At the moment it was little more than a rise of caked soil and buried seeds fed by drip irrigation, but one day it would sprout mint and basil, peppers and chamomile.

Enormous floor-to-ceiling windows opened the corner

penthouse to the world, downtown looming twelve miles to the east, Century City high-rises taking a bite out of the sky to the south. Twenty-one stories below, constipated traffic worked its way through the infamous Angeleno congestion, automotive peristalsis encouraged by horns and expletives.

Evan finished enhancing the bullet-resistant Lexan windows with sensors that detected shattering glass, approaching foreign objects, and any significant compression sound signatures from the quartz rocks layering the balconies. He stepped away from the transparent wall, wiped his forehead, and stared at the vast interior space.

It was cold. Lifeless.

Safe.

Not nearly as tidy as usual, with stray tools, tarps, and the occasional plastic water bottle left over by the legitimate construction crew or one of the clandestine night-shift workers. The discreet armor sunscreens, a fetching shade of periwinkle, still had to be hung. They lay on the floor, rippled like chain mail. Composed of a rare titanium variant woven together in rings, the shades provided an additional layer of protection from sniper rounds or explosive devices, a feature that had been put to the test right before his grudging defenestration.

The elaborate alarm system had been installed and its firmware updated. As well as the front door that hid interlocking steel security bars and a water-filled core that dispersed the effect of a battering ram. The wood façade matched every other residential door in the building and ostensibly complied with code, a veneer sufficient to keep Hugh Walters, the officious president of the homeowners' association, at bay.

Evan had managed to swap out the standard half-inch residential Sheetrock with five and eight-tenths commercial grade for soundproofing and protective rigidity in the event someone gave up on the front door and tried to come through the walls themselves with a fire ax, a chain saw, or Wile E. Coyote shot out of a cannon. A coat of paint layered the unsanctioned upgrade out of sight.

Why was he going through all this rather than finding a new burrow or drifting from city to city as he had before, anonymous and solitary? This stretch of floor, the taste of this air, the views from these windows, they'd become a part of him. He'd never understood what it meant to have a place in the universe, and now that he had one, he was loath to give it up.

Then there was Mia Hall, nine floors down. Single mother, district attorney, beauty mark at her temple. And her son, Peter, on the cusp of turning ten years old. With a raspy voice and charcoal eyes, he was innocent and mischievous, the kind of boy Evan might have been in another life. For years Evan and Mia had skirted the issue of what Evan actually did, a dance made necessary by the fact that what Mia actually did was prosecute people who – like him – broke the law.

He shook off the thought. He wasn't intent on staying here for Mia and Peter. It was the view. His fortress. The Vault.

The Fourth Commandment: *Never make it personal.*

Evan crossed to the kitchen, his boots leaving dust impressions on the polished concrete. He soothed the OCD compulsion gripping his brain stem. The footprints could be swept up and cleaned, any trace of his movement eliminated. The rebuild had his mind on permanent alert, his visual scanning for imperfections at a high level. Everywhere he looked, there were splinters to sand and scratches to buff and trash to haul, a mess that constantly replenished itself. All these signs of life and human imperfection were hard to bear for a man who preferred to leave no trace, who'd always kept his refuge here above the city more spotless and stainless than a mausoleum.

On the broad island, his RoamZone rested on its stand, charging and ready.

Of everything in the penthouse, the encrypted phone was the most important.

The process was simple. After he completed a mission, the only payment he asked was that his client find someone else in an impossible situation, someone who had nowhere else to turn. That they pass along Evan's number. The new client dialed 1-855-2-NOWHERE as had the preceding client and every client before.

The call would be converted into digital packets, encrypted, shot through the Internet, and routed through more than a dozen virtual-private-network tunnels in nations ranging from Andorra to Zambia. The RoamZone would ring. He would answer.

The first question was the same every time.

Do you need my help?

As a government assassin pulled from a foster home at the age of twelve and trained in the deep-black Orphan Program, Evan had an arsenal of skills at his disposal that few people on the planet could match. He'd been raised by a handler and father figure who'd bucked procedure and tradition to keep Evan's sense of morality intact. Jack Johns had forged him into a weapon while never letting him forget that the hard part wasn't being a killer. The hard part was staying human.

For about a decade, Evan had neutralized targets unofficially designated by the Department of Defense. He did not technically exist, drifting in the shadows, nourished by heavily stocked bank accounts earning interest in nonreporting countries around the world and known only by his code name: Orphan X.

When he'd fled the Program, the powers-that-be had designated him an unsafe asset, a man who knew too much.

Now he had to live his life below the radar, a challenge complicated by his pro bono work and his desire to live here among ordinary people, both of which were attempts to keep the pilot light of his humanity alive.

Most days he was Evan Smoak, boring Castle Heights resident and importer of industrial cleaning supplies.

But when the RoamZone rang, he became something else.

The Nowhere Man.

It was his way of paying penance for the blood he'd spilled in European alleys and Middle Eastern sweat lodges, in South American *plazas* and African fields.

His own moral compass, pegged to his own true north.

Staying human the only way he knew how.

Now he picked up the encrypted phone and checked it for missed calls, though he'd been within earshot of it every waking minute. In keeping with the spirit of his remodel, he'd given the RoamZone some additional upgrades. The organic polyether thioureas screen with a capability to stitch itself together when cracked was ensconced in an 'antigravity' case, able to cling to most flat surfaces. He tested it now, flipping the phone at the Sub-Zero, the nanosuction backing enabling the RoamZone to stick in place.

He drained a glass of water, washed and dried the cup, and put it away. Then he popped the RoamZone off the refrigerator and padded across the empty great room, stripping off his clothes.

He dumped them and his boots into the fireplace, struck up a fire, and burned them. It was habit, destroying DNA and trace evidence of anything on his person at the end of a mission or a day when he interacted with strangers or unusual materials.

He continued down a brief hall at the north-facing side of the penthouse and into the partially rehabilitated master bedroom suite. In the corner a king-size mattress lay on the floor, neatly made up with white sheets. Normally it rested on a metal slab that floated three feet off the ground, suspended by neodymium rare-earth magnets and tethered by steel cables, but the explosion had loosed it, sending it flying up to smash into the ceiling.

In the bathroom the plumbing had been replaced – toilet, tiled stall, shower arm sticking out of the wall – but there was still no cabinetry and the new barn-hanger shower door had not been installed.

He threw the RoamZone at the wall, where it stuck upside down, and stepped into the stream of water from the metal pipe, rinsing off. When he was done, he gripped the hot-water lever, waited for the upgraded embedded electronic sensors to scan the vein pattern in his palm, and turned the lever the wrong way.

A hidden door, disguised seamlessly by the tile pattern, swung inward to reveal the Vault, an irregular four-hundred-square-foot space that served as his mission-planning room. Given its concealed position, buffered behind the rest of the space, it was the only part of the penthouse that hadn't been destroyed by the explosion. An L-shaped sheet-metal desk piled with electronics. Server racks and gun lockers, ammo crates and surveillance devices, all positioned neatly beneath exposed beams and the underbelly of the public stairs to the roof, which crept downward in Escheresque fashion.

The equipment had slid around from the force of the blast – a few cables snapped, a server rack on tilt, a toppled Yagi directional antenna. A few of the 2.57-millimeter-thin OLED screens that covered three of the rough concrete walls had cracked, fissure marks etched through their invisible surfaces like forks of lightning.

Evan's sole companion, a pinecone-sized aloe vera plant

nestled among blue cobalt pebbles in a glass bowl, had died in his absence in the weeks following the explosion. Vera II, second of her name, faithful companion.

Dripping wet, he walked over and picked her up. Brown leaves, brittle core.

He said, 'Rest in peace,' and dropped her into the trash can.

Emerging back into the bathroom, he toweled off, then plucked his phone from the wall to text Joey Morales, an Orphan Program washout who had inexplicably wound up in his charge. At sixteen years old, she was the finest hacker he'd ever encountered, with a processing speed matched only by her smart-assery. For reasons they neither understood nor fully acknowledged, they had become family to each other.

He thumbed in:

> Need your help to make repairs on the nails.

Less than one second later:

> nails?
>
> I meant vault. Autocorrect.
>
> bummer, x! was hoping we could do some french manicure action just get over here.
>
> or maybe like gels you could get em in black so youd still feel all orphan-y
>
> Joey.
>
> i'm just glad yr finally getting in touch w your feminine side Josephine.
>
> fine. c u in 10.

Trudging out, he moved to the stacks of clothing resting in the corner of the bedroom. Gray V-neck T-shirts, tactical-discreet cargo pants, dark blue 501s, boxer briefs – eight each, folded in perfect squares. Though the bedroom was spotless, their proximity to the floor made his brain itch, so he dusted off each item before donning it and made a mental note to check when the replacement bureau was coming in.

The walk-in closet was empty save for eight hanging Woolrich shirts, eight watch fobs made by Vertex, and eight Original S.W.A.T. shoe boxes.

No, wait.

Seven.

Seven Original S.W.A.T. shoe boxes.

He stared at them, willing it not to be. He'd gone through an extra pair of boots today when a circular saw had bitten a chunk out of the sole, and now there it was, a stack containing one fewer item than the others. That made his face twist with discomfort.

He scratched at the back of his head.

Stared at the boxes. Counted them. Counted them once more.

Still seven.

He'd ordered to replenish his supply but hadn't accounted for the stagger in numbers.

He buttoned up a Woolrich over his T-shirt and tugged on a fresh pair of boots.

Now there were seven of each. But six of the boots.

By the time the new articles of clothing arrived, the numbers would still be off by one.

It was okay. He could handle this.

He started to walk out.

Halted at the threshold of the bedroom.

His place was a mess, covered with sawdust and tools and fucking half-drunk water bottles with germs of other people on them. He could manage this – barely – along with the unfinished state of the penthouse, but having his clothing count misaligned was too much. Distress roiled in his stomach, pressed at the backs of his eyes.

He reversed course, plucking one item from each stack on the floor. Then one hanging shirt and watch fob from the closet.

Holding the mound of brand-new items against his chest, he walked back to the fireplace, tossed the RoamZone to stick against the rise of the flue, and threw the clothes into the fire.

Now there were six of everything and order had been restored to the universe.

With an exhale he uncramped the muscles around his neck. Stared into the flame. Took measure of his breath. Felt the coolness at his nostrils, his throat, the expansion of his ribs, the belly.

A sound pierced his awareness.

The RoamZone.

Ringing.

He stared at the phone stuck magnetlike to the chimney before him. The tech enhancements he'd made to his Roam-Zone included a holographic display incubated by Chinese and Australian researchers at RMIT University in Melbourne. Visible without 3-D glasses, the images thrown beyond the device were twenty-five nanometers thin – a thousand nanometers skinnier than a single strand of hair.

Right now the pop-up visual displayed a phone number with a South Texas area code.

Evan tapped the holograph to answer, the RoamZone reverting to speaker mode.

Adrenaline and anticipation converged into something dangerous and delicious. The start of a mission that could lead to his death or another piece of his salvation.

He took a breath. Exhaled to calm.

Then said, 'Do you need my help?'

6. A Catalog of Horrors

The voice from the phone was deep, resonant. 'Will you help *anyone* who is in need?' Holographic electric-blue sound waves augmented the audio, rising and falling with each consonant.

Evan's question had rarely been answered with a question. He felt the heat of the fire against his chest, his face. 'If they're worthy.'

'I don't know, then.'

'What?'

'If you'll find me worthy.'

An unusual start, unlike any preceding mission. Evan let the man breathe. He sounded troubled. A faint kiss of a Hispanic accent, a formality to the cadence of his words. Unrushed, composed. A man accustomed to being listened to.

'So that's what you do?' the man asked. 'You help people? Outside the law? People who no one else is willing to help?'

'Yes.'

'What do you want for it?'

'Nothing.'

A note of incredulity. 'Nothing?'

'No money. No credit. And no permission.'

A long silence. Then the man said, 'A man who needs none of those things can move the world.'

'How did you get this number?' Evan asked.

'From the Esposito cousin. Rogelio Esposito.'

The young worker with the forearm scar. Evan had given him the phone number less than twenty-four hours ago.

The man spoke again. 'He has family in Eden. My town. An aunt and her boy who nature has been unkind to. They are good people. He is a good boy, too.'

'Describe him,' Evan said.

'He's a Mexican,' the man said. 'Brown hair, brown eyes, brown skin. A scar on his forearm.'

'What's it from?'

'Hot-mix asphalt. I had him put to work here one fall. He went to school briefly with . . .' A slight hesitation. 'With my daughter.'

'What is your name?'

'Aragón Urrea. Perhaps you have heard of me.'

'I have not.'

A very long silence. 'I have heard of you. The Nowhere Man.'

The conversation was stilted, long pauses and awkward hitches. Evan asked carefully, 'Why do you think I would have heard of you?'

'I am not a good man. And now, now God has punished me.'

'How have you been punished?'

'My daughter has been taken. By my enemy.'

'Who is your enemy?'

'Cartel.' Aragón breathed. 'My competitors.'

Evan stared at the RoamZone stuck to the flue at eye level, the dancing blue light emitted from the screen sculpting the contours of the voice.

'You're cartel?' Evan said. 'And you're calling *me*?'

'I'm not cartel. I am an unconventional businessman.'

'Assume I've already heard every version of that argument,' Evan said. 'So we can skip this part. You said you know who I am. So I'll ask you again: Why are you calling me?'

'Do you know of La Familia León?'

Evan did. He gave the revelation the respect it deserved. The Leones had muscled in on the Zetas in Nuevo León, one of the Mexican states floating below the border of South Texas, and they had affiliate franchises starting to metastasize throughout the American Southwest. There was only one way to take on the Zetas – the most vicious cartel in the world. To be *more* vicious. Inspire *more* fear. Project *more* terror. Stories had spread, some apocryphal, some not, a catalog of horrors.

Mass graves in the desert, desiccated limbs sprouting from the sand like gnarled roots.

Crack-blitzed teenage initiates carving organs from their rivals and eating them while the hemorrhaging victims looked on.

Kingpins smuggling lions onto their ranches and cultivating in them an appetite for human meat.

Gunmen storming nightclubs, hurling decapitated heads across dance floors.

Home-invasion squads forcing *federales* to watch the violation and dismemberment of their wives, their sons, their daughters.

An orchard of fifty-five-gallon oil drums sprouting in an abandoned salvage yard, each one plugged with a concrete-encased corpse.

Journalists mummified in duct tape, left to bake to death in the trunks of abandoned cars, the metal dented from their feet and heads.

Ex-girlfriends found stiff and eyeless in alleys, the Leones gang sign carved between their shoulder blades with butcher knives.

'I've heard of them,' Evan said.

'Years ago a distant associate of mine was taken,' Aragón said. 'They call it white torture. Blinding bright light beamed into his eyes as they hung him from a rail for five days, arms behind his back. And then? Darkness. And silence. Removing

39

each sense one by one until you don't know if you are dead. Until the only way you know you are alive is from pain. Your senses revolt and long for it. Pain. They said he begged to be crucified again, that he beat his head against the floor until the cartilage of his nose was smashed flat to his skull. Just to feel.'

The fire leapt before Evan, a dance of orange and red.

'I visited him sometime afterward in a facility,' Aragón continued. 'He was broken, twitching, a living tremor shaped like a human body. His eyes were dead. He had no light left inside him. I have never seen a human being look like he looked. I had to pause outside his hospital room and sit to catch my breath. For me, with the things I have seen, the things I have done. For *me* to need to catch my breath . . .' The thought trailed off and died.

The pain in his voice was tangible, a deep ache thrumming beneath the surface of the words.

'These savages,' Aragón said. 'They obey no rules. My eighteen-year-old daughter is in their hands. She is a beautiful girl. She is pure of heart. She is untainted by who I am and what I have done. She is good. She is as good as I am not. And they have her.'

'Why are you calling me?'

'When I was a little boy, I vowed never to let fear in again. Not all the way. Until now. Now it has gotten in. And I think I might die from it.'

There was such desperation in him, raw and unformed, the desperation of a man who had long forgotten what it was to be desperate.

'You asked if I need your help,' he said. 'I do. I need your help. Will you help me?'

When Evan reached out to pull the RoamZone free from the metal rise, his hand was the slightest bit unsteady. He swiped the screen, disabling the holographic mode, and pressed the screen to his warm cheek.

He heard the faintest sound, like broom whiskers brushing dryly across a floor. The sound of Aragón Urrea weeping. Evan ran his thumb across his hairline, freeing beads of sweat.

He said, 'I don't know,' and disconnected the line.

7. The Dark Man

The crossing at Laredo had been seamless. ICE, Border Patrol, Mexican customs officers – none of their focus was on people being smuggled *south* across the border.

So here Anjelina was, away from the reach of her father or any law and order she had ever known, trapped in the gilded cage of this god-awful estate that felt more like an homage to *Scarface* than anything of the real world.

Gaudy gold sconces, Carrara marble floors, a bed the size of a small boat on which she floated like Ophelia in the stream in that one painting Mr Hirsh kept on the homeroom wall. Anjelina felt just as lifeless, just as transformed. One hand resting on her chest, one on her stomach, willing her heart to slow. It thumped against her palm as if begging to be let out.

She'd been ensconced in an upstairs corner room with two large windows facing the front and side of the mansion. Between billowing tassel curtains parted like a bodice, she could see men patrolling the resortlike grounds with assault rifles. A swimming pool out of some MTV party show, rock waterfalls and bikinied girls with glazed eyes and flat laughs. And somewhere the one everyone talked about. The one everyone feared.

El Moreno.

The Dark Man.

She couldn't see him, but she heard the low hum of his voice, how the others hushed in reverence when he spoke, and she could make out a curling wisp of cigar smoke lifting through the beams of the pergola.

She turned her head from the window and stared at the high ceiling. A garish chandelier billowing with glass beads. Or maybe they were diamonds.

She'd learned from her father that wealth could be limitless. It could be so large that it became an abyss impossible to fill.

She wasn't crying, not exactly, but she felt tears sliding down her cheeks. She couldn't muster the strength to sob. She felt the specter of death hovering about her. In a sense she had died already and could not know if she'd be reborn.

With her fingertips she pressed on the puffy edges of her eyes. She ached all the way through, terror soaking her to the bone. She'd never imagined she could feel like this.

From outside, she heard the voice once more. She couldn't make out the words but their cadence was intense, aggressive, drug-fueled. Only the one voice spoke. There was silence for El Moreno.

She turned away from the window onto her side in the fetal position. She clutched her stomach.

And at last she sobbed.

8. Easily Traumatized

Evan was standing in the glass freezer room at the kitchen's edge contemplating the sparse vodka options when his front door burst open. By the time he caught up to himself, he had cleared the threshold, mist streamers spilling over his shoulders, ARES 1911 drawn from his Kydex holster.

He was aiming at Joey's center mass.

She smirked at him, sticking her hands above her head. Her Rhodesian ridgeback padded in at her side, then sat, cocked his head, and regarded Evan with a wrinkled brow.

'Hey, X,' Joey said, 'Shoot a girl, why dontcha? It's not like *you* texted *moi*.'

He holstered the pistol back in the appendix carry position beneath his shirt. 'I'm not used to traffic through here.'

She lowered her hands, heeled the sturdy door shut behind her, and smiled, showing off the hair-thin gap in her front teeth and putting a dimple in her right cheek. A strip of her hair was shaved on the right side above the ear, a subtle undercut that gave a punk flair to her tumbling black-brown waves. She wore a T-shirt that read HACKING IS MY LOVE LANGUAGE and had an army-surplus rucksack slung over her shoulder. One leg was kicked out, the top of her Doc Martens boot rocked away from her shin, her hip shoved to the other side. She was beautiful and abrasive, quintessentially teenage.

The ridgeback, whom Joey had ingeniously named Dog, padded over and nuzzled Evan's palm.

'Why so jumpy?' Joey asked.

'I had a call.'

'Like a *call* call?' She affected her pompous Orphan X voice. '"Do you need my help?" "Are you eating enough fiber?"'

'I'm mostly certain I don't sound like that.'

'You know how they say you can't hear what your own voice sounds like?'

Evan scratched Dog behind the left ear, and the dog leaned his big head into the touch. 'I told you you can't bring him here. You know how uptight they are about pets.'

She waved him off. 'A new mission, huh? Is that why you're in there self-medicating and it's barely six o'clock?'

'Is it still called self-medication if you're really good at it?'

'Uh, *yeah.*' She turned the latter word into two syllables. 'But you can't do another mission yet. Don't we have to find your birth father?'

Evan's last mission had introduced him to the mother he'd never known and a half brother who he was still figuring out what to do about. He'd discovered that he'd been the product of a brief failed affair and had learned the name of his biological father – Jacob Baridon. Baridon had been a no-shit rodeo cowboy, a hackneyed development that Evan still couldn't get his head around. The databases had turned up little else about Baridon, and given the fact that Evan's living quarters had Chernobyl'd, he had turned to more pressing concerns. But Joey wasn't one to let an uncomfortable matter lie.

'I've had enough family reunions for the foreseeable future,' Evan said.

Joey breezed past him, smelling of bubble gum, and dumped her rucksack on the kitchen island. 'C'mon, X. What if he's out there somewhere? Don't you *have to* know? What if he's homeless? Or an oil tycoon? What if he died in, like, a tragic manscaping accident?'

'Manscaping?'

'Gawd. Read a magazine.'

'Why does everything you say sound like an accusation?'

'Why are you so dim-witted and judgmental?' She arched an eyebrow at him. 'See what I did there?'

Evan looked at Dog the dog. Dog looked back at him with sympathy.

'Oh – I brought you something.' She stuck her hand in the rucksack. 'Wait for it. Waaaait for it. And . . . *wa-la*!' She pulled out a crystal dish holding a baby aloe vera plant nestled atop a rainbow assortment of glass pebbles. She stared at him, beaming that high-wattage smile. 'Vera III!'

All the colors jumbled together caused discomfort to swell in his chest. 'Too many colors,' he said. 'I don't like rainbows.'

'Homophobe.'

'That's not –'

She thrust the tiny plant at him. 'You need someone to look after you. 'Cuz – God knows – no human would take that job.'

He poked at the pebbles and then started sorting them by color. She slapped at his hand. 'Stop it. You're violating her personhood.'

'She's a *plant*.' He scowled at her.

Joey was lit up now, really enjoying herself. 'Did you just microaggress me?'

'You're gonna get a macroaggression if you keep this up.'

She ticktocked a finger at him. 'Trigger warning.'

'Josephine!'

'Okay, okay. Jeez. Get with the times, X.' She poked her finger into the soil of the living wall, and he clamped his jaws shut to stop from reprimanding her. 'Now that you've *not* thanked me for my gift' – she made a kissy face at

Vera III – 'I'm sorry, pretty girl, that you have to have such a self-absorbed daddy – do you want to *not* thank me for schlepping over here to fix your hardware?'

'Schlep?'

'LA's a Jewish town, X. A girl's gotta code-switch.'

'Code-switch?'

'That thing where you just repeat the last thing I said but sound stupid? Not so charming.'

'Noted.'

'Now. Tell me about the phone call and this mission we're going on.'

'There's no "we." I'm not even sure if *I'm* going on this mission.'

At last her face turned serious. She hopped to sit on the island, and Dog the dog mirrored her, plopping down at Evan's side. 'What? Don't you have to? Isn't that, like, unofficial Nowhere Man rules?'

'I don't know,' Evan said. 'I don't know what to do.'

She stared at him, dumbfounded. 'Say more.'

He told her about the phone call, giving her what sparse information Aragón Urrea had offered. When he finished, she sat quietly, nibbling the inside of her cheek, her face suddenly full and youthful. He imagined what he might feel if she were in the hands of La Familia León. What he might do.

The thought was too much to bear, and he pushed it away before it had fastened onto his mind with specifics. It was the first time he could recall having to terminate an imagined scenario.

She was watching his face, watching him closely.

'Once you fix the gear in the Vault, can you do a deep dive on him?' Evan asked. 'I need to know everything.'

The doorbell rang. Evan and Joey stared at the door, and

Dog the dog emitted a low growl. Evan said, 'Hush, boy,' and Dog silenced.

Walking to the door, Evan glanced at the security monitor embedded in the wall. Hugh Walters, HOA president, stood outside, arms crossed so his navy-blue blazer pinched at the shoulders, fingers drumming briskly on opposite triceps. Peeved body posture.

Evan gestured for Joey to hide Dog in the back, but before she could move, Hugh called through the door, 'I know you're in there, Mr Smoak. And I'm quite certain you're aware that HOA regs expressly forbid any pets on premises.'

Evan scrunched his face up, set his hand on the door handle, and summoned fortitude. He could deal with kidnapped girls and homicidal cartel kingpins, but interfacing with Hugh Walters over HOA 'regs' made him want to put his face through the Sheetrock.

He pulled open the door and Hugh leaned in, wagging a finger imperiously. 'We've discussed this before, and –'

Joey piped up from behind Evan. 'My bad, Hugh. It is okay that I call you Hugh?'

As Hugh walked in, Evan lowered his forehead to the heel of his hand and closed his eyes, praying for forbearance.

'I prefer Dr Walters,' Hugh said. 'I have a Ph.D. in city planning –'

'My dog here is actually a service animal.'

Joey's tone, curt and professional, was like none Evan had heard her employ. He looked up to see that somehow in the intervening seconds she had produced a red SERVICE DOG vest and wrapped it around Dog the dog.

Were he not so dumbfounded, he might have grinned.

Hugh hesitated a few steps into the penthouse. 'I wasn't aware that . . . er, that Mr Smoak required . . .'

Joey continued with her simulation of a prissy yet pleasant

boss. 'Oh, yes, Dr Walters. Evan has *special needs'* – she lowered her voice to a stage whisper, and Evan's notion of grinning evaporated. 'He's easily traumatized by small things you and I might not understand.'

As Hugh swung his head to take in Evan, Joey smirked behind Hugh's back and pointed theatrically to the rainbow-color pebbles in Vera III's dish. Evan was trapped, unable to glare at her, a calm expression frozen on his face for Hugh's sake.

'He suffers from nighttime enuresis,' Joey said, pressing her advantage. 'You know, bed-wetting.'

Hugh's bird's-nest eyebrows hoisted. 'Bed-wetting?'

Evan felt his face reddening, perhaps from embarrassment. It was hard to tell given his rising aggravation.

'Oh, that's only *one* of the symptoms,' Joey continued. 'Really, anxiety. Crushing anxiety. Panic attacks sometimes. He requires a special-needs dog to settle his nerves.'

Hugh looked skeptically at Dog the dog, who licked himself, lost balance, and fell over. Still licking himself.

Joey nudged him with her foot. 'Gross,' she whispered at him. 'Put the lipstick away.'

Dog lifted his large head sheepishly.

Hugh composed himself, squaring his shoulders. 'Even so,' he said, 'all service dogs must be preregistered with the HOA –'

'I'll take care of that ASAP,' Joey said. Even her posture was pantsuit-crisp all of a sudden, indicative of the social-engineering training she'd received during her Orphan days. 'In the meantime we must ensure that there's no interruption in care. There are vigorous laws for the disabled.'

'Indeed there are,' Hugh Walters conceded.

Dog stood up, his back arching like a Halloween cat's. His head lurched forward twice, telescoping his neck, and then he vomited a Frisbee-size disk of puke on the floor, dotted with tree bark.

Evan stared at the mess, his OCD redlining.

'Oh,' Joey said. 'That's unfortunate.'

Hugh had withdrawn across the threshold, looking intimidated and mildly disgusted. 'Mia has asked for your presence downstairs at Lorilee's place,' he said to Evan. 'She said it was an emergency.'

Evan felt an uptick in concern. 'An emergency?'

'That's what she texted.' Hugh held up his phone, bolstering his case. 'If you can pause your . . . therapy, perhaps you could run down and check on her?'

'That's okay,' Joey said. 'I can approve that.'

Hugh gave an unsettled nod, adjusted his horn-rimmed glasses, and vanished up the hall.

'Well,' Joey said with a self-satisfied grin, 'you can thank me later.'

Evan heard his teeth grinding and suspected that she could, too. '*Disabled*?'

'Let me just . . . uh' – her hands made humorous pointing gestures in all directions – 'clean this up, fix the gear in the Vault, and get on that research for you.' She backpedaled dramatically. '*Bu*-bye, now.'

Against his better judgment, he left the penthouse at her mercy.

9. A Sharp Detour

Evan heard the buzz of conversation issuing through the door of 3F. Puzzled, he rapped three times.

Lorilee Smithson swung the door open, a glass of red wine in one hand. She wore a loose crocheted sweater that dipped off one shoulder and draped like batwings beneath her arms. A recent round of Botox injections had left her face looking like a shiny plastic mask, her lips ballooned to cartoon proportions. 'Ev! So glad you made it.'

Evan leaned to peer past her. Her condo, which he'd never visited, was a collage of white and off-white shabby-chic furnishings that collapsed the place into two-dimensionality. Some of the residents, including Mia and Peter, were spread around a puffy cream sectional, gazing down at a collection of candles arrayed reverently on a plush vanilla area rug.

Peter popped to his feet, his nine-year-old body humming with excitement. 'Evan Smoak!'

Evan stared at Mia. Her brown eyes were wide, gleaming in the artificial light. Even from here he could make out the rust-colored flecks in them.

As always when interacting with Castle Heights residents, he felt uncomfortable. 'I was told there was an emergency.'

'Oh,' Lorilee said, goosenecking a hand at him. 'That was just me being silly. I used Mia's phone.'

Mia stood up, patted her pockets, found her phone on the cushion beside her. 'You used my —'

'We're having an artisanal-candle party,' Lorilee said, pressing her hands together, her manicured fingernails tepeeing. 'It's the new Tupperware party!'

'I'm sorry,' Evan said. 'You called me down here for . . . candles?'

Mia stood up angrily. 'Lorilee, I cannot believe you used my phone to text Hugh.'

Lorilee said, 'Well, I couldn't find Evan in there, and I knew Hugh would fetch him. I figured Evan would show up here for *you*.'

'That is not the point,' Mia said, blushing slightly. 'I am a state prosecutor. My correspondence is confidential. You can't just *use someone's phone*.' Flustered, she gathered up her things as the others looked on and started to storm out, purse knocking against her hip. 'C'mon, Peter.'

Peter plopped back on the couch, suddenly boneless. 'But Ms Smithson said if I helped her pack up the candles, she'd take me for frozen yogurt.'

'Traitor.'

Despite the evening hour, Peter still had bedhead, the cowlick at his part sticking up like a miniature blond rooster comb. 'I already had to suffer through all the old-people talk. Might as well get cookies-and-cream out of it.'

Mia hesitated. 'That's a valid argument.' She pointed at Lorilee. 'Child size. No chocolate toppings or you're keeping him tonight.'

Lorilee held up three fingers. 'Scout's honor.'

'Don't push it,' Mia said. 'You're an unreliable witness.'

She stomped out, and Evan followed her down the hall and into the elevator. Mia ran her fingers through her wild chestnut curls and exhaled. 'That woman. I swear I want to stick her face to a window using her duck lips for suction.' She gave him an up-from-under look, lips twitching just shy of a grin. 'Did you really come down here because you thought I said it was an emergency?'

The faint freckles across the bridge of her nose were visible in the elevator lights. She smelled of lemongrass lotion.

He said, 'I did.'

'To rescue me.'

'Damsel in distress.'

'From the artisanal-candle-it's-the-new-Tupperware party?'

'If ever a damsel needed rescuing.'

The elevator stopped at the twelfth floor. She cocked her head. 'Walk me to my condo? You know, in case I get mugged on the way and my police-grade pepper spray malfunctions?'

They were walking side by side. Evan said, 'I've heard the mean halls of the Castle Heights Residential Tower have reached dystopian levels of violence and treachery.'

Mia fumbled with her keys. 'The other day a retiree passed me with spiked tennis balls on her walker.'

Inside – the smell of laundry detergent and Elmer's glue, the brightness of throw pillows and crayon art. She dipped her shoulder, dumping her purse into an armchair, and rubbed her neck.

'And I seem to recall someone's penthouse mysteriously blew up a few months back,' she said. 'Do you remember whose that was?'

'I believe that was Judge Johnson?'

'Hmm.'

His stare was on her nape, the gentle dip between the splenius muscles. In a Gothenburgian port warehouse, he'd once slipped a push dagger through that very spot, severing the brain stem of a morbidly obese child trafficker. But he wasn't thinking of violence, not now.

She reached behind her, arms pretzeling beneath her

shoulder blades. 'Can you just . . . undo me? This bra is killing me.'

Through the thin fabric of her blouse, he slipped a finger beneath the catch, and it snapped and gave way. He heard her lips part in a faint sigh.

She turned around into him, her mouth on his, her hands pressed against his chest. She'd caught him off guard, and yet it was not unexpected at all.

With their mouths fastened, they stumble-walked down the hall to the bedroom as she kicked off her block-heel sandals, one thunking against the wall. Into the master, falling onto the bed, her fingers at his sides, fighting his shirt up and off, the bite of her nails against his ribs. He pulled the holstered pistol free with a snap, mopping the shirt around it before she could take note, and set it down next to the bed.

She yanked her blouse up. It tangled on her earring. 'Ouch. Wait. Fuck. Help.'

He steered the fabric clear, and she stared at him, her cheeks flushed, mouth ajar, lips swollen from kissing. Thumbing out her earrings, she took in his chest and stomach, smirking with mock irritation. 'God, you're so annoying. Can you please eat more carbs?'

She reached up and hooked his neck, pulling him down, and he was lost in her, the smell of her, lemongrass and citrus, her skin impossibly soft. His fingers interlaced in hers, pinning her hands to the mattress, and then with a swivel of her body she was on top of him, holding his arms above his head, her hips moving, moving, moving. Her hair swaying down, brushing his collarbones.

Side by side now, their legs locked, ankles clawing for purchase in the sheets and against each other's legs.

'Hang on,' she said.

'Bad angle,' she said.

'Yeah,' she said.

'There,' she said.

'Mmmm,' she said.

'Slower.'

'Slower.'

'Slower.'

They were barely moving, her face twisted over her shoulder, facing him, their foreheads touching, her mouth ajar, his mouth ajar, breathing each other's breath. A shudder and a cry, and then she lay atop him, spent, her body sealed against his with sweat, panting into the side of his neck, and he was looking at the ceiling, his vision pixelating with static from exhaustion or ecstasy or oxytocin or a triple cocktail of all three.

For a time they just breathed. He trickled his fingertips along the dip of her waist. Her hip was pushed high against his, a fan of muscle and bone and gracefulness.

'Know why I like you?' she asked, her voice still breathy.

'My artisanal candle-making?'

'Besides that.' She dipped a finger in the sweat pooled in the hollow of his neck and traced a line down his chest. 'You see things like a woman.'

Her head bobbed slightly on his chest as he breathed.

'I'm going to wait and hope there's more coming,' he said.

'You check for things like we have to,' she said. 'Dark patches on the sidewalk at night. Looking at window reflections to see who might be following. You're alert. You know what it's like to feel vulnerable. All girls learn that. We don't have a choice. That's why you can be trusted.'

He said nothing. He was unsure what to say.

'And you, you don't really belong anywhere,' she said. 'You fit in, sure, but that's different from *belonging*.' She had a perfect curlicue of hair sweat-pasted to the intimate spot beneath her ear. 'You probably don't even get it. How different you are from other men and their concerns. Like status. What car they drive, the best restaurant. I mean, don't get me wrong. You have so many flaws –'

'Granted.'

She laughed. '*So, so* many flaws. But you have the good parts without the bad parts. Or I mean the *usual* bad parts. The day-to-day stuff that most men let . . . I don't know, *diminish* them. They put blinders on and come to think that how they see the world is how the world is. They still think it's real.'

'What's real?'

'Everything out there that glitters and shines.' Their proximity turned the arresting brownness of her eyes translucent, revealing a hidden layer the color of champagne. 'When Roger died, all that died for me for good. I only saw beneath. What was real. You see that, too. All the time.' She paused, and he felt on the verge of something he'd never felt before. Something different. And then she said, 'But.'

He braced.

'We don't have real intimacy,' she said. 'I don't know if I can have it without knowing anything about you. I mean, the *usual* stuff about you. And yet that's also the stuff that makes other men . . . other men.'

'Why's it necessary?' he asked. 'Knowing the usual stuff.'

She dug her fingers in her hair and heaped it to the other side, the soft bedroom light bringing out shades of honey and cinnamon. 'I don't know.'

'Zen Buddhists think that's all that matters. All we are. The present.'

'No,' she said. 'No.'

'It was worth a try.'

She laughed once more. 'I want you to come with me and

Peter to dinner at my brother's house next week,' she said. 'Wally's kind of an idiot, but a *lovable* idiot.'

He forced his muscles not to stiffen beneath her. The last time she'd invited him to a meal with her brother, Evan's penthouse had exploded, providing him with a reasonable excuse to decline. And yet here was the request raised anew. Why now? It seemed like a sharp detour, irrelevant to the preceding conversation. And yet it was related, too, in a way that was even deeper, that carried with it some great mythic importance for her that he couldn't fully comprehend.

He stayed still, let the flurry of emotions beat at the cage of his chest. A lifetime of training to not get involved, to not forge personal relationships and certainly not *extended* personal relationships. Going to meet her brother's family was the last thing and the worst thing he would ever want to do.

He drew in a breath. 'Okay,' he said.

She looked up at him now, her lashes long, her throat still flushed from exertion. 'Really?' She sounded as shocked as he'd ever heard her.

He pressed his lips softly to her warm forehead and then slid out of bed. 'Mind if I use your shower?'

'Just leave a quarter on the counter.'

'Cheap date.'

'Reminder: You're not taking advantage of me. I'm taking advantage of you.'

'Noted.'

She rolled off the mattress and grabbed a water bottle from atop the bureau. He paused and took her in. She was built from the ground up and the top down. Her hips, pushed wide, etched here or there with the feathered kiss of a stretch mark. She was lovely. She was imperfect. She was soft and firm and complex and alluring.

She was a woman.

57

He gathered up his clothes around the ARES 1911 and stepped into the bathroom. Turning on the shower, he leaned his crown into the hot stream and let the water run down his face.

Mia's brother's house. Dinner.

For the first time in a very long time, he felt out of control.

10. Seriously Dangerous

Evan slipped through the hidden door in the shower into the Vault to find Joey cocked back in his chair, bare feet up on his desk, a cordless keyboard in her lap. She was typing more quickly than seemed humanly possible. The three walls horseshoeing the desk were lit up, the OLED screens filled with streaming logs and text editors and decompiled assembly code.

Vera III sat in her position near the mouse pad, the rainbow-colored pebbles discordant in the cramped concrete room. Joey flopped a Red Vine from her mouth into Dog's, who nibbled off a chunk. Then she flopped it back into her mouth.

Evan said, 'Leaving aside how disgusting that is, you shouldn't feed the dog candy.'

She was back at the keyboard, not even dignifying him with a glance. 'What happened with Mia's emergency?'

Evan halted awkwardly. With chagrin he noticed that nondescript noises were coming out of his mouth. He forged them into an excuse. 'It was just a misunderstanding.'

Her eyes finally ticked north and froze. 'Wait a minute. Why's your hair wet? Did you *shower*?' The seat tilted forward, her feet slapping the floor. '*Oh*-em-*gee*. X. Was it a *loooove* emergency?'

'What did you find on Aragón Urrea?'

'Was Céline Dion beneath the couch serenading you with a flautist?' Joey thwacked down the keyboard hard enough to make Vera III jump and came around the desk. 'Or was it more, ya know, *boom-chicka-wow-wow*?'

He took her by the shoulders, spun her in a 180, marched her around the desk, and deposited her back into the chair. 'Make useful things come out of your mouth now.'

'Fine.' She risked one more gleeful peek at him, throwing in an overwrought winky eye. 'Hope you didn't throw your back out during your *misunderstanding*.'

He palmed the top of her head and directed it at the screens tiling the walls, many of which sported surveillance photos of a grave-looking man, stocky and dignified, with a fleshy nose and deep-set, soulful eyes.

'Talk,' he said.

'Okay, okay.' She took a breath. 'Aragón Urrea isn't cartel. At least not like any cartel we've ever seen. He's more like . . .' She cocked her head. 'An unconventional businessman.'

'So I've heard.'

'Most of what I got was from the DEA and IRS databases,' Joey said. 'They've kick-started a dozen investigations into him and given up each time.'

'Why?'

'Imagine being so smart at business that you're literally outside the law.'

'Above it?'

'*Outside* it,' she said. 'Like, an anarcho-capitalist who uses the principles of twenty-first-century entrepreneurship to plug into the unsanctioned gray areas of global commerce. He uses the gig economy, hires and fires fixers, cybersecurity experts, bookkeepers, suppliers, and networkers using virtual communications run through surrogates so his name doesn't appear on any transaction. Never uses the same workers twice so there's no one to flip on him, because they don't know who he is, what he looks like, or anything about his operation. They don't even have any idea what the job is, just their little piece of it, which is fully siloed.'

'Like an Orphan.'

'Exactly like an Orphan.' She gnawed down another Red Vine with lawn-mower proficiency. 'Lets him scale up fast for a job, scale down just as fast. Plus, it keeps infrastructure costs low. He outsources means of production, outsources trafficking, outsources equipment – everything. Doesn't even need locations, just rents them like people job by job, so if you're law enforcement or rivals, good luck finding any physical location, let alone attacking it. Anytime anyone gets close, he cuts bait and disappears. Everyone else takes the risk and the fall.'

'He's the unseen enemy,' Evan said.

'Yeah. And he's also a kinda-sorta digital-age multinational company of one that doesn't require a footprint. It's all about disruptive innovation. No wonder the cartels hate him. If they're Blockbuster, Urrea is Netflix. He's . . . dunno, Amazon to their Walmart.'

Evan walked around the desk and stared at the information covering the walls. Shell corps and business fronts and interlocking corporations. Hundreds of servers completely torn down and spun up hourly in countries with lax regulations, many of which Evan used himself to stash funds or park his phone service. The Comoro Islands, Djibouti, Ghana, Israel, Mauritius, Mozambique, Papua New Guinea, Seychelles, Tanzania, South Africa, Vietnam, and a host of the other usual offshore suspects. Anonymous e-commerce run through cryptocurrency, stored for transfer on Trezor hardware wallets, and processed out through Bitcoin exchanges in Chile, Seoul, Nigeria, or the Netherlands.

The tangle of red tape, interfering jurisdictions, and discrepant governmental regulations was sufficient to make Urrea's criminal enterprise – by any practical consideration – extrajudicial.

His digital operation, expounded upon in an internal DEA chart, showed a confusion of lost trails and dead ends – satellite links, private clouds, digital middlemen, dark fiber, encrypted messaging apps, anonymizers, file dumps, carding, warez, and dark-web transactions.

'The sheer manpower required to crack an operation like his makes it virtually uncrackable,' Joey said.

She came around next to him, marveling at the rise of data. Three screens alone held an accounting of dismissed felony counts.

She pointed to an elaborate flowchart. 'Look at that deal the DEA tried to run down. Freelance Serbian thugs brought in for a one-off to buy four tons of Peruvian cocaine. The deal conducted through surrogates using Tor with Tails on a USB stick in a browser over the dark web. Traffickers from the Philippines are rented to bribe customs officials and smuggle the dope through Lubang' – she traced that route with a gnawed fingernail – 'avoiding actual Chinese waters, which are monitored like a mofo, and then they sell it to Hong Kong triad and backdoor it through Shenzhen into the mainland.' She whistled. 'Urrea could put all this together using nuthin' but an ORWL machine and a secure Linux distro without even leaving his La-Z-Boy. That's a street value of what?'

'Quarter billion,' Evan said.

'He's impossible to get a handle on, so he can't be brought down.'

A family tree had been constructed by the IRS, complete with photos. A scattering of mug shots displayed Urrea's known associates. His top lieutenants were identified as Enrique Pérez, aka 'Special K', a dumpy guy with a drooping mustache and baggy eyes. And Eduardo Gómez, aka 'Special Ed', a big man with a face like a pug's: Wet, downturned lips shoved up high beneath his nose. Severe acne scars mottled his cheeks.

Joey tilted her head at Special Ed's photo. 'You'd think as a public-health consideration they'd airbrush out the blemishes, but then there'd be nothing left of the guy. I mean, can you believe *that dude* was someone's fastest sperm?'

Evan tuned her out and walked over to the north-facing wall, his eyes scanning the screens. 'They have a location on Urrea. This two-hundred-and-fifty-acre compound in Eden.'

'Why's he parked way the hell down in South Texas?' Joey asked.

Evan thought for a moment. 'Texas gun and privacy laws are the most extensive in the Union. You have stand your ground, open carry, aggressive privacy regulations, stringent search-and-seizure protections, and broad self-defense allowances. So you're starting with strong distrust of the government, which increased exponentially after the Branch Davidian siege in Waco. Now, as for the *specific* location . . .' He considered. 'El Paso's a hub of fed influence since SouthCom, BorTac, and DEA South are there, but the farther south you go, the more Wild West it gets. In fact, South Texas and Alaska might be the last places in the country where law enforcement would want to roll up on a property and have a look-see.'

He went around the desk once more and zoomed out slightly on the Google Earth image. 'Hidalgo County's got a long and distinguished tradition of corruption. Cops, elected officials – graft is a cottage industry there. And that's before you get the Zetas, Leones, Emmis, and Gulf Cartel involved with bribes. A few years back, they had the chief of police personally waving drug caravans across the border. And the terrain's rough enough for serious home-court advantage. I think most federal agencies would just as soon give that chunk of land back to Mexico.'

Evan stared at the satellite view of the compound. Beyond the map coordinates, there wasn't much to see, the image blurred out. At the edge of the pixelation, a stretch of security barrier was visible, topped with military-grade razor wire and equipped with numerous cameras. He said, 'The security –'

'Of course, being the resident genius . . .' Joey paused. 'Well, that's not fair. There are two of us. Isn't that right, Vera III?'

Vera III looked on with approbation.

'Being one of *two* resident geniuses, I already dug in. Turns out the IRS did some recon a few months back, hit a wall when they determined that Urrea's running ZoneMinder on an OpenBSD system with closed-circuit cameras – air-gapped from the rest of the Internet. Which makes it impossible to hack. If you're not me.'

Evan rolled his hand to keep her going. 'And if one has the good fortune of being you . . . ?'

'If you're so blessed, you hack into the Amazon account Urrea's staff uses, see that the compound orders a shit-ton from them like anyone else. And being me and having access to all sorts of deviant behavior through the dark web (Note to self: There's a bizarre uptick in Aussie mail-order husbands, so I might grab me a Hemsworth), then you can social-engineer someone who works in one of the Amazon warehouses to include a jailbroken cell phone with Wi-Fi enabled in the next package heading into the compound. Which means . . .'

'A remote pivot into the network.'

'Aw, look who showed up for class. Then I ARP spoof the router to slam a man-in-the-middle proxy directly into the air-gapped network, intercepting the video feed, and set it to be remotely controlled through a reverse tunnel over Urrea's own public Wi-Fi network for good measure, and guess who's steering the ship?'

She made muscley arms, popping her slender yet defined biceps, which he had to concede looked fairly impressive. Dog the dog's tail thumped the floor. Human happy, dog happy.

'If I were able to see beyond the filter of my deeply engrained humility, I might point out that this guy?' Now Joey jerked this-guy thumbs chestward. 'Is gonna pull off some shit that the IRS and their combined eighty thousand employees couldn't manage.'

'They do have the misfortune of having to abide by the law.'

'Tell me more, Orphan X.' A flash of a smile, here and then gone. If she weren't so goddamned winsome, he would've throttled her. 'And now that this is soon to be accomplished, I have something to ask of *you*.'

'Pay for your psych eval?'

'Not funny.' Joey took a breath, held it. 'Once I help you through this mission, I want to go on a road trip.'

At first Evan thought he'd heard wrong. As soon as he fitted her words to meaning, he was assailed with images of Urrea's daughter in the hands of the Leones. He thought of the uneven cadence in Aragón's voice, the cracks of a man on the verge of crumbling.

'A road trip?' he said. 'Alone?'

'I'll take Dog with me. He's a protective companion.'

'Who lacks opposable thumbs.' Evan walked over to one of the gear lockers and started flipping through various passports and driver's licenses, choosing a fresh identity. The work, supplied by the finest counterfeiter on the West Coast, was unassailable.

Joey was at his heels. 'Hear me out. I never got to be on my own in a good way. I went from the foster system into the Program, out of the Program, on the run, and then here stuck going to UCLA taking computer-science classes I could've taught when I was in, like, preschool.'

'Switch majors. I've heard that Nordic studies has an opening for mouthy reprobates.'

'It'd just be for a few months.'

'A few months!' Evan felt suddenly thrust into the role of suburban father, stuck in a version of another human being more normal than he was.

'Why can't I?' Joey said, an uncharacteristic whine creeping into her voice.

'Because you don't have full myelination of your prefrontal cortex.'

'Do too! I'm sixteen. That's, like, almost an adult.'

'No. Sixteen is further from an adult than an eight-year-old.'

'Hi. Know math much?'

He turned to face her. 'Joey, there's no way. What are you gonna do if you get into trouble?'

'Have you met me? That's all I do. Get *into* trouble. Then get *out of* trouble.'

'With me watching your six.'

'Oh, so I'm nothing without you.'

'Joey, two-thirds of what you do online is illegal. If you're out there' – he pointed idiotically through the concrete wall, an ill-advised gesture intended to encompass the vast menacing world beyond – 'and get busted and they figure out that your ID showing you to be eighteen isn't fully backstopped, what are you gonna do?'

'That's a problem for Future Joey.'

'And that's precisely why you're not going on a road trip. You want to wind up like Aragón Urrea's daughter?'

'Oh. I get it. Young women shouldn't ever be independent 'cuz abusive assholes try to control them.'

'Not at sixteen they shouldn't be independent.'

'You: "Oh, no! Joey might get a paper cut! That makes my

Jane Austen teacup clatter against my saucer with anxiety!"
Also you: "I'm gonna stick my thick head into a satanic cartel
and see what happens."'

Evan said, 'Me taking risks is different from you taking
risks.'

He was at the computer now, searching flights. To
obscure his trail, he'd go out of Long Beach, connect
through Phoenix, switch airlines, set down in San Antonio –
an inconvenient and therefore unexpected choice – and
drive from there.

He heard her cross her arms behind him, a curt rustle of
her T-shirt. She was breathing hard, upset.

'Besides,' he said in a conciliatory tone he didn't recognize,
'I need you to stay here and take point on the remodel.'

'Wahoo.' She twirled a finger with a deadly lack of enthu-
siasm. 'Living my best life.'

Flight booked under the alias David Bannor, he spun
and rose. She followed him out through the shower and
into the master bedroom, where he threw a few things into
a bag. Dog the dog stayed at her side, claws clicking on the
concrete.

'Are you gonna be reachable?' she asked. 'To, like, pick out
lacy curtains and dust ruffles?'

'Very funny. You know me. Handle it yourself. I trust you.'

'Okay,' she said to his back. 'I have a smaller favor you
might be willing to grant in return. Some advice.'

He paused, relieved. 'Of course.'

'How would you dispose of the body of an annoyingly
controlling uncle-person?' she said. 'Asking for a separate
person who is not me.'

'Joey –'

'I mean, is lye more effective for the body, or would you go
with concentrated hydrofluoric acid?'

67

'Concentrated hydrofluoric acid,' he said. 'But make sure you don't do it in a porcelain tub, because it'll eat through.'

'The good news is, I've been tasked with overseeing a remodel,' she said brightly. 'So I'll be sure to install a copper soaking tub. That should work, right?'

'Right.' He offered his hand. 'Best of luck.'

She gave him a professional shake. Then her front dropped. 'Are you really going down there?' she said. 'Into this guy's compound? What if he's lying?'

'He's not. I heard it in his voice.'

'But, I mean, this guy's not like the other people you've helped. He's serious trouble. And seriously dangerous.'

'You're right,' Evan said. 'Which is why I'll have to approach him differently.'

'Even so.' She chewed her bottom lip, her eyes worried for the first time. 'Can you save a bad man?'

Evan looked over her shoulder, catching sight of himself in the mirror hanging on the inside of the closet door. Average size, average build, a guy who'd blend right in. If you didn't consider his eyes, dark with memories, it might be easy to forget the body count he'd left in his wake. The things he'd done. The manner in which he'd done them. His hands hung at his sides. The things they'd done, too. A shuffle of images moved through his mind – pallor-mortised skin and petechial hemorrhages and a fine mist of blood issuing from a tracheal slit.

He said, 'I ask myself that every day.'

11. Hell

Aragón dreamed of coughs rife with blood, the glassy fish-white eyes of drowned men, turgid dark waters, severed feet, stained slaughterhouse walls, rusty blades, corpses slow-twisting on meat hooks, wakes of vultures, unseen footsteps, shards of bone, noxious fumes, coiled whips, hanks of human hair, hooded figures, fingernails scratching windowpanes.

All the horrors of the world and his daughter lost among them.

He woke up drenched, the covers kicked below his feet. He'd sweated through the sheets, the pillowcase, the pillow itself. A fan turned lazily overhead. The king-size bed felt unsteady around him, like he was at sea rocking on a rescue boat that was never going to be rescued.

Hell.

This was what hell felt like.

His daughter. His baby girl.

The last moment he'd seen her, she'd thrown her arms wide across the dance floor, summoning him for a hug. Business had interfered. The image of her floated in his mind's eye. Arms spread, eyes smiling. And him gesturing. *Be right back.*

He pulled himself from bed, every tendon and fiber aching. Found his feet unsteadily. Shuffled into the bathroom and emptied his stomach into the toilet. Hands on his knees, leaning over the bowl afterward, he didn't understand the shuddering in his chest until he realized he was weeping.

Shuffling down the carpeted hall toward the room where his wife slept, he leaned on the walls for support. At ghostly intervals Anjelina peered out from rounded frames. Her school pictures, the same smile on her evolving face. Pre-school, in sixth grade, now a senior portrait. That rare perfect gem, never a brooding stage.

He would kill the world before he would let harm come to her.

And yet that wasn't an option.

Belicia's door was slightly ajar. She lay in bed, facing away as she always did. It struck him that he was thankful for this; he couldn't bear to have his eyes on her face right now. He could hear the rasp of her breath. Was she sleeping? Or breathing in the darkness, aware of his presence in the doorway?

She did not turn to him.

He wanted the comfort of a wife. No, the comfort of a mother in the arms of his wife. He was diminished, a boy-child, standing on trembling legs, pathetic and broken.

His shame overwhelmed him. The fraudulence of who he'd pretended to be, of who he'd convinced himself he was. No, he was still a terrified little boy and had always been nothing more. He was scared to face his wife, to see his failure to protect his daughter reflected back at him through her grief. All the pain Belicia had been through, and now he'd caused more. So much more. So much worse.

The sweat dried cold across his body, his nightshirt clinging. He was trembling. He put his shoulder blades to the wall beside the doorjamb and slid down to the carpet.

Be right back, he'd gestured to his daughter. *Be right back.*

He bowed his head to his knees, the hellish memories of the nightmare moving through him. He was too exhausted to cry. He shook and he ached and he told himself to take a breath. And then another.

It seemed impossible that he would make it through the night.

12. Virile and Dangerous Men

Anjelina rustled in bed, turned over sleepily to find Reymundo Montesco in the doorway, watching her. She jerked upright.

The Dark Man's son was very handsome – two days' stubble, strong jaw, dimpled chin, and light green eyes made more arresting given his complexion. Adrenaline hammered in her veins. She drew the sheet up beneath her chin by instinct.

'I'm sorry I startled you,' he said gently.

She took a few shallow breaths, nodded.

'He wants to see you.'

'Your father.'

'Yes.'

She was fully clothed beneath the covers, wearing the ill-sized articles they'd provided her because fleeing the country in a vibrant *quinceañera* dress wouldn't exactly be inconspicuous. Staying dressed made her feel safer, though she knew that safety was an illusion. She rose on numb legs, her thoughts compressed beneath the sheer weight of her panic until she didn't know what she was thinking or if she was thinking at all.

They'd reached a rustic oak door, architectural in height with a rounded top. She had a vague recollection of walking down long, narrow halls and descending tight spiral stairs to arrive here.

'It's okay,' Reymundo said. 'It will be okay.'

He turned the doorknob. They stepped inside a vast room that looked like a telenovela version of a powerful man's study. Mallard-green walls, dark bookshelves with scarce books, brass fittings, and a rolling ladder.

Behind the desk was an aquarium viewing glass looking into the spa-blue water of a tank beyond. A naked woman floated within, twirling in slow motion, her long dark locks porcupining out and washing across her face. Anjelina wondered if the window was a portal to the extravagant pool. She wondered how a woman could have breasts that large on a rib cage that slender. She wondered what kind of upbringing a girl would have to have endured to be a living pornographic display for a monster and his cohorts.

At last she drew in a deep breath and brought her eyes to the Dark Man himself. Raúl Montesco sat behind a theatrically large desk in a saddle-leather wing chair. He was flanked by men and scantily clad women who spilled across the couches arranged before him. Almost as handsome as his son, but with an off-skew cast to his features. That mouth a bit too wide, unsettlingly carnivorous. Far apart eyes segregated by a broad, flat bridge of the nose. Wild dark hair, shiny curls tumbling from a severe widow's peak to brush the top of his right eye. On his inner forearm, a lion tattoo rendered in black and burnt orange, eyes glowing ghostly blue. The gang logo displayed with pride beneath a cuffed-back sleeve.

Among Montesco's men were two *sicarios* whom she identified from their ink. One had a meth-ravaged face, a shiny bald head, and a full collar of neck tattoos. Inked across his throat were the words DARLING BOY. The other looked to be a new generation of killer – bushy black hair, pretty features with youthfully full cheeks. He wore a suit, his shirt unbuttoned to reveal similar heavy work on the neck, his alias inked out in an Old English font: JOVENCITO.

Montesco extended a hand, snapped his fingers, and a

slender man with pronounced teeth laid a rolled cigarette in his palm. Thumbing up a flame from a gold-encased butane lighter, the Dark Man passed the fire beneath the paper, vaporizing the powder, and then sucked in a deep inhale. A crack-laced cigarette, smoked *a la mexicana*. Anjelina had come across them before in the mouths of vagrants at truck stops and the more unsavory kids at high school.

Montesco leaned back, thunked the blocky heels of his ostrich-skin cowboy boots on the leather blotter, and shot smoke at the high ceiling.

His eyes found her, flicked up and then down, undressing her to the bone. 'You're quite beautiful,' he said in accented English. 'You know that.'

Her voice sounded far away. 'I've been told.'

'That's not what I asked.'

It was striking how much menace he could pack into five words. He studied her anthropologically. There was to be no lying. Not with this one. Because of who her father was, she'd been in the vicinity of virile and dangerous men and had learned a few ground rules.

'Yes,' she said flatly. 'I know I'm beautiful.'

'But you're not vain, like these ones.' He chinned at the women on the couches as they examined their nails or smoothed down their microminis. 'Why?'

She searched deep for the truth and found that she actually knew it. 'I didn't think I was pretty when I was younger,' she said. 'Around sixth grade I had a bad awkward stage. And I remember . . .' Her voice trembled, gave out.

He snapped his fingers for her to continue. Behind him the swimming woman spun, arms Jesus-wide, pale sinewy legs drifting, toes pointed like those of an Olympic diver. Darling Boy stared at her with dead, sunken eyes. He had a thin line of a mustache, and the skin of his face was baggy,

73

sliding off the cheeks, showing the shape of the skull beneath. She couldn't look at him without feeling terror beneath her own skin, at the base of her brain. But she couldn't look at El Moreno either.

She found her voice again. 'I remember that girls who were vain about their looks, it felt like a double insult.'

'How?'

'Because you know they're prettier than you to begin with. But when you see them . . . notice themselves so much, you realize that's how they view everyone. Which means you know they look at you that way, too. They notice how *not* pretty you are. I never forgot that.'

Montesco smiled, but there was no mirth in it. He looked glazed, his pupils blown wide, the dark, dark eyes of a shark. 'She's a peach, eh?' He glanced at his men. '*Nacho, tráeme tres vestidos de novia blancos.*'

The skinny guy slid off his perch on the arm of the couch, opened a wall safe, and removed a Baggie of coke. Nacho's teeth were large, protruding outward at an aggressive enough angle that it seemed his thin lips couldn't close over them. As he brought the bag over, the Dark Man lifted an MP7 from behind the desk and held it sideways.

Growing up in Texas as her father's daughter, Anjelina was more familiar with submachine guns than she would have preferred. Nacho arranged a few lines on the flat side of the grooved magazine, and the Dark Man snorted them all. He passed the MP7 to Nacho, who circulated it among his men as Montesco squeezed his nostrils and blinked his red-rimmed eyes. Jovencito took a noseful, but Darling Boy held up a hand, declining the offer. His drug days might have been in the rearview, but he still wore the wreckage all over his face.

Montesco rocked forward and stood up, leaning to steady

himself on the desk. His hand fumbled at his pocket and came up with a folding knife that snapped open with a click.

She stiffened and took a step back.

He circled the desk and came lurchingly at her, leading with the knife.

She tried to retreat again, but he seized her, palming the back of her head, the knife held low at his side. She heard the noises escaping her, squeaks of fear. She couldn't see the blade. His eyes were filled with something beyond loathing, an urge to desecrate, to raze.

'*Papá*,' Reymundo said. '*Papá!*'

But the Dark Man did not move.

Staring directly into her eyes, he slid his hand down to the nape of her neck and squeezed it, a grotesque approximation of a lover's touch. His knuckles drifted forward, grazed up her cheek. He gripped a thick lock of her hair and bent it across the blade. It gave readily.

A tendril sagged free in his fist.

'A girl who is so virtuously not vain should not mind this,' he said. His breath was dry and sour, webs of cotton at the corners of his mouth.

'*Papá*,' Reymundo said. 'She understands.'

The Dark Man released Anjelina and swung his heavy-lidded eyes to his son. He cracked that awful smile once more. Reymundo shriveled on his feet.

'Oh, I get it,' Montesco said. 'This one's different, right? She's different from all the others. She needs to be treated *special*. Is that what you're telling me?'

He stepped aside to go nose to nose with his son, clearing her view to the aquarium window behind the desk, the swimming woman rotating slowly into view. As the broad fan of hair lifted from the face, Anjelina saw that the woman was not swimming at all. Bubbles trapped in perpetually open eyes. The flesh not so much pale as ashen. The cheeks bloated, distorted, crowding waterlogged lips.

Anjelina knew better than to scream. So she turned it inward, felt it scorch through her insides, felt it burn into her cells, where it would remain until – unless – she was ever safe enough to let it out.

She was faint-headed, falling backward, her back striking the door with a resonant thud, and then she was out in the hall, sprinting barefooted across the tiles toward her room, the Dark Man's cackling chasing her each step of the way.

13. The Kind of Exchange
You Regret Later

The rented Buick Enclave rumbled along the rutted, unpaved roads of South Texas, passing dirt and ranches, dirt and farms, dirt and bramble. Now and then an intimation of civilization thrust up from the barren landscape, a skid of auto garages, liquor stores, budget tire shops, and the occasional dentistry outfit that Evan wouldn't venture into if his molar exploded through his cheek.

At one point the route dipped far enough south to bring the Rio Grande into view across a broad sandbar that faded into a morass of thorny puckerbush. He passed a river floodplain with a few ancient mesquites twisting apocalyptically from the bare blanched earth, an abandoned slaughterhouse being inexorably reclaimed by scrub, kids playing volleyball using a half-assed border fence as a net. Textile factories brimming with cheap Mexican labor strobed by through the slats of the barrier, and then the road veered north to spit him out onto a long, flat stretch of baked caliche and brown desert grass.

He pulled over and relieved himself on the side of the road near an ostrich farm, the air thick with the reek of bird shit. Saguaro cacti thrust up from the loam as if posing for postcards, prickly arms lifted hopefully toward a bone-dry sky of forever blue.

He was wearing a casual button-up shirt with an adversarial pattern designed to thwart facial-recognition software. The design, engineered in an MIT lab for resilience against fabric deformation that came with pose changes, confused machine-vision algorithms into believing that the people wearing them were invisible. The shirt also featured magnetic buttons that parted to allow a quicker pistol draw. Like its owner, the shirt looked like not much to speak of.

He drove on for another three hours through dusk and nightfall and then pulled off to fill the tank at the next town. While the old-fashioned reel meter clicked like a slot machine, he watched two mechanics over by the garage pouring beer on the head of a diamondback who thrashed and snapped at the thin air. A well-put-together middle-aged Hispanic woman in church clothes walked by, pursued by a shady character on a kid's BMX bicycle so small that his knees rose to his chest when he pedaled. He wore stained ass-crack blue jeans and whistled at her through spotted-black meth teeth, making menacing shark circles around her. She kept her head high and her shoulders pinned back and paid him no mind.

As she neared, Evan said, '*Necesita mi ayuda?*'

Without breaking pace, she said in perfect English, 'This ain't none of your business.'

The bicyclist gave him a rotting grin, and they continued on their conflicted way.

Evan removed his RoamZone and called Joey.

'I'm five hours out,' he said. 'Are you into Urrea's security system yet?'

'Does the pope shit in the woods?'

'Not as a distinguishing habit.'

'Fine,' she said. 'Does the pope *not* shit in the woods?'

'I'm not familiar with apostolic excretory behavior.'

'*Fine.* Yes, I'm in, okay? Gawd.' She crunched ice loudly in his ear.

'Are you drinking soda over my keyboard again?'

'What? Can't hear you. Going through a canyon.' She made static noises with her mouth and then hung up.

He looked over at the mechanics and the diamondback. Found himself rooting for the snake. The meter clicked off, and he seated the nozzle and drove away.

Hours more of hammered flat terrain, and then all of a sudden the road smoothed out, fresh asphalt with bright lane markings pointing the way. Illuminated in the headlights, the ranches and farms looked cleaner, with nice tractors and split-rail fences and cotton crops blooming from well-tended soil.

As he neared Eden, he saw that the lower-middle-class houses were also better cared for, pride of ownership evident in the paint, swept gutters, and curated lawns and gardens. The high school boasted a new-looking sign announcing THE EDEN RATTLERS. A reroofing job on the main building was paused for the night, bundles of asphalt shingles and tar mops awaiting a new day.

He steered through the two stoplights and scattering of shops that constituted town. A saloon-style bar showed signs of life through neon-glazed windows. The florist next door had nothing to offer but empty window displays and barren interior shelves and refrigerated units; a Magic Markered sign hung on the door proclaimed SOLD OUT – CLOSED UNTIL FURTHER NOTICE. A coffee shop and a grocery market, a taquería and a thrift store, a barbershop and a tattoo parlor. A lawyer who'd hung out a shingle seemed to have cornered the market on wills, personal-injury claims, and SERVICIOS LEGALES DE INMIGRACIÓN.

Ten minutes past the town, up a long and deserted road ideal for surveillance and ambushes, loomed the razor-wire-topped twelve-foot-high concrete-block wall surrounding Aragón Urrea's vast compound. Spotlit by the enclave's high beams, it looked impregnable.

Two men stood at the huge main gate. Everything about

them screamed private military contractors – Timberland boots, CASIO G-shocks, desert-colored canvas pants, slate-gray Rothco tactical softshell jackets over Nike DRI-FIT polo shirts. The PMCs held AR-15 clones with what looked to be sixteen-inch barrels, noteworthy for a number of reasons. Unlike the MP7s or full-auto AK-47s favored by the cartels, AR-15s were legal for private civilian use, which put these guards on the right side of the law. The 5.56 NATO ammo that the semiautomatic rifles employed was readily available in this area of operation, which meant the men were Boy Scout prepared. They kept their AR-15s off sling in a parade carry over their right shoulders, hands cradling the butt plates. A lazy, undisciplined carry method that reached back to when foot soldiers hauled spears and pikes, it subsisted because certain mouth-breathers thought the pose looked good enough to post on weapons-porn websites.

Evan parked at a good distance and opened the door immediately, wanting the dome light to afford the PMCs a reassuring view of him. Unrushed, he got out, standing so the fan of zip-ties rising from his back pocket remained out of sight. Surveillance cameras atop the wall swiveled to note his progress. He wondered how many more he had passed along the desolate road here. How many more heavily armed PMCs there were around the perimeter. And how many more inside.

He drew in a breath, reaching for the Ninth Commandment: *Always play offense.*

And then he approached.

As he did, the PMCs moved their long guns to a port-arms position, angled diagonally across their chest, muzzle above their support-side shoulder. An improvement from parade carry, which wasn't saying much.

The broader of the two PMCs said, 'Can we help you, sir?'

'I'm here to see Aragón Urrea. At his behest.'

'We can neither confirm nor deny that he resides here.' The man smacked his gum a few times. Blond hair buzz-cut tight enough that a pink, sunburned scalp showed through. The edge of a sleeve tattoo peeked out from his cuff, no doubt a snake or a skull or some combination thereof. 'This is an unannounced visit on privately owned land.'

His polo shirt sported a crest with wings, some private company no doubt licensed and vetted and in tight with the DoD. As expected, Urrea was covering all his legal bases.

Evan halted a few feet from the men, dead center between them.

'Sir,' the guard continued in a slightly bored drawl. 'I'd like to edify you that these firearms are registered in accordance with state and federal law. And that Texas is a stand-your-ground state. We have every right under state law to shoot you, as you are trespassing on private property after dark.'

'Consider me edified,' Evan said.

The partner piped up. 'We are within our legal rights to respond with deadly force if you don't heed our commands.' His words, too, were flattened, rehearsed. 'I would like to make clear: We don't want to start a fight. But we will finish one.'

Buzz Cut again. 'We will ask you a second time to evacuate the premises. Your unlawful intrusion and unwillingness to obey our clear sequence of commands is being recorded right now.'

Evan squinted thoughtfully and gazed up at the surveillance cameras topping the front gate. The units looked like robotic heads atop articulated necks. 'Is that right?'

A whirring sound drew the guards' attention.

The camera heads were shaking their heads back and forth. *No.*

'Looks like you lost your backup,' Evan said to the men.

Again to the cameras: 'Do you think these gentlemen have any idea what they're in for?'

Another whirring sound as the cameras shook their heads once more.

'Should I do it now?' Evan asked.

A different pitch of whirring as the cameras nodded.

The guards gazed slack-jawed up at the treacherous surveillance equipment, trying to process this sudden perfidy.

Evan closed the distance between himself and the PMCs with a single long lunge, grabbing both barrels a half foot above the hand guards and shoving them to the right. The men reacted reflexively by yanking the barrels to the left. Evan reversed direction with them, augmenting the momentum and smacking the front sight towers against their temples.

They crumbled in tandem.

Evan stripped their rifles and then crouched over the men, zip-tied them at the ankles and wrists, and rolled them to the base of the wall. He drew a key card from the breast pocket of the bigger man and held it against the pad beside the gate. The gate clicked and swung open accommodatingly.

Evan looked up at the cameras, doffed an imaginary hat at his sixteen-year-old niece-person on the other side of the digital connection, and entered.

What struck him first was the open stretch of land, partially lit. Whitewashed adobe storage facilities rose at sporadic intervals, along with a massive propane tank, a water tower, and a generator visible through the open door of a shed. As he neared the shed, a chubby man exited holding a Styrofoam take-out box filled with Chinese noodles, plastic fork halfway to his mouth, a massive pistol shoved into a hip holster. Evan recognized him as Enrique, aka Kiki, aka Special K.

He came face-to-face with Evan, started, and dropped the box.

Evan knocked him in the larynx with a four-knuckle strike just gentle enough not to collapse his windpipe. Kiki choked and reached for his throat with both hands. Evan flipped the pistol free of the holster, tossing it behind him, then slid one leg behind Kiki's ankles, took him firmly by the shoulders, and dumped him onto the ground.

'You're okay,' he said. 'You'll find air in a moment.'

He zip-tied Kiki and turned him onto his side, resting a hand on his well-padded ribs until the lungs released to let in a screech of air.

'Don't scream or shout, or I'll hit you again,' Evan said. 'Understand?'

Kiki nodded, his cheek burrowing in the dirt.

'How many more of you are there?'

Kiki's eyes strained up to take Evan in. Then his mouth twitched upward, a smile Evan caught a second too late.

He jerked away, a haymaker coming from behind him, glancing off his shoulder, and knocking him to the ground. Another man, the size of an NFL linebacker, stood over him.

Special Ed was just as ugly in real life, but much larger than Evan had anticipated.

Now that Evan was clear of Kiki, Special Ed readied his right hand, which happened to be holding a Glock 21 with a shiny chrome slide.

Evan swung a steel-toed boot into Eduardo's crotch, and the man coughed out a clump of air, doubling over, pistol tumbling. Evan snatched at his wrist, ripped the arm toward him, and spun around Eduardo's torso as he fell. The man struck the earth flat on his back, hard enough to raise a puff of dust, one of Evan's legs scissored around his wide neck, the other knee wedged into his armpit. Evan arched away, holding him captive in an arm bar.

The tumble brought Evan face-to-face with Kiki, who

looked on with bulging eyes, sweat beading on his forehead, mustache fluttering with strained exhalations. They stared at each other as Evan held pressure on Eduardo's arm.

The limb strained a centimeter or two shy of the snapping point, the joint bent the wrong way across the fulcrum of Evan's inner thigh. The back of Evan's knee cinched down on Eduardo's neck, choking off his air supply. Evan lessened the pressure only slightly, listened to Eduardo take in a sip of air.

'I'm going to let go,' Evan said. 'And you're going to let me cuff you. Understand?'

Eduardo's voice came strained. '. . . break my arm . . . you're . . . not getting to Aragón.'

'I'm not here to hurt him. He asked for me.'

'. . . don't care . . . see what happens . . . you let go of me . . . motherf—'

Evan cinched off his air again. Eduardo thrashed a bit but had nowhere to go.

'This is the kind of exchange you regret later,' Evan said quietly. 'Not just immediately after when the pain hits and you're curled up here in the dirt with your elbow dislocated and the tendons snapped. But the months of rehab. When you're old and the arm aches in the morning, in the winter, when you can't sleep on your side.' He leaned back another millimeter, his shoulders seated firmly against the ground. At his side he could hear Kiki breathing hard. 'And that's assuming I stop at your arm. So weigh your anger now against a lifetime of pain. I'm going to give you until three . . . two . . .'

Eduardo tapped Evan's calf twice, a show of surrender, and Evan released him and swung quickly away. The big man kept his word, cradling his elbow for a moment and then rolling onto his stomach. Evan got the plastic cuffs around his ankles and wrists, leaving him facedown in the dirt next to his pal. Then he patted Eduardo's pockets, found a laden key ring in his left cargo pocket that pulled free with a promising jangle.

'Do I need to gag you?' he asked.

Both men shook their heads.

Evan popped up and moved swiftly toward the interior of the compound. A few other PMCs walked patrols in the distance, but it was clear that their guard was down here inside the razor-topped walls. He waited for them to drift away. As he came clear of the last of the maintenance structures, he found himself confronting an open plain of land without any cover.

Nowhere to go but forward.

He ran, keys hard against his palm, praying for something to hide behind.

Ten meters. Thirty.

Still nothing.

He'd gone about the length of a football field when suddenly the main residence resolved from the darkness. At first Evan wasn't sure he was seeing what he was seeing.

He paused a moment to behold it.

It looked as though a two-story house had been spatula'd up out of a middle-class suburb and plunked down directly on the hard Texas dirt. Even the land itself seemed to have been transplanted, perfect green sod rolled down over the unforgiving terrain. A standard front yard complete with a decorative white picket fence and a mailbox with a red flag.

Given the grandiosity of the concrete-block wall, the two-hundred-fifty-acre sprawl of the compound, and the vastness of Urrea's operation, Evan expected a mansion fifteen or twenty times the size of the modest house before him.

He gazed in disbelief.

White clapboard, black trim, gables, shingle roof, a humble porch with a swing. A few sprinklers *chop-chop-chopped* a fine mist across the perfect strips of Bermuda grass. It was as surreal as finding a perfect square of turf grafted onto a parking lot.

Evan turned a slow 360, scanning his surroundings, but there were no guards in view, no other buildings even, nothing but the steady sawing of cicadas reverberating in the humid air. As he finished the full circle, it struck him that he half expected the house to have disappeared, proving itself a figment of his imagination. But no, there it was, set down as if by sleight of hand or alien intervention.

He stepped across onto the edge of the lawn, his boot cushioned by the soft blades. It felt like stepping into another reality. The smell of fresh-cut grass was sharp enough that he could taste it. Out of respect for the carefully tended sod, he moved to the paved front walk. With a creak, a knee-high gate gave way under his knuckles.

He checked the darkness at his back once more. It struck him that the house was withdrawn from the perimeter activity for privacy's sake. A normal family home.

He walked up to the front door, his fingers searching the key ring for the most likely candidate. The lock gave on his first try.

He took a deep breath and eased inside.

14. Strange Bedfellows

The first thing that hit him was the scent of roses. He moved through the short foyer, a living room unfolding to his right, the kitchen to his left. Flowers blanketed every surface, and his mind tracked back to the florist he'd passed on his way here: SOLD OUT – CLOSED UNTIL FURTHER NOTICE. He lifted a card from a bouquet of sunflowers and read a scrawled prayer for Anjelina, signed by a family of four. A spray of sterling roses on the crowded mantel sported a similar sentiment from a different family.

The design of the house – the layout, art, appliances – was wholly unremarkable. Department-store sofa set, family photos on a glass coffee table, framed prints of sunsets and fruit bowls. There was mail on the kitchen's tile counter, dishes in the sink, shoes set in a basket by the front door.

A few drips of a coffee stain marred the carpet of the fourth stair. Evan's footfall was silent on the way up. Four bedrooms upstairs, three closed doors. The open one let into a small, empty study.

He figured the room on the end for the master.

He withdrew his Strider knife, snagged the shark fin topping the blade against the outside corner of his pocket so it snicked open.

Photographs lined the walls, Anjelina through the years.

The door handle was cheap brass, cool beneath his palm. The hinges were silent.

A king-size sleigh bed made of light oak that showed the grain and knots. Pale gray early-morning light starting to leak around the edges of the curtains, bringing into relief the single form slumbering beneath the sheets.

Evan padded across the room silently and stood over the man.

Aragón Urrea slept on his side, his eyelids puffy. Even in sleep his mouth had a patrician set to it. A dense shock of dark hair shot through with silver, pronounced chin, the pressure of his cheek against the pillow coaxing jowls into distinguished existence.

Evan lowered the blade against Urrea's Adam's apple.

Aragón's eyes opened.

Moving only his pupils, he stared up at Evan.

'You called,' Evan said. 'Here I am.'

Aragón blinked up at Evan a few times, taking his measure.

'Thank you,' Aragón said. 'I will do anything to get my daughter back.'

'What's it worth to you?' Evan asked.

Aragón cleared his throat, his stubble rasping against the blade. 'Everything.'

'Your kingdom?'

'Yes.'

'Your life?'

'Yes.'

'If I help you,' Evan said, 'I will make demands of you. Some of which you will not like.'

'I understand.' Aragón remained perfectly frozen, perfectly calm. 'As I understand why you make this point at the edge of a blade.'

From across the room came the sound of a throat clearing. Aragón still did not move, but his eyes pulled to the doorway as did Evan's.

La Tía – the woman who had raised Urrea – stood in the doorway. Already dressed for the day, she wore a high-necked blouse, and her white hair was elaborately blow-dried upward, striking a contrast with her deep brown skin.

She regarded the two of them down the length of her nose disapprovingly. 'Is this him?'

Aragón said, 'Yes, *Tía*.'

Her gaze shifted to Evan. He kept his fist around the knife handle, the blade resting against Urrea's throat.

'It's enough, *muchachos*,' she said with a measure of irritation. 'Downstairs. I'll cook you some eggs.'

She withdrew.

Evan looked back down at Aragón.

'You heard the woman,' Aragón said. 'If you think *you're* tough, wait till you see what happens if we're late for breakfast.'

Evan heeded Aragón's advice and removed the knife from his throat.

It was the best goddamned plate of migas Evan had ever tasted. Steaming-hot eggs scrambled with chorizo, pico de gallo, diced jalapeños. He ate heartily, shoving mouthfuls onto his fork with the edge of a griddle-warmed corn tortilla. To his side a sliding glass door let out onto a stretch of rolled sod and hard land, the perimeter fence little more than a dark streak in the distance.

Aragón watched him, arms folded high across his chest. 'Here, try this,' he said, spooning up tomatillo chipotle salsa from his plate and dolloping it across Evan's food. He used his fork to mix it a bit, took a bite from Evan's plate to sample. 'There,' he said. 'Good.'

Evan fought down his OCD, tried another forkful. Even better.

Over at the stove, La Tía had not stopped bustling. She'd moved the flowers onto the floor, clearing her operating space. Her motions seemed choreographed – kneeing the refrigerator door closed, sliding pans from high burners to medium, pivoting to put away a dish, drying it until it slid from her towel-covered hands into place in a cupboard. 'I use a soy chorizo,' she said to no one in particular, her back still turned. 'For his cholesterol.'

Evan finished and rose from the round wooden kitchen table to clear his plate. Without looking at him, she said, 'Sit.'

He obeyed, and she whirled around the counter to pluck his plate off the table. She eyed Aragón's. 'Something wrong with my migas this morning?'

'I can't find my appetite.'

She scowled at him. 'At some point you'll have to. Your daughter needs you strong.' She swept his plate away and busied herself washing dishes in the sink.

Evan said, 'May I help you clean?'

'No,' La Tía said. 'Would you like more juice?'

A glass jug of orange juice rested on the counter between them. Evan said, 'Yes,' and stayed put.

She brought the jug to him and refilled his glass. He nodded his thanks, and she withdrew to the sink once more.

Aragón studied Evan. 'Señor Nowhere Man,' he said. 'Flesh and bone spun into a legend.'

'No one measures up to a myth.'

'No. And yet here you are,' Aragón said. 'Inside a home. A real home. And just as you tested me upstairs, you have been tested here.'

'How?'

'Everyone is appraised when they share a meal. Do you belong here? Do you pay attention? Will you abide by the rules of our family? Will you show respect?' Aragón nodded toward La Tía, vigorously scrubbing a pan under steaming water. 'Two times you offered to help. A man who doesn't offer to help cannot be trusted. Two times she rebuffed you. The third time you didn't ask.'

'What's that tell you?'

'That you're not too eager to please. That also cannot be trusted in a man. You were raised right.'

'I was raised rough.'

'That's irrelevant,' Aragón said. 'It has nothing to do with rough or gentle. Privileged or broke, everyone has their own path to the light. Sometimes those of us who came up hard are forced to see what actually matters. If we survive, that is. The world doesn't allow us *not* to see. We are forced into understanding, into grace. It's either that or prison, or drugs, or the cold, hard earth.'

Evan looked into the family room. A row of antique volumes lined a bookcase. They were sorted by height, except for one that was out of place, higher than its neighbors. The sight of it scratched at Evan's OCD, and he returned his focus to the table, aligned his fork and knife with the edge of the place mat.

He wondered what he was doing enjoying a home-cooked breakfast in the middle of an armed compound in South Texas. He wondered at the closed bedroom doors upstairs and why Aragón slept separately from his wife. He wondered what Anjelina was doing right now – or what was being done to her.

'You didn't ask me here to discuss manners,' Evan said. 'Or grace.'

'Didn't I?' Aragón said. 'How can I trust someone with my daughter's life who is not a good man?'

'And yet you're a drug lord.'

Aragón shrugged. 'I'm a captain of industry.'

'That doesn't interest me,' Evan said. 'Tell me how your daughter was taken.'

'A cadre of armed men. Eight of them armed with MP7s.

Día de los Muertos sugar-skull masks, Leones ink on their forearms. They stormed the community center, snatched her, took off in three black SUVs.'

'I'll want to see the place,' Evan said. 'Talk to witnesses.'

'Of course.'

'What was she wearing?'

Aragón went to a small desk in the corner of the kitchen and came back with a stack of photos – glittery signs announcing Anjelina's eighteenth birthday, paper tablecloths, what looked to be half the town in attendance. Anjelina wore an orange dress with frilly arm cuffs, a basque waist, and a matching shawl draped modestly over her front side, a not-too-revealing sweetheart neckline peeking through. She was glowing – dimpled cheeks, perfect grin; it seemed it was impossible to take a bad picture of her. Evan took out his RoamZone, thumbed up the camera, and captured the photographs digitally.

'The gold locket she's wearing,' Evan said. 'What's in it?'

'A wedding photograph of me and my wife.'

'Your wife, she lives here?'

Aragón stiffened slightly. 'Yes. She prefers to keep to her room. She's less social than I am.'

'Can I talk with her about this?'

'It will upset her.'

'That's not what I asked,' Evan said.

Over at the sink, La Tía had stopped scrubbing to eaves-drop more intently.

'If it becomes necessary,' Aragón said. 'But she knows nothing. She wasn't there.'

'She wasn't at your daughter's birthday?'

'No.'

Evan stared at him. Aragón stared back. Not open for discussion.

'Have the Leones made contact?' Evan said. 'Asked for anything?'

'No. And that is even more terrifying.' Aragón rubbed at his eyes, the pouched skin shifting beneath his thumb and forefinger. 'To everyone *their* child is different, yes? On Santa's knee, going down a slide, first day of preschool. It's new to the world, like this is the first time it has ever happened. They are special. We all were once.' A weighted pause. 'The rules of life hurt me at a young age. I can barely remember who I was before that. I hardened myself. But then? I had her. And I remembered who I once was. Even though I didn't know it, my whole life had been spent trying to earn this honor, being her parent. I wasn't ready. Maybe no one is.' He smacked his hands together. 'Once you have a daughter, she forces you to become a man. Or a failure.'

'Which are you?'

'You never know if you succeed. Only if you fail. That's the joke, you see?' Aragón took in a breath, held it. 'When Anjelina was a little over a year, we started taking her to Zihuatanejo for Semana Santa. And Belicia – my wife – had the stomach flu. So I had this child with me all day every day. Riding my shoulders across the sand.' He held up his large hands, the veins pronounced beneath the knuckles. 'She held my hand to walk to the water's edge and clung to me, squawking against the cold. That belly laugh. There wasn't a single minute that whole week when we weren't touching, like we were a part of each other and always would be.' There were tears now on his cheeks, glittering streams, and he made no move to wipe them. 'If they . . . harm her . . .' He halted, tried again. 'To lose a child, it's not just her dying. It is the death of the future. It is the death of the entire world.'

The pan hit the sink with a clang. 'Stop it!' La Tía barked.

'She is not going to die. You will not let it happen. Your self-pity doesn't help.'

Aragón waved her off, aggravated.

Evan gave the remark a moment to dissipate and then asked, 'Have you talked with the authorities?'

'The authorities.' Aragón snorted, wiped his face. 'The rule of law is not an option. If someone steals from me, I can't go to court. If someone harms me, the police root for them. If someone takes my daughter, they assume it is a problem of my creation, a consequence of my choices. And they are right. I am outside the law. I make my own way, live by my own code, enforce my own rules. Like you.' He leaned forward, and for the first time Evan sensed menace in his deep, dark eyes. 'There is nothing the law can do that I cannot do better.'

'Then why don't you go to war?' Evan asked. 'Hire up an army of mercs and crush them?'

'Because if we go in through the front door, they will kill her. They will move her. They will make her suffer. But you know this. So why do you ask?'

'I'm gauging your temperament.'

La Tía bustled over with a coffeepot and filled mugs for Evan and Aragón. She lingered by Evan. 'You seem acceptable,' she said.

'Good thing,' Evan said. 'Or your nephew would have me shot the minute I walk out of the house.'

She gave a single-shoulder shrug. 'Details.'

A sudden commotion at the sliding glass door drew their attention. Six PMCs, including the gate guards and Special K and Special Ed. Eduardo was still babying the arm Evan had declined to break.

They were banging on the glass, sounding an alarm. In the background others trotted by, surrounding the house, weapons at the ready. Evan had instructed Joey to take out the phone system as well, which had bought him some extra time.

As Eduardo took in Evan sipping coffee with Aragón, the pockmarked skin of his face shifted with surprise, then anger, then something like envy. La Tía unlocked the door and slid it open.

'We were coming to alert you to an intrusion, *Patrón*,' Special Ed said as the PMCs faded away behind him. 'But it seems you've discovered that.'

At his side Kiki folded his arms, the long-suffering buttons of his shirt straining to reveal lozenges of belly flesh. A powdering of dirt clung to his cheek and one ear. Raw red streaks at his wrists from the zip-ties. The heel of his hand rode the butt of his holstered .44, and he looked as eager to make use of it as Special Ed looked ready to beat Evan senseless with his bare fists.

'Boys,' La Tía said, 'come eat.'

'No thank you, *Tía*,' Special Ed said.

'It's my migas,' she said sternly. 'Sit.'

Not a question.

They sat.

She produced another two plates and set them down.

As the men chewed, their eyes bored holes through Evan. Evan sipped his coffee and returned their stares. Aragón watched with an air of wry amusement.

'"Misery acquaints a man with strange bedfellows,"' he said. 'Get all the *verga*-measuring out of the way now, *hombres*. *Tenemos trabajo*.'

15. In the Hands of Savages

There was nothing to be learned at the community center. Nothing to be learned from the witnesses. Nothing to be learned from a half dozen interviews with Anjelina's friends.

The townsfolk spoke of Anjelina as if she were part local mascot, part village deity. They showed Aragón the utmost respect, and Evan had no sense that it was feigned. Surveillance cameras at the town's periphery had captured the SUVs, but the windows were tinted and the license plates removed. Aragón figured she'd been smuggled across the border to Mexico on the night of the party, which put her beyond reach in a multitude of ways.

With Aragón at the wheel, they rattled back to the compound in a Jeep Wrangler flanked by security vehicles brimming with PMCs. Evan sat up front, Kiki and Special Ed crammed unhappily in the back with a few spare gas cans, waiting for an excuse to kill him.

The tires shoved through the sun-bleached loam, churning up reddish clay from the subsoil, dust powdering the air. Confused by the weather, a few Guayacán trumpet trees remained in bloom, full crowns of golden flowers massaged by the breeze. White yucca flowers thrust phallically from nests of sword-shaped leaves. A lifeless bull snake sprawled across the road like a speed bump, smashed flat at axle-wide intervals. It truly was another world here.

'What next?' Aragón said.

They passed a field of cattle, the stink hitting them on the hot air. Evan considered the Fifth Commandment, his least favorite: *If you don't know what to do, do nothing.*

'I'm not sure yet,' he said.

'This Nowhere Man is very impressive,' Eduardo piped up from the back.

'Yes,' Kiki said. 'So far he's eaten breakfast and asked a bunch of useless questions. Maybe once he's had lunch, he will graduate to only being *partially* useless.'

Aragón waved them off.

Evan shared the men's frustration at the snarl of dead ends. He'd searched Anjelina's room before they'd left. Posters and makeup and fluffy throw pillows, the sugary residue of a cinnamon candle tingeing the air, a piano keyboard with dog-eared sheet music on the stand. He'd leafed through her yearbooks, read the inscriptions – BFF vows, tentatively flirty entries from boys, and glowing praise from teachers. An extraordinary yet ordinary young woman. In the hands of savages.

'The night she was taken, I hired a man to infiltrate the Leones,' Aragón said. 'We will need inside information if we hope to find her. Especially if she's already in Mexico.'

'When will you hear from him?' Evan asked.

'He's so far undercover that he will barely be able to breathe. We can only wait and pray.'

'Have you initiated contact with the Leones?'

'Through a proxy. I was told they will contact me when they are ready.'

'What do you think that means?'

'I have no fucking idea.'

'Any precipitating event between you and the Leones?' Evan asked. 'Recent turf dispute? Cutting in on their market or they on yours?'

'Nothing,' Aragón said. 'We operate in different lanes.

They're heavy into hard drugs, human smuggling, and gun-running. I got word that their Reynosa franchise was moving shoulder-fired surface-to-air missile launchers for thirty-five K a unit.' He scowled at the thought, his chin doubling. 'I used to dabble in small arms. No more. We are very different. The Leones are big into posses and entourages, prostitutes and clubs. I keep a clean nose.'

'For a transnational drug kingpin,' Evan said.

Aragón shrugged. 'It's relative. After Anjelina was born, I decided to diversify my portfolio, move to online retail. She inspired me. Maybe not to be good. But to be less bad. To . . . *yo no sé*, do less harm.'

'How so?'

'Why so many questions?' Special Ed asked from the back.

'I have to understand your operation,' Evan said, 'to understand why you were targeted.'

'*Patrón*, how do you know you can trust this –'

Aragón held up his hand. 'Remember where my daughter is. Trust is the least of our concerns.'

The road narrowed, crowded by a green burst of chapote, hard persimmons knocking against the door panels like children begging at a border crossing.

'I only sell what our government sells,' Aragón said. 'Correction: what our members of Congress – with their pockets stuffed with lobbyist cash – *allow* big pharmaceutical companies to sell. Oxys and Roxys and the like.'

'Manufactured where?'

'China used to be promising, but they require end-user certification, and it takes too long. Lately I've been bringing in pharmacy-grade stuff out of Mumbai. The bribes are heftier, but they're more reliable than the Chinese. They ship it here labeled as pool chemicals.'

'Ship it here how?'

'Congress passed a law requiring electronic data tracking for all FedEx and UPS packages. So guess who we use now?'

'The United States Postal Service,' Evan said.

'That's big government at work for you.' Aragón chewed his lip, eyes on the road. 'For the European market, I warehouse it in Liberia. A beautiful laissez-faire country. Strategic location, political anarchy, modern technology. I try to make sure the meds are conflict-free, fair trade, like coffee. Not quite like the coca growers' unions in Bolivia, but I do my best to work with manufacturers who provide some measure of social benefit to their communities. You'd be surprised at how accountable business practices ensure silence, loyalty, and make more profit, too.'

'Do you sell direct to consumer?'

'Sometimes. We keep our sales online. In the US we target states that treat off-prescription drug sales as civil violations rather than as criminal. I am insulated regardless, but that makes us less likely to draw attention. When we do, we shut down that website and port it over to another URL. Generally I can have a fresh operation opened within the hour. The digital age is so easy. What did the Colombians have back in the seventies? Coca seeds, speedboats, a few rusty Cessnas. And yet they built one of the biggest world economies. *Cojones* like soccer balls.'

'How's the money come in?'

'The cheapest e-commerce call centers can be contracted in Manila and Haifa. The Filipinos are polite, the Israelis . . . are not. But both are cheap, discreet, and process credit-card authorizations through different financial institutions in cities with loose regulations – Pretoria, Dar es Salaam, Addis Ababa, and the like. And after that? Zurich and the Caymans have drawn scrutiny lately, so I move the money through

Dubai now. Then currency-swap over to dirhams, rupees, rands, rubles, gold, whatever.'

'I doubt the Leones are tangled up in that,' Evan said. 'Or even care. How about bulk sales?'

Aragón shrugged. 'Conducted through middlemen, encrypted comms, and cryptocurrency. As with everything else, I maintain total operational security. I'm never the face of conflict.'

'But you can't ship bulk in through the post office.'

'No. We bring bulk in from the south, paying off the entities that control points of access.'

Evan's interest perked. 'Like who?'

'Smuggling families. Armed bands. Mexican officials who control ports, airstrips, border crossings.'

'That's your most likely overlap with the Leones,' Evan said. 'You use the official checkpoints?'

'The men I pay to take the risk do, yes.'

'How do you do it?'

'They load the product into a trailer with a false bottom. Sew it into the upholstery. Stuff it into spare tires, gas tanks, false roofs. You know how long border agents have to assess each vehicle? Forty seconds. They only get around to inspecting two percent of cars. You'd take those odds at a casino any day of the week. Now, human smuggling is trickier. Humans are bigger, produce waste, need oxygen.'

Evan caught up to Aragón's words at the same time, it seemed, that Aragón did himself. The parallels to his own daughter in transit.

Aragón's anger intensified. 'That's why the bastard *guías* and coyotes forgo checkpoints and drag them through the desert wasteland, don't care if they live or die. But drugs? Legal checkpoints make much more sense. In fact . . .' Aragón checked his phone, thumbing across a few messages. 'I have a load coming over now.' He jerked the wheel to the right, hammering over a ditch to vector north. 'It's a big one. Since you are so curious, I will make an exception to go myself and show you.'

The rest of the convoy screeched and veered to course-correct before settling into a protective phalanx around the Jeep once more. In about a half mile, they left the paved road, rumbling onto a dirt path that cut through head-high stalks of sugarcane. The fields stretched for an eternity, crops thrashing against the open sides of the Wrangler, forcing Evan to lean toward the center console.

The path was nothing more than a memory of tire tracks and a slight parting of the tall stalks. The way forward grew increasingly claustrophobic until it seemed they were forging into the sturdy grass itself, the fender serving as a jungle machete. Through the windshield Evan could see only the crops beating at the glass, but somehow Aragón knew where he was going.

All at once they were spit through into a cleared circle of land where a brazilwood tree rose, framed by a squat tangle of bramble. Twilight was coming on, leaching color from the world, dusting everything into shades of sepia.

The other vehicles swerved into the clearing behind them and halted. For a moment everyone waited for the dust and grit from the wheel wells to sulk away on a limp breeze. The dirt near the center was fanned out in a familiar pattern, two long strokes showing where helicopter skids had recently set down. The sugarcane rimming the circle leaned outward, beaten down by rotor wash.

Aragón emerged, Evan at his side, and headed for the bramble. Without bothering to don gloves, he reached for a thorny clump and tugged it aside. It came readily, unattached to the earth.

'They call this *huisache*. It means "many thorns" in Nahuatl. Useful stuff.' As Aragón swept the brush away, a hatch came clear in the ground. A few creaky twists of the metal wheel and the hatch swung open on rusty hinges, revealing a storage tank below filled with wax-encased bricks. 'The helo sets down right over this bramble. They unload from the belly of the chopper straight into the earth. Invisible from the eyes of drones.' He snapped his fingers, pointed down.

Kiki tried to swing into the tank but wound up clinging to the lip, wheezing, the tip of one boot circling the hole.

Aragón rolled his eyes. 'Enough with this. Someone help him. He's going to have a heart attack.'

Special Ed hoisted Kiki out and dropped down into the hatch himself.

Kiki kicked at the dirt sheepishly with the pointed toe of a cowboy boot. 'Sorry, *Patrón*. I have to go back on the Weight Watchers.' He patted the bulge of his belly.

Special Ed hoisted himself out of the hole bearing one of the bricks. He thumbed up a blade and sliced the wax surface, the slit brimming with white pills.

Aragón grabbed a few and admired them in his palm. Indistinguishable from prescription meds, they were circular or oval and bore various stamps. 'They're getting good at disguising it as Tramadol and OxyContin.'

'What is it really?' Evan asked.

'New China White. Pure.'

'Fentanyl.' Evan stared down into the hatch. 'That's . . . what? Eighty kilos?'

'A hundred.'

'It's fifty times more potent than heroin,' Evan said. 'So we're looking at almost a hundred million overdoses?'

'If taken improperly.' Aragón tilted his hand, let the pills spill back into the slit package. 'If people don't want to follow the instructions, that's on them.'

'No,' Evan said. 'It's not.'

Aragón's face tensed.

Behind him Special Ed and Kiki went motionless. Even the PMCs at the edge of the clearing had gone on alert, perfectly still, AR-15s held at a slant, barrels aiming at a spot in the dirt between their boots and Evan's.

Aragón's shoulders tightened, and he drew himself fully erect, an unsettling effect like that of a cobra unfurling. The shift in posture gave him another few inches, forcing Evan to look up at him, Aragón's size apparent for the first time.

Aragón's lips barely moved. 'What did you say?'

'You heard me,' Evan said. 'If you want my help, you're going to burn those pills.'

'Are you threatening me?'

'I'm making clear my terms,' Evan said. 'I told you I would make demands of you that you would not like. This is the first.'

'Oh, the *first*?' Aragón's eyes had a touch of wildness in them now. They'd grown larger, the sclera more pronounced. Even so, his tone was calm, measured. 'Are you going to go after the Big Pharma companies as well? Make them change their business practices?'

'They didn't ask for my help.'

Aragón took a step toward Evan. Evan held his ground. To his side he sensed Kiki's hand drift to the grip of the big .44 at his hip. Special Ed hiked his shirt up, showing off the gleaming pistol nestled against its tattooed outline on his washboard abdominals.

There was, Evan realized, a good chance this would all go sideways.

He charted the choreography. Half step to pivot behind Kiki, counterclockwise momentum putting the fat man between him and the others. Choke hold with his left arm, right hand shoving Kiki's .44 back into the holster on a tilt, firing down through the top of Kiki's thigh. If Special Ed dared to shoot, Kiki's mass would be enough to absorb the 230-grain rounds from the Glock 21 in the three-quarters of a second it would take for Evan to clear leather with Kiki's gun and fire into Ed's chest at close range. The big round would knock Ed over into Aragón. Kiki would be collapsing by then, aided by Evan's knee to his kidney, which would shove him out in front. That would block the sight line of the PMCs long enough for Evan to cinch up Aragón from behind, leaving the guns for hire with nothing to target but a sliver of his face and the thin band of his forearm across Aragón's throat. Three of the PMCs stood in the open, which gave Evan easy target acquisition. He'd have four cartridges left in the .44, one for each, but the fourth man would likely park his critical mass behind an armored SUV door before Evan could get to him. He'd have a decent shot at the guy's ankle, and he'd use the precious second and a half as the man collapsed to choke-drag Aragón to the ground so he could grab Special Ed's Glock 21, loaded with fourteen rounds minus whatever he'd fired into Kiki. By then the fourth PMC would be in the dirt, his vital organs visible beneath the SUV door given Evan's lower vantage, which meant the follow-up shots would penetrate gut or rib cage. In case Kiki hadn't bled out from his femoral by then, a bullet would put him down for good, removing him as a distraction.

Then Evan would have Aragón, three vehicles of his choosing, and a world of possibilities.

Evan kept his gaze locked on Aragón. In his peripheral vision, he sensed the heel of Kiki's hand resting on the grip of his pistol, Ed's fingers trembling above his .44. If either of them drew, Evan would have to move, and then there would be no stopping it.

The PMCs wouldn't dare open up first with the big guns from across the clearing, not with Aragón in the mix.

Aragón lifted a hand, pointed at the open hatch. 'This load is worth one hundred sixty million dollars.'

'How much is your daughter worth?'

Aragón lowered his hand to his side. His face remained placid, but there was an ice-hard coldness beneath it that reminded Evan how little he knew of the man. Aragón's nostrils flared ever so slightly, close enough that Evan could feel the heat of his breath. He kept his vision sharp yet diffuse – Kiki's hand, Special Ed's posture, the position of the PMCs. Every slight movement bringing a commensurate adjustment to the plan he hoped not to execute.

The moment stretched out and out, and then – finally – Aragón stepped back.

'Get the gas cans,' he said.

Special Ed and Kiki stared at him in disbelief.

'Move,' Aragón said.

They unstuck themselves and ambled back to the Wrangler, returning with gas cans.

Aragón seized one, spun the cap off, and sloshed gasoline down through the hatch. He shook the can empty, let it tumble into the subterranean storage tank. 'Well, what are you waiting for?'

Kiki and Special Ed scrambled into motion, emptying the contents of the remaining cans into the tank.

Aragón pulled out a silver lighter and thumbed up a flame. He held it at chest level, peered at Evan over the finger of orange light. 'You ask what my daughter is worth?'

He flung the lighter into the storage tank. It was slow to catch, but finally a whoosh announced ignition, the earth belching a cloud of heat. Evan stepped back from the toxic chemical stench, watching the black smoke rise to the clear blue sky.

After a time Aragón kicked the hatch shut and turned to Evan. 'I have enough money for a hundred lifetimes.' He shifted his focus to Kiki and Special Ed. 'None of them are worth living without Anjelina. Do you understand me?'

Eduardo said, 'We understand, *Patrón*.'

For a moment there was nothing but the crackling of the buried fire expending itself inside its metal prison. And then the sound of an engine cut through the noise.

The PMCs fanned out, readying their AR-15s. Special Ed and Kiki had their pistols in hand, too. About a quarter mile away, the stalks began to wave.

They all stared at the edge of the clearing, waiting to see what emerged. The curved edge of sugarcane stalks fluttered slightly in the breeze as if respiring.

The sound of an engine grew louder, and then another SUV pushed into sight. Everyone relaxed. Before it stopped moving, the passenger door flung open and another PMC emerged, breathless, holding a square FedEx box the size of a basketball. A pink sticker on the side read PRIORITY ALERT.

'This arrived for you, *Patrón*. It came special delivery.'

Aragón's voice came dry and cracked. 'You scanned it for explosives?'

The man nodded. 'No return address. But there is a name. It says it's from . . .'

Aragón's face had gone bloodless. 'From whom?'

'From El Moreno.'

Aragón's gaze went loose, unfocused. He stared down at his boots, took a shaky breath. And then another. Fighting his way to composure. Everyone waited for his face to stop trembling.

At last he lifted his eyes, and the man handed him the box.

16. The Gravity of the Situation

Aragón stared at the FedEx box. Sweat trickled down his pronounced brow, and he shrugged a shoulder to mop it with his sleeve. 'It is cold.' His hands were shaking. 'The box is cold.'

He set it on the ground. They stood around staring down at it.

Aragón held out his palm toward Evan. 'Your knife.'

Evan gave him the Strider.

Aragón thumbed it up. His chest rose and fell, his breathing audible. He took a knee over the box. Slit the tape. The cardboard flaps lifted upward, emitting a sigh of mist.

Aragón reached inside and pulled out a cooler, dry ice spilling in its wake. Bloodred lettering across the side: HUMAN ORGAN FOR TRANSPLANT.

Aragón's breath caught. He set the cooler down on the earth gently, as if it might shatter.

He reached for the lid. Hesitated. Closed his eyes. Jerked in a few breaths.

Opened it.

He peered inside, and his face sagged. He clutched his stomach and gave a low moan.

It took a moment for Evan to realize that the sound was relief.

Kiki inched forward and peered over Aragón's shoulder and then walked backward, stumbling on the blocky heels of his boots, hand over his mouth, gagging.

Special Ed regarded the contents evenly. 'I guess FedEx doesn't scan for severed heads,' he said.

Aragón's knees cracked as he rose. A piece of paper fluttered in his hand, a simple note, the penmanship smeared with moisture from the dry ice.

'Try again and your daughter's head will be delivered next.'

Evan stepped forward and looked down into the box.

Greasy hair, crusted eyes, sallow skin. Gaping mouth with cracked pale lips, a black well where the tongue should be. The decapitation mark was clean, no marks from a serrated edge. A big blade, probably a machete.

Evan cleared his throat. 'Your undercover man?'

Aragón nodded, the color starting to return to his face. 'Send his widow and children money,' he said to Special Ed.

'How much?'

Already he was walking back to the Jeep, his gait now steady. 'Whatever they need.'

The PMCs at the compound noted the caravan's arrival, the armored front gate rumbling open as they approached. Evan's rented SUV remained where he'd left it, parked at a slant facing the wall. Aragón didn't slow, the Jeep nearly clipping the Buick before squeezing through the moving gate with no more than a few inches to spare on either side.

They rattled across the hard earth for a time, and then the bizarre square of suburbia came into view. Aragón pulled into the driveway, a middle-class father returning from a day's work.

They unpacked from the vehicle, the night air crisp in Evan's lungs. As Aragón and his men headed inside, Evan said, 'I need a minute.'

Aragón didn't seem to register that he'd spoken at all.

Once the men disappeared into the house, Evan strode the property's perimeter, walking that razor's edge between inhospitable South Texas dirt and the lush grass where the yard began. The house was more than a house; it was an act of will, stubbornly nourishing a patch of civilization to life.

Shadowed beneath the eaves of the house, a row of surveillance cameras swiveled to hold him in sight, the glint of their lenses barely visible in the darkness.

He took out his RoamZone and called Joey.

She picked up against a white-noise storm of commotion in the background – the clatter of equipment and men speaking in raised voices. 'You're alive,' she said. 'Good. Now you can come home and deal with construction guys who are, like, *tha worst*. Especially to people with girl parts.'

'Joey –'

'I mean, the cable guy's all like, "I'll be there in this six-hour window." And I'm like, "Of course. Why would I expect you to actually be able to set a human-being time like, dunno, a brain surgeon or senior partner in a law firm?" And then they're all like –'

Evan said, 'I don't need cable.'

'Whatevs.' Fuzz filled his ear; Joey must have pressed the phone against her chest, though it barely muted her shouting, 'Uh, 'scuse me! Does the so-called Excelsior Package include someone who knows how to install wireless speakers right side up?'

Evan couldn't make out the muffled retort, only the guy's disconsolate tone.

'Well, I appreciate your concern, but I *do* want to worry my pretty little head about it,' Joey said. 'Oh, and I should warn you, I subsist on the bitter tears of dude-bros, so please keep pushing me. I haven't been fed yet today.'

'*Joey.*'

'What!'

'I'm in the middle of something here.'

'Is it as stressful as a remodel?'

'Probably not.' Evan eyed the cameras once more. 'Are you still in Urrea's surveillance system?'

A faint *tap-tap-tap* of her footfalls as she moved to privacy. He could only imagine the dude-bro installer's relief. 'Nope,' she said, lowering her voice. 'They closed the loophole, kicked me out right after our little stunt. I can't have your back anymore, X.'

'That's okay. Aragón and I are coming to an understanding.'

'Do you know how insane you sound?'

'Yes.'

'Don't forget who he is,' she said.

'I'm texting you pictures of Anjelina from the night she was taken. What she was wearing, jewelry, all that. And some images of the SUVs that took her, though I don't know how useful they'll be, since they ditched the plates. I need to know anything you can find about the Leones, everywhere they're operating in Mexico, the US, all of it.'

'Okay. The pictures are coming through now and – *HEY, PONYTAIL!*'

Evan started, nearly dropping the phone.

'Pro tip!' Joey yelled at someone. 'Don't show up drunk to a job requiring nail guns.' Muted sounds of remorse. 'Sure you're not drunk. Dude, you have Cookie Monster eyes. *Out!* And eat a sleeve of Mentos.' Back to Evan. 'I have to go. The tile guys just showed up, and they only speak Croatian.'

'Do you have Bosnian?' Evan asked.

'Nope.'

'Serbian?'

'Nope.'

'Polish?'

'Passable.'

'Forty-percent overlap.'

'I was today years old when I learned that.'

'Between Polish and Google Translate, you should muddle through.'

'I always do. Don't do anything more stupid than usual. I don't have time to come rescue you.'

'Your concern is heartwarming.'

'Hey, wait. These are supposed to be ceramic, *not* porcelain!' She started yelling in Polish before she cut the line.

Evan stood a moment beneath the vast Texas sky before heading inside.

The men were sitting around the kitchen table, the mood somber, the FedEx box centered between them like a salad bowl.

Aragón nodded to a chair, and Evan sat. Aragón tugged at his mouth, pulled it down hard enough to make the outer edges of his eyes sag. He gave a sigh, the stale air reaching across the table. His hand pressed firmly across his mouth, thumb shoving his cheek up at one side. Wrinkles bunched at the corner of his right eye, his gaze haunted.

The misplaced book on the shelf in the living room called to Evan's OCD, but he kept it purposefully out of his line of sight, not giving in to the compulsion to glare at it.

Aragón set his palms on the table as if grounding himself against the wood. 'There is a tear inside most men's brains through which they sometimes glimpse the things they don't allow themselves to think. And it scares them so much they do everything in their power to wall themselves off from that place. From the unthinkable.' Pleading eyes, the eyes of a man consigned to hell. 'I live in that place. Among those thoughts. That's where my daughter and I are together right now. *This?*' His gesture took in the kitchen and the men, the house and the world beyond. 'This is a dream to me.'

'We find her here, though,' Evan said. 'Not in your nightmares.'

Aragón steadied himself with a breath. 'I think you're right about the border crossings being the likely point of contention between me and these *putos*. I've dug up plenty of intel on the Leones. So now that Plan A came back to us in a FedEx box, I will send these two' – a nod to Kiki and Special Ed – 'to find out what loads the Leones are moving. Where they are vulnerable, overextended. Perhaps that will shed light on what they want from me.' He suddenly looked weary beyond his years. 'They poison their product. Heroin with chocolate-flavored baby milk, meth with MSM, cocaine with laundry detergent.' He waved a hand. 'Or worse.'

'Unlike you,' Evan said. 'The organic drug dealer.'

Aragón's dark eyes lifted to meet Evan's. They did not look amused. 'I do not cheat my customers. I treat my people with respect. I do not lie. I am not like them.'

A rapping on the door interrupted the stare-off, and Special Ed rose to answer. Three PMCs crowded the doorway with their body armor and semiautomatic rifles. They conversed with Ed in hushed tones, and then Eduardo turned to face them across the foyer.

'There's a problem with the García boy, the eldest. He's in the SUV.' A pause. 'I told you he was no good.'

'We were all no good,' Aragón said. 'Until we weren't.' He waved them in. 'Bring him here.'

'Are you out of your mind?' La Tía had appeared at the top of the stairs, clutching her bathrobe at her throat. Her hair was up in curlers, her face a ghostly white, smeared with some kind of cream. 'It's too late to do business here at the house. You'll wake Belicia.' She came down a few steps and halted, shoulders back, chin aloft. 'What's in the FedEx box?'

'A head,' Aragón said.

'I see. Well, whatever you boys have to contend with

tonight, you can contend with it outside this house.' She fluttered her hand, shooing them all.

The PMCs had halted sheepishly in the foyer. 'Should we meet you elsewhere, then, *Patrón?*' one of them asked.

Aragón rose with a groan, pressed a hand to his lower back. 'Out back.'

They shuffled out beneath La Tía's disapproving gaze.

Evan didn't fully comprehend the gravity of the situation until it was too late.

The men were gathered well back from the house, light spilling from the downstairs windows and one upstairs. La Tía became visible in the second-story room, glaring out at them before shaking her head and clicking off the light. Evan could have sworn he sensed the curtain stir in the neighboring window – Belicia's room – but couldn't be sure.

Where the backyard ended, there was nothing but flat earth stretching unbroken into the darkness. Before them at the lawn's edge, a half dozen rolls of sod were stacked like massive log cakes, dark soil wrapping green interiors. The dirt had been churned up in anticipation of the sod's being laid, a trio of shovels protruding from the ground. A waning crescent moon looked down with disinterest, illuminating the men, a thicket of salt cedar in the distance and little else.

The García boy stood before the semicircle of men. An unattractive kid, he looked to be in his midteens. Pimple-faced, slump-shouldered, a few wisps on his upper lip. Surly but scared enough that he didn't dare conjure attitude.

One of the PMCs leaned on a shovel.

García hugged himself against the cold and tried not to shiver. He wore a black T-shirt, the skin of his arms goose-bumped against the night. He was doing everything in his power not to look at the shovels or the sod ready to unroll across the waiting earth like a coffin lid.

Evan took measure of the weaponry. They had enough firepower to bring down an armored truck. He had a knife and a bad angle.

Aragón swung his heavy-jowled face to the first PMC. 'You have me out here dealing with this while my daughter is missing. So get to it. What did he do?'

'He was supposed to deliver a car to that judge in Hidalgo,' the PMC said. 'With the briefcase in the trunk. Never got there.'

The García boy emitted a low moan of terror. The air smelled of mulch and fertilizer and decay.

Aragón asked, 'What happened?'

'He won't say.'

Aragón cocked an eyebrow, studied Garcia. 'Won't you?'

'I did. They just won't believe me.' The boy jerked in a few breaths. 'There was a checkpoint outside of Mercedes. Cars backed up for a hundred yards. I got nervous. I . . . I left the car.'

'Says he just ran away,' the PMC said. 'From the car and the briefcase in the trunk. No sign of the car now, of course.'

'Do you know what was in that briefcase, *mijo*?' Aragón asked.

Garcia shook his head.

'That's good,' Aragón said. 'None of you do.'

'I should have stayed with your vehicle, *Patrón*. I should have turned around and driven off and fought them off if they came after me.'

'No,' Aragón said. 'No. If you're ever going to get caught, you run or surrender. We can always handle it in court. You don't *ever* threaten the life of a police officer. Do you understand?'

García nodded.

Evan eased out a breath.

'That's not all,' the PMC said. 'His payment? For the delivery? He says it went missing. That he left it in the car as well.'

Something in the quality of the air seemed to shift. Special Ed and Kiki alerted, their eyes flashing. Aragón drew himself upright as he had before Evan in the clearing.

'You left the envelope,' Aragón said flatly. 'In the car.'

The boy nodded.

'An unusual choice,' Aragón observed. 'It could fit in a pocket, correct?'

The boy's cheeks flushed, bringing up splotches under the acne. His arms trembled, and not just from the cold.

The land felt dark and open and desolate, the stars out in force, the only witnesses to what might take place.

Evan felt the thrum of his heartbeat in the side of his throat. The Tenth Commandment: *Never let an innocent die.*

He edged a half step forward, but Special Ed drew his pistol, aiming at the ground in front of Evan's toes. The PMCs eased back, bringing their barrels to a casual slant, sighted at Evan's thighs. He wouldn't get two steps without losing both legs.

Aragón took notice of nothing but the boy, his eyes remaining locked on the kid's. 'Why would you drive to Hidalgo County and keep that kind of money on the passenger seat?'

'I . . . I don't know.'

'Or in the glove box. Is that where you kept it? The glove box?'

García's lips moved, but no sound came out at first. Then a whisper, the words barely audible: '– *siento lo siento lo siento* –'

'You're sorry?' Aragón said. 'What are you sorry for? Leaving the money in the car?'

García blinked sweat from his eyes and shook his head, sweat-heavy bangs swaying across his greasy forehead. 'I lied.' He could barely choke the words out. 'I gave the money to my *mamá*. She has the bone disease, osteo-something, where everything breaks. Her wrist, her hip. She's been rationing her pills, cutting them in quarters. They are so expensive. And she can't work, and my dad isn't around, and my brothers, they are little. And I promised her I'd be bringing in money for her pills. But the checkpoint . . .'

He started crying. White residue at the corners of his mouth gummed up as he sobbed.

'So you decided to steal from me instead of coming to me honestly and asking for what you need?' Aragón said, leaning in, his nose inches from the boy's.

Evan said, 'Aragón –'

Aragón's hand shot out so quickly that Evan almost grabbed it instinctively and goosenecked the wrist. But it stopped just shy of his face, finger raised in a shut-the-fuck-up warning. Aragón never even broke eye contact with García.

If they went to kill the kid, Evan would have to move to stop them. Which seemed unlikely to result in his staying alive.

If he got cut down here and buried beneath the sod beside this unappealing teenager, he wondered if anyone would miss him. He thought about Mia's mouth at his ear, her hands pressing his wrists to the mattress above his head. For the first time in a long time, there would be something for him to lose.

García's voice came dry, little more than a squeak. 'No.'

'No?' Aragón asked. 'What do you mean "No"? The answer is "Yes," is it not?'

The boy nodded, wiping at his cheeks.

In the darkness a coyote bayed, seemingly on cue. And then the silence asserted itself once more, black and heavy.

Aragón leaned back, crossed his arms. 'What do you think we should do with him, Kiki?'

Kiki hooked his thumbs through his straining belt loops on either side of the oversize buckle. 'Teach him a lesson, *Patrón*. Break both arms. Shoot out a kneecap. He knew the rules.'

'Eduardo?' Aragón said.

Special Ed considered for a moment. 'You have to put him in the ground, *Patrón*. Your reputation. Word will spread. These are uncertain times. You can't have people stealing from you and living to talk about it.'

García gave a sob. The PMCs looked uneasy.

Aragón nodded somberly once, twice. Then reached into his pocket.

García's knees buckled, but he kept his feet.

Aragón pulled out a fat bankroll and peeled off a dozen hundreds. He held them out to the boy. 'For your *mamá*'s pills,' he said. 'If your family needs something, you come to me. Never lie to me again. Understand?'

Tears streamed down García's face as he took the bills and stuffed them into his front pocket. 'Thank you, *Patrón*. Never, *Patrón*.'

A held breath burned the insides of Evan's ribs. He let it ease out through clenched teeth.

'Change never comes in the perfect future,' Aragón said. 'It comes in the messy here and now.' He patted the boy's cheek, lighter than a slap but just barely. 'I believe in you. I believe you know how to change.'

García nodded again. 'God bless you.' He stepped backward, tripped over his heels, went down, and got back up, moving away the whole time. 'God bless you, *Patrón*.'

Aragón said to the PMCs, 'See that he gets home safely.'

The three PMCs departed.

The skin of Aragón's face looked battered, his eyes a thousand years old. He put his hand on the ledge of Evan's shoulder. 'Come with me,' he said, lumbering for the house.

He got a few steps and then paused, spit in the grass, looked back at Kiki and Special Ed.

'Don't give a boy's advice to a man,' he said.

17. Recalibration

Aragón moved wordlessly, soft-footing through the dormant house. He led Evan upstairs and into the study. Fabric couch, bookshelves, a built-in desk with nothing on it. Not a true working space. Above the couch a wood-handled rifleman's dagger was framed in Lucite for no apparent reason. A rose-gold-and-white marble bar cart in the corner hosted a variety of high-end liquor bottles that seemed at odds with the rest of the middle-class decor.

Aragón noted Evan's gaze and said, 'Gifts.'

'Of course.'

'I could use an *amigo de borrachera*,' Aragón said. 'Now more than ever. Do you drink?'

'I've been known to have a sip now and then.'

'Should we indulge?'

Evan leaned against the desk. 'I could use a finger.'

'I have some fine mezcal with worm salt from Oaxaca.'

'I prefer vodka.'

'Vodka,' Aragón said dismissively. 'I know, I know, it has the most impurities removed. They say that makes it cleaner, but I think it makes it boring. Give me impurities any day. Peat, smoke, wood.' A surprisingly warm smile. 'But you're the guest.' He lifted a black bottle with bold red lettering. 'Have you had Blavod? It's a German vodka. Black. Like our hearts.'

He poured a bit of the ebony liquid into two crystal old-fashioned glasses, handed one to Evan, and they clinked.

'It derives its color from catechu,' Aragón said. 'A heart-wood extract from Burmese acacia trees. But that's probably more information than you care to know.'

'You'd be surprised.'

The vodka washed down Evan's throat, coated the inside of his stomach, seating him in his body. He exhaled in full for the first time in nearly forty-eight hours, and Aragón matched him, sinking down onto the couch.

Evan said, 'Bit of spice in the aftertaste.'

'The biggest trick alcohol ever pulled was making us believe we like the way it tastes.' Aragón held the glass aloft, peered through the inky wash. 'What if we called it what it was? Medicine. Panacea. Tinctures to turn the dial of our moods this way or that.'

Evan stared down into his drink, thought of what little he knew of his mother and half brother, the current of alcoholism that ran through his genes like a live wire. Discipline and force of habit kept his affection for liquor in check, but he felt the draw of it in his cells now and again. To loosen, to unclench, to give up and give in. From the way Aragón eyed the cart, he knew that his host heard the siren call as well at times like these.

'What's with the framed dagger?' Evan asked.

Aragón unbuttoned his shirt and slipped it off one shoulder. A thin white scar carved six inches to the left of his sternum just beneath the collarbone where someone had gone for the axillary artery.

'Back in the day,' Aragón said. 'When I was still – how would you say it? – more hands-on. A transaction that went wrong. It didn't go deep.' He smiled. 'Not on *me*, at least.'

'So you framed it? Like your first dollar bill?'

'No. To commemorate the price of my stupidity. And his.' A scattering of gray hair covered Aragón's chest, the musculature surprisingly pronounced for his age. 'I came home, and Belicia about took my head off. Anjelina' – at the mention of his daughter's name, a shadow moved across his face – 'she was a newborn. So my wife demanded changes.'

'And you obeyed?'

'"Obeyed"? That is not a word we use in our marriage. I *listened*.' He tasted his vodka. 'My home has always been my refuge. Even when Belicia and I fought, even when we threw plates and screamed, that's been true. My wife has kept me safe from my own worst self. But never by trying to neuter me. Not like the games your suburbanites play. Mommy wives and their little-boy husbands. No, I didn't obey. I waited until I understood why she is almost always right.'

'*Almost* always?'

'I have to hold out hope.'

Leaning over, Aragón gave himself another healthy pour. Swung the bottle in Evan's direction, but Evan declined.

'It sounds like a cliché. That my wife is the wisest person I know. But, my friend' – and here Aragón leaned forward and grew intense, even threatening – 'you haven't met *my* wife.' Amusement reshaped his face, that unorthodox handsomeness showing through. Leaning back on the cushions, he took a gulp, let the liquid swirl in his mouth.

Evan felt it, too, a touch of heat about his temples.

'The measure of a man is how tough he can be to the world and how sensitive he can be to women.' Aragón took another sip. 'Women are fucking Swiss Army knives. Throw anything at them and they figure out which part of them to use to fix it, care for it, make it better. They can hear if a baby's cough is just a cough, can smell if something's burning in the next room. They can see when our arrogance is serving us. And point out when it's not.'

His tone was angry, but Evan sensed what was beneath it, a current of remorse, self-disgust. Grief.

Aragón was looking at Evan, but his eyes were glazed, distant. 'I have a wife who used to dance in the kitchen while she cooked dinner. When I was in my right mind, I'd sit and just . . . *marvel* at her. And before you get modern on me, she could do the same thing while running a corporation or performing open-heart surgery. She could do *anything*. Women don't have to compete with men. Men aren't fit to kneel at their altar.' He stared into his glass. 'But I wore her down. I wore her down with my childish needs. No – she wore *herself* down trying to make me less stupid. And I dressed up my cowardice by calling it manliness.'

Evan thought of his conversation with Mia, the postcoital flush still high on her cheeks, her body warm against his. The coming dinner at her brother's house, the day-to-day realities that ground men down. But also – maybe – that could build them up.

Aragón stared at him, his eyes brimming. He blinked hard a few times, heavy eyelids holding everything back. 'A few years ago, I could have gone fully legal. I could have had marijuana grow houses as big as Costcos, teams of lawyers making sure every t was crossed. I have enough money already. Nobody would get hurt. But it's force of habit, yes? Chasing the thrill. Feeling like a big shot.' He sneered. '*El Patrón*.' The last of the black liquid drained into his mouth. 'My choices and my choices alone put Anjelina at risk. Along with everything else.'

Genuine curiosity stirred in Evan's chest. Aragón's flaws were prodigious, perhaps fatally so, but he knew things Evan did not. For an instant he felt how much he missed Jack, the first person who'd treated him with care. There'd been a comfort in knowing that there was someone ahead of him on the climb, who'd seen a broader vista.

Aragón reached with a groan to offer the bottle again, and Evan told himself it would be rude to refuse. The sloppy pour splashed a few drops onto his knuckles.

'I considered myself a wise man,' Aragón said. 'But I didn't understand humility. Why it's adjacent to wisdom. Maybe even the same thing.'

'How so?'

Aragón lifted his glass, the black vodka threatening to slosh over the top. 'My daughter's kidnapping has forced me to confront the full measure of my blindness. And maybe now – finally – I will find the courage not to turn away. If I confront myself for the fool I am without drowning in shame, then maybe I will be granted the wisdom to make things right.'

And there it was, the slightest tug at Evan's insides, a recalibration of the man sitting before him. Was it possible that he actually *liked* this man, an accomplished drug dealer and innovator of illicit markets? What did that mean about Evan's hard-and-fast rules, the carved-in-stone Commandments? There was a softness in Aragón's face, a vulnerability behind the eyes.

Aragón shifted on the couch, elbows on his knees, glass dangling in both hands. 'I feel like a hermit crab. You ever have one of those growing up?'

'Those were for rich kids.'

Aragón smirked, but there was no meanness in it. 'As they grow, they have to shed their shells to search for new ones, bigger ones, that will accommodate who they might become. I feel like I've outgrown my old shell, but I can't find a new one. It's like I'm at the bottom of the ocean scuttling across the sand, predators swirling overhead.' He drank again. 'Talk, talk, talk. Listen to me. None of this is helping us find my daughter.' He screwed a fist into one eye and yawned. 'I need to sleep. I will give you everything I know about the Leones tomorrow.'

He offered his hand.

Evan shook it. Aragón's grip was firm but not too firm, the confident grip of a man with nothing to prove.

Evan said, 'You have until I find her and bring her back.'

'Have until then to do what?'

'Figure out how to leave all this behind. The drugs, the trafficking, the money laundering.'

Aragón's cheeks bunched high around that bulbous nose, his face raw and rough like something carved from mahogany. 'Or *what*?'

'Or I'll come for you.'

'Ah,' Aragón said. 'Only you get to decide who lives, who dies. Only you know what is right. Only you have the unassailable moral compass.'

'No. Not just me. But I can choose what I do. And for whom.'

'And you don't find me worthy?'

'No,' Evan said. 'But your daughter is.'

Aragón grinned, though his teeth were clenched. 'Quite a position you put me in,' he said. 'Given my love for her.'

'Your love for her,' Evan said. 'Maybe that's what will save you.'

'From you?'

'No.'

Aragón blinked at him a few times. Some kind of understanding passed between them, but it was too complicated to put into words.

Evan set down his glass, half full. 'I should get going.'

'Nonsense, nonsense.' Aragón moved to the closet and racked open the flimsy slatted bifold doors. He removed a set of sheets and a pillow, tossed them on the desk. 'Come, help me pull out the sofa bed.'

'No, thank you. I won't stay here.'

Aragón slid the cushions off the couch and strained to tug out the folding bed. 'The motel in town is shitty. Trust me, I own it. You stay here, grab a few hours of sleep. We have much to review and can't waste time with you driving off and breaking back in to hold a knife to my throat.'

Aragón threw one side of a fitted sheet across the bed to Evan. 'Come on, come on.' He gestured once more, his manner impatient and disarming, and Evan found himself dumbly listening, pulling the elastic corners into place.

Aragón laid down the top sheet and blanket while Evan chinned the pillow into a case.

He had never made a bed with someone else. The act was oddly intimate.

'Bathroom's up the hall on the left,' Aragón said. 'Fresh towels on the rod, toothbrush in the drawer. Do you need a mint on your pillow? A burned fentanyl tablet?'

'The black vodka and Dagger of Damocles should suffice.'

Aragón came around the end of the bed, crowded in the small room, and rested his powerful hands on Evan's shoulders. 'Thank you. I'm glad we didn't kill each other.'

He embraced Evan, wrapping him in a bear hug that Evan was too stunned to return. Then he was gone.

Evan stood a moment, pillow in hand, replaying the bizarre domestic episode in his head to determine if it had actually happened.

It seemed it had.

By the time he'd stripped off his shirt, kicked off his boots, and moved out into the hall, the master door was closed. He walked quietly to the bathroom, where he found a toothbrush in a drawer as promised. He brushed his teeth and then washed his face with French milled soap shaped like a snail. Feeling insufficiently settled to shower, he pulled off his shirt and rinsed off in the sink, then dried himself with a fluffy lavender towel.

When he emerged, slinging his shirt over his shoulder, one of the doors in the hall was slightly ajar.

Belicia's.

There was no more than a few inches of black at the door-jamb. Had she cracked the door to listen to him? Or had air from a vent in her room suctioned it open?

He set his bare feet down silently on the carpet, heel-to-toe easing toward Belicia's room.

He stopped just outside. The black interior gave up nothing. He was at a disadvantage backlit here in the hall, a welcome target for bullets or carbon-fiber arrows or a tomahawk throwing ax if someone got creative. And yet curiosity pinned him to the spot. The air leaking through the gap smelled of air-conditioner freon and something else, something vaguely medicinal.

He strained to listen, his face inches away. He sensed the air tremble, and then the door pushed shut abruptly, the brusque snap of wood in the frame startling him.

He stood a moment bare-chested, drops of sink water cool across his chest, embarrassed to realize that his breathing had quickened from the scare.

Moving back to the makeshift guest room, he sat cross-legged on the bed, debating whether he had it in him to meditate. He didn't feel like it in the least, which was usually a sign that he needed to.

But every time he tried to focus, his thoughts pulled out of shape. To being a guest in someone's home and the unfamiliar mix of vulnerability and obligation that elicited in him. To

Aragón's mysterious wife who'd soft-slammed the door in his face. To La Tía also slumbering right up the hall. To Anjelina wherever she was sleeping or lying awake in terror.

His mind raced, the alcohol converting to sugar in his bloodstream, his mind jumping across the mission, picking at details, yawing wide and zooming in. The photos from the party, laughter and lipstick. The saccharine cinnamon scent of Anjelina's room. That caravan of dark SUVs conveying her away like a stolen princess.

He couldn't catch the rhythm of his respiration, couldn't reduce himself to his breath.

The sheets were not his sheets, and the bed was slightly uneven, the taste of the air unfamiliar. He'd been in plenty of unknown places, but being *part* of an unknown place, not just a trespasser moving through, felt intensely uncomfortable. He pictured the books downstairs ordered by height except for that one, sticking up out of place, an affront to its neighbors.

He gave up on meditating, turned off the light, and drew the covers over him.

Still that fucking book disrupted his thoughts.

Five minutes passed. Then ten. Above his head the entombed dagger stared down at him, and he stared back.

Finally he slipped from bed, tiptoed down the stairs, crept into the living room, and confronted the offending hardcover on the bookcase.

He took it off the shelf, slid it along the line of ascending spines until he found its proper spot, and then seated it in place.

He exhaled. Without knowing it he'd broken a sweat, but staring at the books restored something in him to order.

He headed back upstairs.

All the doors were closed, including Belicia's.

He returned to the study, closed and locked the door behind him, and climbed back into bed. At last ready for sleep, he shut his eyes, laying one hand on his chest and one on his stomach, letting his breath rise through his palms.

He was just drifting off when he felt a vibration in his pocket.

The RoamZone.

Caller ID showed Joey.

He clicked to pick up, but before he could say anything, her voice came in a rush, strangled and tight and devoid of its usual sardonic edge.

'I found her,' she said. 'Jesus, X. She's already dead.'

18. Other Unfavorable Lowlifes

The thin gray air of early morning found Special Ed and Kiki parked surreptitiously in an alley between two ratty houses on the American side of the Pharr-Reynosa International Bridge. Special Ed drove an eight-wheel pimp-white Eldorado with custom body panels to cover the stretched chassis, so surreptitious was relative. Aside from his longtime pal Kiki, the car was his favorite thing in the world.

The bridge was for commercial crossing only, an endless stream of box trucks and semis arcing from the Mexican state of Tamaulipas above wetlands on the four-lane bridge, bringing in oil, natural gas, fruits, vegetables, and countless kilos of drugs. The shortest crossing time of any port in the state made it popular for smugglers.

A Leones *teniente* nicknamed Chango ran a stash house where the goods were cached before being dispersed to various cities in the Southwest and on the West Coast. His bailiwick was product storage, oversight, distribution, and logistics, banal front work that removed him from the orbit of *sicarios, halcones,* and other unfavorable lowlifes who might draw the attention of local and federal law enforcement.

Part bookkeeper, part CFO, Chango was a key point of access, running one of several hubs for the Leones operation. The stash house was unguarded, unalarmed, no cameras to memorialize the business conducted within. Anyone sufficiently streetwise to understand what went on behind that vinyl-sided exterior would never dare to rob it.

Eduardo and Kiki sat in the maroon velvet seats, cowboy

hats pulled low on their brows, pistols resting lengthwise on their knees, sunglasses turning their eyes insectlike, predatory. They had a thin manila folder, a schedule of Chango's comings and goings, a bowie knife sporting the decal of the Gulf Cartel, and two shotguns in the backseat in case an escalation was in order.

'So . . .' Eduardo took another beat to mentally process what Kiki had just divulged to him. 'You're gay.'

Kiki frowned, his bushy mustache shifting. '*Sí, amigo.*'

'And you never told me.'

'Don't see why you'd care.'

'Huh.' Special Ed cast a glance across at his friend. Unshaven around the messy mustache, bulge of flesh pushing over his belt buckle, shirt buttons barely holding on. The polyester fabric, a yellow that had faded to off-white, hadn't been ironed for at least a few outings, the wrinkles sprouting subwrinkles at the elbows. 'I thought you were supposed to be like two people in one. A guy *and* a girl. Have nice clothes and shit.'

Kiki shrugged. 'Yeah, I didn't get that part.'

'And I thought you was supposed to worship Lady Gaga and have a flat belly like them oiled-up *maricones* in the music videos.'

Kiki looked down at his belly. 'What do I know? I grew up in this dumpy-ass body.'

'You fuck anyone I know?'

Kiki shook his head, his double chin rasping against his overly starched collar. 'No.' He tapped a sausage finger against his thigh opposite the .44. 'Wait. That one guy from the job in Tempe.'

'The cabana-boy-looking motherfucker we shot in the swimming pool?'

'*No.* No. The manager at the hotel.'

'*That guy?* That guy wasn't gay.'

'Coulda fooled me when I had his –'

'Okay, okay.' Special Ed contemplated the revelation, squinting into the rising sun. Then he grabbed Kiki by the scruff of his neck and jogged him a few times roughly in his seat, grinning widely. 'Fuck, Kiki. Look at you, getting some ass at the Red Roof Inn.'

'It was a Red Roof Plus. And let's not get excited and make this a big deal.'

'It *is* a big deal. It's you. Have you told your *mamá*?'

'Are you fucking crazy?'

'I bet she knows,' Special Ed said. 'On TV the moms *always* say they knew all along.'

'She doesn't know. And can we just –' He stopped and pointed. 'Look. There's that monkey-faced motherfucker.'

They watched Chango pull in to the driveway in a businessman-gray Hyundai Elantra. The garage door shuddered up unevenly.

The Eldorado jogged on its shocks as Special Ed and Kiki got out, Eduardo tapping the fuzzy die for good luck. He tucked the folder into the waistband of his jeans at the small of his back.

The Elantra eased into the garage. They strolled across the street, ducking beneath the creaking door as it closed.

Chango had already entered the house, so they paused in the dank garage to get their bearings. Shrink-wrapped pallets lined the far wall, bound bundles advertising coffee and carrots and pineapples. They took a moment to admire the quality of the packaging.

Eduardo used the tip of the enormous bowie knife to flick through the side of pineapple, releasing a trickle of white powder. '*Piñas*,' he said approvingly. 'We should try that shit.'

The door to the house was unlocked. Most of the floor

was covered with stacks of products on pallets – cardboard boxes and cartons and plastic tubs. The short hall led to a living room equally crammed, a narrow path carved through the rise of product. The foyer remained relatively clear, no doubt to allow the flow and egress of the packaged goods, but the kitchen where they found Chango looked like a hoarder's paradise, boxes climbing the walls all the way to the soffits.

Chango stood over the sink, his back turned, shoulders jiggling as if he were washing a dish. Eduardo and Kiki eased quietly through the doorway. An MP7 rested on the round wooden table to their side.

They raised their pistols, Special Ed keeping the blade low by his thigh.

Kiki cleared his throat. ''Scuse me, friend.'

Chango turned around. Circular ears stuck straight out, echoing his round face. They were the feature that had no doubt earned him the nickname, though the others competed. A thatch of dark stiff hair formed an improbably low hairline, the result of bad transplant work, bad genetics, or both. He was spectacularly ugly.

Small beady eyes took note of them, then pulled to the submachine gun out of reach at the kitchen table. 'Hello, my friends,' he said, with an unctuous grin. 'I was just making guacamole.' He tilted the yellow bowl in his hands to prove his point. 'We've been branching into avocados. Legal and expensive. Green gold, we call it.'

'I understand,' Kiki said. 'We have debated doing the same.'

'Perhaps I can serve you some,' Chango said. 'My grandmother's recipe.' He started for a cupboard. 'Let me grab us some chips.'

'Allow me to get them for you,' Kiki said, sidling forward

and opening the cupboard door. A Beretta rested on the shelf above a bag of blue-corn tortilla chips. He plucked the bag out, handed it to Chango.

Chango nodded. 'Thank you, my friend.'

While his hands were occupied, Kiki patted him down.

'I trust you understand who this house belongs to.' The neck of Chango's T-shirt stretched wide, showing off a ball-chain necklace and sweat glistening at his collarbone.

'Indeed we do,' Kiki said.

'That's good. I wouldn't want you to underestimate the amount of danger you are in.'

'We have not. Though your concern is appreciated.'

'The house is wired with surveillance cameras,' Chango said. 'Right now this very conversation is being live-streamed to my bosses.'

'We know that is not the case,' Kiki said. 'The risk of recording who and what moves through here is too great. Perhaps you have this confused with another stash house.'

'Perhaps so.' Chango considered them both. 'I have a delivery due any minute. A big crew coming in to unload it. Roughnecks from Ziracuaretiro. The avocado belt, you see. They are quite difficult to control. I fear that they might interrupt our discussion.'

'I'm afraid you might be confused,' Kiki said. 'The Ziracuaretiro delivery isn't due until three o'clock, which gives us plenty of time.'

The bowl and bag of chips sagged in Chango's hands.

'Perhaps we can sit at the table,' Kiki suggested.

'That would be good.'

Chango walked across the kitchen, and they sat. What little light might have made it through the closed venetian blinds was blocked by a rise of tomato crates. The overhead bulb flickered a Morse code of hideous yellow.

'Let me clear this,' Kiki said, sweeping the MP7 off the table. 'For the guacamole.'

'Very thoughtful.' Chango set down the bowl and the chips.

'Well,' Special Ed said. 'Aren't you gonna open the chips? We are your guests.'

Chango popped the bag and slid it around to face the other men. Eduardo scooped a healthy heap onto a chip and thrust it into his mouth. 'Hey, this shit *is* good. Your grandmother knew what she was doing. Cilantro and – Wait, don't tell me . . .'

'A tiny bit of mango to take the edge off the jalapeño.' Chango sat stiffly, his face expressionless. A bead of sweat worked its way from that dense hairline, curving down in front of one of his unfortunate ears. 'I assume you want to take something. Product, cash. I have plenty of both. Perhaps we can save some time if you tell me what you require.'

Eduardo guided another heaping chip into his mouth. 'I'm thinking I can't believe my buddy here' – a chin jerk to Kiki – 'just came out of the closet.'

Chango's head pivoted to Kiki. 'Really?'

'Yeah,' Eduardo said. 'Times are changing. I mean, the Sinaloa are even using *sicarias*. They're hot bitches, too. Have Instagram profiles, posing in G-strings with tigers and gold-plated machine guns. So I'm thinking' – he chewed some more – 'that in this day and age my best friend here won't have to suffer any discrimination.'

Chango cast a sympathetic gaze at Kiki. 'I never would have guessed.'

'Funny, that,' Special Ed said. 'Looks like your gaydar's as shitty as mine. But yours? Yours should be better.'

He reached behind him, and Chango flinched. But Eduardo came up with the folder, which he tossed onto the table. An eight-by-ten photograph slid out, showing Chango in a compromising position with a young man. The young man was without pants, but he was wearing a backward baseball cap with a logo matching the one carved into the handle of the bowie knife: C.D.G., inked in the green, red, and white of the Mexican flag.

'See, that's how it came up between Kiki and me,' Eduardo said. 'We were reviewing these pictures, and I made a – What'd you call it?'

Kiki said, 'Derogatory remark.'

'That's right. So he came clean with me. To make sure I was more respectful about him being a *maricón*. So I guess we have you to thank for clearing that shit up for us in our friendship.'

'It's true,' Kiki said. 'We are grateful.'

The sweat running down Chango's face had quickened, his T-shirt spotting. He chinned at the photo. 'I assume you know who that is?'

Eduardo picked up the picture, regarded it with a squint, then turned it sidewise and squinted some more. 'Looks like you.'

'I mean the man I'm with.'

'The son of the president of the Austin affiliate of the Cartel del Golfo. Just turned twenty. Promising future. I'm sure El Moreno wouldn't want you putting your dick in the enemy. I'm sure he'd know that a rival would need to protect his family name by eliminating a pedo –'

'He is a legal adult!'

'– even if that meant going to war. So to answer your question, no, we don't want product or money. We will touch nothing in this house. Except you.'

Chango lifted the collar of his T-shirt to wipe off his forehead. 'You still can't kill one of us. When a León bleeds, we all bleed.'

Eduardo took the photograph and used the knife tip to

carve out the face of the young man in the picture so that it couldn't be used against him after they left the photo behind. 'Then I suppose El Moreno will have to take that up with the Gulf Cartel.'

'May I . . .' Chango's voice went dry, soundless. He tried again. 'May I ask who you represent?'

'Aragón Urrea. You might be familiar with him. He has a daughter who is the center of his universe.'

Chango went to wipe his face once more with his shirt, but then grabbed through the fabric and stuffed something into his mouth. Eduardo's hand shot out, clamped around his throat, and squeezed. Chango's chest heaved a few times in silent despair until Eduardo released his grip and Chango coughed something into the guacamole.

Eduardo dug it out. A USB zip drive. The broken ball-chain necklace swayed beneath it, coated with guac.

Chango hacked some more, a squiggly vein bisecting his forehead. He caught his breath. 'You'll never crack it. You'll never –'

Eduardo swiped the knife across Chango's throat. His beady eyes flared, and his legs pumped under the table high enough that his kneecaps tattooed the wood. Then he fell forward, hands spread on either side of his face as if he were taking a nap.

A crimson slick expanded beneath Chango's head. Eduardo plucked up the photograph before it was sullied.

Holding the picture up against the wall, he drove the knife through the center, pinning it in place. The hilt proudly displayed the CARTEL DEL GOLFO logo. Special Ed used a handkerchief to wipe off his prints.

Eduardo tossed the zip drive to Kiki, who slid it into his pocket.

Together they headed out of the kitchen.

19. Terrible Things

Evan reached the morgue an hour after sunrise. Deep into Leones territory toward the last grimy outskirts of Guaridón, where the wind-blasted buildings grew more sporadic, civilization yielding to scrubland. He'd crossed the border at Brownsville in the trusty Buick Enclave, using a passport in the name of Ryan Miller. Then he forged three hours northwest into Nuevo León, heading for the location Joey had named for him.

The view was monotonous, deadening. Dirt and greasewood bushes and cacti, everything a smear of brownish yellow. The imprimatur of La Familia León proliferated, the blue-eyed lion spray-painted on rusting traffic signs and rendered on the sides of abandoned sheds, watching everyone and everything.

Evan smelled the morgue before he saw it, the air through the vents tinged with something vile.

A converted restaurant set back from the road, cracked adobe with orange and pink paint that the sun had vanquished to a pale memory. He pulled in to park, coaxing a pellet spray of sparrows from a desiccated ebony tree at the lot's edge.

He opened the door, and it hit him in the face, the inside-out smell of rupture and rot and a terrible sweetness. He crouched for a second outside the car, hoping the air close to the ground would be clearer.

It wasn't.

He drew himself up and entered.

The door gave a cheery chime, a remnant of restaurant days. Candles everywhere, *veladoras* of Mary, San Toribio Romo, and the Virgin of Guadalupe breathing vanilla and apple-cinnamon. Copal incense burned in abalone shells. A sacerdotal ambience, sure, to respect the deceased, but its primary failed function was to disguise the undisguisable scent of decaying flesh. The air-conditioning kept the place cold, but not cold enough.

A woman with a long, bookish face sat behind a counter so crowded with files that she was visible only between the stacks. She looked intimidatingly intelligent.

She did not glance up as he drew close but continued scribbling away on a form. He waited patiently. The corridor behind her was crammed with stretchers, one pinning back the swinging doors to what used to be the kitchen. A massive freezer unit beyond had a thick glass door, showing a large interior crowded with bodies to the point of bursting. A few zipped black bags waited outside the door. He sensed movement out of sight.

A closer glance showed the files surrounding the woman to be postmortem packets. Several had spilled over, exposing death certificates, field reports, digital photos of ruinous faces, sloughs of skin, and shiny white teeth protruding from baked-adobe gums. Others showed the bodies where they'd fallen, mired in desert sands like fossilized specimens from an extinct past, their mouths filled with dirt where the winds had buried them alive.

One picture showed a gruesome pietà, a dead mother with a desiccated baby at her breast, mouth fastened in a vain attempt to nurse. They'd been mummified in their own flesh, their skin turned to cracked leather like a horror-movie effect.

Close-ups captured tattoos, dental work, shoes, underwear, wallets, jewelry. Evan stared down at a glossy depiction of a coroner's latex-covered hands violating a woman's mouth, spreading blackened lips to show off a gold-rimmed incisor.

Evan lowered his voice with respect. *'Perdóneme.'*

She started, jerking back in her chair, then looked up at him with black-rimmed eyes and a hundred-yard war-zone gaze.

He said, *'Estoy tratando de identificar el cuerpo de una joven que usted tiene aquí.'*

'Identify a body?' she said in crisp English. 'Are you Migra? PD?'

Sensing that she was not someone who could be lied to, he shook his head.

'Family member?'

'I'm here on behalf of a family member.'

'I'm sorry. There are legal issues. Confidentiality.' She jotted a few more items on a form. 'You like to think we don't care about such technicalities here, but we do.'

He remained quiet. Thirty seconds passed. Another thirty.

Finally she dropped her pen in frustration and looked back up. 'What?'

'You go to extraordinary lengths to try to identify these bodies for the family members,' he said. 'Posting photos of tattoos and personal effects on the database. I represent a father who is wrecked with grief and concern over his daughter. Will you please allow me to confirm if he needs to start making arrangements?'

She stared at him. He wondered if she ever smiled. He wondered if it was even possible after doing this job.

'Why do you think she's here?'

'In the personal effects you documented was a locket necklace,' he said. 'Given to her by her father.'

He held up the picture on his phone. She took it in briskly, then typed at her computer for a moment, the monitor's glow illuminating her reading glasses.

Abruptly, she scooted her chair away from the counter and walked back to the kitchen. It took a moment for him to realize he was to follow her.

The air-conditioning blasted in the kitchen but was no match for the bodies on gurneys shoved against the walls. Two of her co-workers moved among the dead, taking photographs, jotting notes on clipboards. A few corpses were laid out on the stainless-steel counters and rolling worktables that had once been used to chop lettuce and whisk corn meal. A faint hospital hum of machinery, tubes feeding the bodies, preserving the flesh.

'Is it always this crowded?' Evan asked.

'This is the overflow morgue. That's why we are here on Sunday. Seven days a week.' She gestured at a NEGRO MODELO sign hanging in the sole window, its neon tubes coated with dust. 'As you can see, we make do with what we can. Today is worse than usual. They found an ice-cream truck abandoned in Chihuahua. Fifteen bodies locked inside. The smell, it hits you like a paste.'

She snapped on latex gloves and walked around, checking toe tags. Evan followed, breathing through his nose, fighting to hold his gag reflex at bay. Behind them a camera flashed and clicked.

'The *pinche guías* don't care about anything,' she said. 'They take their money and pump them full of coca or diet pills to power them through the desert. Some have heart attacks. Some are left behind, alone beneath the sun. And even if they *do* make it? The cartel gets their filthy hands on their children back home, makes them work off an endless ransom. It's slave labor. The people working all around you, in your hotels and fields, mowing your lawns.'

She halted before a parched form on the prep counter. Lipless and noseless, skin shrunken around the skull, features demolished by triple-digit desert heat. A clipboard rested beside the corpse, showing basic identifying information and the coordinates where her body had been discovered.

'Here. This is your Juana Doe.'

It was difficult to believe that the shriveled form before him was once a vibrant human. More difficult yet to think that it had been Anjelina.

A plastic bag tied to her ankle held the locket and chain, three rusted hair clips, and a tube of melted lipstick oozing maroon. The woman loosened the bag on the ankle, removed the locket, and handed it to Evan. He clicked it open. A posed wedding picture, young Aragón beaming in a tuxedo, Belicia in flowing white, their hands clasped before them in a way couples never held hands in real life.

He thought about Anjelina's room, posters and fluffy throw pillows. The tears on Aragón's cheeks as he recalled them at the beach when she was a baby. Evan's thoughts bled into Joey's wanting to go on a road trip, out alone in the world where things like this happened to young women, where one minute they were smiling at their birthday party and the next laid out on a stainless-steel prep table in a makeshift morgue.

The Fourth Commandment: *Never make it personal.*

He cleared his throat, cleared his mind. 'How am I supposed to confirm her identity?'

'Wait,' the woman said, picking up the stick-dry arm and examining the hand carefully. 'She might be ready.'

From a nearby drawer, she removed an ink pad and a blank notecard. She inked the corpse's prints and tried rolling them onto the pad, to no avail. 'The fingers are not plumped up enough yet,' she said. 'And even when they are, the prints might be ruined.'

'Sometimes you can slide the skin off the hand,' Evan said. 'And wear it like a glove to press the prints more fully.'

She stared at him, her long face growing even longer. 'Who *are* you?'

'I've seen terrible things, too.' He gestured at the body.

She nodded.

He reached for the hand and tugged gently at the skin, but there was no give. It had been baked onto the flesh.

He leaned on the table, regarding the body.

Knobby knees turned inward, ribs visible, collarbones pronounced.

And there, an unnatural curve beneath the leathered flesh of the breasts. A kind of roundness not found in nature.

Evan looked at the woman, gestured at the breast. 'May I?'

She nodded once more.

He pushed the skin at the side, felt the hard silicon edge beneath.

His heart quickened, a surge of hope. From what little he knew of Anjelina, he thought it unlikely that she had gotten breast implants.

'Can I . . . Do you have a scalpel?'

The woman must have read the emotion in his face, because she got a scalpel and returned to his side.

'I will do it,' she said.

She carved a six-inch incision down from the armpit and applied gentle pressure until the translucent yellow implant popped out. She ran it under the faucet to clear the body fluids and then placed it beneath a desk lamp clamped to the sink.

The serial number, rendered in soft relief.

Before touching his phone, Evan washed his hands and then washed them again, keeping the water hot enough to turn his flesh red.

A quick Google search brought up a legal website for breast-implants showing which models were eligible for recalls and which were considered safe..

He typed in the number. Realized he was biting his lip. Stopped biting it.

The surgery had taken place at Centro Médico Internacional on Sexta Sur y Avenida Longoria.

Eleven years ago.

Anjelina would have been seven.

He exhaled, lowered his head.

'What?' the woman asked.

'It's not her.'

She rested a hand on his shoulder blade. He appreciated the gesture but didn't like being touched with hands that had just touched the dead. 'I'm happy for you.'

'Thank you.'

'This will help us, too. We can find her family. And perhaps get her a proper burial.'

He looked her in the face, taking in those black-rimmed eyes. 'You do important work,' he said.

'Yes,' she said. 'I do.'

He left her there among the bodies.

The air outside provided little relief. Pausing by his car, he thumbed off a text to Joey:

NOT HER.

He drove with the windows down and the air conditioner high. The smell was in his hair, his clothes, his pores. He passed a motel and pulled over, paid cash for a room. The clerk wrinkled his nose as he handed over the key.

Evan grabbed his duffel bag from the trunk, went inside, and stripped naked, piling his clothes in the corner. He took a shower, scrubbing himself from head to toe, and then

143

dressed in an identical set of clothes. By the time he emerged from the bathroom, the stench of death had emanated from his clothes and hung heavy in the room.

He found a metal trash can in the alley behind the motel, dumped in his clothes, and burned them. But he couldn't get the smell off his hands.

Back inside, stripped down again, another shower. He dried off with a fresh towel, flossed his teeth, clipped his fingernails. Stole a bedsheet to sit on for the ride back until he could air out the seats.

He wanted to have Guaridón in the rearview before the afternoon came. That's when cartel violence intensified, peaking by design just before the six-o'clock evening news – menace and marketing hand in hand.

He rode the whole way with the windows down.

It was dusk by the time he arrived back at Aragón's complex.

Special Ed and Kiki were waiting at the front gate, bullshitting with a few PMCs. Eduardo was cradling the arm Evan had nearly hyperextended but released it quickly when he recognized the car.

Evan slowed, stuck an elbow out the window.

'You don't just leave whenever you want,' Eduardo said.

'That's exactly what I do.'

'Keep talking back,' Eduardo said. 'And you'll see what happens.'

'How's your arm?' Evan said.

Kiki smirked a little, and Eduardo glared over at him.

Evan held up Anjelina's locket, let it dangle beneath his fist. 'Open the gate,' he said.

They opened the gate and hopped into a Jeep to follow.

As Evan coasted up to the house, the front door opened and Aragón came out onto the porch.

Twisting one hand in the other, he walked toward Evan, meeting him at the driveway.

'I came from the morgue,' Evan said. 'It wasn't her. But I found this.'

Aragón took the locket, and his knees buckled. Evan steeled him with an arm across the small of his back.

'I'm fine,' Aragón said irritably, pulling away. 'I'm fine.' He stared at the locket, then clenched it tight and pressed his fist to his forehead, shutting his eyes, his lips moving in a silent prayer.

The Jeep remained at the curb, Kiki and Special Ed keeping a respectful distance.

After a time Aragón lifted his head and looked at Evan.

Violent men and trauma victims often recede behind their faces, shrinking back and in, leaving flat eyes to face the world. Aragón's eyes weren't like that. They held a staggering depth of knowledge and pain and life lived unflinchingly and close to the marrow. Soulful eyes, the eyes of survivors who do more than survive, of war veterans and the terminally ill and the grateful living, the eyes of those who refuse to give up or look away or retreat into numbness.

His voice came hoarse and cracked. 'And now?'

'The Leones,' Evan said. 'What do you have on them?'

Aragón's jaw shifted left and then right, as if resetting itself. 'I know them better than they know themselves.'

Evan said, 'Tell me everything.'

20. Filthy and Subhuman

Anjelina was tired of lying in bed. Her head throbbed, and she felt nauseated and hot beneath the slow-turning paddle fan on the high ceiling. She cast off the covers, and then a freeze hit her so she pulled them on again.

She sobbed quietly for a time, curled inward, one hand pressed to her stomach, the other held over her face as if she could close her eyes to the desperation of her situation. Her pillow was wet with tears, her sheets damp with sweat, and she was exhausted from trying not to make noise.

She was hungry and sticky and completely unmoored.

Her father had always said to take the world on in your own terms, to hold true to what you felt was right and force reality to organize itself around you, good or bad. That's what she'd have to do now. Even now.

She slipped out of bed, anticipating the cool floor, but even the tile had been warmed by the satanic heat.

Cracking the door, she peered out into the hall. It looked clear.

She started to step out when a low ticking noise came from the hinge side of the door. She yelped and spun around.

Darling Boy sat on a chair, back to the wall, eyes glimmering at her. A guard post. He was scolding her, making a clucking noise with his tongue against his meth-rotted teeth. The inked band around his neck rippled with the movement of his Adam's apple.

She drew another sharp intake of breath. 'Why are you here?'

'El Moreno wants you watched. All the time.' He made a horrible grin by stretching his loose lips outward, seemingly pleased by the opportunities that watching her might afford.

'Where's Reymundo?'

'You don't get to choose who watches.'

She realized she'd drawn back behind the door, hiding her body, peering around the edge at him. 'I'm hungry. I need to eat.'

'Food will be brought.' Even at this distance, his breath smelled like death.

'I need . . . I need a towel.'

He rose, his bald pate shiny from the light. 'I will fetch it for you.'

As she withdrew into the room, he shoved the door from the outside, scooting her in quicker. A metallic click announced itself. The dead bolt was reversed, the latch on the outside. She ran her palm across the smooth wood.

The first time they had locked her in the room.

She moved backward on wobbly legs and sat on the bed.

After a time she heard Darling Boy's footsteps ticktocking across the tile, drawing closer. Revulsion churned in her stomach, climbed the back of her throat.

The door unlocked. He entered, holding a towel in his hand. A chemical smell wafted off him, meds and body chemistry gone bad.

She took the towel. It was soft and fluffy and felt brand-new.

She stared at him.

He stared back.

In a foreign country. On a guarded cartel estate. Behind a door. Alone.

With Darling Boy.

It took a moment for her to find her voice. 'Will you excuse me?'

'As I said.' Another gruesome smile. 'You are to be watched.'

She entered the bathroom. Shut the door behind her. No lock.

It was vulnerable-making to undress, but she felt filthy and subhuman, layers of panic sweat dried on her skin, her hair greasy and tangled. She started the water, stared at herself in the mirror. A thin line of broken capillaries where the necklace had been torn from her neck; it had caught on the seat belt when she'd been hustled out of the SUV for the sole bathroom stop they'd allowed.

She no longer had the photograph of her mother and father the locket had held.

She no longer had anything of who she had been.

The steam began to mist the mirror, and she stepped into the shower, easing the sliding glass door shut. She lathered herself up, using soap for her hair, feeling the blunt edge where Montesco had taken a lock of it. Scrubbing beneath the stream. And then she sensed it, the faintest squeak of the hinges.

Panicked, she swiped suds and water from her eyes.

Through the fogged shower glass, she could see Darling Boy filling the doorway, a dark cutout from the light beyond.

She didn't breathe, didn't move.

He didn't either.

Fixing her stare on him, she rinsed off as quickly as she could. Her breath kept hitching in her throat, and she made an effort to draw full inhalations so she wouldn't pass out.

She turned off the water.

Still he didn't move.

The fog was lifting from the glass. In another minute he'd be fully visible to her. And her to him.

She eased the door open. The towel rack just beyond reach. No way to get there without exposing a breast.

She leaned out, snatched the towel, jerked back into the false safety of the shower stall.

The mist carried the scent of him; it seemed to fill the room.

She wrapped herself up.

He stayed in the doorway. Staring. Unblinking.

The last bits of fog evanesced from the glass.

She was trembling from the cold. She hadn't dried her hair.

He wasn't smiling that awful smile. He just stared at her, his eyes focused with longing and something beneath it, something hard-edged and aggressive. He looked underfed.

He took a step forward.

She reached out and grabbed the handle to hold the shower door shut.

'Hey!'

A voice from behind, from the bedroom.

Reymundo stepped into view. 'What are you doing? What are you *doing*?'

Darling Boy hesitated. 'Your father told me to watch her.'

'Not like that. Do you understand me? Not like that.'

Reymundo was breathing hard, and Anjelina sensed fear in him. He was heir to the throne, yes, but Darling Boy was a *sicario*. He had done things that a young man like Reymundo and an eighteen-year-old girl like her could scarcely imagine.

She used the distraction to slip past them both into her room. She grabbed her clothes and stood in the corner, facing the wall, holding her towel in place as she slid on her panties and jeans, her bra and T-shirt.

Behind her the men murmured, their voices low and angry.

Finally she turned around, toweling her hair.

'I have to go,' Reymundo told her. 'He understands now.'

'He doesn't understand anything,' she said.

Darling Boy watched them mutely. She knew she was risking his wrath by taking a stand, but if she didn't, she would be here alone with him.

'I want to go with you.'

Reymundo said, 'Where I am going isn't safe for you –'

'I don't care. It's safer than me staying here.'

'My father will be there. You don't want to see what he is going to do.'

She looked at Darling Boy. Those eyes. That skin. That hungry look.

'I don't care. I don't want to stay here. I don't care what I'll see.'

Reymundo bobbed his head sadly. 'I will find you a jacket.' He paused at the door, looked down at the floor. 'You might regret what you ask for.'

21. Lack of Professionalism

Aragón led Evan, Kiki, and Special Ed through the living room with its array of floral scents, down a brief hall devoid of decorations and art, to a room in the back of the house. Even here at the heart of the guarded compound, three dead bolts secured the door. Using a key hung around his neck, Aragón coaxed them back into their housing and knuckled the metal door open.

It swung inward to divulge a wide room nearly filled with an enormous Faraday tent. Nothing rimmed the perimeter aside from cables and power sources snaking across spotless white carpet.

It was an impressive setup – double-wall construction, metal mounting frame, good ventilation. No electromagnetic or radio frequencies would be leaking in or out, protecting the system from intrusion. A soft whir issued from the RF noise-source generators parked just outside the zip doors.

In single file the men whispered through the slick fabric, entering the inner sanctum. A giant computing powerhouse. Six stations with screens and hardware. TEMPEST-certified computers, GigaFOIL V3 filters on the Ethernet lines, EMI-EMP signal and data filters for the power sources. The nerve center of Aragón's operation.

'I'd like to bring in my associate,' Evan said. 'To pool our resources. She knows more about tech than anyone I've met.'

'The person who hacked our system yesterday?' Special Ed interjected.

Evan ignored him, keeping his attention on Aragón. 'Can you open up a secure messaging channel to her?'

Special Ed and Kiki bristled at the suggestion, but Aragón held up his hand, quelling their protests. 'Is this person to be trusted?'

'I've trusted her with my life.'

'You are asking me to share intel,' Aragón said.

'We need to figure out how to infiltrate the Leones. And we need to do it better than the last guy you sent.'

Aragón's mouth pulsed as he chewed the inside of his cheek. 'I expect you to maintain impeccable control over your underling.'

Evan gave a hesitant nod. Stepping out of the Faraday tent, he called Joey.

She answered in a telemarketer's cheery voice. 'Covert Former Government Assassins Are Us.'

'Joey. Knock it off. I'm going to open a channel for you into Aragón's operation, okay? I need you to play this serious. Understand?'

'Okay. Jeez. Call 911 – your sense of humor's gone missing. Oh, wait, I forgot. You don't *have* a sense of humor.'

'Put appropriate audio modulation and visual filters on,' Evan said. 'Vocal disguise, facial recognition cloaking, and make sure everything runs through virtual-private-network tunnels. I want two dozen software telephone switches –'

'It's so adorable when you mansplain to me about encryption. Any hair advice? I'm thinking of doing frosted blond tips, and that also seems to be right in your bailiwick.'

'Joey. This is different. I'm plugging you straight into a connection with a cybersecurity mastermind.'

'Once I'm done shuddering with anxiety, I'll be on my best behavior.'

'*Josephine.*'

'What? I'll play it straight, okay? Texting a link now. Gawd, X.'

She hung up. His RoamZone chimed.

He re-entered the tent and keyed in the link on one of Aragón's computers. A window popped up. Blackness, and then the connection came through.

Evan saw Joey's avatar and heard the sound of his molars grinding.

She had disguised herself using a manga filter that gave her giant neotenic eyes, fluffy alien antennae, a cute bunny nose, and a wagging dog tongue.

'Greetings, Boomers,' she said, the tongue shedding cartoon saliva droplets. 'What are you doing? Listening to Neil Diamond? Comparing Social Security statements? Reading blogs on gut health?'

Evan felt three sets of eyes swivel to rest on him. His mouth opened, but no sound came out.

'I heard we're swapping lipstick,' Joey continued. 'Is that right, Cartel Guy?'

Aragón cleared his throat, which sounded in need of clearing. 'I would prefer you not refer to me as –'

'"Cartel Guy"? But "Anarcho-Capitalist Megalomaniac" is a mouthful, and I figured since we'll be working together, we'd better establish some shorthand.'

Evan turned to Aragón, managed to get words to come out of his facehole. 'My associate has an unorthodox sense of humor.' He glared into the monitor.

Joey's bunny-dog mouth panted affably at him.

'Perhaps you could try a more professional filter if we're going to –'

'Righto.' Joey's hands – which Evan noted with dismay had been transmogrified into furry bear paws – fluttered across the keyboard, and then she was ensconced in a fat filter, chins billowing, eyes rolling in a watermelon head. 'Hang on, haaaang on.' Now a giant bobbing mustache sprang to life. 'Better?'

'Is this some kind of fucking joke?' Special Ed said. 'Is this little girl for real?'

Aragón turned crisply to Evan. 'I'm not certain I trust this associate of yours sufficiently to grant her access to my databases.'

'Well, that's a shame,' Joey said. 'Since I'm already in.' Her giant fingers splayed and typed, the monitors all around them populating with windows, code, images.

Eduardo said, 'How the *fuck* did she –'

'Duh. Turns out this video chat? It ain't just a video chat. And you know what else? Ah wanna be paid in *jelly doughnuts*!' She was speaking, inexplicably, in what seemed to be a southern accent.

'Your accent is terrible,' Evan told Fat Joey. 'Are you supposed to be southern or French?'

'Ah'm not French, boy-ah.'

'I'd asked you to handle this with maturity –'

'You want maturity? 'Kay. How 'bout some grammaflage?' Joey clicked over to an old-age filter. She looked like the off-spring of Gollum and old Picasso.

'I'm sending through the location of the body that was mistaken for your daughter's,' Ancient Joey said through wrinkled lips. 'And the files. I've charted out various travel-route trajectories along which she might have lost her necklace. They're on your left monitor. No – your *other* left. I see you have, like, tons of intel on the Leones on your end, but I'll also send through everything I've compiled here. And Raúl Montesco, or as he likes to be called, El Morrrrreno' – she laid on the accent, Aragón stiffening at the mere mention of the name – 'plus his son Reymundo, his *sicarios*, lieutenants, accountants, all that. Their main HQ, a super-secret Bond-villain lair rumored to be somewhere outside Guaridón squares with the route trajectories. But that's dead center of their territory. There's no getting at it. As far as I can tell, if someone sneezes near Guaridón, the Leones hear about it.'

Aragón was ashen. 'You think that's where she is? In Guaridón?'

'Dunno,' Joey said. 'But I'm guessing even the Nowhere Man isn't dumb enough to walk through there knocking on doors and asking questions.'

'No,' Aragón said. 'There is Guaridón. And then there is the rest of the world.'

'Which is why I've traced a bunch of secondary compounds. Conveniently located *outside* of hell on earth.' Ancient Joey clattered away for a moment, peering down her aged nose. 'I see you have more information on the affiliate chapters he's flirting with in the US. And your shipment and transaction intel is more up to date than mine. All these comings and goings . . .' She tapped a venerable finger against her liver-spotted cheek. 'Interesting. What's Kontact?'

'A new synthetic marijuana delivery' – Aragón caught himself. 'Wait a minute! Are you exporting all my data?'

'Just on the Leones. I'm going to drill down on the loads heading into cities here. Baltimore, Butte, Chicago, Dayton, Mesa, Oklahoma City, San Bernardino, Toledo. Wow, they're really sizing up with freelance muscle and contract hitters. Aaand . . . what's over here? You guys took out Chango? Left a calling card from the Gulf Cartel? Did the Leones answer yet?'

Kiki said, 'They killed one of the Gulf *sicarios* this morning. . .' He trailed off beneath the heat of glares from Aragón and Special Ed.

Joey was undeterred. 'So you started a gang war. Useful.' The screens around them illuminated, exporting, uploading, and scrolling code. 'What's the play, X? You not gonna track them down in Nuevo León, are you?'

'El Moreno's stranglehold on the community makes Guaridón operationally impossible,' Evan said. 'Even if we did find the location of their HQ and determine that they're holding Anjelina there, I couldn't penetrate it without them knowing I'm coming. We have to figure out another way.'

Aragón frowned at Evan. 'What other way?'

'I have to bring them to me.'

'And then?'

'Have them escort me back to Mexico.'

'How will you do that?'

'I don't know yet.' Evan nodded at Ancient Joey. 'But my colleague and I will figure something out.'

Joey turned her baggy eyes to Evan. 'I just need some time to get inside all this data, and then I'll ping you back.'

'My daughter's life is at stake,' Aragón said. 'And your colleague's lack of professionalism is *completely* unacceptable.'

A rustling at the tent door, and then La Tía entered with a tray of sandwiches. 'Hello, boys. Would you like some lunch?'

Aragón reddened. 'I told you not to come in here, *Tía*.'

'And *I* told *you* you have to remember to eat. Now, what'll it be? Ham or cemitas?'

La Tía spotted Elderly Joey on the screen and gave a little wave, which Joey returned, old woman to old woman.

'Your aunt's right. Eat lunch. I got it from here.' Leaning forward for her keyboard, Joey gave a faint grin. '*Boys*.'

A click of her finger and the connection was cut.

22. Sylvan Scene Turned Diabolic

Raúl Montesco drove the front truck. He'd demanded that his son ride shotgun, leaving Anjelina in the backseat of the two-row cab beside Jovencito. The youthful *sicario* scarcely spoke at all, but from time to time he whistled softly and beautifully. The caravan was four vehicles deep, each León armed to the teeth. They blazed across the Tamaulipan brushland, heat beating down through the metal roofs, cooking them in their seats. They passed petrochemical plants belching black smoke and forged onto dirt roads carved through fertile lowlands, the Sierra Madre Oriental mountains rising beyond.

A tablet phone rested in Montesco's lap, his hand in constant motion, dialing, texting, scrolling. It was a wonder he could focus on the road. The whole time he kept a running monologue directed at his son about their operation.

Montesco's tablet lit up for the tenth time or the thirtieth. He thumbed to answer. Said nothing. A slight delay as the call worked its way through the encryption.

A gravelly voice, no greeting. 'We have him. We are holding him at the lab, as you asked.'

'Name?'

'Luis Millán. The *sicario* they use to handle business in Hidalgo. The bowie knife left behind? The one that cut Chango's throat? Is Millán's calling card.'

'He will regret ever setting foot inside one of my stash houses. Do you have the rest of what I asked?'

'I'm sending you the license plates now.'

Montesco flicked at the screen. 'This is his wife? His brothers, cousins, *madre*?'

'Sí, *Jefe*. His sister, too.'

'Tell your men to plant drugs in each of these cars and alert the *federales*. I will pay twenty-five thousand dollars for each arrest. I will see him soon enough. I will deliver him news of what he has done to his family, where they will spend the rest of their days.' Montesco knuckled the bridge of his nose and snapped it back and forth, the cartilage supple, eroded from within. 'When a León bleeds, we all bleed.'

He hung up and continued his tutorial for Reymundo. 'And you have to get certificates for weaponry if you're gonna buy them from Eastern Europe. Look to Eritrea or Congo, places where weapons outlast war and the governments take bribes. Are you listening to me, *hijo*?'

'Yes, *Papá*.'

'I won't be here forever. You must learn. We have to diversify now to stay ahead of the Tijuana Cartel and these Gulf motherfuckers. We need a bigger piece of human smuggling. We already have the transportation setup, the supply chain. Some product we have to import, but we make plenty of women in Mexico.' A belly laugh. 'Most important, though, is drugs. Our foundation. We can never become lazy. We must always innovate. That's why I want you here today. I need you to see it with your own two eyes.'

'See what?'

'The next generation of drugs. Colombian government's been locking down import of precursor chemicals for cocaine.'

'That's what we're running in the trucks now?' Reymundo asked.

'That's right. We build our *own* labs here, eh? That way we can import cheap, unrefined coca base from Bogotá and upgrade it here for the US market. We're playing with synthetic marijuanas, too – cheaper, stronger high. That shit'll blow the top off your head, take you to heaven. We're expanding into US cities, building out affiliates to hold pace with the market. Decentralization, *hijo*. Franchisees who know their own streets. Leones Las Vegas. Leones Miami. Leones Philly. If we take over America, we can take over the world.'

Dusk turned everything charcoal. Soon enough there was little more than the headlight beams burrowing through the darkness.

El Moreno lit up a crack cigarette, lowering the window a few inches to shoot his smoke out into the humid night. His driving grew more sporadic, his energy wilder. Brake, gas, brake, gas, the speed gradually increasing.

Reymundo cast a nervous look back at Anjelina. '*Papá*. Watch the road.'

'Watch the road, eh?' Montesco finished his last long, crackling draw and flicked the cigarette butt out the window. Droplets of sweat clung to his cheek, his hand tightening atop the wheel. 'I'm a night predator, *hijo*. I see in darkness.'

He turned off the headlights.

Pitch-black ahead. The windshield an impenetrable screen.

From the trucks behind them, they heard whooping, and then the sets of headlights went off one after another, following his lead. The caravan hurtled invisibly through the black night.

There could be a turn in the road, an abandoned truck, a wayward cow. The engine screamed, changing gears until there were no more gears to change.

Anjelina wrapped her hands in the seat belt, closed her eyes, murmured the Lord's Prayer. Reymundo was shouting, 'Okay, *Papá*! I get it, *Papá*!'

The dashboard was dark, so she couldn't see the speedometer, but they must have crossed sixty miles per hour and now maybe seventy, and the chassis was starting to shimmy and there seemed no way that they could be holding the straight line necessary to keep them alive on the narrow dirt road when –

'*Papá!* There's too much money in these trucks if one crashes!'

At last Montesco looked over at his son, but he kept a heavy foot on the gas pedal.

Darkness flew past them. Anjelina clawed at the seat belt, muscles locked, limbs contorted, another second passing miraculously without impact and then another yet. At her side Jovencito looked completely unruffled, wearing a faint smile, the breeze from the cracked window riffling his hair.

And then Montesco's arm moved, his shoulder pulsed, and the road materialized once more. They'd veered across to the wrong side, shrubs clipping the side mirror, and the Dark Man laughed as he course-corrected, the truck wobbling one way and then the other. Headlights strafed the rear windshield as the trucks behind them found their lanes again, tires smoking, brakes hissing, and then all at once everything evened out and they were coasting along as though nothing had happened.

Jovencito looked across at Anjelina. 'You're sexy when you're terrified.'

She barely had time to slow her breathing before they swung off into a fallow field overgrown with weeds. A half mile in, a black wall of the forest's edge appeared, a fringe of pine-oak woodlands blanketing the rise beyond.

They rumbled between tree trunks, bouncing violently in their seats, until they reached not so much a clearing as a miniature settlement – tents and sheds constructed of rust-flecked corrugated iron.

As Montesco's crew unpacked from the trucks, other men bearing AK-47s emerged from the woods to greet them.

In a daze Anjelina spilled out onto the moist forest floor. Her senses were assaulted. There was no gentle woodland scent, just the sting of industrial solvents hitting her in the face. The air smelled flammable, coating the inside of her throat and firing her nasal passages.

A crew of workers wielded screaming gasoline-powered hedge trimmers, dipping the blades into oil barrels. Bits of dry coca leaves flew up, powdering their surgical face masks. A row of pickup trucks were being gassed up like race cars at a pit stop, washing machines strapped to their beds, product churning inside the makeshift centrifuges. One by one they roared off to trundle around the forest, dispersing the risk of capture or detection.

Amid the chaos she shrank against a door of the truck. She was shouldered aside by Jovencito as he reached for the 120-gallon propane tank bolted behind the cab. He removed the fake valves and pipes seemingly feeding the engine to reveal a Bondo'd plate beneath. The drivers of the other trucks readied their respective tanks in like fashion.

A man with round John Lennon glasses appeared from one of the corrugated-metal sheds, his thinning scalp beaded with sweat. A crew emerged in his wake with various tubes and storage barrels. '*Jefe!*' he barked. 'Which is which?'

Montesco pointed to his truck. 'Potassium permanganate.' The second truck: 'Hydrochloric acid.' The third and fourth: 'Cannabinoids.'

'Which chemicals?' the bald man said. 'In the cannabinoids?'

'What chemicals *aren't* in that shit?' Montesco laughed, but the man did not. 'This is for the contact lenses.'

'We have them ready now.' The man produced a matchbox-size cardboard box from his pocket with the word KONTACT on the side and handed it over.

Montesco slid out the tiny drawer, peered down, and grinned. 'Looks like some real shit. Should have no problem getting these across the border.'

The men went to work extracting the chemicals from the tanks on the truck, Kalashnikovs swinging at their sides. Because of their curved magazines, Anjelina's father called them *cuernos de chivo*. Goat horns. Just another element of the sylvan scene turned diabolic – the eye-watering fumes, the strobing lights, the scream of rent metal.

Montesco crossed his arms, lit up a cigar, and watched them work.

'*Jefe*, you don't want to smoke a cigar here,' the man with the thinning hair said.

Montesco looked at him flatly. 'Yes,' he said. 'I do.'

The man hurriedly got back to work.

'Where is Luis Millán?' Montesco asked. 'This grand assassin of the famous Gulf Cartel?'

The man pointed into one of the tents and went back to siphoning liquid from the altered propane tank. 'Tied up in there as you asked, *Jefe*. We haven't laid a hand on him.'

'Jovencito! Let's go already.'

Jovencito was up in the truck bed, straining and grunting. He kicked down the tailgate and wrestled something off and onto the ground.

An industrial floor buffer.

To steer it through a mud puddle, he tilted it back on its heavy-duty wheels, revealing two rotary wheels capped with abrasive pads.

Anjelina nearly lost her knees. She leaned against the fender.

162

Jovencito paused to unbutton his thin cotton shirt, revealing a long rosary tattoo, inked beads traversing his torso, the cross pendant at a tilt beneath a floating rib. He set his shirt back in the truck. 'So I don't stain it,' he said.

And he grinned.

He rolled the buffer past Anjelina, so close it nearly ran over her toes.

Montesco held out an arm – *after you* – and followed him into the tent. Pausing halfway in, Montesco said, 'Reymundo.'

His son was in the rear truck, helping unload the tank. His head snapped up, brow wrinkled with dread.

'Come.'

Reymundo straightened up, slapped his hands together as if to dust them. 'I'm helping here.'

'No. This. This is what you must learn.'

Reymundo hesitated once more. '*Papá* –'

'*Now*,' Montesco said.

Reymundo lowered his head. Walked past Anjelina, his head down as if he could not meet her eyes. He entered the tent.

Montesco followed.

Anjelina thought, 'I will wait in the truck,' and a moment later she realized she'd said it aloud.

There was no one there to stop her. There was nowhere for her to go.

She climbed into the truck. Shut the door behind her. Stupidly put on her seat belt.

A moment later she heard it. The rev of the floor buffer. The ten-grit sound of contact.

And then a screaming unlike any she'd ever heard. Like someone was being split open and the noises were coming directly from their insides.

'No,' she said to herself. 'No.'

She closed her eyes. Covered her ears.

But she couldn't block out the sound.

Revving.

Sobbing.

Revving.

Pleading.

It was pitch-black here inside her skull. She squeezed her eyes shut, lowered her head.

Breathe in. Breathe out. Don't vomit.

Rocks crackling beneath deadweight. Something being dragged to right outside the truck. She could feel the vibration through the seat. A man panting like a dog. Wet words pushed through ruinous lips: '– *no lo hice, lo juro, no toqué a Chango –*'

And then El Moreno's voice. 'Better for ten innocent men to die than for one guilty man to go unpunished.'

She was safer here in the darkness, with her eyes closed.

'Reymundo, take this.'

'*Papá*, I cannot.'

'*No. No no nooo! Espera, sólo –*'

'Take it!'

'I can't.'

A blow. A squelch – something hitting mud.

'Then I'll show my *coño* son how it's done.'

'– *por favor por –*'

A thud. An expulsion of air. Tearing. A chicken-bone crackle.

Things being hoisted. Things being slammed.

Breathe in. Breathe out. Don't vomit.

Montesco: 'Now tie him to the back of the truck. That's right. Around the legs.'

Noises behind her. Rope whistling around a trailer hitch.

Doors opening. Doors closing.

She could smell them now, the men in the car with her. Perspiration and deodorant and coppery tang of blood.

Montesco: 'Look at that one, eh? So delicate.'

They drove.

Uneven ground. Something dragging behind them, bouncing across ruts.

If she didn't open her eyes, it wouldn't be real.

Rocks skittling up against the undercarriage.

They drove, and she stayed here in the pitch-black and breathed and tried not to throw up.

At last the truck rumbled to a halt.

'Out,' Montesco said.

The driver's door opening. The door next to her opening, Jovencito sliding out.

A rustle in front of her, Reymundo turning around, his voice dry and cracked. 'I told you. I told you you did not want to come.'

'*Out!*'

The passenger door opening, sounds of Reymundo being hauled out in the open air.

Montesco's voice, moving away. 'Grab a tank of gasoline. Come, we'll build a fire. Jovencito, get the cooler from Armando. Let's have some *cerveza*.'

Breathe in. Breathe out. Don't vomit.

The voices of men laughing, taunting one another, moving away. Jovencito's whistle, dead on key, a haunting Ennio Morricone melody.

She could taste her own breath, bitter with panic. Her lips were cracked, her hair pasted to her face with sweat.

The whoosh of a conflagration. The crackling of a fire. And then a distant stench.

That's what finally did it.

The smell.

She jerked her seat belt free, fingers scrabbling at the door handle. Leaning outside, she emptied her stomach onto the ground. When she was done heaving, she lifted her gaze slowly, dread filling her insides. Through the tangled hair across her face, she looked upon the scene.

A fallow field, choked with weeds. Twenty yards away Montesco and his men sat on logs, gathered around a bonfire, crack cigarettes floating like fireflies before their faces. They smoked and they clinked bottles and they laughed.

Atop the fire she could barely make out the shredded torso of Luis Millán, flames licking up through the holes of his skull.

She realized that hell wasn't a faraway place in another realm.

It was here.

23. Your Stupid Face

After a few more hours digging into Leones distribution channels and an exquisite dinner of pozole and mole chicken,
Aragón and his men retired to the living room. The bulk of
the flowers had been removed, but their scent still perfumed
the air. Aragón took up a kingly perch on a leather armchair,
his men flanking him. Evan asked La Tía if he could help with
the dishes, and this time she granted him a stern matronly nod.
Hands in the suds, side by side, they worked in silence as a
stream of townsfolk entered to have an audience with Aragón.

Evan glanced over his shoulder. 'What are they doing?'

'He receives visitors on Sundays. It is part of his responsibility. To be a respectful *padrino*.'

'Even with Anjelina missing?'

'Responsibilities don't stop in times of hardship. They
become more essential.' La Tía took a plate from him to dry,
admiring his work. 'You are good at this. Most men are not.
Or at least that's what they tell themselves until they believe
it. And so they can use incompetence to get out of work.'

'How you do anything is how you do everything.'

'Excuse me?'

'Nothing.' Evan ran a soapy sponge around the rim of a
coffee mug. 'You're very close with your nephew.'

'Yes. Sometimes there are special relationships like that in
families, you know?'

He did not.

She continued, 'Where there is no static in the line. You
just *get* each other.'

'He seems to have that with his daughter, too.'

She considered. 'Complete understanding is harder between a father and daughter. His love for her? It is fierce beyond the winds. There is a weight there, the pressure of his love for her. My father loved me like that. It was wonderful, all-encompassing, frightening in its intensity.'

Evan thought of that closed bedroom door upstairs. The scent seeping through the gap last night – freon and something else. 'And his wife?' He trod gently. 'I still haven't met her.'

'Belicia is a real woman. From the very beginning, Aragón understood what he had in her. He knew not to ruin that.'

'I don't understand.'

La Tía held a glass to the light, checking for water stains. 'A woman should have many loves in life. Maybe it's dancing. Painting. Travel or hiking or drinking mezcal. Spending time with girlfriends who . . . recharge them. Most husbands seek to kill their wives' loves so we'll love only them. They are insecure little boys. Then they resent us when we get old, less full of life. I raised Aragón better than that. I raised him to stand on his own two feet so his wife can stand on hers. So she can be . . . *full*.'

'Then why does she stay holed up in her bedroom?'

La Tía turned a stare on Evan that he felt in his spinal cord. Discussion over.

They cleaned for a time in silence, and then he glanced over his shoulder into the living room. A line of townspeople had formed, backed up all the way to the foyer. An elderly man sat on the couch before Aragón, clutching his hands in his lap, his head bobbing in a tremor. Aragón jotted something down on a pad of paper and handed it to him.

'What's he doing?' Evan asked.

'Ah. That is a note to the pharmacy in town to put the

man's prescription on Aragón's tab. He makes fake loans to the elderly. They will never pay him back, but it allows them to have their dignity.'

Fascinated, Evan watched as the man took Aragón's hand in both of his and bowed his head in thanks.

'*Narcolimosnas*,' La Tía said. 'Drug alms. You saw the surrounding towns. Why do you think the roads are better in Eden? Who do you think pays for the soccer and baseball fields for our children? Equipment and uniforms? Who sends a repair crew to the high school when the roof leaks? Who pays for the irrigation and fencing for our farmers? Tractors and threshers? Who funded the construction crews for the new church? Who bought Christmas presents for the impoverished *niños* last year? Provided credit to young people struggling to start businesses? Who paid for trash collection for three months when the county budget was overdrawn?'

'The addicts who bought drugs from Aragón,' Evan said.

La Tía turned an irritated eye on him, snatching a plate away more crisply than seemed necessary. Her perfume was bitter and yet oddly pleasant, an olfactory analogue for the woman herself. 'Good intentions purify money. Transform it. Just as a person who has been corrupted can transform himself.' A pointed stare at him. 'I would think you might know something about that.'

Evan took this in.

She pressed on. 'Would you rather the money be spent on guns, more violence, more drugs?'

'I'd rather the money not be raised off sick people.'

She laughed. 'That's what capitalism *is*, child. All those companies with their "social responsibility" doctrines. Dodging hundreds of millions of taxes on the one side and then planting a few trees for the cameras. These people here in South Texas? What help do they get from the state? From

D.C.? I'll tell you what they get. Potholed roads. Soaring hospital bills. A legal system designed to protect the rich and powerful. Poverty. Suicide. Hopelessness. They pay taxes for what? To subsidize corporate welfare? Tax breaks for billionaire *cabróns*?'

'Aragón's a billionaire. Many times over.'

She shrugged. 'Who knows. We've lost count. The point is, the big pharmaceutical companies make more than a trillion dollars a year. With a *t*. They pay an army of lobbyists, falsify data, spend billions in marketing. And when they're caught? They settle. Cost of doing business. A price for every lost life. Last year over fifty thousand people in America died of opioid overdoses. Most of them had legal prescriptions.'

It was clear where Aragón had inherited his business acumen.

La Tía wasn't done: 'The black market is a tiny fraction of the sanctioned system. Aragón's business is no less corrupt than what is legal. It's simply a different system of pain and priorities and sacrifices. Except at the end we get schools. And safety. And money in the community.'

'A lot of things are sanctioned,' Evan said. 'And legal. That doesn't make them right. I know something about that as well.'

'Perhaps. But why should the white men in suits have all the money? Capitalism is a blood sport. I raised Aragón to compete as well as anyone else.' As she took the sponge from Evan, she caught him focusing once more on Aragón in his regal armchair in the adjoining room. 'Go sit. Listen.'

Evan drifted into the living room, half expecting to be stopped, but Aragón waved a welcoming hand. After firing off a text to Joey – **update?** – Evan sat to the side to observe.

A grandmother had taken her turn on the couch, embracing a newborn. At her side was a young teenager with xv3

170

tattooed on his forehead, branding him the property of the 18th Street Gang.

'– never should have come to America.' The grandmother's voice was tremulous, her English poor. The boy kept his head bowed, his big brown eyes soft and doleful. 'His mommy and daddy, they are work now every day. For to give him opportunity. And his brothers and baby sister. But look at him. He wear the mark of the devil now on his face. And he is oldest, to set example.'

The RoamZone vibrated on Evan's knee, Joey coming back: im deep into u.s. affiliate chapters. who they r hiring + how. urrea's intel stronger on the mex side + central ops so im filling in blanks.

Evan thumbed back: good. hq will be harder to penetrate. pick at the edges.

duh. thats what i just said.

is there a leones los angeles chapter? closer to my base of operations preferable. better ground truth.

Plus, that gave him a chance to get back for the dinner with Mia's brother that meant so much to her. But he didn't need to tell Joey that.

doesn't look like it, Joey texted. sinaloa cartel 2 strong. san bernardino closest.

get me everything asap.

kay, Joey texted.

The lowercase 'kay,' from her, was attitude.

eta? he typed.

4–5 hrs should have good handle on their us operations.

When he looked up and refocused, the grandmother was holding back tears. 'His daddy never should have bring him here because he find trouble anyway.'

'No, no, no.' Aragón said. 'Any good man with *cojones* would try to get his family here. Back in El Salvador? One out of ten men are murdered. This boy with his foolish face paint, he'd be dead by now. Or in Zacatraz. These prisons, they're the job centers for the gangs.' He narrowed his gaze on the boy, who'd folded into himself. 'That tattoo on your forehead? Know why they put it there right on your stupid face? That means you can't work anywhere else. That means they own you forever. Into the grave.'

The boy's lower lip began to tremble, but he pinched it between his teeth. The baby began to cry, and the grandmother bounced her in her lap, clutching her with arthritic hands.

'Look at me,' Aragón said.

The boy couldn't bring himself to lift his gaze.

'*Look at me.*'

The boy did. The baby's wail grew louder. The grand-mother tried to lift her but struggled, her hands gnarled, her grip weak.

'Do you want to be a scourge on your family?' Aragón said. 'A scourge on your people? A scourge on this new coun-try that offered you an opportunity?'

The boy shook his head, mumbled something unintelligible.

'What? If you have enough machismo to brand it on your forehead, you should be man enough to talk loud enough to be heard.'

'I don't want that,' the boy said. 'But it is too late now.'

'Yes,' Aragón said. 'Yes, it is. After everything your father and mother risked for you.'

The baby grew more agitated, squirming against her grandmother's chest, the cries coming staccato fast. Aragón stood up and held out his hands.

With disbelief the grandmother handed her over.

Aragón scooped up the diaper bag and brought the baby back to his armchair. He unsnapped the onesie with a prac-ticed flick of his fingers and tugged the baby's scrawny legs up, swiping at her rear end with a wipe.

The RoamZone went again. WHILE IM SLAVING AWAY WHAT R U DOING?

Evan thought to reply to Joey, looked up at the newborn's pale rear end aimed at the ceiling, and then, at a loss, pocketed his phone without responding.

The baby wailed and wailed. Aragón continued to clean her, hushing her tenderly, not looking up at the teenage boy. His last words – *it is too late now* – hung heavily in the room.

Aragón cleared his throat. 'Unless . . .'

The boy leaned forward. 'Unless *what*?'

Aragón folded the dirty diaper into itself like someone performing a magic trick and secured a fresh one on the baby. He tugged a pink blanket out of the bag and swaddled her so tightly that Evan thought he might cut off circulation. The bound baby resembled a larva, a plump body with a red face poking out of the top. Aragón rose and hoisted her with confident firmness, pressing her to his chest and tapping her back. Evan wondered how he could handle something so fragile without breaking it – the birdlike limbs, the attenuated spine, the tiny nose and mouth that seemed insufficient to take in oxygen. And yet the baby settled in his grasp, her cries turning to coos before fading into silence.

'I can offer you a job at one of my online centers,' he said. 'So no one has to look at the shit on your face. I will pay you one thousand dollars a week.'

The grandmother lifted a gnarled hand to cover her eyes. Her shoulders shook.

The boy looked stunned, poleaxed.

'If you do this job poorly or if you go back to those *putos perdedores* who scribbled on you, you will be fired and wind up in prison or dismembered in an oil drum. But if you work hard and make it through three months, I will fly you to Austin. There is a tattoo-removal clinic there that does excellent work. Three months. You will have earned the right to show your face in public again.'

Aragón slid the baby now into an upside-down cradle, his hand forked through the legs, her cheek smashed into the bulge of his biceps, a one-armed football tuck. He swayed her, and she dozed contentedly.

He nodded, indicating that the consultation had come to an end.

The boy rose, head still lowered. 'Thank you, Señor Urrea—'

'*Cállate*,' Aragón said. 'You don't thank me with words. You thank me with actions. Ninety days.'

The grandmother reached for the baby with her knobby hands. Aragón nodded to her respectfully and instead offered the sleeping baby to her brother.

The boy hesitated and then took her awkwardly.

Aragón lifted the diaper bag, held it out next.

It hung in the air between them.

The boy hesitated another moment and then took it and slung it over his shoulder.

He started to say something once more, but Aragón cut him off. 'I'm not interested in talking to you for three months.'

The teenage boy shuffled out, cradling his baby sister. The grandmother clutched at Aragón's forearm and stared up at him with wet eyes. He looked back at her. She patted his arm twice and departed.

Aragón lowered himself back into his armchair, a sound between a groan and a sigh escaping him. The house seemed empty in the relative silence.

'Hey, *Patrón*,' Special Ed said. 'Kiki has something to share with you.'

Kiki rested his folded arms across his paunch and glowered at Eduardo. 'No, I don't have something to share. I told you I don't—'

'He's gay!' Special Ed exclaimed.

Aragón took in his men. 'So what?'

Special Ed grabbed Kiki by the neck and rocked him back and forth roughly. 'I told you! I told you he wouldn't care.'

Aragón said, 'Have you discussed this with your mother?'

'No,' Kiki said with an edge of aggravation. 'I haven't told my mother.'

'She probably knows already.'

Special Ed said, 'That's what I –'

'*Enough*,' Kiki said. 'Don't we have more pressing matters to discuss? We still have heard nothing from the Leones. Why don't we call that crazy associate girl of Cabrón de Ningún Lado here and see what sort of headway *she's* made?'

Evan said, 'She needs a few more hours.'

Aragón rubbed his eyes. 'If there is nothing to do for the moment, then I need a drink.'

Evan found himself in full agreement.

Aragón started for the door. 'Let's go.'

Kiki and Special Ed rose, but Aragón shook his head.

'No.' He pointed at Evan. 'Just him.'

24. Just Another Sunday-Night Drink

The sole white-tablecloth restaurant in Eden featured American fare and a surprisingly impressive bar. Towering glass shelves, illuminated from beneath with a cool cobalt glow. As Aragón was greeted with customary warmth by the proprietors, Evan took in the bottles, his eye gravitating to the selection of clear liquids.

It took them some time to reach their booth, everyone rising to receive Aragón. He tried to wave them aside. 'Please, please. Enjoy your meals.'

They slid into the cushioned seats: Evan and a cartel leader.

Just another Sunday-night drink.

The waitress came over, a woman in her twenties with a stout build and a mess of red curls twisted up around a pencil. 'Greetings, Señor Urrea. Should I bring your usual?'

Aragón confirmed – Blanton's on a single big cube. Before she could turn to Evan, Aragón said, 'Miss?'

She hesitated. Played with her wedding band. She had a stain on her jacket by the lapel.

'Last time I was here,' Aragón said, 'I recall I gave you a big tip.'

'Yeah,' she said. 'Like a grand on an eighty-dollar check.'

'You weren't happy,' Aragón told her. 'Why?'

She set a fist on her hip. 'You really want to have this conversation?'

'Yes.'

Her lower jaw shifted left, right. 'It was like . . . like you

176

were saying you're better than me. Like if I didn't thank you profusely, it would bug you. Like, enough to bring it up later.'

At this she gave him a look.

Aragón frowned thoughtfully and nodded. 'Thank you for telling me.'

Her attention tracked to Evan. 'What'll you have?'

Evan said, 'Would you mind if I go to the bar to see the vodka selection?'

The waitress nodded. 'Suit yourself.'

Evan excused himself and crossed to the bar, leaning on the counter and examining the vodka. Just seeing the bottles there, illuminated with a cool sterile light, gave him a charge in the bloodstream.

The bartender, an older white gentleman in a well-worn suit, came over, sweeping a rag across the burnished wood. 'Help you, my friend?'

'The Polugar, please,' Evan said. 'Up. Bruise it.'

The man filled a martini glass with ice to chill it and then set to work with the stainless shaker. The loud rattle of ice would have been unpleasant if it didn't presage what was to come.

He paused, readying to pour, but Evan said, 'More, please.'

The bartender gave the shaker another trouncing, raising it up by his ear like a maraca. When he finally flicked the cubes from the martini glass and filled it with vodka, a thin sheet of ice crisped the surface.

'Olives?'

'No thank you,' Evan said. 'Not for the Polugar.'

'I understand.'

The single-malt rye vodka smelled like dough. A throwback to the pre-ethanol distillation process that produced the Russian breadwine enjoyed by literal and literary nobility from Ivan the Terrible and Peter the Great to Pushkin and

Dostoyevsky, *Polugar* meant 'half-burned.' The term signified the outstanding portion of liquid remaining after the excess had been burned away. Far off the beaten path in the woods of Poland, the vodka was not aged in oak barrels but triple-distilled in copper and filtrated with egg whites and birch coal.

The first sip struck bready hints of dill and honey, the aftertaste tinged with hazelnut on the fade. Evan felt the dopamine hit right away, the endorphin release hazing his mood at the edges. After the day's long journey into night and the moral confusion it had brought, he needed something clean, an antiseptic. He tasted the vodka once more, closing his eyes into the burn. Unlike the warm, earthy whiskey hues that Aragón preferred, it tasted elevated and azure and unpolluted – the taste not of grounding but of altitude.

The bartender observed him. 'You understand it,' he said. 'Alcohol.'

Evan nodded.

'We are honored by Señor Urrea's presence. You are a friend of his?'

It took Evan a moment to identify the sensation the question had elicited in him, surprised to discover that he felt offended. 'A friend? *No.*'

The bartender studied him. 'Ah,' he said. 'You know of his livelihood.'

'Doesn't everyone?'

The bartender set his rag aside and busied himself spearing olives. 'I've known him for twenty-three years. As for many in Eden, he is my first call when I'm in trouble. And never once in hours of conversation has he given me advice tainted with envy or arrogance or vanity. Not one time. I've heard that he has darker dealings. I don't know, and I don't care.'

Evan set down two twenty-dollar bills. 'I'd best be getting back to the table.'

'Wait one moment.' The bartender removed another martini glass from the freezer and transferred the remainder of Evan's drink. 'I was waiting for this one to frost.'

Evan lifted the glass in thanks and headed back to the booth. At an adjoining table, a trio of young women in spandex dresses took pictures of their food and of one another, applying various filters, flipping their hair, tilting their chins just so. It looked more like a confabulation between phones than a social meal.

Aragón observed them. 'All our sins and temptations at our fingertips all day. We carry them in our pocket. Our technology outweighs our character.'

One of the women came over, plucking down her dress to cover her ass. She traced a finger along Aragón's shoulder. 'Señor Urrea.' She brushed a hip against his elbow. 'I am so appreciative for everything you've done for, like, the town. And I know things are . . . distracting at home. If you ever want to talk . . . ?' She pinched a puffy lower lip between perfect white teeth.

Aragón finished the last of his bourbon, the block of ice clinking when he set down the glass. He did not look at her. 'My wife is sleeping two miles from this very spot, and I do not need a whore.'

She retreated, her color rising to match her makeup. The women and their phones made a swift exit.

A cloud had lowered over Aragón. He rolled his empty glass back and forth in the sweat ring it had left on the table.

For a few minutes, neither man spoke. They were into it now, the bone-weariness of waiting for the next thing to do, the horror of the situation held barely at bay.

Then Aragón said, 'Last night I dreamed I was eighteen

179

years old. And I chose to go to university. I became an anti-corruption lawyer, and I fought for the very things that matter to me now, but I did it better, cleaner. And my wife, she was happy and clear-eyed, and there were no savages at the gates baying for my blood, and my daughter was safe in my house, and it was not hidden in an armored compound but set on a street like every other street.' His face was still downtilted, so he glowered darkly at Evan from beneath the ledge of his brow. 'Then I woke up.'

A pause so long that Evan wasn't sure if the story was finished.

But Aragón continued, 'And I realized that yes, that girl in my dream was safe. But the girl in the dream, she wouldn't be *my* Anjelina. She'd be the daughter of a good man.'

Evan didn't understand why Aragón was telling him this.

Aragón set the glass down, pushed it away. 'Maturity is graduating from the belief that the world misunderstands you to the awareness that you misunderstand the world.' He laced his fingers together. 'Who I have failed to become is the story of why my daughter suffers. That load of product I burned yesterday? I could have burned it, burned them all, two years ago or three. And then maybe she would be safe. I didn't need you to tell me to do it. I didn't need you. But clearly I did.'

Evan thought again about how he'd recoiled from the bartender's question: *A friend? No.* He wondered what he was doing here in this booth talking with Aragón while Anjelina was out there somewhere, terrified and alone. And he wondered if somehow this very conversation was taking some tiny step toward setting things right, things so deep in the design of Aragón's life and maybe even Evan's that they lived beneath the tectonic plates, mired in the primordial sludge of emotion and fate that drove the whole confusing enterprise.

This was not a language he spoke, an outlook he trafficked in.

'Why didn't I take steps sooner?' Aragón peered into his glass as if hoping it had refilled itself. 'I was still afraid, though I didn't want to admit it. Afraid of being soft and weak, of being like everyone else. When life comes at you and bad shit happens, it knocks off your edges, wears through your veneer. Makes you more *ordinary*. That's why there's so much resentment at people who act entitled. Rich people who think they're special and better, above it all. They aren't special. They just haven't yet learned they're ordinary like everyone else. All those *cabróns* with their fancy university degrees, they learn everything but humility. And I thought *I'd* learned it. But I hadn't even begun.' He looked at Evan with something approaching deference. 'You're different. You've learned humility without having to be ordinary.'

'I never had the chance to be ordinary,' Evan said.

Aragón's eyebrows lifted with curiosity. He was fully engaged, his focus like a beam of energy. Evan couldn't recall being the subject of such attention, of having an opportunity to be seen the whole way through. It was every last thing that his training sought to protect him from, and it felt uncomfortable and liberating and intoxicating all at once.

The words came before Evan had considered them. 'When I was young –' He halted.

'Please.' Aragón waved a hand.

Evan looked down at his glass and realized that he had never spoken about what Aragón's words had just called to the surface. Though he'd known it somewhere beneath awareness, he'd never hauled it into the light, given it form, set it to words.

He cleared his throat, steeled himself with another sip.

The vodka warmed his temples, the tips of his fingers. 'When I was young, I shut myself off to the world. It wasn't safe to . . . to take in too much. It was like I was on an airplane and I closed all the windows. Everything blocked out except the view through the windshield. The way forward. There wasn't much . . . light. Or color. Warmth. Comfort. Feeling. Just . . . darkness.' He stared at his hands, the frost receding from the rim of the martini glass. 'I needed something extreme just to feel. To feel anything. Danger. Risk. Pain. But it served me to live that way. To keep everything muted. With the windows closed, there were no distractions to see. There was only . . . only the path ahead. It kept me alive.'

The textured pouches around Aragón's eyes seemed a part of his eyes themselves, his focus conveying a care and warmth Evan had rarely – never? – felt directed at him.

'Lately –' He halted again. The next sip of air felt cool traveling down the spirit-fired channel of his throat. 'I've started thinking about opening some of those windows. Letting in more light. But I worry . . .'

Aragón leaned forward. 'Yes?'

'I worry that if I let in the light, I won't be able to do what I do. I worry that I won't be able to go as fast and with such . . . singularity of purpose. Do you understand?' Evan felt something twisting in his chest, a need to be heard, to be understood, and that need was as foreign to him as a mother's caress or a baby wanting a diaper change.

Aragón bobbed his head, drawing him out.

Evan continued, 'When I think about how much I've missed all these years, all my life, I feel . . .'

He couldn't find the word. *Angry? Resentful? Vengeful?*

'Grief?' Aragón offered.

The word slid between Evan's ribs.

'I don't know that I know how to do anything else,' he said. 'To be anything else.'

'I understand,' Aragón said, and Evan saw in his eyes that he did. 'How could you not feel loss at everything you've missed? You've traveled way beyond what most people know, over uncharted lands, and you haven't even seen them.' He paused, giving the statement its due. 'But if you dare? To open those windows now? You will look down at a different view than anyone else. Perhaps that is the reward for your sacrifice. If you have the courage to take it.'

The waitress approached bearing the bill, and without breaking eye contact with Evan, Aragón held up his credit card to her. She read the table and retreated without a word.

Evan's mind churned and churned, and he felt unable to shape any of its content into words. Aragón gave him the silence.

The waitress returned with the check folio, which Aragón flipped open.

Evan read the bill upside down. The tip of Aragón's ballpoint hesitated over the slip.

Aragón tipped 20 percent.

Crossed it out.

He left twenty-five.

'If you look "patient" up in the dictionary, you know what there's a picture of?' Joey's voice over the RoamZone, despite being ping-ponged through two dozen virtual telephone switch destinations on six continents, was undiminished in its aggrievedness.

Evan sat cross-legged on the sofa bed in the upstairs study of Aragón's house. It was dark, moonlight falling in stripes across the carpet. 'I'm guessing something you think is clever that winds up insulting me?'

He'd tossed the RoamZone to nano-stick on the wall at eye level. It conveyed Joey's words holographically in sound waves with angry peaks and valleys.

They projected spikily in the darkness, electronic blue daggers: 'It's a picture of you with a *Ghostbusters* slash sign around it.'

'What's a ghostbusters?'

'Oh. Em. *Gee*. You're kidding, right? It's the red slashy sign. That means, like, the *opposite*.'

'A bend sinister?'

'What's a bend sinister?'

'A diagonal red band on a coat of arms. It's a sign of bastardy.'

'O*kay*, Jack.'

'Or you could call it a circle-backslash or an interdictory circle.'

A thumping sound, probably Joey banging her forehead against her keyboard. 'Never mind! Just . . . *stop*! I already *told* you I've almost got a handle on the San Bernardino delivery. I'm getting into some of their phones even to track correspondence. The more you bug me, the longer I'll take. So just leave me to my Red Vines and Red Bull, and I will call you when I'm done. *Gawd!*'

Click.

Evan pried the phone off the wall and checked his watch fob. It was nearing midnight. He didn't want another day to pass without getting a step closer to Anjelina. If she was still alive, whatever danger she was in would be worsening with every passing hour. Hostage situations wore down as they wore on. Strained patience. Frayed nerves. Appetites no longer held at bay.

He listened to the silence of the house. Aragón had excused himself upon their return, leaving Evan to the converted guest room. His unease returned, an eerie sense of connection with the other sleeping bodies under the same roof.

Out in the hall, a door creaked open.

He was on his feet, padding quietly to the threshold. He peered out.

Belicia's door was once more ajar an inch, maybe two. It had been shut minutes before.

He emerged from his doorway, moving silently toward her room.

He halted outside. The same smell, air-conditioning and something else, the weight of unvented air within.

A voice, husky and feminine, said, 'Come in.'

25. Something Else Entirely

Evan pressed the door gently, and it yielded under his knuckles. The room was dark, blinds closed, no night-light. A dark form sat in the bed, pressed up against the headboard, comforter across her legs and lap, face lost to shadow.

He entered.

An odd feeling of violation, of intimacy, being alone in a bedroom with someone's wife as she lay in the sheets. Aragón and La Tía were so guarded when they spoke about Belicia; Evan had no idea why and no idea what to expect now.

'Come,' the voice said. 'Sit.'

An antique oak accent chair with a round back, curved arms, and Victorian print fabric was positioned bedside, illuminated faintly by the seam of light from the doorway. Against the wall, a humidifier rasped, leaking tendrils of fog. The air felt thick and wet and vaguely cool.

He drew closer and sat.

She was motionless; he couldn't even see her mouth move. 'You are here to save Anjelina.' Belicia's voice was low, throaty, and she spoke in the perfect, heightened diction of a well-learned second language. Evan recalled from Joey's research that Belicia was born in Bosques de las Lomas, a wealthy *colonia* on the west edge of Mexico City.

'Yes,' he said.

'Aragón trusts you.'

'I believe he does.'

'Is he right to?'

'Yes,' Evan said. 'Why do you stay in here? Hidden?'

'Is that what I am? Hidden?'

He had no answer.

'I stay in here to keep my thoughts locked on the horrifying business at hand,' she said. 'Until my daughter is back in my arms, I choose to live in the worst of anything that could happen to her.'

The humidifier spun cottony chimney smoke from its spout. The wet air smelled of freon and petroleum jelly and Lysol.

'A baby takes everything from you. Everything you were before.' She waved a hand, a ghostly flicker in the blackness. 'Your time. Your figure. Your looks. They take your sleep until you don't know how to function. But all that is just a disguise for the most important thing they take from you: your selfishness. And that's the true gift of parenthood.'

Her hand went to her mouth, touching her lips, and for a time her chest rose and fell with emotion. 'Men think that giving big lessons is the way to raise children properly. But it's not. It's *us*. All the tiny things. Leaving the door open this much at night. How to turn the toothbrush handle so the bristles don't hurt the gums. Which stuffed animal to pack for a trip. The right smell of laundry detergent, how thin to cut the slices of cucumber for lunch. All those things men dismiss as unimportant. Our child's pains and fears and comforts are the only things that matter, and a thousand times a day we tend to them. That's what we do to help them grow and trust. And you men think it's from words you put together more nicely. Lessons you learned. How you did it in your day. Values. Discipline. Standards.'

Evan felt an unexpected surge of protectiveness for Aragón.

'All necessary,' Evan said.

'Yes. But not all that *is* necessary.'

'You're saying that Aragón is a bad father?'

'*No*. He is a *wonderful* father. But it's not so black and white. It's gray and messy. Family teaches you that.'

It made sense then that Evan had never learned it.

'This horror we are in now? It is my failure that I couldn't get him to understand what he needed to understand. Maybe . . .'

'What?'

'Maybe you will have more luck making him see.'

The humidifier puffed and puffed.

'That isn't what I do,' Evan said. 'This isn't my language. It's not who I am.'

'Maybe not,' Belicia said. 'But that is why I asked you to come in. Hope is . . .' Her voice seized, and she paused to collect herself. 'With my daughter's life at stake, hope is the hardest thing of all right now. I needed to see if you are someone worthy of pinning hope on. If you are someone *I* can trust as my husband trusts you to conduct this awful, awful business. If I can let you in knowing that it might tear my heart right out of my chest.'

Evan's RoamZone chimed, and Belicia started, rustling against her pillows.

Joey: I HAVE SAN BERNARDINO DELIVERY TIME + PLACE. 1ST THG TMRW. U NEED 2 GET BACK HERE NOW.

Evan rose. 'I have to go. I have a line on the Leones.'

'Wait.'

He paused.

'Come back. I'd like to see what you look like.'

Confused, he hesitated. Then eased back to her.

'Closer,' she said. 'Closer.'

She reached for him, and then he understood. Bending over her, he let her palms come to rest on his face. She felt the contours of his cheeks, his nose, running a hand along his brow. At this proximity he could see her pupils, white and cloudy. At the edges of her eyes, instead of crow's-feet were patches of scar tissue no bigger than a thumbprint, shiny with some sort of medical lubricant.

She released him, and he pulled up and away, letting her recede back into shadow.

He'd reached the door when she said, 'You didn't ask. Whether I decided if I could trust you.'

'You're right,' he said.

'You don't care what anyone thinks,' she said. 'That will only slow you down, muddy the way forward.'

'That's right.'

'You care only about saving her.'

'Yes.'

'That,' she said, 'is why I can trust you.'

He closed the door gently behind him.

In the guest room, he unlaced and relaced his Original S.W.A.T. boots meticulously, grabbed his duffel bag. Then he crept downstairs. Out into the hot, wet, night air, the same purgatorial air of Belicia's room, of South Texas.

He'd just reached the rented Buick when a voice called after him.

'*Amigo.*'

He turned to look across the hood of the Enclave. Aragón stood at the edge of the driveway in a gray bathrobe one size too big, bare feet against the concrete, face swollen with exhaustion.

'You saw her? Belicia?'

'I did.'

Aragón pawed at his mouth. 'The last time we went away for Semana Santa . . .' He drew in a breath. 'They replaced my eyedrops with drain cleaner.'

'Who did?'

'Who do you think?' Aragón said.

'Why?'

'I'd been exploring whether to route a supply line through Nuevo León. At the periphery. A single conversation, no more. I think he wanted to send a message.' Deep breath. 'He didn't claim credit for it, so I cannot know for sure. I can never know. And –'

'What?'

'We were swimming all day in the ocean. Belicia and I had been fighting. Nothing important, one of those marital disputes you don't remember the next day. She went back to the room first. Eyes red from the ocean.'

His face looked loose, undone.

Evan said, 'I'm truly sorry.'

'It's the way of the world. Sometimes it's so cruel it seems designed specifically to punish you.' Aragón fastened the sash on his bathrobe, looked at the Enclave. 'You are going?'

'I found a way in,' Evan said. 'I'll be in touch when I can.'

He started to get into the Enclave, but something in Aragón's expression stopped him. Barefoot and lost, standing out beneath the moon.

Aragón opened his mouth. Hesitated. Then said, 'The night before my girl was taken, she was playing on her keyboard in her room and singing. It was a Beatles song. "Let It Be." And I stood out in the hallway where she couldn't see me. And I watched and listened. I didn't think it could be real, you understand? That I got to have it. That moment. I thought that if I took it in all the way, all my joy, all my pride . . . I thought that she would die, you see? Because how could I have a moment so perfect? I feared that if I stayed, if I let myself have it, if I let myself say, "This is all I will ever need," then the other shoe would drop.' His cheeks were wet now,

190

glittering in the moonlight. 'The other shoe has dropped,' he said. 'And you're all that we have.'

A breeze cut through Evan's shirt, tightening his skin against his ribs.

'You're not the strongest man I've ever met,' Aragón said. 'Not the most vicious.'

'No.'

'Nor the best man.'

'No,' Evan said. 'I'm not.'

'You're ... something else entirely.' There was a heft behind the words that implied it was a compliment.

Evan ducked into the SUV and headed out of this patch of faux neighborhood, out of the guarded facility, out of Texas.

And toward the black, black heart of the Leones.

26. The Fallen and the Dead

The park in San Bernardino was an idyllic slope of grass in a non-idyllic neighborhood. A gritty low smog had curled in from the San Gabriels and layered over the flats. An optimistic yellow spot of sun bled through, creating a confusing two-dimensional effect that flattened the surrounding body-detail shops and working-poor homes. The park's slopes and parameters had no logic to them; it seemed that this misproportioned patch of land was all that had been left over after the neighborhood had hammered itself into place.

Evan gave a quick scan, checking the few folks out and about. A mother tapped at her iPhone with press-on nails, listlessly pushing her infant son in a creaky bucket swing between scrolling. Beneath a sturdy oak tree, a wholesome family of five had laid down a picnic, wicker basket and all.

Evan had taken a circuitous route back to California, picking up his Ford F-150 at Long Beach Airport's long-term parking and beelining straight here to head the Leones' drug delivery off at the pass.

Joey had downloaded him on the basics. Kontact was a new synthetic marijuana with a snappy delivery system. Place it on the eye like a contact lens and let it seep right into the bloodstream. The Leones San Bernardino chapter that had received the load was one of the newest, composed mostly of poached Verdugo Gang members from the East Side who brought with them infrastructure and distribution networks. Their primary push to market came through a rickety two-story trap house at the top of the park.

With its high crime rate and scant city investment in law enforcement, San Bernardino was a smart place for the Leones to sink resources. Established market of users, crumbling schools and communities, citizens worn down to the bone with hard work and despair. That's how gangs thrived, by feasting on the wounded sheep.

After surveilling the surrounding blocks, Evan decided to approach from the base of the park, abiding the Third Commandment: *Master your surroundings*. Strolling with his hands in his pockets, he focused on parked cars, rooftops, and windows. He noted alleyways and read the flow of traffic on the bordering streets. All of it rendered in that odd flat light, like a painting.

His boots crunched across sun-scorched spots of dead grass. Rusting chains locked the plastic picnic tables in place, their plastic benches gone mosaic from their time in the sweltering heat. The mom at the swing set was FaceTiming loudly now, phone flat beneath her chin. 'I never said that. Uh-uh. *Ne-ver.*'

Upslope the trap house was backlit by the sun, a dark rise. The prefab house next door had been half eaten by a fire, the demolition job seemingly stalled. Most of the parking meters had their heads lopped off. Bike frames impaled with U locks clung to the others, rusting into the pavement.

Drawing in a deep breath, Evan opened up his senses. Warmth of the sun. Dryness in the eyes. The mom's streamed altercation intensifying: 'You tell her to come say that to my face. Not just Insta-ing that shit. To my *face.*' The *creak-creak-creak* of the swing. Scent of Kool-Aid wafting over from the picnic, aggressively sweet, the kids' laughing mouths stained Joker red.

A shift in the earth's rotation brought the sun behind a bank of clouds, muting it further. Just as abruptly everything around Evan changed.

The mother had stopped talking.

The phone fell from her hand, plopped in the sparse tanbark.

Her mouth was ajar, rimmed with orange lipstick.

The swing slowed: *creak-creak-creak.*

The children on the picnic blanket had stopped laughing.

Their father on his feet, grabbing the youngest around her waist, legs and torso flopping.

The mother and older kids tripping to gather everything up, plastic cups rolling, painting the blanket tropical-punch red.

Creak-creak-creak

As if in a dream, Evan swept his gaze upslope.

A wispy-faced druggie stumbling toward them down the slope, his legs buckling but somehow keeping him upright. He was bleeding from his eyes, hiccupping frothy red flecks across his lips.

Spread behind him like a zombie horde, another half dozen users spilled from the house. One clutched the post of a street sign in a football tackle, shoulder sliding down the metal, bare feet scraping the ground. A young teenage girl vomited foam down the front of her shirt, stumbled and fell. She sank her yellowed fingernails into her eyes.

Now a metallic jangle to Evan's side, the mother ripping the boy from the bucket swing, his dimpled legs stuck in the hot black plastic, mouth wide and wailing.

Evan picked up his pace, jogging upslope into the horde.

The family of five blew past him hustling the other way, the girl weeping, the father repeating a mantra through clenched teeth: – *don't look baby don't look don't look* –

A hollowed-out man who might have been twenty or sixty stumbled between the trees, pants loose at his ankles, the buckle of his belt dragging along the ground, crotch bared to the world. He was grinding the heels of his hands into his eye sockets and emitting a prophet's howl. To his side a woman with tangled witch's hair sprawled on her stomach, grinding her face into the ground. Another lady staggered by her, mouth drooping, teeth red, bleeding from her gums. Two crimson stains ran jaggedly down the thighs of her jeans.

Anguished cries emanated from the trap house, more bodies pouring from the front door and the shattered windows, bubbling out like ants. Screaming and clawing and cackling, lost in the horror-trance of the spiked drug. Passersby all up and down the street backpedaled in terror and sprinted off. Everyone moving one direction out, – away.

And Evan bucking upriver, cutting through the walking dead, running to the source.

Heat in his chest, his face, his heart fluttering. He was used to all varieties of pressure but had never waded into something like this.

Trash covered the porch – hamburger wrappers, syringes, and empty Mountain Dew two-liters rolling underfoot. He shouldered in through the front door, reeling from the smell.

Mayhem inside. A husk of a man sat on a ratty couch, chewing off his own finger.

'No,' Evan said. 'No.'

The man looked up with blackened eyes and smiled, his chin sleek and dark.

More on the floor, moaning and puking and hacking. Someone seizing on the stairs, a blind throng trampling him on their way down.

Evan started upstairs. The balustrade had rotted away, and a man wearing filthy rags had tripped, impaling his thigh on the jagged rise of a snapped newel post. Blood sheeted down his leg, dripping off his bare toes to the ground floor.

Evan hit his knees, ripping off his belt, looping it around

the guy's leg above the gash. His hands were sticky and wet, but he managed the cinch. 'Hold this,' he said, shoving the tail of his belt into the man's hand, but the fingers pried open slowly and Evan looked up to see that he was already dead.

Evan rose, heartbeat thundering, sparks of static jittering across his visual field. His mind was racing, threatening to overload, so he extracted his breathing from the mess of his nervous system and set it on its own separate course. Two-second inhales, four-second exhales. Muscle memory, the click of a mental knob to start his internal metronome, and he could leave it to run in the background.

His vision cleared as he reached the second-floor landing. Garbage layering the floor like fallen leaves. The chemical reek was stronger here, overpowering the scent of human filth. Junkies lounging in various bedrooms, littered across floors and ratty couches, moaning and sobbing. Something in the horrid tableau – primal utilitarian space, packed human bodies, decay and poverty – brought him back to the foster home of his childhood. Sleeping in a room crammed floor to ceiling with bunk beds, the perennial battle for more food in the ant-infested kitchen, the indelible smell of despair and the marrow-deep sense of worthlessness that came from living in it.

A shirtless blonde staggered into his path, knocking him from his reverie, streams running from her eyes and nose. She couldn't have been older than sixteen. She pitched forward, and he caught her beneath the arms. Her momentum took him by surprise, boots sliding out from under him until he struck the floor, still cradling her.

'Are you okay?' he asked dumbly.

'Oh, sure,' she said. 'I'm fine.'

Then she arched back violently, wrists and ankles pronating, lids fluttering over destroyed eyes.

He grabbed her cheeks, forced her mouth open, cleared her tongue from the airway. The smell lifting off her – industrial cleaner and ammonia – made his eyes water.

'Hang on, just –'

She shuddered once more and then went limp – full cardiac arrest. He eased her to the floor, thumped her chest. More people spilled out of the big room ahead, their knees banging his shoulders as he started compressions. The girl rolled to her side, rag-doll limp, and expelled a stream of fluid from her mouth.

Someone ran into him squarely, knocking him off her, and by the time he found his feet, she'd hemorrhaged out.

Blood on his shirt, his pants, his hands.

His feet felt numb as he pushed into the big room.

Folding tables lined the far side beneath a smoke-hazed window, hundreds of white packets laid out with KONTACT blazoned across them in alluring bubblegum pink. Other options abounded – meth Baggies, vape pens, preloaded syringes. Plastic tubs brimmed with thousands more. Past them in the bathroom, funnels and beakers filled a curtain-less shower. The tiles and toilet were covered with hoses and propane tanks, tubs of solvent and an open blue barrel labeled ETOH. Chemicals burned the back of Evan's throat, his eyes, nostrils. It was like breathing chlorine.

Two dealers scrambled around the room's periphery, throwing handguns, scales, and grimy balled currency into duffel bags. They wore ribbed sleeveless undershirts, their arms sporting full Verdugo Gangster ink, the branding not yet converted to that of the Leones.

'– get the fuck out before po-po –'

'Grab the ledgers, man, or Rondo'll kill us.'

Rondo.

Evan knew the leader's name and the names of most of the

affiliates in the local chapter, gathered up along with other intel in a neat virtual bundle by Joey. From the phones she'd hacked into, he knew most of their movements and schedules.

The men continued their scramble. 'The ledgers! All them ledgers!'

They stopped and took in Evan. His hands gloved to the wrists in blood and grime, clothes soiled, sober upright posture.

Somewhere in his subawareness, his breathing kept on – two-second inhale, four-second exhale.

The skinny one near the bathroom had veiny tennis-ball biceps. A crack cigarette burned down to his lips, cherry burning beneath a solid inch of ash.

He spoke in a stunned monotone. 'Bad batch, man. We didn't know. No one knew.'

His colleague froze, stooped over the duffel, a gleaming .22 in reach. He made no move for it.

Evan heard his voice as if from afar. 'Is this the main stash house?'

The second man straightened up. 'No, man. It ain't here. We was just seeding the market. The wider rollout comes tomorrow.'

'It kicks in *after* the high, so we didn't know,' the skinny guy said, the cigarette bouncing in his lips, a cartoon effect. 'The poison and shit, it hits later.'

The exchange was conversational, even civil, any strife paved over by the trauma all around.

The back of Evan's throat felt dry and cracked. One, two on the inhale. Push out the exhalation. He kept his stare on the other guy. 'Where, then?'

'HQ, man. Rondo at HQ's got the main load.' He broke off eye contact with Evan, turning to his friend. 'Get the fucking ledgers and let's split.'

The skinny guy nodded, backing up.

Evan saw the jugs behind his heels.

The hanging ash of the cigarette.

The lidless barrel of ethyl alcohol.

Even before the puzzle pieces connected, Evan turned and ran, hurdling the dead girl in the hall.

He heard the guy's heels strike something, the yelp of surprise.

Evan passed the landing, lunging down the steps four at a time.

Nothing yet nothing yet nothing y—

A whoosh thrummed the bones of the house, and then the pressure wall of the explosion rushed his back like a giant hand, sweeping him off the last few stairs. He got a foot down in the foyer, miraculously dodging fallen bodies. Knee buckling, other leg driving, like a running back dragging line-backers into the end zone.

Doorway – porch – *boom!* – flames licking his back.

Then he was rolling across the dead front lawn, the hair of his arms scorched. He found his feet and looked behind him. Flames eating the interior, flapping out the upstairs windows in bright orange sheets. The smell was indescrib-able. The taste of death and lesions, like necrosis withering his lungs.

He drooled and coughed and found his feet.

Ambulances, cop cars, and fire engines screamed up and down the street, a respectable first response mustered from San Bernardino's paltry resources. Uniforms covering the park, tending to the fallen and the dead.

Evan shook his head, trying to clear his senses.

Someone was screaming, a higher pitch than the rest.

He lifted his gaze to the blown-out front window. Behind a thin wall of flame, he saw a young man with rotted teeth pacing in drugged agitation, rubbing his arms. He looked like he'd just woken up. '– help me – oh, Jesus –'

Evan rose, steadied himself on his feet.

A cop yelled at him from the curb. 'Get back! Sir, get back!'

Evan took a step toward the house, but the heat was too strong, propelling him back on his heels. One of the Mountain Dew two-liters rattled across the dirt, caromed off his boot. He looked down at it.

Then at the neighboring house, half burned to begin with, the demolition stalled. A pile of scorched nails, a rusty sledgehammer with a broken handle, a few wadded paper dust masks streaked with ash.

Whipping his Strider knife out and open, Evan snatched up the two-liter bottle and sprinted for the heap of refuse next door. His hands working of their own accord, sawing off the bottle at the lowest seam, carving away the dimpled four points of the bottom. He sliced a U through the label, ending two inches from the cap.

Evan kicked the mound of trash, scattering the white orbs of the dust masks. They were all heavy with ash, but he plucked up the least battered and rammed it into the severed bottle, seating the gauzy disk at the base of the U. It wedged into place, an imperfect seal, but it was all he had.

The cop had stopped yelling at him, aiding paramedics on the sidewalk, waving over an ambulance. From the trap house, Evan could still hear the guy screaming.

Sprinting back to the house, jabbing a few holes through the lime-green bottle cap, ramming the makeshift gas mask to his face. The jagged edge where he'd sawed through the plastic cut into his cheeks.

Up the porch into the foyer, eyes streaming tears, lungs burning. Flames billowing down the stairs, the scent of poison and burned hair and angry periodic elements. A feminine form shuddered facedown at the base of the stairs. Evan got the toe of his boot beneath the body and flipped it over. Flames rose through her mouth; she was long dead, on fire from the inside.

The man still paced erratic circles behind the couch, lost in a drug haze. Holding the mask in place, Evan lunged through the flames, grabbed him around the ribs, and swung him toward the door. The guy tried to resist, but he was light as a scarecrow and Evan muscled him through the flames.

High-stepping over corpses, sucking oxygen through the tiny holes, trying not to cough, because if he started, he'd never stop.

Out into the bright light of day, half falling off the stairs, staggering toward the paramedics. The cop was gesturing wildly. Another explosion made Evan's shoulders jerk, and he lost his grip on the mask.

He fumbled the man over to the paramedics, the cop grabbing Evan's shoulder and shaking him – 'You crazy? You fucking crazy?' – paramedics stabbing penlights into the guy's eyes, his chest lurching with dry heaves, trying to hack out the toxins he'd inhaled.

The junkie's head lolled to the side, and vomit spilled from his throat. Evan backed away, the puke spreading toward his toes, the cop still yelling at him – 'Fucking junkie gonna die anyways! You can't just run into a –'

Evan's heels hitting first as he kept backing away and more ambulances wailing into view and EMTs triaging, the park covered with movement. He turned, lowered his head, and walked downslope, away.

His hands were shuddering and his heart thumped wildly, but he realized that he was still breathing at the right setting – two in, four out – and as long as he had his breath, the rest of his body would find its footing again. His neck felt blistered, his cheeks raw from the jagged plastic of the make-shift mask.

Neighbors were at their windows and on their front steps, glassy-eyed and pointing, hands clamped over mouths. Cops and firefighters and paramedics now pouring in and Evan moving once more alone against the current.

Finally he reached his truck and crouched by the driver's door, palming the scorched nape of his neck, the grilled-meat smell still pasted through his nasal cavities, his gorge rising.

He vomited twice into the gutter and was relieved to see nothing like the foamy poison that had spilled from the mouths of the victims. He spit to clear his throat and then again and again.

This wasn't war. These weren't soldiers or hired guns or mercenaries. These were poor huddled masses, broken and useless, human refuse scraped from the bottom of the barrel. Throwaways.

Just like him.

He peeled off his bloody shirt, wiped his hands imperfectly, and stuffed it down a storm drain. Got into the truck and turned over the engine. Sweat dried across his bare chest, sticky hand on the gearshift, but he couldn't manage to pull it into drive.

All he could manage to do right now was breathe.

Two in.

Four out.

27. A Journey Through the Underworld

Evan kept a number of safe houses scattered around Los Angeles County for this kind of contingency. Inside a stuccoed bungalow abutting a check-cashing shop on the Eastside, Evan burned his clothes and then showered. The place was one square room with a kitchenette and a nook of a bathroom. He held the deed under the name Xavier Francis and stopped by semiweekly to turn on different lights and clear the mail. He stood in the garage now for a time with his hand on the hood of his trusty Ford F-150, gathering himself.

He wanted the comfort of home, a comfort he'd been missing sorely for the past six months through the destruction and rehabilitation of 21A but never as sorely as now in the middle of a mission that had turned into a journey through the underworld. His penthouse with every last thing in its place. All the surfaces able to be scrubbed clean, polished to a reflective sheen. Each item steel and concrete, immune to the ravages of time and decay, as hard as every last bit of his training. No traces of the grime and decay of the outside world, of human beings, of confusing emotions that dragged him through the morass of his past and reminded him that he was as stained and dirty as everyone else.

Vodka to purify. A floating bed on which to meditate. His Vault to plot and plan.

He would make them answer. Every last León who had unleashed this hell. He'd start at the periphery and work his way inward to the glowing-hot center, to El Moreno, the

Dark Man himself, who held Aragón and Belicia's daughter captive in the hateful grip of his hateful enterprise.

Driving back to Castle Heights, Evan felt the nape of his neck still burning beneath the skin, though there was little visible damage. Scratches from the mask left his cheeks lightly scraped; a day's stubble would shadow it under.

The radio was lit up with breaking news of the carnage. He listened for a time and then clicked it off. The air conditioner smelled like the freon of Belicia's room, so he cracked the window the two inches allowed by the Kevlar armor hung inside the passenger door panel. Hot tar and exhaust returned him to the stink of the morgue. On the inhale he could still taste the blackened flesh of the trap house, a bitter tang riding the back of his throat. He rolled the window up again.

It didn't help.

He was *in* the mission. It was all around him, in his mind and his body, everywhere he looked, in the air he breathed, the whole world flattened to that two-dimensional light of the park and those who had perished there. He had flattened himself, too, in order to fit into this world, in order to make sense of it and engage with it on its terms. He'd entered the prison of his OCD, all thinking and sensation hammered into a plane.

The valet at Castle Heights started to rise from his director's-chair perch in the porte cochere but recognized Evan's truck blasting by and sank back down in defeat. Descending into the mouth of the underground garage, Evan parked between the two pillars that bookended his space.

Out and up into the lobby, mere minutes from the sanctity of his own space.

Lorilee and Hugh were arguing near the front desk, Joaquin caught in the middle, his security cap low over his eyes as if that could make him vanish. Grateful for the diversion, Evan slipped behind Hugh's back, gesturing at Joaquin to summon the elevator.

'Mr Smoak!' Hugh wheeled on Evan. 'Do you see the mayhem you've caused? We are dealing with a real crisis here.'

Evan halted. His voice still felt chalky from the fire, and he had to push out the words. 'Not sure I understand.'

Lorilee pivoted next, a teacup poodle wedged between her biceps and the side of an augmented breast. 'Hugh is freaking out over my cousin's dog coming for a sleepover –'

Hugh adjusted the black frames of his eyeglasses, peering peremptorily at Evan. 'Had you not set a precedent with service animals –'

Lorilee made cutesy lips. 'This lil' guy's more like my nephew –'

'– Mrs Rosenbaum has terrible allergies –'

'– this baby has terrible allergies, too. You wouldn't believe the amount of yeast in most dry dog foods. We had to go to a line-caught salmon diet because he gets ear infections –'

'– Ida had to go on Zyrtec, which interferes with her blood-pressure meds –'

'– good thing poodles have hair, not fur, so they don't shed –'

'– and health-code violations are not to be taken lightly when –'

Evan felt his teeth grind, enamel and bone. 'I'm sorry,' he said. 'I've had a trying day at the office. Can we deal with this later?'

'No,' Hugh said. 'I'm afraid not.'

The elevator arrived, and Evan got on. They both followed him. As Hugh continued to berate Evan, the poodle scrambled in Lorilee's arms, lunging at him. It looked like a mop or a merkin or the paw of a properly sized dog.

'Ooh, wook how sweet,' Lorilee said. 'Boba wants Ev cuddles!'

Evan was unsure how to convey how close he was to snapping the dog's neck. And Hugh's. And perhaps Lorilee's for good measure.

'I need some personal space,' Evan said.

'"Personal space." Come ooon, Ev.' She laughed. 'Looks like someone's caught a bad case of the sillies.'

The dog came at him, panting fish breath in his face, triangular pink tongue poking out beneath a Monopoly Man mustache. Evan made direct feral eye contact, and the dog stiffened and recoiled, curling into Lorilee's surgically enhanced bosom.

Undeterred, Hugh continued with his monologue into the side of Evan's face. '– norms keep us safe. We have to look out for one another. Like when Ida got mugged. Or Judge Johnson had prostate surgery. We take care of each other. We give our time. Our care. Our *support*.'

Evan returned to combat breathing: two in, four out.

Boba stared at Evan warily.

Hugh's Adam's apple jogged in his tanned throat, and Evan had the flash of an impulse: backhand strike to crush the larynx. That would make the words stop.

Not nice.

The elevator opened. They'd ridden up to the top floor with him.

Evan emerged. Did his best to assemble words suitable for whatever circumstance this was. 'Thank you for the input.'

They stared at him blankly.

'I am . . . sorry for the service-animal complication.' Evan felt his face form what he hoped was a pleasant expression. 'And for Mrs Rosenbaum's allergies. And Judge Johnson's prostate operation.'

Evan stepped out. Just seeing the clean hallway was cause for relief. Hugh stayed at his heel. 'It's not just about feeling sorry –'

Evan turned and looked him in the eye.

Hugh shrank from the heat of his gaze, and his mouth snapped shut. He retracted back into the elevator.

Evan exhaled. Just a few more steps to carry him to his sanctum.

Key in the door, the clank of internal gears shifting, the faint whoosh of water within. The door creaked open to the sound of giggling.

At first he did not believe what he was seeing. Joey and Peter were wearing giant black bulging suits made of – was that *Velcro*? – circling each other like sumo wrestlers. A wide vertical stripe of black fabric covered the wall to his left from floor to ceiling. There was a disco ball hanging from the ceiling near the fireplace. A disco ball. A fucking disco ball. They'd placed Vera III in her nest of ludicrous rainbow pebbles on a chair next to them so she could get in on the fun.

Heat rose from the pit of his gut, claiming his chest, clawing up his throat, firing his face.

The kids hadn't noticed him. Peter took two waddling steps and flung himself at the wall with a movie-karate cry. 'Hiii-*ya*!'

He stuck sideways three feet off the floor, arms and legs pinned to his sides, his hands waving helplessly. Then Joey helped pry him off, the ripping sound of hundreds of tiny Velcro hooks peeling from loops. They collapsed on the floor together, belly-laughing.

Evan took another step into the great room, and they saw him for the first time. Joey rose, stumbling in her giant suit, peeling herself away from the nine-year-old.

'Evil E! You're back. Wait, I have a surprise for you.' Joey snatched a sleek remote from the hearth of the freestanding fireplace, aimed it upward, and clicked a button. 'Wait for it. *Waaait* for it.'

The disco ball began its rotation, flashing lights around the penthouse, music blasting from unseen speakers: *Night fevah, night fevaaah, we know how ta show it!*

Evan felt a cinching at his temples. 'Joey.'

Now she and Peter were doing diagonal pointy fingers at floor, then ceiling.

The ball strobed light in Evan's eyes. 'Joey.'

They linked arms and do-si-do'd, waddle-dancing preposterously in their Velcro suits.

'*Josephine.*'

At his tone they both stopped. Joey looked at him. Some of the color drained from her face. She clicked the remote, and the music and lights stopped abruptly. They stood absurdly in their absurd suits. The silence was painful.

Evan said, 'Peter. Home.'

'But we also hafta show you the cool nozzles in the shower that hit *all* your parts –'

'*Now.*'

Peter stripped out of his suit, tumbling over and then kicking his way free. His tiny footsteps pounded past Evan, out the door, and up the hall.

Evan closed his eyes. Saw the blond girl in his arms, her body arced as if an electric current were passing through, her insides gone to jelly, leaking out her nose and mouth. The raw skin at the nape of his neck prickled. The inside of his mouth, raw from chemical residue. All those fallen bodies littering the park. His need to come back to a space of his own, designed to his specs, something that reflected the state he tried moment by moment to achieve in his mind.

When he spoke, his voice shook with anger. 'This is *my* place.'

Joey flipped her hair out of her eyes with a quick jerk of her head. Sweat glistened in the strip of shaved hair over her right ear. She tugged her arms free of the suit so it hung down at the waist like a coveralls bib. She looked wounded and foolish and utterly ridiculous. 'Maybe it's not anymore,' she said bitterly, fighting her way free of the puffy legs.

'What does that mean?' His voice wasn't raised, but there was a coldness in his tone that he'd never used with Joey.

'It means you asked me to get all this done for you. And I did. *And* over the weekend. Tile guys and appliances and painting and – You know what? Never mind.'

'I asked you to help restore my place. Not add a bunch of shit that I don't want.'

'When you ask for help, you don't get everything exactly how you want it, X. It's impossible for anyone to get everything exactly how you want it.' She kicked the suit aside. 'You know why? Because you're impossible.'

'It's a stretch to think that I might not be ecstatic with Velcro and a disco ball?'

'I thought it might cheer you up!' she said. 'Know what you told me? "Handle it yourself, Joey. I trust you."'

'I *thought* I could trust you.'

'What?' Her mouth fell open. That dimple appeared in her right cheek, and not from smiling. 'What did you say to me?'

It took everything he had to hold his tongue.

'You can't trust me because I did something to cheer you up?' She blew the hair off her forehead once more. 'Just 'cuz the world is dark and miserable doesn't mean you have to be, too. You *choose* it. You choose not to trust anyone. You choose to be an asshole to people who care about you. Sure, you're nice to some girl you don't even know – Anjelina or whatever

209

princess's name is. You run off to save her. Do anything for her. But *me*? I'm here fixing your place up and you won't even let me go on a road trip by myself.'

The road trip now.

Two in. Four out.

Not working. Images cascading down on him.

His defiled penthouse, Velcro and a disco ball.

The blonde shuddering in his arms, bleeding out.

Anjelina in the hands of men who decapitated their rivals and suffocated journalists with duct tape.

Joey out in the world he'd protected her from all this time, out among men like the Leones who lie in wait for vulnerable girls like her.

Too much for him to manage and also save Anjelina. Too much weakness and emotion to hold in his heart to go after those he needed to go after. He tried to access what was right, but he couldn't. He was trapped in two dimensions, inside the painting of this horror of a mission.

Joey was still going, mouth wavering, anger in her glare. 'Just 'cuz you can't figure out how to have freedom doesn't mean you can take it away from *me*.'

'You want to leave, Joey?' His voice low like a growl and even more controlled; rather than revving up, he was simmering down, eradicating emotion. 'Go, then.'

She looked suddenly unsure of herself, even frightened. Like she didn't recognize him. 'X . . . ?'

'*Get out*,' he said.

Her eyes flared, those big glossy lashes parting, emerald irises shining beneath the strokes of her eyebrows. She was wide open – her face, her heart, everything stripped bare.

She collapsed, hitting the floor on her side, head resting on her biceps, fetal and sobbing.

He stared at her in disbelief.

He had never done that to another human being. With words.

He couldn't make sense of the noises coming from her.

'Joey,' he said in a strangled tone that was completely foreign to him.

She shoved herself up with her palms, got her legs under her. She was shaking her head, looking down, away. Hurt glowed from her, and something worse.

Shame.

She walked past him, giving him a wide berth, no eye contact. Not storming for the door so much as sweeping herself out before she went to pieces.

The front door slammed behind her.

A terrible silence asserted itself. No giggling, no belly laughter, no tearing of Velcro.

He didn't understand what he felt, but he felt it everywhere. In his fingertips. His scalp. Tongue numb against his teeth.

Vera III looked up at him in her stupid fucking rainbow pebbles.

Then she was in his hand, hurled against the wall, the glass dish shattering, brightly colored pebbles raining down across the poured-concrete floor, skittering past his boots.

Belicia's words returned to him like an echo: *It's not so black and white. It's gray and messy. Family teaches you that.*

Right now Evan had to turn away. Had to flatten himself out again, knife-thin, nothing but purpose and intent with a tapered point.

Because of the bodies scattered across that park. The remainder of the Kontact waiting at the Leones San Bernardino headquarters. The other batches creeping their way into America, spreading toxic tentacles through cities and towns, stash houses and bloodstreams.

He thumbed his RoamZone on, dialed Aragón.

'Yes?'

'I tracked down the first shipment of Kontact,' Evan said.

'And?'

'Turn on the news.'

He waited while Aragón grunted, no doubt rising from his armchair. There was a click, the sound of a commercial, channels flipping. Then a newscaster's voice hitting a strained note of empathy.

'My God,' Aragón said. 'My God.'

'I'll handle the San Bernardino chapter.' Evan still maintained that flat, dead tone. 'Every other channel you have a bead on from your or my associate's intel, you leak to the DEA. Give them everything and see if they can backtrace to the original lab in Mexico. Blame the leak on the Gulf Cartel. Blame it on whoever you need to. But get it done now so they can stop those loads from hitting market, so they can snuff this out at the source. Understand?'

Aragón sounded shocked by whatever footage he was seeing. 'I understand,' he said quietly, his voice touched with remorse. 'Those people in the park . . . all those people.'

'It ends,' Evan said. 'Right here. Right now. No more drugs. No more anything like it ever again. Burn whatever product you have. Destroy whatever you have in transit. You do it now. Or you'll never hear from me again.'

The pause stretched out. Evan wasn't sure he'd be able to hear the reply over the blood thundering in his veins.

'Okay.'

'Give me your word.'

Aragon said, 'I just did.'

'I'm going in,' Evan said.

He cut the line.

28. Beginner's Mind

Hands shoved in his pockets, head down, Evan came up on the headquarters with nothing on his person. No ARES 1911, no Strider knife, no backup mags in the streamlined inner pockets of his cargo pants.

All he had was himself. They'd search him at the front door. They'd pat him down ankle to crotch to ribs, make sure he had nothing on him before they'd let him pass through.

Jack's timeless advice returned to him: You *are the weapon.*

The back end of dusk, stagnant water standing in the gutters, drawing mosquitoes. The spaced-out houses somewhere between mobile homes and prefabs, blue TV light flickering against windowpanes, folks cocked back in easy chairs, grandmothers fanning themselves with magazines at screen doors.

A portable chain-link fence guarded the onetime auto-repair shop at the end of the block. A sentry stood guard outside, beefy and neckless, arms so bulky he could barely clasp his hands in front. He took note of Evan's approach from a hundred yards out, straightening up, shoulders back, ready to rumble.

There was no time for a strategic approach. The bigger Kontact rollout was planned for tomorrow. Evan knew from intercepted texts that the Leones San Bernardino crew was in an emergency meeting right now regrouping after the disaster in the park and that they were expecting a visit later in the night from a member of El Moreno's inner circle. Given the fatalities, Evan didn't know if the Leones would pull the load back or try to dump it into the marketplace to recoup what they could. The latter seemed unconscionable, but Evan had lived with the unconscionable for the bulk of his life and was unwilling to put off a confrontation in order to give human nature the benefit of the doubt.

And so he would enter the headquarters with open eyes and beginner's mind, see everything as if for the first time. No assumptions. No thought patterns. No neurological pathways.

That was the aim.

To see nothing that wasn't there and to see everything that was.

To pay attention.

Fifty yards out.

Now forty.

The ground firm beneath the tread of his boots. Air keen in his throat.

Thirty yards out.

Twenty.

Taking note of the red eye of the security camera on the roof, Evan made sure to square himself to the lens to allow the active camo of his shirt to have full cloaking effect.

The sentry had an MP7 in hand now. His head cocked back, beady eyes looking down his nose at Evan, ready to kill or fight or frisk him.

Ten yards.

Holding his arms wide, palms bared, Evan released the jumble of thoughts tumbling through his mind and sharpened his focus until every last detail was crystalline.

The sentry's hands were huge, encompassing Evan's calves, thighs, biceps as he patted him down. Evan recognized him from the files as Alce. The guy straightened back up, seeming to rise and rise, and then he breathed out through flared nostrils into Evan's face.

'Fuck you want?'

'I'm here to talk to Rondo.'

'Ain't no Rondo here.'

'I have a message straight from El Moreno,' Evan said. 'You're gonna want to let me in now.'

A sea change in attitude. 'Oh, shit. Okay. *That's* why you're not packing.' Alce set his massive palm on the metal door and hinged it open. 'I wasn't expecting you to be so . . .'

'White?' Evan said, drawing up next to him and side-eyeing the MP7, noting the selector switch's position – three clicks down for full auto.

Alce nodded somberly. 'I apologize for the disrespect.'

Up a long hall. Through another rusting metal door. Across the defunct floor of the garage with its car lifts and oil stains and a few disused cargo vans. And into a surprisingly pristine lobby-office.

The members were spread out on vinyl couches or perched on mesh chairs rolled out and away from the front desk, which hosted a few dated security monitors streaming live feeds from the property.

Eighteen men, tattooed and rawboned. Gold incisors and dangling cross pendants. Forties of malt liquor and crack cigarettes. The cubicle walls of two-thirds of the room had been torn apart and stacked like firewood to make room for dozens and dozens of clear industrial plastic tubs stuffed with Kontact packets.

Rondo had a soft, boyish face with sad, seal-like eyes and whiskers at the edges of his upper lip. Scruff tufted from his chin, glistening in the low light. He sat on a throne built of shrink-wrapped bricks of five-hundred-euro notes, his black British Knight high-tops propped up on an ottoman fashioned of like currency.

Nicknamed the 'bin Laden,' the banknote was favored the

world over by high-rolling reprobates because it packed the most punch for its weight. A million bucks in hundred-dollar bills weighed nearly twenty-two pounds, whereas the same amount in bin Ladens came in at a fifth the weight and size.

Everything about the Leones operation was designed for maximum efficiency.

Evan entered at the tail end of a conversation.

'– having some growing pains, that's all,' Rondo was saying. 'Complications. It's a trial-and-error process, and the chemists down south are aware of the imperfections in the product.' His eyes snapped over to Evan, and he leaned forward, clasping his hands.

'This is El Moreno's guy,' Alce said.

'I didn't catch a name,' Rondo said.

'No,' Evan said. 'You didn't.'

'Take a seat.'

Evan took a spot in the circle of loosely arrayed couches and chairs and weighed their eighteen beating hearts against the forty-seven no longer beating hearts in the park. For a moment he saw through their cocky bearings, saw their full humanity, saw them as sons and fathers and grandsons. A sacred pause he sometimes took before the kill.

Alce had sauntered over to stand at Rondo's side, leaving Evan on the couch between Arturo, who tapped a pencil nervously against a ledger, and Beltrán, cleaning dirt from beneath his nails with a stubby button-lock knife. Lengua Larga leaned against a pallet stack of Kontact tubs, tapping a crowbar in his palm. A few pieces were visible, a blinged-out .38 resting on Pancho's thigh on the far side of a footrest and of course the big gun in Alce's hands, ready to spit 950 rounds per second.

Rondo flared his hands. 'Well?'

'Quite a mess at the park,' Evan said.

Rondo bobbed his boyish face. 'Yes. Yes.'

Evan was unsure what he was reading from Rondo's expression. Remorse? He caught himself. The First Commandment: *Assume nothing.*

'Too bad about that,' Rondo said.

'Yeah,' Lengua Larga said. 'It's a mess, a real mess, amirite? All them dead junkies and shit, can barely believe –'

Rondo silenced him with a glance. Returned his attention to Evan. 'The product, the product we trusted you to deliver, is tainted. We are unwilling to kill any more of our consumers.'

Maybe there would be a way out for these sons and fathers. It struck Evan that he knew how to walk into a room filled with men and walk out with them all dead and him alive. He was less sure how to extract himself from the situation with them still breathing.

'I know you bring a suggestion for what we should do with the remaining product.' Rondo swept a hand to indicate the thousands of packets brimming from tubs, each one a lethal dose. 'And we respect greatly the wisdom of El Moreno. We are honored to be newly pledged Leones.'

Evan waited and breathed and paid attention.

'But.' Rondo held up a finger. 'I understand it will be some time for your labs to figure out the proper ratio of chemicals for the next batch, so –'

'Seriously,' Lengua Larga cut in. 'Gotta get that figured out. Spraying the right synthetics and shit, amirite?'

Rondo patiently continued, 'In the meantime we laid out six point five million of our own money for this. We are overextended. In order to recover our cost . . .'

Evan felt nothing but his breath, his heartbeat, and the faintest *ticktock* of the second hand on his watch fob.

'. . . we would like to dump the bad product in other cities.

217

Wholesale if we have to. We can recover what we can while preserving our market here. And start fresh once you've squared away your end of the operation.'

Evan felt it then. High clarity, sensory precision, utter stillness. The whole world slowing down. *Ticktock.*

The curl of smoke from Rondo's cigarette. The sharpened tip of the ledger pencil three and a half feet to Evan's side. Arturo's pupils. The tilt of Beltrán's head. How Beltrán's shoulders were persistently elevated, his neck foreshortened, showing diminished confidence. He'd be slow to move. Lengua Larga displayed a beta body-language cluster as well, lowered eyes, forehead creased. He carried tension in his left shoulder, and his left eye had the faintest flutter – a potential flinch point Evan filed away for later.

Ticktock.

With his jewel-encrusted handgun, Pancho was overconfident, facial muscles relaxed. The sight line of the horizontal barrel aimed vaguely to the side; with a shove it could be controlled, a thumb dug through the trigger guard from above. Alce's fluttering nostrils betrayed his nerves, as did his right trapezius raised in a partial shrug, which showed not firmness of purpose but unease.

Ticktock.

'I'm not with El Moreno,' Evan said. 'I'm not with anyone.'

Rondo's features contracted. 'Then who the fuck are you?'

'The Nowhere Man.'

Rondo gave a short stutter of a laugh, but on the tail end he made a gestural slip, lips stretching horizontally in an effort to conceal fear. He raised a finger to point at Evan, his right forearm slightly bigger in circumference than his left, showing his favored side. 'Whether that's true or not, friend, you just made the last mistake of your life.'

Another fear microexpression undermined his words, brows lifted and pressed together in a straight line, eyes showing upper white but not lower, the bottom lid drawn up.

The discussion was over though it was still continuing. Evan had already moved the entirety of his focus to the chessboard. Noting every minuscule movement, each flash of the eyes, angles and sight lines. His body was completely relaxed. He was attuned to every last element in the room, waiting for the precise moment when they would all align.

This entire time they were still talking.

Evan had already done the whole *Look at me, look at me closely and ask yourself: Do I look scared?* bit, which they had not seemed appropriately impressed by. Now they were on to the part where they would inform him how stupid he was to come in here without a weapon and tell him what they were going to do to him.

'You're so fucking stupid to come in here without a weapon,' Rondo said. 'Here's what we're gonna do to you.'

It was almost piteous, what they couldn't see.

That Evan had already won even though it hadn't yet begun.

The pencil was nearest. He would start with the pencil and upgrade from there.

The gears and cogs turned – *ticktock* – and all at once there it was, the needle's point of an opening.

Evan's hand shot out, closing around Arturo's, fist over fist. Slamming the sharpened tip up through his eye. A wet exhalation across Evan's knuckles, but already he was pulling the pencil out, snapping the wrist, ripping Arturo's arm across his own body, and slamming the point down into Beltrán's thigh.

Tick.

Beltrán screamed, jerking upright, hands flaring, and Evan

219

went for the battlefield pickup, trading pencil for blade, stripping the button-lock knife from his fingers, nicking the right carotid on the rise and uncoiling over the couch back, coming at Lengua Larga hard from the left side – *flinch* – and punching the knife once through his axillary artery in his armpit, the crowbar tumbling from his grip.

Tock.

Catching the crowbar as it fell, Evan whipped in a half turn, slamming it down across Pancho's forearm just as his gun hand began to rise from his thigh. A satisfying crunch as the bone snapped, the arm jellying, Evan thrusting his hand over Pancho's at the .38 revolver, thumb through the trigger guard, fifteen-degree rotation and clutch, the round shattering Alce's hip an instant before Evan jerked the barrel north and fired up through Pancho's chin.

Tick.

Evan was airborne now, leaving the revolver in Pancho's dead claw, rolling over the currency brick of an ottoman, the cigarette falling from Rondo's parted lips. The men at the periphery moved in slow motion to draw, but it was too late, they were all too late, and Evan grabbed the MP7 with both hands, reversing the submachine gun to fire a burst into Alce's gut, the big man tumbling back as Evan swept the weapon in an arc, trigger depressed, rounds riddling torsos, necks, tufts of stuffing spitting from the couch, chairs tumbling, tubs rocking. He finished 270 degrees of rotation, the heated muzzle stopping inches from Rondo's face, the magazine spent.

Rondo had drawn with his right hand as Evan knew he would, body weight shifted in his stupid-ass makeshift throne, Evan sliding one foot behind him as he completed the rotation so that Rondo fired in the spot he'd just vacated.

One hand to Rondo's chin, the other palming the back of

his head, a crisp torque of the hands, and the king sagged bonelessly over a royal armrest.

Tock.

Rondo's cigarette finally struck the floor, freeing a scattering of ash.

Detritus had been kicked up from the gunfire, bits of couch and dust motes sifting through the air, settling across the tableau like a fine mist of snow.

Evan was untouched. No blood on him. Not a spot. No bruising either, or injury of any sort.

That was unanticipated. Of all the things he'd counted on for what was needed next, emerging spotless was not one of them.

The hard drive and four of the five security monitors on the desk were shot to shit, but on the intact one a movement caught his eye.

A man strolling up to the front gate, pretty features, lightweight suit, lips pursed as if whistling. Passing beneath a streetlight, his *sicario* markings came clear.

Jovencito.

The Dark Man's right-hand man arriving early.

29. Call Me X

Evan searched the pockets of the dead. None of them packed everyday carry knives, it seemed, and he wasn't about to use the one jammed through Lengua Larga's armpit.

He made out the distant opening of the front door, the sound of a whistling approach.

Moving quicker, he patted down the men, at last finding a pocketknife clipped to Arturo's key chain. It would have to do.

Evan made two notches just back from his hairline at the front of his scalp, right through the dense grouping of blood vessels. The flow was immediate, mixing with his sweat, warm rivulets forking across his eye, running down his face.

The whistling grew louder now, echoing off the hard interiors of the neighboring garage.

Evan smeared blood up and through his hair and then wiped his hand across the side of his neck, leaving dabs there. Then he grabbed Pancho's embellished .38 and slumped at the side of the throne, sitting with his head nodded forward.

The whistling cut off abruptly.

Evan heard the creak of the door. A shoe tapping down. Another footstep. Another.

He waited until he sensed the presence approaching the circle of seats and then emitted a pained cough and lifted his crimson mask.

Jovencito was staring down at him over the barrel of a polished chrome Desert Eagle .44.

Blood was gumming up in Evan's eyebrow, and he mopped at it, his eyesight blurring. '. . . Gulf Cartel . . .' he rasped.

Setting the revolver on the ground, he slid it over to Jovencito, then rolled heavily to a forearm and gagged a little.

Jovencito kept the pistol trained on him. 'Who are you?'

'Xavier Francis,' Evan said. 'Call me X.'

'Rondo didn't mention you.'

Evan propped himself up, pressed the heel of his hand to the cuts in his scalp. 'He hired me freelance when they sized up for the affiliate chapter. Wanted someone clean, outside. I'm a close-protection expert.'

Jovencito surveyed the damage. 'Didn't do a very good job.'

'I winged the motherfucker and put him on his heels before he could take the product,' Evan said. 'You spot a blood trail coming in?'

'No.'

Evan shoved himself to his feet, pretended to get woozy. He leaned on the back of the throne. Jovencito watched him closely with brown, soulless eyes. The Desert Eagle came back up, pushed gently into the corner of Evan's jaw.

He searched Evan's pockets, came out with a wallet.

A bunch of hundreds and several credit cards in the name of Xavier Francis. Driver's license, too, with the address of Evan's Eastside safe house.

The muzzle backed off. Jovencito slapped the wallet against Evan's chest, and Evan took it with a blood-sticky hand.

'We'd better bolt,' he said. 'Cops're probably en route already.'

Jovencito slid the pistol into his waistband. 'Help me get the cash on the dolly first.'

They moved quickly, disassembling the throne and stacking

shrink-wrapped bricks on the steel-end dolly. Jovencito gave a tug, and it started moving.

'Wait,' Evan said. 'What about the product?'

He assumed he knew the answer but grew nervous when Jovencito hesitated to think. 'Leave it.'

Evan exhaled silently, and they continued pushing the wall of euros.

They got through the door into the garage when Jovencito said, 'Why didn't you take the money and split?'

'Wasn't my job,' Evan said. 'Ain't my money. I was paid fair for what I did.'

Jovencito studied him. Gave a faint nod. 'What did the guy look like?'

Evan glanced back at the doorway. 'You think *one guy* could do that?'

'How many?'

'Three. Came in loaded for bear.'

'They say anything before they opened up?'

'They said this is their territory. That Leones don't understand "LA tough." They said that's why you guys had to open an affiliate franchise. 'Cuz El Moreno doesn't have the balls to come here himself.'

Jovencito's forehead pulled taut enough to crinkle above his eyebrows. 'That's what they said?'

'Yeah. That he's afraid to show his face here.'

At last something lit up in Jovencito's eyes, burning deep beneath the polished brown. He tore his focus from Evan, scanning the garage. 'Any of these vans work?'

'Dunno.'

Jovencito climbed into the nearest cargo van, let the keys fall from the visor. The engine turned over on the first go. Leaving it running, he hopped back out and swung open the rear doors. 'Help me load. Let's go.'

They hurled the bricks in one after another, the empty dolly rolling away to kiss one of the car lifts.

Jovencito knocked the first in a row of garage openers with his elbow, and on the south wall a segmented door rattled up. Sirens pierced the night air, far away but growing louder. He climbed back in, his tattooed elbow V'd from the rolled-down window. 'Need a lift?'

'Nah, thanks, man. My rig's that way.' Evan pointed out into the dark night.

The sirens grew more piercing. Four blocks out, maybe five.

Jovencito yanked the column gearshift down into drive. Looked back at Evan. 'Be seeing you.'

As the van drove off, Evan felt himself return to his body for the first time since the episode in the park. As if it were safe to open up again, to let the world return with all its depth and contours. The sensation came with a rush of relief, followed by a hazy sense of remorse. A remembrance of everything he'd cast aside to enter this state.

Empathy. Grace. Patience.

He sensed movement in his pocket. Blinking away blood, he fished out the RoamZone with a tacky hand.

heading to my brother's for dinner in 30, Mia's text read. where r u?

Evan said, 'Fuck.'

30. A Confusion of Arcane Etiquette

Jumping in his truck, clearing the area, bloody face turned away as patrol cars screamed past him. Six blocks out, pulling over beneath an underpass. Spare gear in the back, change of clothes, baby wipes to clear the crusted blood from his face, Los Angeles Angels hat to cover his clotted hair.

Beelining across the city, closing the seventy-five miles to Castle Heights in fifty-three minutes. Lowering his head so the brim of his cap shaded his face. Running the stairs, into the lobby.

And smack into Ida Rosenbaum.

'Excuse you!' she barked.

'Sorry, ma'am, I'm just late for . . . a dinner party.'

'Well, I hope you're not going dressed like *that*.'

'No, ma'am.'

She squinted, nose quivering, then extracted a wadded-up tissue from her sleeve, failing to get it past her chin before she sneezed in his face. 'It's all the goddamned animals they're letting in here. It's like a zoo.' She assessed him once more, seemed underwhelmed per usual. 'I hope you're going to bring something.'

It took everything Evan had not to edge past her and make a break for the elevators. 'Sorry, ma'am?'

'To the dinner party. My Herb, may he rest in peace, had a golden rule. Would you like to know what it was?'

Evan felt a bead of blood starting to work its way from beneath his cap down his forehead. He tilted his head back slightly to slow its pace. 'Yes, ma'am.'

She jabbed an arthritic finger at his chest, her aggressively floral perfume crowding out the oxygen. 'Never show up empty-handed.'

For once her unsolicited advice struck home. He hadn't even begun to think about what to bring to Mia's brother. 'What would you suggest?'

'Something environmentally friendly,' she said. 'The young people today are all about climate change and whatnot.'

'What's an environmentally friendly dinner gift?' Evan asked.

'I don't know,' she snapped, shuffling by him. 'I'm not your personal shopper.'

Evan had forgotten about the disco-Velcro motif of the penthouse until he barreled in the front door. Hurrying through the great room, he halted by the empty chair where Vera III had sat before he'd hurled her against the wall. Something pinged in his chest. Guilt?

He reversed course to the kitchen, yanked open the trash compactor. There she lay atop the other garbage in a pile of glass shards and rainbow pebbles. Crouching, he picked her up gingerly and brushed off her exposed roots.

'Sorry.'

She glowered at him.

'We're not having this conversation right now.' He set her in a glass salad bowl on the island, hesitated, then plucked a leaf from her. Snapping it in half, he dabbed aloe on the reddened skin at the back of his neck. 'Thanks.'

Through the great room, down the brief corridor to the master, passing beneath the seventeenth-century katana sword that Joey had remounted on the wall. The same ping in his chest intensified as he pictured her curled up on the floor crying, punctured by his words.

No time for that either.

Through the bedroom, stripping off his clothes. Into the bathroom, the shower retiled and finished, eight rain nozzles sticking out of the walls to hit the body at various heights. Another Joey embellishment.

Aggravated, he stared at the confusion of nozzles for a second before turning the handle to hot and climbing in. The water ran pink at his feet, the jets washing him clean. It was different, foreign, new, scratching at his OCD compulsion that demanded that everything be kept as it was.

He hated to admit just how much he enjoyed it.

Evan screeched up to the curb, grabbing the bottle on the passenger seat before it could roll into the footwell. The mailbox was ensconced in a miniature decorative re-creation of the house itself, a cornflower-blue old-school Valley house befitting the Tarzana neighborhood. As he hopped out, Mia appeared at the door, strolling up the walkway to meet him.

She smiled big. Her chestnut curls were for once tamed into a semblance of order, cascading down the right side of her face. 'You're usually so punctual.'

'Hung up with a work thing.'

'Look at you, all dressed up. Are those your *fancy* cargo pants?'

'Fresh back from the dry cleaner.' He touched a finger to her chin. 'You okay? Your coloring seems off.'

'Proximity to family makes me blanch.' She looped her arm in his, pivoting them up the walkway.

He did a double take at the mailbox. Beneath the trim a cutesy hand-painted sign read WALLY AND JANET DONKERSGOOD. 'Your maiden name is . . . ?'

'We don't talk about that,' Mia said.

He was grinning, so she poked at his ribs.

'It's Dutch,' he said.

'That's a nice way of putting it.' She tipped her head toward the house. 'C'mon now. I should warn you about my brother. He's a bit . . . let's just say he'll be the craziest person you've met this week.'

Evan said, 'I doubt that very much.'

Wally Donkersgood lowered a twenty-four-ounce can of Bud Light from his mouth and gestured magnanimously at the spread of gherkins, beet stew, and rookworst. He wore a Santa Monica Police baseball cap, a T-shirt, and – inexplicably – a piano-keyboard tie. 'Lord, please demonstrate your mercy by blessing this food. My wife's an awful cook, so it really needs it.'

From the kitchen: 'I *heard* that!'

Peter was rubbing his tongue back and forth across his teeth. 'I just got my braces off, and everything's all slimy. Feel!' Grabbing Evan's hand, he rammed his index finger into his mouth, swiping it across his front teeth.

Evan withdrew his finger, wiped it on his napkin, resisted the urge to go wash his hands with soap and water. Mia watched him, mouth brimming with amusement, keeping herself from smiling.

Evan felt unmoored here, less sure of himself than when he'd walked into the Leones affiliate headquarters with nothing more than his bare hands and a focused mind. He'd known the rules of that situation, how to engage. Everything reduced to life and death, the age-old dominance hierarchy, kill or be killed. The Donkersgood home presented a confusion of arcane etiquette and unspoken rules, and his finger was moist with a nine-year-old's spit.

Evan raised the Air Company vodka he'd brought, housed

in what resembled an old-fashioned milk bottle. His movements felt stiff, mechanical. 'This is . . . uh, a carbon-negative vodka. It's made from thin air, so it's . . . um, environmental. Which people like for dinner parties. I've been told.'

Wally was staring at him, beer can frozen halfway to his mouth. Mia hid her lips behind a fist, but her eyes were laughing.

To Evan's chagrin he realized that he was still talking. 'The conversion reactor they employ is solar-powered,' he was saying, 'so they manage to eliminate the agricultural process. No irrigation or crops, no greenhouse gases, and each bottle . . . uh, is equivalent to eight trees in terms of daily carbon intake, so . . .' No one seemed engaged, Peter least of all. Evan's voice continued to fade. 'It's got a bit of sweetness, so maybe pair it with a dry vermouth for a . . . martini . . .'

He ran out of steam.

Wally blinked a few times. Then produced a surprisingly good-natured smile. 'A drinker!' He offered a toast with the tennis-ball-tube-size beer, then set it aside and reached for a Bordeaux glass. 'In that case you'll enjoy this fine vintage, I believe.' He gestured to Evan's overpoured glass and then lifted his own and made a big show of swirling the wine around beneath his nose. 'Good legs,' he remarked, and took a sip. 'Earthy finish.'

Janet entered from the kitchen, bearing an honest-to-God casserole between oven mitts. 'Oh, honey, we were out of the good stuff, so I opened the box wine from Costco.'

Some of the wattage left Wally's grin. 'Oh.'

Evan glanced at Wally's shiny face, shadowed with stubble and wearing a smile that seemed a permanent fixture. That Evan was here at Wally's of Tarzana drinking box wine rather than at Wally's Fine Wine and Spirits in West LA perusing fine vodkas at the end of a night like this seemed a particularly cruel twist.

'And watch your blood sugar,' Janet said. 'We don't want a repeat of the Almond Joy incident.' A pleasant-looking blonde, she wore neat, dated bangs and an apron that said, DON'T KISS THE CHEF! in goofy lettering. 'Evan, so glad you could come for a bite. We were happy to hold dinner.' She came at him with the Pyrex pan.

He pivoted to protest gently. 'I'm not actually that much of a casserole aficio –'

But her manicured hand set down on his shoulder, turning him firmly around in his chair. A spoonful glopped onto his plate and then another.

He cleared his throat. 'I'm really –'

His shoulder bumped her serving arm, spilling casserole down the front of his active camo cloaking shirt. 'Heavens to daisy,' Janet said. 'I'm so sorry. Let's get you out of that right away.'

Now she was pulling at his shirt, the magnetic buttons yielding with painful ease.

Abruptly he was shirtless.

Evan folded his arms across his chest, going for casual. Janet's gaze lingered on him. 'I'll just . . . throw this in the wash and get you one of Wally's shirts.'

She vanished.

Mia looked at Evan. 'Nice six-pack,' she said. 'Do you, like, work out?'

He scowled at her.

Wally was talking at him. 'So Peter here tells me you're into gear. Samurai swords and whatnot. I'm a bit of a gearhead myself.' He grabbed his tie and wagged it at Evan. 'This was a gift from the guys at the station. It plays musical notes.

Touch-sensitive polyester fabric, plastic speaker hidden here at the knot. See?' He leaned forward. 'Want to play it?'

'No thank you,' Evan said.

'I will!' Peter popped up to his knees in his chair to face Wally. He typed furiously against his uncle's sternum, but nothing happened. 'It doesn't work.'

Wally grimaced down at the tie, his double chin tripling as he read the back label. '"Batteries not included." It takes triple-As. *JANET! DO WE HAVE TRIPLE-A BATTERIES?*'

Janet's disembodied voice floated down the hall. 'Stop yelling from the table!'

Wally ripped off the tie and cast it aside, dejected.

Peter on turbo speed. 'Uncle Wally. Uncle Wally. *Uncle Wally*. Would you still love me if I looked like this?'

Flared nostrils, buck teeth.

Wally said, 'Yes.'

'How 'bout now?'

Underbite, tongue sticking out.

'Yes.'

Janet returned with a shirt, which Evan pulled on with relief. He stared down at the large red lettering: CERTIFIED BIKINI PAGEANT JUDGE. Mia looked away, her shoulders bouncing. He noted tears at the corners of her eyes.

Janet reclaimed her seat and the plates began to circle. 'Hat off, Wally.'

Peter: 'How 'bout now?'

Fish cheeks, crossed eyes.

'No,' Wally said. 'Absolutely not. That's where I'd draw the line.'

Mia had caught her breath. 'Peter. Eat.'

She speared some smoked-sausage segments onto his plate. Peter tentatively poked at them, his sleeve dragging through the anthill of ketchup he'd soft-served onto his plate. He considered his cuff, shrugged, then sucked it clean.

Mia said, 'Have some stew, too.'

Peter leaned forward and sniffed the serving pot, crinkling up his nose. 'It smells like sour-feet milk.'

Mia face-palmed, but Janet seemed undeterred. 'Wally. Please take your hat off at the table.'

Grudgingly, Wally removed his cap, revealing a nasty red lump above his left eyebrow.

'Your forehead,' Mia said. 'What happened?'

Wally waved her off. 'An on-duty incident.'

Mia set down her fork, concerned.

'He locked himself in a Porta-Potty with a wasp,' Janet said. 'And bonked his head trying to get out.'

Mia grimaced. 'You're kidding.'

'You know I'm allergic,' Wally said.

'You think *he* got it bad,' Janet said, 'you should see the Porta-Potty.'

'Funny, Janet,' Wally said. 'A real crack-up.'

Mia turned to Evan. 'Wally works Santa Monica. A bike cop.'

Evan realized a response was required of him. 'Motor unit?' he offered.

'No,' Mia said. 'Bicycle.'

'First of all,' Wally said, 'it's a *mountain* bike. Okay? Easier for pursuits on the Promenade. And it's called the *Bicycle Coordination Unit*.'

'Well, then,' Mia said.

'Listen,' Wally said, jabbing at Evan with his fork. 'Civilians don't always understand the requirements of the job. Given the high pressure, the constant risks, you need the right tools. And a mountain bike is the right tool for maneuverability and transport in that particular area of operation.'

'Sounds like it.' Evan was having a hard time not staring down at the red lettering emblazoned across his chest.

'Just be grateful you have a nice safe job pushing papers, Evan, importing cleaning supplies and whatever. That you're not out there every day, a potential target. That's why I'm always alert. See here? I'm sitting with my back to the wall, right? Facing the door. That's how I always sit. And I check reflective surfaces, right? Like I could hold up my spoon.' He demonstrated. 'If I need to see over my shoulder.'

'Subtle,' Evan said. 'Cutlery tradecraft.'

'Yep. At the academy they taught us to read people. You have to develop a nose for it. You never know when you could be looking at a stone-cold killer.'

Evan poked at the casserole's spongy edge, which resumed its shape like Jell-O when he let go. 'Sounds dangerous.'

'It's a duty we bear, but we bear it proudly.' Wally glugged down the rest of his wine. 'We're working on cracking a theft ring this week.' He shot a wink at Peter. 'Sunglasses going missing left and right at the Loews Hotel. Twelve pairs last week, seventeen pairs this week. And that's only what's *reported*.' His nod moved horizontally in and out, a birdlike jutting of his head. 'We're thinking of putting a coupla UCs in place.' A glance at Evan. 'That's "undercovers." Seeing what we can stir up.'

'Does the hotel sell sunglasses?' Evan asked.

'Yeah. There's a shack at the pool.'

'Have you talked to the owner?'

Wally smirked a bit. 'Why would *he* need more sunglasses?'

Evan chewed a chunk of the sausage, which needed chewing.

'Oh,' Wally said. '*Oh*.' He nodded a few times, then a few

times more, then stood and hitched up his oversize pants. 'I gotta make a quick call.'

Keys clenched in his fist, Evan sat at the kitchen counter as Mia helped Janet clean up at the sink. They'd spurned his help but asked for Wally's, though Wally seemed to be in a foul mood since reporting in to his superior officer about the newest suspect in the sunglasses caper. He sat gloomily in the adjacent living room with a tiny eyeglasses screwdriver, fixing his piano-keyboard tie with surgical intensity. At his side Peter peered down at the failed dissection.

'Let's put on some music,' Mia said.

Wally at last lifted his head. 'I just downloaded the new Josh Groban Christmas album,' he said.

'It's *August*,' Mia said. 'Plus: Josh Groban.'

'He can knock a ballad outta the park.'

Mia was already calling something up on her phone, and a moment later Oscar Peterson's piano trickled out through wireless speakers. Janet passed off a wet dish to Mia, who wiped it down, starting to dance. She caught Evan looking at her and smiled, and their eyes locked.

All at once it was as though he'd passed through a threshold where he could see her at all ages — bashful bangs and girlish cheeks, the flirty coed with intelligent eyes, and all her lush maturity as well, crow's-feet and womanly hips. For a moment he felt like he had all of her, she was showing him all of herself.

Mia and Janet were dancing together now, laughing, and they twirled over and collapsed into the kitchen chairs.

'Evan,' Wally said. 'Evan, can you help with this goddamned thing?'

Evan walked over, plucked the screwdriver from Wally's hand, and lifted the battery cover from the back of the tie.

Wally pressed in two slender batteries and the tie lit up, playing a crazy polka, Peter clapping his hands with delight.

Evan felt an unfamiliar warmth in his chest but then he heard Janet calling out, 'Wally! Evan! It's an emergency!'

His first thought went to the last time he'd been called to a Mia emergency, which had turned out to be an artisanal-candle party. But Janet's tone was hard and sharp, the kind of tone he was accustomed to not from this world but from his. He moved swiftly to the kitchen.

Mia was slumped back in her chair, eyes rolled to white, face as pale as death.

31. All the Everything

Two quick strides and Evan had Mia out of her chair, cradled in his arms, lying her flat on her back. Fingers at the side of her throat, counting seconds and heartbeats, all the noise behind diminished to background fuzz.

Her eyes came back online.

'I got you,' he said.

'You . . . Your name. I don't know your name.' Her panicked glance moved past him. 'Peter. Peter, honey, it's okay.' She tried to prop herself up on an elbow but seemed to get faint.

Evan eased her back down. 'Janet, call 911. Wally, get your diabetes kit. And a flashlight.'

Wally swooned a bit.

'Never mind. Sit down. Peter, get your uncle's diabetes kit. Probably in the bathroom?'

'Nightstand,' Wally said weakly, and Peter shot out of the room.

As Janet spoke hurriedly into the phone, Mia blinked up at Evan. 'I know I recognize you, but I can't . . . I don't know words.'

'What's it feel like?'

'Like I'm light inside. Gonna pass out. Legs not working.'

Janet came back from the phone. 'They have an ambulance in the area. They said they'll be right here.'

Evan squeezed Mia's thigh. 'Can you feel this?'

'Yes.'

'Good.'

He checked her other limbs. 'This?'

'Yes. Yes. Uh-huh.'

Peter flew in with a leather kit and a flashlight.

Evan thumbed Mia's left lid gently open, clicked the light, and watched her pupil constrict nicely. Fumbling through the pouch, he got out a test strip and a lancet, raised a bead of blood on her fingertip, and fed the sample into the glucose reader. It blinked up at 85.

Peter was crying quietly, mouth ajar, cheeks flushed red.

Evan said, 'Janet, get a cold washcloth, put it on the back of Wally's neck. Peter, your mom's gonna be fine. Let's all take it easy until –'

The doorbell rang. Janet scrambled out to answer.

The paramedics hustled in.

Evan said, 'Light-headed, lost words, pulse slightly elevated at ninety-seven. Pupils reactive, sensation in all limbs, able to speak. Not diabetic, blood sugar at eighty-five.'

The first paramedic said, 'Are you a doctor?'

'No.'

They got the stretcher down – 'On my count, one, two, *three*' – and slid Mia onto it.

Janet's hands were curled inward at her chest. 'Can I ride with you?'

The paramedic didn't look up. 'No one in the ambulance, but you're welcome to follow.'

'We will.' Janet shook Wally's shoulder gently. 'We will.'

'Wait,' Mia said faintly. 'I can't go. My son . . .'

'We've got him,' Janet said.

'. . . don't want him at the hospital. He . . . hates it since his dad . . .' Mia's eyes found Evan. 'Don't remember your name –'

'Evan.'

'– but . . . trust you. Will you watch him?'

The Seventh Commandment fluttered at the edge of his mind: *One mission at a time.*

Evan thought about the look Jovencito had cast back at him before driving off. *Be seeing you.* The safe-house address Evan had allowed him to discover. Anjelina under the thumb of El Moreno. Aragón and Belicia waiting day and night, every second passing like barbed wire pulled through a fist.

He looked over at Peter. He'd backed up into a kitchen stool, gripping it behind him, cowering beneath the counter overhang.

He looked again at Mia.

He said, 'Yes.'

At Peter's request, Evan transferred Peter's school stuff from Mia's car into his truck before driving them home. As they walked through the lobby, Evan carried an unwieldy model of the solar system, the planets made of tennis balls and foam spheres that bobbled around the unripened cantaloupe core of the sun and threatened to bonk him in the face.

Together they shuffled onto the elevator, Evan still wearing the fucking CERTIFIED BIKINI PAGEANT JUDGE shirt. He held the doors for Peter, who trudged through, shoulders slumped beneath the weight of his Batman backpack. Rotating in after the boy, he managed to dodge Saturn but almost got clocked by Neptune.

'Did you see Mom's eyes?' Peter said. 'They were all like . . .'

He demonstrated.

Evan said, 'I did.'

As he fumbled to hit the button for the twelfth floor, Peter grabbed his hand, pulling him off balance. Evan ducked Uranus, but Mars came around and sucker-punched him in the temple.

They made it to Condo 12B without any more planetary mishaps.

Peter ran into his room and slammed the door.

Evan stood in the living room, unsure what to do. He set the treacherous solar system down on the kitchen counter. A yellow Post-it was stuck to the bottom of the cabinet, but instead of featuring the usual life lesson in Mia's neat handwriting, there were two words written in Peter's sloppy scrawl: *'NEXT TIME.'*

The two best words in the English language. Freedom and possibility. Progress, not perfection. Just do something a little bit better than the last go-round and your place in the world would get a little bit clearer.

That's what Jack Johns had told Evan and what Evan had shared with Peter. And now Peter had taken up the mantle, penning his own rules to live by, not Mia's or Evan's but commandments of his choosing.

Evan was entangled in something here that he did not understand. A different kind of burden and responsibility that felt ungovernable.

There was a bottle of lotion near the phone. He popped the lid and sniffed it.

Lemongrass. The smell of Mia.

The scent hit his memory centers – her in the sheets, her naked back when he kissed her between the shoulder blades, her laughing in the lobby with one hand holding up her mane of curls, her soft, soft mouth, her dancing in her brother's kitchen holding eye contact, the most intimate and vulnerable look he'd ever had directed his way.

His thoughts were spinning, and his chest felt tight.

There was a nine-year-old in the other room, he had no idea what to do, and the person most suited to give him advice on the subject was in the emergency room incapacitated.

He stared at Peter's closed door, one of Jack's Commandments tapping gently at the back of his brain: *If you don't know what to do, do nothing.*

So he stood for a time in the mess of his emotions, watching them inundate his body, wreak havoc with his nervous system, pull him to and fro. Two-second inhale. Four-second exhale.

Reluctantly, he fished out his RoamZone and dialed.

Straight to voice mail.

He called again.

'What?' The word like a dagger.

'Joey.' He felt a vein throbbing in his forehead. 'About earlier . . .'

'An apology's not good enough. Not right now.'

'I know –'

'Then what?'

'I need your help.'

'Finish your own mission.'

'It's not that.'

He told her what happened to Mia.

For a time Joey was silent. 'What do you think it is?'

'Some kind of neurological event.'

'Serious?'

'Could be. But I don't know what to do with Peter.'

'The Fifth Commandment,' Joey said.

'I know. But I have to go in there, right?'

'Right. But don't do anything. Just let him lead. Sometimes you have to read what other people want and not try to fix them.'

'Okay.'

'And not try to make them *exactly like you* so you can judge them *all the time* for how they come up short.'

'Okay.'

241

'Or not let them go on road trips 'cuz you're, like, super controlling and self-deceptive and won't look at your own shit.'

'Joey.'

'Right. Sorry. Good luck.'

She hung up.

He walked over to Peter's door and tapped gently. No answer.

'Can I come in?'

'Sure.' Peter's voice, huskier than usual.

Evan entered. Already in his pajamas, Peter was sitting with his back to his race-car bed, legs kicked out in front of him. He was hot-gluing crayons of all different colors along the bottom border of a corrugated sheet of cardboard, points aimed inward. He'd gotten glue on his pants and the carpet. To his side lay several dismembered action figures, a lump of dried-out Play-Doh, and his mother's hair dryer.

Evan sat down next to him and watched.

Two minutes passed in silence.

'You know,' Evan said. 'A crayon can burn for fifteen minutes. They're made from wax. You just snap the point off and light the paper wrapping at the top. The paper acts like a wick.'

'Why would you do that?' Peter said.

Evan said, 'No reason.'

Another two minutes passed in silence, Evan pondering his failed overture. *Don't do anything*, Joey had said. *Just let him lead.*

Evan considered a different approach. 'Can I play with you?'

'Sure.' Peter chinned at the Crayola ninety-six-count flip-top box, all those vibrant tips poking up like warheads. 'You can pick the next colors.'

Evan slid out the white and black crayons and offered them to Peter.

'Not *those*. Those aren't even colors.'

Evan put them back. He stared at the array before him. There was no order to this, no design. How did one choose arbitrarily?

Peter said, 'Come on.'

Evan chewed his lip. Selected Atomic Tangerine and Wild Blue Wonder.

Peter glued them in place, completing the neat row at the cardboard's edge. Somberly, he held up the electrical cord of the hair dryer. 'Plug this in.'

Evan did.

Peter popped up to his knees, clicked on the blow dryer, and angled the hot blast of air down over the line of crayons. After a few moments, they started to melt, trickling tributaries up the cardboard. The streams blended together, forming different colors, spreading and spreading until the sheet of cardboard transformed into a ferocious piece of abstract expressionism.

Peter clicked off the hair dryer. 'Unplug it,' he said. 'Or Mom'll kill me.'

Evan did.

They sat and stared down at the colorful mess.

'Makes me happy,' Peter said.

'Why?' Evan asked.

''Cuz it's all the everything.'

The words opened a hole in Evan's chest, just the wind whistling through him, exposing the emptiness within. And yet it felt hopeful, too. So much space to be filled.

'What now?' Peter said.

'Bedtime?'

'I don't want to sleep alone.'

'I guess we could have a slumber party.'

'Well, technically it's not a slumber party if it's only two of us. It'd be a sleepover.'

He scrambled up into his sheets and lay there, staring at the ceiling. 'I have a crocodile blanket that looks like it's eating you when you're in it.'

'That sounds dangerous.'

'It's in the closet.'

Evan retrieved the blanket, clicked off the light, and stretched out on the carpet, the threads marred by spills and hot glue and a mashed crayon. He set one hand on his chest and one on his stomach.

'No pillow, no nothing?'

'No nothing,' Evan said.

''Kay.'

They both stared at the ceiling. Peter's race-car bed was low to the ground so Evan could see the side of his face. His blinks grew longer. Then his breathing steadied out.

Evan did not move. He'd been trained for this, to sit motionless in a tree or wedged in a crawl space or lurking beneath a sewer grate, belly down in a sniper's perch or frozen in a low-kneeling position, face streaked with camo paint, spiders crawling across his cheek, pissing in place, barely blinking, barely breathing.

All that training now in the service of not waking a traumatized nine-year-old boy.

Hour two ticked by. Hour three. The dead heat of August night, midnight, 1:00 A.M.

At half past one, he heard a key hit the front-door lock.

A purse hit the kitchen counter. The soft padding of Mia's feet.

Her form in the doorway. She leaned against the frame with a forearm, staring in at them.

244

Her whisper low and husky, edged with amusement. 'I see the crocodile got you.'

Evan sat up, kept his voice low. 'It's been a ferocious struggle.'

'Did you brush your teeth?'

'I did.'

'Need to go potty?'

'I went before bed.'

'Glass of water?'

'That would be lovely.'

He rose, and she brushed past him, leaned over her son, pushing his bangs up. She planted a soft kiss on his forehead.

Back in the kitchen, she and Evan sat at the table, hands cupped around their glasses.

Her eyes stayed low on her knuckles. 'They said it was a seizure, even though that's not how I picture a seizure. CT'd me.' Deep breath. 'And they found something. Some kind of small mass or an aneurysm. They want to image it with contrast. I have an appointment with a neurologist tomorrow.' An unconvincing laugh escaped her. 'Maybe it's nothing.'

Evan nodded.

'Thank you for watching Peter.' She smirked. 'This was all a bit more than you bargained for when you said you'd come to dinner.'

'To be honest, nothing could shock me after the piano tie.'

She smiled, but it was a sad smile. 'Fuck, Evan.'

'Yeah,' he said. 'Fuck.'

'I'm gonna fall into bed.' She rose. 'I'll keep you posted.'

She embraced him. She smelled like hospital – conductive gel and disinfectant. He could sense dread and fear coming off her in waves.

She saw him to the door.

As it closed behind him, he turned his internal dial away from emotion, the color of the hall lights fading to an antiseptic yellow.

Back on mission.

32. Come with Me

A full moon glow cast the Eastside safe house in a spotlight, illuminating the chipped stucco. After leaving his truck in an overnight parking lot five blocks away, Evan strolled to the bungalow, pretending not to notice the window-tinted dark SUVs parked at intervals along the block.

Not unlike the ones that had borne Anjelina off into the night.

These sported Hertz rental license-plate frames. Someone had flown into town in a hurry, likely on a private jet. Since Evan and Jovencito had parted ways at the auto shop, there'd been no Guaridón–Los Angeles direct commercial flights, and none of the connecting flights matched the time frame either.

As Evan entered the big square room, he was already picking at the scab a half inch behind his hairline, freeing a trickle of blood. Tucked under his arm, a plastic bag held the crimson-crusted baby wipes and the bloodstained clothes he'd changed out of beneath the underpass.

Moving quickly, he scattered the wipes across the bathroom counter, dropping a few on the tile for good measure. He flung the dirty clothes on the floor by his bed when he heard a faint whistling from outside. Seconds later someone rapped on the front door.

Snatching a tissue from a box, he pressed it to the cut on his forehead, braced himself, and opened the front door.

Jovencito grinned that blank grin as he entered, trailed by a stream of men. A second *sicario* with DARLING BOY inked across the front of his neck eye-fucked Evan before patting him down, liberating his ARES 1911 and Strider knife. He rose and put his face kissing distance from Evan's, medicinal breath leaking through meth-rotted teeth. He wore a fixed-blade combat knife in a leather sheath on his belt, angled down his hip like an old-fashioned beeper. They stared at each other unblinkingly until Darling Boy finally moved on.

The men storm-troopered through the house, opening cabinets, flinging papers from drawers, and racking back closet doors. The bungalow offered scant opportunities to search, but they left no space unexamined.

Evan stood against the wall, letting the night breeze wash through the open front door. The men finished and halted, Jovencito raising a phone to his rosy cheek. 'Okay, *Jefe.*'

He slid the phone back into the breast pocket of his cotton blazer. His youthful features and thick head of black hair contrasted with Darling Boy's gleaming skull and sunken cheekbones.

Everyone stood in silence, hands crossed at their groins, eyes lowered in respect.

Out in the night, a coyote howled and a car alarm bleated twice and someone yelled something from a passing car.

Evan swiped blood from his brow before it could trickle into his eye.

They all waited and waited some more. At last the sound of footsteps tapped up the front walk, a leisurely pace. A shadow fell across the threshold, a man's form carved from the streetlight glow.

El Moreno entered the house.

He walked past Evan through the stone-still flanks of his men to the neatly made bed. He hopped onto the mattress, stretching out, crossing his ostrich-skin boots on the sheets, showing Evan the soles.

An impressive bit of theater.

Raúl Montesco took in the small room, his right cheek drawn up, crow's feet pinching the temple. Contempt – the only emotion expressed lopsided on the face.

But when he looked at Evan, his features smoothed into a mask. 'You didn't take my money.'

'No, sir.'

'You didn't take my product.'

'No, sir.'

'Rondo was bringing you in? To be a member of his team?'

'Yes.'

'You want to be one of us? A León?'

'Yes.'

The Dark Man rose from the bed, leaving scuff marks where his boots had been. He walked over and stood in front of Evan. They were the same height, nose to nose, eye to eye.

That wide, oft-broken nose. The sharp V of his widow's peak, crazy curls cascading over his forehead. Mouth stretched too wide, square teeth spaced out. And on his forearm a lion inked in fiery orange, predatory eyes glowing an icy blue.

He smelled of cigarettes and spicy cologne.

He stared right into Evan, and Evan stared back. Evan could see himself mirrored in the Dark Man's pupils, the shape of his head and torso like a generic paper shooting target outlined in the obsidian blackness. He wondered if Montesco was looking at the same reflection in his own eyes.

'Come with me,' El Moreno said, and strode for the door.

33. A Guy with a Limited Set of Skills

The after-hours club was all velvet and pumping bass, the air a liquid swirl of too-sweet perfume and blended scotch. El Moreno and his men commanded a massive leather booth at the periphery. With a nod of his head, he indicated for Evan to sit at his right elbow. Bespoke drinks flew out of the bar, delivered by fetching Vietnamese waitresses, and an impressive array of food issued through the swinging kitchen doors – filet and lobster, sea bass and roast veal.

Several sturdy-legged Southeast Asian women worked poles onstage, the vibe more luxury indulgence than strip club. One of them stopped, catching Montesco's eye, and laced up a pair of hot-pink heels, an across-the-room show for one. The straps crisscrossed all the way up her muscular thighs, stopping like garters just shy of the panty line.

Practically vibrating, Montesco kept his eyes locked on hers. 'I love yellow meat,' he said. 'Girlish faces, dick-sucking lips, that tan, tan skin.' Sweat beaded across his brow, a drugged blood level on the wax or wane. 'What's your type?'

Evan said, 'I always figured men who have a type lack imagination.'

Big round tables and four-tops rimmed the stage. Lots of men flashed cash, but there were a good number of elegantly appareled women as well. The high-low mix felt out of place and time, a wartime haunt or a speakeasy from the Roaring Twenties.

Montesco licked his lips, watching the dancer tie her pink

ribbons into a bow at the inner thigh. 'Girls. I need so many of them. Three, four a night. They never satiate me.'

'Maybe you should try dating a woman.'

Montesco laughed. 'You're boolsheeting me, right?' He lit up a Romeo y Julieta cigar, prompting the manager to scurry over.

'Sir, I'm sorry. There is no smoking in here.'

Montesco gave the manager a dead stare, smoke lifting from the tightly rolled Cuban leaf. He made a lean-in gesture with his fingers, and the manager bent over.

Montesco put his mouth to the manager's ear, whispering something Evan could not make out over the music. The manager straightened up, his round eyeglasses fogged at the bottoms. Nervously, he swept a loose lock of hair over his thinning pate.

He moved swiftly away through the swinging doors, returned a moment later with a heavy glass ashtray, set it down before Montesco, nodded deferentially, and departed.

Montesco blew a smoke ring and watched the dancer some more. As a waitress passed, he hoisted a hand, flagging her down. 'A round of Pho cocktails.'

Grimacing, Evan flipped open the cocktail menu to read the description. *'A variation on the British Bullshot, the Pho-King Good Cocktail cranks the umami up to eleven with atomized beef broth, cardamom, fish sauce, and Vodka Hanoi.'*

Evan was willing to endure all order of corporeal damage for the mission, but drinking a Pho-King Good Cocktail was one bridge too far.

Evan said, 'I'll have a Zu Bison Grass up instead, please.'

Montesco looked at him, brow heavy, that dark complexion growing darker. He spoke softly, but his words were pressurized. He seemed always on the verge of an explosion. 'You don't approve of my order.'

Evan ignored him. 'Actually, we'll take two.'

The waitress nodded unsurely and departed.

Evan turned to Montesco. 'Each bottle has a single blade of grass from the fields of eastern Poland where buffalo roam. It's said to heighten stature, power, and virility. For centuries this vodka is brought out to celebrate hunting successes. I would like the honor of toasting you.'

Montesco's eyes took on a dangerous sparkle. 'Women, vodka. You have a lot of opinions. Are you as sure of yourself when it comes to your job?'

'Yes.'

Farther down the table, Jovencito and Darling Boy sat motionless, watching them speak, attack dogs awaiting a command.

'Close-protection expert, was it?' Montesco sucked on the end of the cigar, making it pop moistly as he extracted it from his lips. 'Do you do wet work?'

'I do whatever I need to advance my employers' interests. Merc work, high-end corporate, private military, gun-for-hire. Battlefields to boardrooms.'

'Un Caballo Oscuro,' El Moreno said. 'You sound usefully flexible.'

'As long as the check clears.'

'Like a ronin, eh? From the old-fashioned movies.'

'Just a guy with a limited set of skills.'

With the glowing tip of his cigar, Montesco gestured down the table at his men and the two *sicarios*. 'I have them. Why do I need you?'

The drinks arrived on a silver tray, the waitress setting down the martini glasses carefully. Another server handed out steaming beef-broth cocktails to the others.

'Because I'm only good at one thing,' Evan said. 'It's not a passion. It's a profession. I don't let myself get' – a glance at the sloppy cocktail mixtures the others were sipping – '*pol-luted*. You have a problem here in Los Angeles. My hometown. You need to protect the name of the Leones. Preserve the brand. I can see what you need to do clearly. No ego, no anger. Just merciless strategy.'

'How do you know I'm not engaged in merciless strategy already?'

'I assume you are. My job would be to support you with clarity. Rondo and his men you ordained . . .'

Montesco leaned in. 'What?'

'They were cheap hires. Not up to your standard. That's why three Gulf Cartel men were able to wipe them out. You want to establish a Los Angeles affiliate that represents and honors the culture of La Familia León.'

'You seem quite clear on what I want.'

Everything the Dark Man said was couched as a threat.

'I understand a leader when I see one,' Evan said. 'If I understood the proper way you built your organization, I could replicate that here in Los Angeles. For you.'

A commotion at the door drew their focus – a young Hispanic man rushing in, rubbing his hands together nervously, scanning the restaurant. He spotted Montesco and beelined over.

Evan stood up, but Montesco clutched his forearm, pulling him down. 'I'm expecting him.'

The man approached, offering a head bow to El Moreno.

Montesco regarded him flatly. 'I invite you to meet with me,' he said. 'You arrive late.' He pursed his lips, dry-spit a fleck of tobacco. 'It's okay. I'm not insulted. I'm bigger than all that.'

The man was trembling. 'I'm sorry, *Jefe*. It took a bit longer than I'd anticipated.'

'Relax, Martín.' Montesco clicked his teeth beneath a cat-like grin. 'Are the arrangements made?'

'Yes.'

'Good. We will meet you there.' Montesco waved a hand, dismissing him. He peeled a dozen hundreds from a fat bankroll, dropped them on the table, and started to rise, his men following his cue.

'Wait.' Evan lifted his glass.

El Moreno raised his as well, and they clinked. 'To . . . what did you say? Stature, power, virility?'

Evan smiled. 'And good hunting.'

Two men knelt before a hastily dug ditch at the edge of a partially poured foundation, towels wrapped around their heads secured with baling wire. Their breaths were audible, groaning exhales and pained gasps, fabric sucked inward at the mouths as they tried to draw in oxygen. Their shirts were torn and soiled, collars ripped wide, jeans split at the thighs.

The construction site, mere miles from the Van Nuys Airport, was a demolished square of land in the middle of a patch of dark warehouses. The convoy of SUVs had pulled through a movable section of chain-link and parked in two facing rows amid the backhoes and cement mixers. The headlight beams crisscrossed over the captives' bowed heads like a saber arch.

The men shuddered and begged.

Evan stood before them at El Moreno's side with the *sicarios*, the other men forming a somber semicircle at their backs. A tumble of gear scattered the ground at their feet – lengths of rebar, rusty bolts, a discarded workman's glove.

Wind blew Montesco's dark curls across his eyes, and he swept them aside, lighting up a crack cigarette, fingers thrumming on his holstered Glock 19. Everyone standing still, the breeze tugging at their edges, rippling their clothes, bringing with it the scent of blood and oil. Evan took in the near-static scene before him, straining at the seams with grandeur and tension and sensuality, a snapshot magnified into something grander, something baroque.

He did not know who these men were or why he was here, but the Tenth Commandment was parked front and center in his cerebral cortex: *Never let an innocent die.*

Montesco said, 'Unwrap them.'

Jovencito and Darling Boy did the honors, the men gasping for air through blood-slick faces. Their features were so battered that it was difficult to identify them as human. Gulf Cartel markings had been inked across their collarbones. They were handcuffed together, each with one arm free.

Private planes rumbled overhead, low enough to thrum the eardrums.

Montesco said, 'These are two of the Gulf Cartel's favored *sicarios* in this region of Southern California.' He looked to Evan. 'Are these the men who killed Rondo and his crew?'

Evan hesitated, the Tenth Commandment speed-looping through his thoughts. They were cartel hit men, sure, but he knew nothing about them, certainly not enough for them to die at his hand. Or his word.

'Well?' Montesco said impatiently.

The men stared at Evan with desperate, pleading faces. 'I don't know you,' the one closer to them said. A subconjunctival hemorrhage had turned his eye wine-red.

Evan spit in the dirt to stall further, taking in the positions of Montesco's men, the distance between him and the nearest length of rebar beyond the toe of his left boot. He tried to run the scenario through, but there were too many of the men too spread out, the weapons not within reach. He'd barely knock over the first two dominoes before he'd be aerated with bullets and dumped in the waiting ditch.

'Not sure,' Evan said. 'They're all banged up. Neither one is the shooter I saw clearest.'

'Well,' Montesco said, 'they'll do for now.'

Sensing their fate was near, the men rose and stood on wobbling legs.

Montesco's eyes ticked to the pieces of rebar on the ground before them, jaggedly cut off, each the length of a tire iron. 'Whichever one of you lives, I will hire.'

They stared at him disbelievingly.

Then the one with the bloodied eye lunged for the rebar, ripping his compatriot off his feet. They scrambled in the mud, swinging and cursing and grunting. The wet thud of reinforced steel meeting flesh. An arm snapped, the elbow joint twisted the wrong way by the handcuff. One of them howled. Their faces grimed with dirt and blood. A collarbone shattered. A shoulder. A head staved in. Both men toppled. One was dead, an eyeball half liberated from the socket. The other had landed on his knees, head angled wrong atop a fractured neck, gasping through a permanently unhinged jaw.

'Oh,' Montesco said with disappointment. 'You're no good now.'

He shot the survivor through the face. The man keeled over, tumbling into the ditch, the handcuff chain yanking his friend in behind him.

Turning to the dark windshield of the concrete truck, Martín rotated a finger in the air. A moment later the chute trembled, and then a torrent of concrete mix flowed forth, filling the ditch, burying the men's bodies in the foundation.

Evan stared at the strip of gray taking hold in the soil, scabbing over the gash in the earth. It had been so matter-of-fact, not so much as a pause to honor the finality of two lives being layered into oblivion.

As the other Leones huddled with Martín, Montesco withdrew to his SUV, sitting in the back. Evan joined him. Darling Boy started over, an aggressive charge in his step, but Montesco dismissed him with a wave of his hand.

He sucked in an inhalation and blew crack-tinged smoke through the gaps in his teeth. An acrid smell filled the car. His wild eyes grew wilder yet.

'I lied to you,' Evan said. 'Those were two of the men who killed Rondo's crew.'

Montesco held the smoke in his open mouth, tasting it a moment before speaking around it. 'Why would you do such a foolish thing?'

'I'm concerned you have a mole. In your organization.'

'My men are loyal to the bone.'

'When those shooters came into the San Bernardino head-quarters, they knew exactly where to go. They were familiar with the space, who to take out first. It had been rehearsed. They'd been given the blueprint.'

Montesco's lips tightened, etched with fine wrinkles. His eyes darted past Evan, out the window, at the conglomeration of men by the fresh-poured river of concrete. His cheek twitched twice, paranoia grinding away inside his skull.

'I was waiting to see if any of your men would speak up in their defense,' Evan said. 'Failing that, I wanted to keep them.'

'Why?'

'To interview them.'

'"Interview" them?'

'Interrogation. Information extraction. Torture. Which-ever term you prefer.'

Montesco took another hit, held it in his lungs, then reversed the cigarette and ground it into his tongue to put it out. 'You're criticizing my decision?'

'You're impetuous,' Evan said. 'Which hurts my ability to get answers for you.'

Montesco unholstered his pistol, set it across his lap, finger curled through the trigger guard, aiming directly at Evan's stomach. 'Who the fuck said I wanted you to do anything for me?'

Evan kept his gaze level, giving nothing up.

Montesco's shoulders and biceps were balled tight, platysmal bands popping in the strained sheet of his neck. A one-centimeter movement of his forefinger and Evan would be gutshot. Not a pretty way to go, hours of agony and internal bleeding, assuming they didn't haul him over to a fresh ditch and bury him alive.

El Moreno's shoulders shook. At first Evan thought he was laughing, but then it seemed he was sobbing, and then the sobs turned back into laughter.

'Okay, X,' Montesco said. 'I'll give you one shot to figure out who my mole is.' He pulled his finger from the trigger, set it straight along the frame. 'I'm taking you home.'

34. Enemies Closer

At first light the Gulfstream II set down on a private airfield in Guaridón. A convoy of matching SUVs waited at the edge of the airstrip. Except these had their license plates removed. Evan had little doubt that they were the ones that had carried Anjelina away.

Raúl Montesco took Evan with him, just the two of them in the back, a mute chauffeur behind the wheel.

Friends close, enemies closer.

Tattered bedsheets painted with the Leones emblem – that blue-eyed lion – flapped from the overpasses, along with various slogans praising La Familia and El Moreno himself. The point of the bedsheets wasn't in the messages written on them. The point was that the authorities did not feel safe to cut them down.

A show of who ran this section of Nuevo León.

Even so, Montesco's chauffeur made sure to stop ten yards back from other vehicles at the first red light they hit, leaving room to escape in the event of a shootout. A blue Dodge Charger with a white stripe idled at the intersecting road before the just-changed traffic light, POLICÍA FEDERAL written in blocky letters on the side. Though the *federal* had the green light, the officer gave a respectful tilt of his head to El Moreno's chauffeur, allowing him to coast ahead through the red light along with the rest of the convoy.

They wound their way through the broken city, the wreckage of brutal cartel rule on display at every turn. Men slinging bodies into the back of a pickup truck, pausing to wipe their foreheads and watch the SUVs speed by. A scrum of boys kicking a ragged soccer ball on a dirt field, a street dog jogging along the sideline with a human arm in its mouth. The boys played on.

The sun rose, achingly bright, making Evan squint even through the tinted windows. They headed out of the city into the bleached light of morning, everything arid and bleak. Heat mirage-wavered the potholed asphalt. Broken glass along the roadside gave off stabbing glares. A waft of sweet musk washed from the not-too-distant Chihuahuan Desert, graveyard to a thousand would-be dreamers.

Across a broad valley, the tarmac washed with desert grit. The dotted center line disappeared at intervals beneath deltas of sand layering the highway into oblivion, a reminder that one day the earth would reclaim all of them and all of this. Rumbling upslope and down as the terrain dimensionalized. Veering off onto a pinched dirt road, heading through ambush-ready walls of wind-carved rock. Evan started to notice power lines and rusty storm-drain grates, signs of encroaching civilization.

A buttonhook right fed the convoy into a path cut through limestone formations.

A majestic wooden archway marked the entrance to El Moreno's estate, featuring carvings of the three monkeys of lore. A trio of sentries with bandido-style face coverings and MP7s manned the gate.

The desert oasis was everything that Aragón's home was not, a Disneyfied sprawl of luxury and wealth. Succulents nested in quartz beds, swans bobbing in man-made rivers, hardscaping and xeriscaping and landscaping. An adobe-style mansion with ranch fixings and a number of smaller buildings trailing behind it like lesser islands of an archipelago. Solar panels, backup batteries and generators, sewer grates up the long driveway and beyond. A pool with a grotto surrounded by a scattering of bikinied women on chaise lounges, a horse corral with no horses. The now-familiar Leones *león* plastered across a water tower, surveying the entire expanse with a king-of-the-jungle gaze.

They arced through a circular white-rock driveway and piled out, Montesco stretching his arms. 'Let's get you fixed up,' he said to Evan. '*Mi casa, su casa.*'

Despite its splendor, the house was designed to withstand a siege. Heavy metal doors with slits just wide enough to fit a muzzle through. Thick window shutters designed to halt sniper rounds. Guards at every entrance.

Rats scurried through the shrubs, intruders in paradise.

Beside the eight-car garage was a building Evan initially took for a horse stable. A second glance confirmed it to be a jail. Women in various conditions and levels of undress were barely visible in the light slanting through the bars. Crammed four, five to a cell. Buckets and mattresses.

'Ah,' Montesco said, 'you are admiring the chicken coop. Come see.' A sweaty hand on the back of Evan's neck as he steered him over. 'These ones are too ugly for personal use. They're for trade. At month's end we ship them to Vegas. I like having them here to look at.' A good-natured grin. 'My own personal zoo.'

They walked past the women, Evan doing his best to ignore the scores of eyes following them. Montesco pointed to a brass-plated skeleton key hung from a nail on a wooden pillar, just out of reach through the bars. 'The key to their freedom, just past their fingertips.' A rumble of a laugh. 'I like to play with my food.'

Moving to the end of the structure, he yanked open an unlocked cell door. A ten-by-twelve space literally filled with currency straps – euros and rubles, pesos and good old-fashioned hundred-dollar bills.

'What do you want to be paid?' Montesco asked. 'It doesn't matter. Twenty million? A hundred million. It's in there, rotting. Come, I'll show you.'

He escorted Evan around the side, yanking open a half dozen other doors, each room filled with the riches of nations. He gripped both of Evan's shoulders, his sweaty face close. A drop of sweat wavered at the tip of his nose, but he didn't seem to notice, his eyes aflame.

'You find the third Gulf Cartel shooter,' he said. 'You deliver the San Bernardino market to me and then Los Angeles? And I will make you a king.' He caught himself. 'No, not a king. A prince. A duke. A very rich man.'

Evan said, 'I can do that.'

'What would you like now?'

Evan eyed a hundred-thousand-dollar brick of hundreds. 'One of those should do.'

Montesco nodded. 'Not too greedy. Smart.' They started back to the main house. 'I will have it brought to your room. Do you want women? Girls?'

'No,' Evan said.

'Boys?'

'Just some rest. I don't like distractions.'

A half step in the lead, Evan froze. Ambling around the side of the house no more than fifty yards away was a full-grown lion. He glided languidly with the confidence of an apex predator. At each step muscles rose at his shoulders like plates of steel. He turned to stare at Evan. His muzzle, bloodred and sopping.

A moment later a handler came into sight behind him, grasping a mosquito-nosed tranquilizer air rifle.

The lion bared his teeth and roared.

Evan felt the vibration at the base of his brain stem.

Bored, the lion swung his head away and sauntered

forward, collapsing in the shade of a palm tree to lick his massive wet paws.

Evan allowed himself a breath. He understood better the rats rustling through the bushes, scavengers awaiting leftovers. The pulse in his neck made itself known. One of the girls in the cell at his back tittered at him.

A flutter of movement in an upstairs window caught his eye – a feminine form shadowed at the pane, mostly lost behind the yellow glare of the day. Anjelina, the proverbial captive princess in the tower? It brought back an echo of Belicia self-quarantined in her room, alone with her grief.

He blinked, and the figure was gone.

Quickly, he returned his stare to the lion, who continued to eye him even as he worked his paws, his sandpapered pink tongue turning redder.

Montesco watched Evan with amusement. 'You're afraid of the wrong lion, *muchacho*.' He pinched Evan's shoulder, shook him roughly yet affectionately, and steered him toward the front door.

35. No Commandments for This

At first glance the mansion's interior looked normal.. But then Evan noted that the hallways were narrower than made sense, fatal funnels intended to slow any potential hostile encroachment. Metal doors at intervals formed barriers. Guards sitting posts at random points along the labyrinthine layout rose as Evan and the Dark Man passed. Each sported a black nylon single-grenade pouch at the belt, speedy access to pop and roll a frag down slender corridors designed to enhance overpressure.

MP7s were clearly the Leones' submachine guns of choice. Chambered for 4.6x30-millimeter cartridges designed to pierce NATO-standard titanium body armor. Compact and light, full auto capabilities, good at distance. And when the forward grip was used with the stock extended, it became a mini-carbine, ideal for close-quarters combat. Like, say, if a firefight broke out inside a cartel leader's adobe-style lair.

They moved along the tile floors, passing metal steps cork-screwing up to the second floor. The tight stairwell ensured that prospective intruders could move between floors only one at a time; ample space around the thin floating handrail ensured that plenty of critical mass was presented during the passage. The stairs led up to where Evan had spied the feminine form in the window.

Darling Boy handed Evan's gun and knife to Montesco, then peeled off and ascended the staircase, his boots clanking against the metal steps.

'What's up there?' Evan asked.

Montesco grinned a wicked grin and kept moving. 'Valuable goods.'

Past a kitchen, a sunken conversation pit with a bar, a freestanding old-fashioned steel safe. Montesco turned the dial on the safe, swung it open. It contained phones, passports, sidearms. He placed Evan's items inside on an empty shelf.

'This is where we park our guests' weapons and phones,' he said. 'So they can be more relaxed.' A grin. 'You can keep your phone, but you won't need your pistol and knife. You'll be safe here.'

Evan followed him down another corridor, through a large wooden door into a couch-lined study. A handsome young man whom Evan recognized as Reymundo Montesco sat behind an enormous mahogany desk, hands resting on the arms of a saddle-leather wing chair.

At the sight of his father, Reymundo scrambled to his feet. '*Papá.*'

The Dark Man said, 'Feeling comfortable in my seat?'

'I was just –'

'It's okay. Tell me. How does it feel? Sitting there?'

Reymundo moved out from behind the desk. A broad sheet of aquarium glass looked into an empty water tank, the rippling water throwing reflections around the room. 'It felt . . . it felt like I should not be there.'

'That's right.' As Montesco stepped close to his son, a tremor tugged the skin beneath Reymundo's left eye. 'It does feel that way for you. And yet I'm supposed to leave this, my life's work, in the hands of a boy who can't even sit behind a desk with confidence?'

Reymundo lowered his eyes.

Montesco extended a hand to Evan. 'This is Xavier Francis. The only survivor to come out of the San Bernardino disaster. He was covered in blood. Do you think he made a single complaint? A single excuse?'

Reymundo extended his hand. 'An honor to meet you, Xavier.'

Evan shook. 'X is fine.'

'Maybe you could learn from a man like him, *hijo*.' Montesco grabbed his son's full cheeks, angled his head to Evan. 'Look in his eyes. You can see he is not afraid. He is a lion like me.' Montesco let go, patted Reymundo on the cheek. 'Do you know what my boy's name means? "King of the world." How far he has to come to live up to that name.' He gestured at a heritage chart and a family tree, both printed on faux-aged paper and memorialized in trying-too-hard ornate gold wood frames. 'This lineage of Montescos I have traced back fifteen generations? It ends with him.'

'I am trying, *Papá*.'

'I grew up in a shanty room beneath a freeway underpass,' Montesco told Evan. 'One-fourth the size of this room. Dirt floors, walls built from waste – planks and trash, some cardboard my *mamá* painted white. No running water. A bedsheet between my brothers and where my *mamá* and sisters slept. One open toilet in a field, three squat holes protected by a rusty metal sheet on one side. We would find corncobs in the trash, pick out overlooked kernels to eat. Anyone used us. Everyone. However they pleased. Drug dealers. Neighbors. Older cousins. We were taught our worthlessness every day. And yet here I am. How am I supposed to pass this on to my son, who is to carry the Montesco name? He who grew up here, eating lobster, vacationing in Zihuatanejo, sports cars and cupboards full of food? He is soft. How do I teach him to run an empire?'

Evan stared at the boy and couldn't help but feel a pang of pity. 'Have him sit in when we discuss the plans for San

Bernardino,' Evan said. 'I need to understand your supply and demand, what resources the Cartel Gulf has in place there, and what you're willing to offer to recruit better muscle and brains into the Leones.'

Montesco walked around the substantial desk, settled into the wing chair with a huff, and pulled a crack cigarette from a drawer. 'Very well,' he said. 'Let us begin.'

As unhinged as the Dark Man was, he could maintain exceptional focus when discussing the intricacies of his dealings. Which chemicals came through which ports of entry, where to route product through Third World customs, how to build out low-cost infrastructure for pop-up labs. He smoked and smoked, dark pupils enlarging until they seemed to consume his eyes entirely.

Evan mostly listened, asking pointed questions where he could, mentally filling in the dossier of La Familia León's enterprise he planned to turn over anonymously to the authorities once the mission was completed.

Reymundo sat silently on the adjoining couch at the edge of the cushions, looking impatiently at the door. One thing was clear: He wasn't built for this.

After a few hours, they moved poolside. Montesco continued to smoke, switching to cigars and adding mezcal to balance out the mix of stimulants. A sipping shot glass, an orange slice, worm salt with ground agave larvae and chili. Evan took a pass, keeping an eye on the guards, noting faces, movements, positions as the Third Commandment demanded.

From their position beneath a pergola, he could see the side window of the room in which he'd spotted a figure from the front yard earlier but sensed no movement inside. He tried not to watch too closely. As the sun continued its path west, he caught a glimpse of a massive chandelier beyond the window, tear-shaped pendeloques casting heavenly winks of light from myriad facets. Beyond that no sign of movement. Or of Anjelina.

As dusk came on, Montesco got stuck in a loop of his own drugged thinking. He seemed unable to escape a spiraling obsession with the third Gulf Cartel shooter, Evan's fiction taking root deep in his awareness.

'I don't know how to describe him to you,' Evan said. 'But I'd know his face if I saw it again.'

'I will figure it out. And when I do, you'll go back to LA. And you'll bring me his head in a box.'

'I'm worried . . .'

'What?'

'That they might come here first.'

Montesco snorted. 'Good luck to them. This estate is built to repel an attack. Every hallway, every room. I have escape tunnels, a helicopter, and a fucking private army.'

'Those measures are worthless,' Evan said, 'if they have an inside man.'

Montesco rose, stumbled, slamming a hand on the table hard enough to make the bottle of mezcal jump. A dagger of sweat had bled through his shirt at the collar, stalactites painting the fabric beneath his armpits. He smelled bitter, smoke and body odor.

'Get Darling Boy down here!' he bellowed to no one in particular. 'He knows the most about those Gulf motherfuckers. I want him to get me the name of the third shooter. And I want him to turn this place upside down to find the mole.'

A few men scrambled into motion, scurrying inside the house, shouting commands. A few minutes later, Darling Boy emerged through the space where the sliding doors had been accordioned open.

As El Moreno explained the problem, it became clear his body chemistry had crossed out of control, his voice rising in pitch and then falling to a whisper. His thoughts grew rambling, desultory, tempestuous. Darling Boy listened attentively with a forbearance that suggested he'd negotiated this type of storm many times over. Reymundo leaned back in his chair, away from the table and his father.

When Montesco's words finally faded off into a low growl of exhaled smoke, Darling Boy spoke. 'I will assemble pictures of Gulf *sicarios*. And I will look into our men. Every last one of them.' While he said this, he kept his cold eyes locked on Evan.

'Now,' Montesco said. 'Now, now, now. And bring this one with you.' He shoved at the edge of his son's chair with the toe of his cowboy boot, causing Reymundo to topple over.

'Yes, *Jefe*.'

Montesco glowered at them all. 'And how is that bitch?'

'She behaves poorly.' Darling Boy unsheathed his knife, admired his reflection in the blade.

'What bitch?' Evan asked.

'We have a prize hen in our captivity,' Montesco said. 'Much too fine to be kept in the coop with the others. Isn't that right, Reymundo?'

Picking himself up, Reymundo dusted off his knees. His bangs fell over his eyes, but he didn't look up at his father.

'I can't trust this one to handle it either,' Montesco said. 'She's been giving us headaches. Doesn't know her place, always chirping at my men, the girls. We don't want to damage that perfect face. Yet.' He ground his cigar into the orange slice. 'She needs to be broken like a wild horse.'

'I've been there,' Evan said, striking a sympathetic tone.

269

'I've guarded trust-fund girls and the daughters of sheikhs. There's an art to it. Keeping them in line. No hassles, no friction. There's a way of making them understand. So they don't behave poorly.'

Montesco studied him, reptilian eyes flat and unblinking. For a moment Evan thought he'd pushed too far too quickly.

Then El Moreno waved his cigar. 'Let's see how good you are, X,' he said. 'Why don't you go get that *puta* in line.'

'Where is she?'

He stabbed the glowing tip of the cigar at the corner bedroom on the second floor and said, 'Take him.'

Darling Boy rose. Evan followed him into the house. Even the back of his neck was inked, blue-black flesh rippling like snakeskin.

They wound their way up the metal stairs. Darling Boy stopped on the landing, waiting as Evan ascended to the second floor, keeping uncomfortably close. Evan's face drew level with his shoes, his knees, crotch, chest, chin. Then they were standing nose to nose.

'I been with him seventeen years,' Darling Boy said. 'Then you come along. Golden boy, straight teeth, pretty face. *White*. And he sits you at his side.'

'Thank you,' Evan said.

Those sunken eyes blinked once, twice. 'For what?'

'For calling me pretty.'

'El Moreno is a great man. He has few blind spots. But you should know . . .' Darling Boy dug the tip of his pointer finger into Evan's chest. 'That I don't.'

He turned and led Evan down the narrow hall. They moved through a pinned-open metal door, and then he gestured to the closed door at the end and faded back toward the stairs. Thumbing through his phone, Jovencito sat outside the room on a chair tilted back so his shoulders rested against the wall.

He didn't bother to look up as Evan approached.

'El Moreno wants me to take next shift,' Evan said. 'See if I can talk some sense into her.'

Jovencito jogged forward, the front legs of the chair clicking against the tile. Pocketing his phone, he stood. 'Don't touch the merchandise.' That handsome grin. 'Tempting as it may be.'

He walked past Evan, brushing his shoulder. Pulling out his RoamZone, Evan called up a white-noise-generating app tuned at specific frequencies to mask voices from being overheard or captured by covert surveillance. He put the phone away and then stood with his hand on the doorknob, waiting for the sound of Jovencito's footsteps to recede downstairs.

A long and winding road had led to this door. There were no Commandments for this, no rules or touchstones to guide him in managing whatever lay in the room behind. He took a breath, eased it out, twisted the knob silently.

She was there, lying atop the covers on the bed, facing away. A tumble of thick black hair strewn across the comforter, head dipped forward, neck bent, a loose approximation of a fetal position.

He entered loudly enough for her to hear his movement and shut the door behind him. 'Anjelina,' he said softly.

She turned, one arm stretching open so she could view him in a half twist across her body. She was so beautiful that it was unsettling to look at her directly, as if he were seeing something he wasn't meant to see. For a moment he felt discomposed, voyeuristic. Then he refocused, clearing the haze of the first impression, seeing her as a girl a few years older than Joey.

'Who are you?' she asked.

'I'm . . . an acquaintance of your father's,' he said in a low voice, inching forward. 'I'm here to rescue you.'

'Rescue me?' She shifted further onto her back, the soft bump of her pregnant belly rising into view. 'I don't want to be rescued,' she said. 'I ran away.'

36. The Meaning of Regret

For the first time in memory, Evan found himself shell-shocked. He had a moment of pure denial, nearly sufficient to convince his brain that he'd misheard her.

The First Fucking Commandment.

He thought about the pictures from her eighteenth-birthday party, how she'd worn a shawl so its ends dangled over her stomach, just enough to distract from the swell beneath.

Anjelina pushed herself up against the plush upholstered headboard, arms protectively crossed over her rounded belly. 'My father sent you?'

Evan still couldn't find words.

'What's your name?' Her voice was deep – not husky and not unfeminine either, but edged with soulful throatiness.

'Call me X.'

Her face was flushed, forehead twisted with consternation. 'Arnulfo – is he okay?'

'. . . who?'

'Arnulfo? He was catering the party. My birthday party. They hit him in the face with the butt of a gun. So much blood – they split his lip. They weren't supposed to hurt anyone. Is he okay? And Hortensia, my God. She must've been terrified.'

Evan finally caught up to himself. 'The caterer? A split lip? Do you have any idea what you've done?'

'What *I've* done? I didn't have a choice. My *papá*, he would've killed me. And worse . . .' Tears sprang to her eyes instantly, glassing them over but refusing to fall. 'It would have *broken* him.'

The pieces slid into place with sudden horrifying clarity.

'Reymundo,' Evan said.

She looked at him, trauma writ large upon her face. Even in grief she was luminescent, lit from within. Impossibly wide eyes, impossibly long lashes.

'Zihuatanejo,' Evan said. 'Both of your families happened to vacation there every year during Semana Santa.' He ran his fingers through his hair, a rare show of aggravation. 'Star-crossed lovers playing games.'

'Don't belittle us. You have no idea what Reymundo's been through. You have no idea how strong he is.'

'So what's your plan? Let your parents believe you're dead? Live out your days here under lock and key? Hope not to get fed to the lions?'

At this her lip trembled, but she bit down on it. 'This wasn't the plan. This isn't our future. Reymundo doesn't want this any more than I do. We're gonna get out of here, and we're gonna start over, and we're gonna –'

'You're not gonna *anything*, Anjelina. El Moreno is a psychopath. This isn't a game. This isn't a movie. They will kill you in the most painful way possible. Feed you to the lions. Cut your eyelids off. Carve your face right off your head. You're on his land, where he tortures and kills people. Your unborn baby is here with these men.'

'I didn't know what to do.' She was refusing to cry, her hands clenched into fists, emotion coming up beneath her smooth skin, inflaming the rims of her eyes and nostrils. 'We didn't know what to do.'

'People have *died*,' Evan said.

'Sorry. I'm sorry.' She pressed her knuckles to her mouth. 'We didn't think it would go like this. I'm sorry. Reymundo thought it would be safe here, that his father would be proud to have a grandbaby, that he would let us leave and start a life. It didn't . . . didn't work out that way. We're not free here. He keeps me watched in here, won't let me see a doctor, won't let Reymundo see me when he wants. But I couldn't have stayed at home either.' Her tone sharpened, and she kept on vehemently, as if Evan were arguing with her. 'It was impossible there, too. Me. The only Urrea child. Aragón's daughter. Pregnant by a León. There were no options. I know who my father is. I know what he's capable of.'

'You think he would hurt you?'

'Not *me*,' she said. 'Reymundo. My dad would've gone to war.'

'He *has* gone to war.'

'You don't understand. You don't know what it's like. I had nowhere to go. They put you on a pedestal, and any way you step, you fall off.'

'What? Who did?'

'I don't know. Everyone. The whole town. My father. You can't move. It's like' – her hand circled helplessly – 'they want you to be a portrait. But it's always *their* painting, you know? And for once' – she sucked in a wet breath – 'I wanted to be the painter. My *own* painter.' Now, finally, she was sobbing. 'There's so much pressure. What they think, what they want, how they'll act if you don't do the right thing in their eyes. You're exhausting. You're all so exhausting.'

'I'm not here to exhaust you. I'm here to help you.'

'Right. You're different.' She tried for sarcastic but only came off heartbroken, despairing. 'I just want to be left alone. I just want to be alone with Reymundo and the baby. Why can't we just –'

'You can't do this right now,' Evan cut in. 'Understand me?' He shot a glance at the door. 'You cannot fall apart.'

'I know. Sorry. I'm sorry.' She tilted her skull back to thunk against the headboard. A moment ago she'd been crying freely, but already she was winding it in, getting herself under control. 'When I was first here, I used to pinch myself, like to wake up from a bad dream.' She showed him the inside of her arm, the tender skin bruised yellow and purple. 'But then I stopped. Easier to just be . . . numb.'

'Be whatever you need to be right now,' Evan said. 'But in front of them, you have to obey me. Completely.'

'Wow.' She glowered at him, face flushed and miserable. 'I knew it. You're not different. You're just like everyone else.'

'If you listen to me, there's a chance Montesco will let me guard you. If you don't, you get Darling Boy. You choose.'

She pulled in another breath, locked it between clenched teeth. Speechless, defeated.

He sat on the edge of the bed, took her bare arms in his grip, held her gaze, hoping she would match her breathing to his to slow it down. 'I will figure out how to protect you.'

'How?'

'I don't know. I don't even know what you want.'

Behind them the door banged open, and she bolted upright, startled.

Jovencito entered, whistling a high fluttering tune.

Evan kept his grip on Anjelina's arms but now made it look menacing, switching modes on a dime – new posture, new bearing, new expression. He stared straight through her eyes, spoke in a cold, hard voice she recoiled from. 'Fuck with me again and I will teach you the meaning of regret.'

She jerked her head in a terrified nod.

'Don't damage the goods,' Jovencito said. 'Romeo will be upset. Which means his father will be angry.'

'No need to damage her,' Evan said, sliding off the bed. 'Not anymore. We've reached an understanding. Isn't that right, girl?'

She looked at him, still breathing hard, nostrils flaring. Behind her long eyelashes, her gaze was wounded, as bruised as the dappled skin of her forearm.

She lowered her eyes, gave a meek nod.

Evan started out, Jovencito signaling his approval, wearing an impressed frown. Clearing the doorway, Evan couldn't bring himself to turn around and see the wreckage on Anjelina's face.

'You continue to surprise, Caballo Oscuro,' Jovencito said. 'Who knows what else you're capable of?'

Evan wondered the same thing.

The bedroom suite was the picture of luxury – marble surfaces, granite soaking tub, high-thread-count sheets. Somehow before this week, Evan had managed not once to play houseguest to a criminal mastermind, but that drought had ended with a twofer. The room looked to have been done by an upscale designer – generic art on the walls, a squat floor vase sprouting curling willow branches, floating shelves filled with actual books, though they were coverless, organized by color, and half were upside down. Montesco could buy everything in the world but class.

Freshly showered, Evan crossed the room, bare feet sinking into the plush carpet, and stared at the array of decorative literature. An urge rose in his chest to alphabetize them. He quashed it.

At the foot of the sleigh bed, a rolling suitcase rested atop a luggage rack, hard-shelled lid raised to display the brick of hundred-dollar bills he'd requested.

That certainly beat a chocolate on the pillow.

To the memory-foam mattress, lying down, a single deep inhalation that he drew up from the soles of his feet. Exhale.

Exhaustion descended over him.

A secret love affair. A pregnant girl. A faked kidnapping. One family destroyed, the other dangerous beyond compare.

And the Nowhere Man tangled up in the middle with a skill set utterly unsuited to addressing a conflict like this. This was the stuff of families – disappointment and passion, resentment and heartbreak, dashed dreams and failed hopes. Intimacy. This wasn't his arena. What had Mia told him? *You fit in, sure, but that's different from* belonging.

He thought of her freckles, the weight of her head in the crook of his elbow, his fingertips at her neck, checking for a pulse.

He tapped her number into the RoamZone, sent her a text: how did it go with the neurologist?

A pause. Now she was typing, the three dots taking their time.

Finally: can you talk?

He felt the weight of the question in his chest.

He texted: no. A moment after the fact, it occurred to him how she might take that, so he added: out of country for work. no privacy.

when are you back?
i don't know.

The screen was blank. Still blank.
Then: . . .
He waited. Impatiently.

i need a consult with a neurosurgeon now.

Evan stared at the phone. Tiny digital words rendered from ones and zeros. Just eight of them. But they packed an awful lot of punch.

day after tomorrow 10 am, she texted.

The doctors were in a hurry. Time-sensitive matters were rarely ideal when it came to neurosurgeons.

He typed:

fuck.

yeah. fuck. Another bubble popped up: good night, mr danger.

good night.

He stared at his phone. The urge to get home to Mia was as alien as any he'd ever felt.

The oval tray ceiling was rimmed with ornate molding and embedded lighting, the drop-down borders in a soothing off-white to accent the scene painted above. Wispy clouds across a cerulean sky, Michelangelo's dome with the day players removed. It was empty, forlorn, a beautiful mural of heavenly nothingness.

Everything beneath this roof was grand and showy, dangerous and cold, so different from Aragón and Belicia's home. Eden felt impossibly remote.

Evan wondered what the hell he'd gotten himself into and how he would possibly get out.

He thought about how when he needed to execute a mission, he flattened the world into two dimensions but how people like Joey, Mia, and Peter demanded three.

This mess, with Anjelina and Reymundo, Aragón and Belicia, would require him to occupy both perspectives at the same time.

Something he'd never attempted.

Not a safe operational space.

All he knew was that he knew nothing.

And that this nothing was deeper and blacker than the nothing he thought he'd known before.

It was time to shut down. He told himself to go to sleep.

And he listened.

37. Fetch the Lion

El Moreno showed his face a bit past noon, and from the look of it, he needed longer yet to sleep off what he'd been trying to sleep off. As he stepped out onto the back patio to where Evan sat beneath the pergola, his terry bathrobe flapped extravagantly, showing off maroon briefs, hairy legs, and ostrich-skin cowboy boots. A cigar hung crookedly from his mouth, adhered to his bottom lip, free of the clamp of his upper jaw. It wobbled as he spoke.

'Caballo Oscuro. Enjoying the view?' His face held pressure lines from whatever he'd fallen asleep on – a pillow, a swirl of sheets, the ergonomic front grip of an MP7.

Evan had spent the morning clocking Montesco's men, watching the guard-station switches, noting which vehicles rolled through the front gate and how often. The side of the house provided a superb vantage to the workings of the estate. Since his arrival Evan had kept a running tally of Montesco's men. On top of the two *sicarios*, his count had reached forty-one.

Topless girls in string-bikini bottoms lounged on poolside boulders or splash-slid into the water like aquarium turtles. A half dozen workers were up the palm trees with razor-tooth saws, thinning out the crowns. Jovencito was guarding Anjelina's room, and Darling Boy had positioned himself at a downstairs window, his ugly face aimed at Evan.

Reymundo scurried out of the house; it was clear he'd been waiting nervously for his father to make an appearance.

'*Papá*, I'd like to see my girlfriend.'

Montesco took his time with the cigar, savoring a puff. '"Your" girlfriend? Nothing here is *yours*, *hijo*. Everything here is *ours*. Father and son is the most important relationship on this planet. For years the Montesco name meant nothing. Until me. Now it is all that matters.' He paced in showy fashion, waving his cigar, walking beneath the hum of the workers overhead. 'You will inherit everything. All that is mine will be yours. Which means that all that is yours is mine. Do you understand?'

Reymundo's head was tilted down, but the muscles of his neck had tightened, as if he were girding himself, and Evan saw something rising in the young man he had not seen before.

'What if I don't want that?' Reymundo's voice trembled, but there was a thread of steel in it.

The Dark Man's face literally darkened, the inner blackness pushed to the surface like toxins fighting their way out. His stare held a cold enmity that Evan had seen on only a few occasions in the entirety of his time as Orphan X. It verged on inhuman, tainted with something preternatural, a kind of evil summoned up, channeled from another place.

Reymundo literally withered before his father's glare.

When Montesco spoke, his voice held an uncharacteristic calm. 'I will line up fifty of my best men and rape her until she falls to pieces. Until her body comes apart.'

Reymundo was breathless. 'You wouldn't do that. Even you.'

'Why not? My life's work, my sweat and blood clawing myself up out of the gutter an inch at a time, it's in you, my son.' Montesco's tone was gentle, even loving, but the sadistic gleam had not left his eyes. 'You want to walk away from everything I've built? Everything I am? When I'm gone, you will turn my legacy into dust, destroy me. You'd exterminate my name, the name of my father. If you're willing to do that to me, don't *question* what I will do to her.' And now he leaned closer, his shadow falling across his son's face. 'What will be left? If you betray all that I've done, all that I am, what will remain of me?'

'What if I'm something better?' Reymundo looked stunned that the words had escaped him. Immediately his posture changed, crumpling inward. '*Papá*, forgive me, I didn't mean —'

Montesco backhanded him, knocking him to the ground, then started kicking him in the ribs, face contorted with rage. His hair tumbled across his eyes, and for a moment it seemed like he'd unleashed something that could never be contained, that he would literally kick his son to death.

As Montesco wound up once more, Evan tensed to intervene, but before he could, a cry came from overhead.

A dead palm frond fell weightily from the sky, striking Montesco at the back of his neck. He staggered and dropped his cigar, embers cascading along the concrete. Knocked down onto a knee, hair thrown forward across his face, his maroon ass hanging out of the bathrobe.

It was as though someone had pressed pause on the world.

Girls frozen in the grotto, mouths ajar.

Darling Boy on his feet inside, one hand pressed to the windowpane.

The guards standing rigidly, as if afraid to breathe.

Montesco rose. Dusted off his knee. Spit a bit of tobacco from his tongue.

There was a hum coming off him, a low vibration of rage. That too-wide mouth quivered. The eyes, offset by that broad nose, had an animal intensity, fire and wounded pride. It was as though he'd been punctured, unveiled as a mere human who could get struck on the head and knocked down like anyone else. Time and time again, Evan had learned that nothing in the world was more dangerous than a weak man who felt humiliated.

The worker was rappelling down the trunk of the palm tree, pulley rope literally smoking in his hands. He hit the ground unevenly, stumbling over to the Dark Man and throwing himself prostrate on the concrete. An older man, quite short, long-sleeved shirt drenched with sweat, missing his front teeth. His name patch read VENUSTIANO.

'*Perdóneme, Jefe. Perdóneme.*' Venustiano was too scared to sob, but his chest heaved as though he were.

Reymundo crawled away, finding his feet, keeping his distance from his father and the newest distraction. Darling Boy had emerged from the house. He stood across the pool, arms loose at his sides.

Montesco looked not at the tree trimmer but at Darling Boy. He swept his sweat-slick locks back over his head, restoring himself to his full height.

'Fetch the lion,' he said.

38. What It Means to Be Ruthless

Time seemed to stand still for another few minutes, Venus-tiano sobbing quietly at Montesco's feet while Montesco smoked his cigar, the breeze riffling his hair.

Reymundo reached a trembling hand to the patio chair and lowered himself into it. Evan sat as well, his mind spinning. He had no weapon. Armed guards every which way.

If he tried to save the tree trimmer, he'd be outed and likely killed, which meant Anjelina would not be saved. The Seventh Commandment decreed, *One mission at a time*, which was all well and good until it collided with the Tenth Commandment.

Never let an innocent die.

Now six of Montesco's men were wheeling an enormous contraption across the parklike lawn beyond the pool. It was a massive cage, not unlike two soccer goals set mouth to mouth with a dividing wall rigged to a handle.

Evan had sworn to help Anjelina. He'd earned the trust of her father and the hope of her mother, and trust and hope were not responsibilities he could jettison lightly.

Now a roar vibrated the bones in Evan's spine. The lion ambled into sight at the back of the house, the handler appearing a moment later, five feet back, tranq rifle in hand.

The lion swung his mighty head to glower at them across the backyard. The handler shouted a command, and the lion lumbered forward into the massive cage.

The door slid shut behind him. Salivating profusely, he stared hungrily over at El Moreno.

Montesco prodded Venustiano with the sharp toe of his cowboy boot. 'Go.'

The old man was sobbing.

'*Go!*'

One of the guards came over, the skinny guy with protruding teeth whom the others called Nacho. He grabbed the tree trimmer by the arms and hauled him across the lawn to the cage. He was boneless, legs dragging limply behind him.

Nacho threw him in the back of the cage. Only the partition separated him from the lion.

Montesco smiled at Evan and Reymundo. 'Come. Let's have some fun.'

They walked over, Reymundo trailing like a beaten dog, wiping blood from his nose and clutching his ribs. Darling Boy joined them along with a dozen of the guards. The women hoisted themselves out of the pool, sitting on the edge, shivering and watching.

The lion pranced and roared, ropes of drool dangling from his jowls. He swatted the metal partition with a paw, the impact like a thunderclap. Venustiano balled himself up in the far corner, knees to chin, head lowered, shoulders shaking.

Something drew Evan's focus to the house. Anjelina at her window, staring down, hand clasped over her mouth. In the blush of youth, pregnant, stunning.

The toothless man, skin leathered from a lifetime of hard work, not much tread left on the tires.

Her whole life in front of her, his mostly in the rearview.

Evan felt Darling Boy's sunken eyes picking across his face, watching him distrustfully. Waiting for a tell.

Montesco stepped forward, gripped the handle.

Venustiano was muttering the Lord's Prayer in Spanish – *en la tierra como en el cielo* – and the breeze carried the stink of his panic sweat and the lion's musk, nearly overpowering at this proximity.

Darling Boy's unremitting stare. Anjelina watching from afar. Feral heat radiating off the lion. Guards encircling the cage, MP7s at the ready. The Seventh Commandment and the Tenth at war inside Evan's chest.

Veins stood out in Montesco's arm. He tensed, ready to throw the handle and lift the partition.

Venustiano's words blurring together – *y perdónanos nuestras deudas* – the creak of the ratchet engaging, the partition shuddering and lifting, an inch off the ground, now a foot, the lion shoving his snout eagerly at the gap –

'*Wait*,' Evan said.

Montesco's head snapped over to him.

Darling Boy's lips peeled back from his cracked yellow teeth in something darker than a smile, something like lustful anticipation.

Montesco released the handle, and the partition slammed back down.

Evan's mind churned for any plausible explanation.

The words left his mouth before he had time to consider them. 'Let me have this one.'

Montesco stepped aside, gestured for Evan to take his place at the handle.

'No,' Evan said. 'Not now. It needs to happen later.'

Darling Boy practically hummed with excitement. 'Why is that? Why does the *gabacho* want us to delay?'

'Yes,' Montesco said. 'Why the change of heart?'

Venustiano lifted his head from the ledge of his forearms. Darling Boy's pistol was drawn, aiming down the side of his leg. He stared at Evan through baggy eyes, pencil mustache rimming his bunched mouth. Reymundo doubled over, hands on his knees, breathing hard.

The Dark Man sidled closer to Evan, brow twisted with confusion. 'I asked you a question.'

'You told your boy he could learn from a man like me,' Evan said. 'You're his father. You can't see him clearly. Even his weakness. You smell it, but you don't understand the way in.'

Reymundo straightened up, legs trembling.

Montesco scowled. He could take it as a challenge or an opportunity. Evan's breath burned in his chest. He had no idea which way it would go.

Then Montesco gave a slight nod.

'He has to carry on your name,' Evan pressed forward. 'Which means he has to toughen up.'

'You want him to do it?' Montesco said.

Evan shook his head. 'There's no lesson in impulsiveness. Anyone can be scared into doing something.' He pointed at Venustiano. 'Throw him in the chicken coop. Make him wait. Make him know it's coming. At the end of the month, before the women ship out. Gather them all around and make them watch, too. Day and night he will think about what's waiting for him. Marinating in the panic with those women. Every minute, every hour. Him *and* your son. Let Reymundo carry the burden of it. Let him learn what it means to be ruthless. The way you learned as a boy. The way I learned.'

Reymundo was quivering, standing askew, one foot a half step back as if he feared toppling over.

Darling Boy eased forward to Montesco's side. *'Jefe –'*

Montesco held up a hand, dismissing him without so much as a glance. 'I like that, Caballo Oscuro.' A snap of his fingers. 'Release him.'

The guards opened the rear door and dragged Venustiano out.

'Now,' Montesco said, cinching his sash and moving for the house. 'Who's ready for lunch?'

39. Virulent Heat

The study was clouded with smoke from the crack cigarettes. The lights were off, the only glow filtering through the aquarium water from above as the day bled into night. Montesco's energy filled the mansion, the entire estate. Even when he was out of sight – yanking mistresses from the pool, drinking in the kitchen, napping in his bedroom – a kind of virulent heat emanated from him, tangible through the walls.

During the course of the day, Evan had made a few gentle insinuations about checking in on the girl, but Montesco either didn't register them or chose to ignore them, leaving Anjelina in the hands of his *sicarios*. After banging around the mansion for most of the afternoon, disappearing at intervals to fuck and smoke, Montesco had summoned Evan to discuss his plans for expansion into Los Angeles.

Evan spoke thoroughly and extensively about the criminal networks he'd become familiar with over the past years, where they laced together in cooperation and where friction had reached a dangerous temperature. Once again Montesco found surprising clarity when it came to business, poking at the picture Evan painted, searching out vulnerabilities and opportunities.

Now he paused, toking deeply before grinding out the butt in a vintage cut-crystal ashtray centered on his spotless leather blotter. In the pen well, ridiculously, rested a Montblanc fountain pen that had likely never been uncapped. 'Your plan. For Reymundo. It's smart.'

Evan nodded.

'Why do you think I keep that girl here? Why do you think I sent my men to take her from her *cabrón* father? So I could have something, something for my boy to care about. So he could learn.'

'Leverage.'

'That's right. A man like you understands.' Montesco steepled his hands, stared at Evan over his fingertips. 'You should pray you never have a son as useless as mine. His weak heart, coming here with that useless bitch.'

'Well,' Evan said. 'Maybe she's not entirely useless.'

'What do you mean?'

'The baby. Can carry on your name.'

Montesco pondered. '*If* it's a boy.'

'Yes, if it's a boy. And . . .'

'What?'

'Maybe Reymundo can become a man. For this. When you became a father, I'd imagine that changed you.'

Montesco leaned back in the oversize chair, dark eyes shining, that burnt-orange lion peering out from his inner forearm. 'It did. It altered the meaning of the world for me.'

'And it can for him.'

'If it's a boy.'

'Yes, if it's a boy. A male baby could teach Reymundo the awesomeness of this responsibility to carry on your name.'

'Unless . . .'

'What?'

'The girl's health,' Evan mused. 'She doesn't come from strong stock like Reymundo does. What if the baby is born all fucked up? Do you know that it's good? Has she seen a doctor?'

'No. I haven't let her leave the estate. She has food and space to rest and whatever else she wants. She doesn't need a fucking doctor.'

Evan waited, watched Montesco's eyes flicker about the room, pondering.

'She doesn't need a fucking doctor,' he repeated. 'Right?'

Evan shrugged. 'How should I know? I don't know anything about babies.'

Montesco inhaled deeply, nostrils flaring. 'But you know how to keep girls like her in line.'

'That I do.'

'It's settled. You will take her.'

'Take her where?'

'The hospital in the city. I will have it all arranged. You'll have a convoy at your disposal.'

'I'm not a babysitter.'

'If I tell you you're a babysitter, Caballo Oscuro, then you're a fucking babysitter.'

Evan let the words land on him, gritted his teeth. Pretended to work something out inside himself.

'Yes, *Jefe*,' he said.

'Tomorrow morning.' Montesco stood up. 'Find out if there's a boy in her belly. If there's not, she'll have an abortion. And I'll put a boy in there myself.'

40. Who Are You?

They stood in the circular driveway just past the portico, the morning light blinding on the quartz stone, everyone lined up as if seeing off newlyweds.

Montesco, Reymundo and Anjelina, both *sicarios*, and a host of Montesco's strongmen, armed and awaiting instructions. Three dark SUVs idled before them, freshly cleaned, spotless windows, chauffeurs ready to go.

In the gardens around them, Evan could hear rats scuttling. Shade fell across the makeshift jail of the chicken coop, the women inside barely visible. Just body parts glimpsed in stray bands of sunlight and the occasional flash of eyes – humans chopped to pieces by light and darkness. The tree trimmer sat in the nearest cell, head lowered, the dim outline of a statue. The brass-plated skeleton key glinted in the sunlight, tauntingly out of reach, winking at the captives. The swans floated on the man-made river beside the driveway, oblivious to human suffering.

Montesco opened the rear door of the middle vehicle for Evan, but Evan shook his head. 'I can drive myself. If there's an ambush, I want to be behind the wheel.'

Darling Boy started forward, boots crunching rocks. '*Jefe*, why would you trust this *gabacho*? He could drive off with her and we'd never see her again.'

'Why would he do that?' Montesco said.

'Who knows what Aragón Urrea would pay for her return?'

'Not as much as I can pay.' Montesco stared at Darling

292

Boy and Evan in turn. 'Remember that.' He snapped his fingers and called out, 'Raudel!'

The chauffeur emerged and tossed the keys to hit El Moreno's raised hand. Montesco dropped them into Evan's palm but then seized Evan's fist, squeezing it firmly around the keys so metal pinched skin. 'Bring her back to me.'

'Of course, *Jefe.*'

'Watch her closely. She is precious cargo. At least Romeo here thinks so.' El Moreno grabbed his son's shoulder and jogged it roughly. Back to Evan. 'My men will flank you on the drive. They'll be with you every step of the way.'

'I understand.' Evan leaned in, lowered his voice. 'Watch your back while I'm gone.'

Montesco's eye twitched, a first sign of paranoia yielding to stress. 'Darling Boy will help me flush out the snake.' Despite his quiet voice, a vein popped in his throat; he was feeling the strain. 'Until then I will keep an eye on *everyone.*'

That was good. The more Darling Boy put the screws to Montesco's men to find the mole, the more it would undermine Montesco's confidence and his men's faith in him.

As Montesco started to turn, Evan gently grasped his arm. 'Can I have my gun back?'

Montesco grinned. 'Not yet, Caballo Oscuro.'

Only once he headed back to the house did Reymundo step forward and embrace Anjelina. 'First ultrasound.'

She nodded into his shoulder. 'I can't believe I'll see our baby.'

'I'm sorry I can't go with you,' he whispered into her hair, his words just loud enough for Evan to register. His voice trembled, and there were tears in his eyes. 'But I know you'll do great. Be strong. *Te amo.*'

'*Te amo.*'

Evan held open the passenger door for Anjelina, and she

climbed in. As he shut it and turned, Darling Boy was standing right there.

'I don't know what play you're running, *gaba*,' he hissed through wrecked teeth. 'But I will figure it out.'

Evan sidestepped him and walked to the driver's door. Jovencito was waiting there, whistling. It was like a *sicario* partner swap.

Jovencito's smile was dazzling, as bright as the gleaming quartz. 'I will be in the front car. This is my number in case we hit any . . . turbulence.' He turned a shitty Kyocera flip phone over, showed Evan the digits printed on a label adhered to the back. 'Follow my lead and we will have no problems.'

Evan jerked his chin down in a nod. Darling Boy had retreated to the mansion, offering a final glare from the front door before disappearing.

'I'm not threatened by you like he is,' Jovencito said. 'Why should I be? I'm younger, stronger, better-looking. Haven't lost a step. So. You and I are good. As long as you remember I'm the best, we will be okay.'

Affable tone, joking twinkle in his eye. He was playing an alpha game, but he wanted Evan's approval, too.

'I remember when I was a young bull like you,' Evan said. 'I wouldn't want to fight me at that age either.'

Jovencito said, 'Then let us hope we never have to.'

Walking to the lead car, he twirled a cattle-roundup finger over his head. 'Let's go, Nacho.'

As Nacho followed Jovencito dutifully to the front vehicle, Evan climbed into the middle SUV. Anjelina started to say something, but he sliced a hand low over the console to quiet her until he got up the white-noise generating app on his RoamZone. He set it in the cup holder, clenched the wheel, stared at Jovencito's SUV ahead, the rear vehicle in his side mirror.

He summoned the Third Commandment, *Master your surroundings*, and scanned the area with hyperfocus. A few storm drains were visible down the long driveway, rusty and weather-beaten save for one in the garden, which looked newly installed and well maintained. Curious.

A moment later they rolled forward, guards shoving open the front gate. They passed beneath the giant wooden archway, two of the three carved monkeys peering down at them.

Limestone formations flashed by on either side, and then they were out onto the dirt road carved through towering walls of rock. He studied the power lines, noted the conditions of additional storm drains and sewer grates, gauged the topography and distance between turns, and plugged them all into the internal map he'd been building since he'd first arrived.

They popped out into the low valley, dunes rolling past like waves of sand, wind sending grit skittering across the windshield. The truck thrummed along the ragged asphalt, the buildings of Guaridón visible in the distance, ugly rectangular slabs thrusting up like a row of tombstones.

Anjelina had remained silent, curled into herself, her face aimed out the window so all he could make out was one smooth cheek.

The sight of her triggered a memory of a similar ride decades ago. Twelve-year-old Evan in the passenger seat of Jack Johns's dark sedan, his first trip out of the Baltimore projects. He'd been no more than a scrawny kid, dried blood crusted on his neck, wrists raw from handcuffs, the somber mood thick enough to choke on. And yet there had been trust there somehow, even before Jack had pulled out his white handkerchief and offered it for Evan to blot his bloodied cheek.

'I saw what El Moreno tried to do to that poor man

yesterday,' she said. 'The tree-trimmer guy. My Lord.' She crossed herself. 'What will happen to him?'

Evan pictured the man balled up in terror, quivering against the lion's roars. 'I have two weeks to figure that out.'

'What happens in two weeks?'

'The chicken coop gets emptied. The women sent to Vegas. The tree trimmer fed to the lion.'

The words seemed to move straight through her, those soulful brown eyes holding something deeper than hurt, something like trauma incarnate. She blinked a few times, reining herself back in, and then blew out a breath. 'Reymundo and I were allowed to see each other for a few minutes this morning,' she said. 'I told him about you. I told him you were good.'

'"Good" is an overstatement,' Evan said. Then added, sharply, 'Can he be trusted?'

She looked at him and coughed out a laugh. 'Clearly I think he can be trusted. I trusted him with my whole life.'

'Your judgment hasn't exactly been exemplary.'

She turned away again, light playing across her face. 'You're all like that. Ready to criticize. Waiting to tell me every little thing I got wrong.'

'You think this is a little thing?'

She clenched her hand and pressed it to her mouth. After a moment Evan noticed her shoulders shake almost imperceptibly. 'You're right,' she said. 'Sorry. I'm sorry.'

'You apologize too much.'

She appraised him over her shoulder. 'That's what my father tells me.'

'He's complicated,' Evan said. 'But he's right about some things.'

The tires hammered over a pothole, causing them to bounce in their soft leather seats. The air conditioner blew cool and steady in their faces. Sealed inside a bubble of luxury, they moved through the wretched outskirts of the city. A dead body lay in a dirt lot, two dogs yanking at the pant leg. It felt like they were manning a submersible, moving through deep waters, scanning an underworld vista from a scientific remove.

Anjelina cupped her hand on the window, fingernails pressed to the glass. 'It's easy for me to think how awful it is to be me. That I'm the only one who could possibly feel this way.' She took a breath greedily, as if oxygen were hard to find. 'I mean, I'm the daughter of a sorta cartel leader who's also a wonderful father who's also cut people's throats – or *had* them cut – who's also the most decent man I know, and here I am with all this money and power and really none at all feeling like I'm so different. But maybe that's how everybody feels. Maybe that's why we're all so lonely.'

Another breath, the words strangled, like she was forcing them out.

'And the way I look, it's like this curse I'm supposed to pretend is a blessing. I walk in a room and every set of eyes moves to me. And they all *want* something from me. It's, like, envy or lust or jealousy. They want to see me naked, they want to see me demeaned, they want to see me fill some role for them. Everyone I've ever met except . . .'

'Reymundo.'

A quick jerk of a nod. 'Have you ever really been seen? I don't mean the way we act every day. I mean like someone really gets *you*. The real part of you?'

Evan gripped the wheel, didn't answer. The direction in which the conversation was headed was out of his comfort zone, into an overgrown tangle of softer emotions he could not afford now or ever. *You fit in, sure, but that's different from* belonging. He thought of Mia's bare shoulders, the warmth of her body curled into his, way in the distant past before

297

seizures and neurosurgeons and tyrant rulers with lions primed for the taste of human flesh.

Anjelina seemed to take his silence as an answer. 'Imagine what you'd be willing to do,' she said. 'To have that. To be with the one person who ever really saw you.'

He debated turning on the radio just to shut her up but then remembered that this mission existed in that space between two and three dimensions, that in order to save her and be true to Aragón and Belicia he might have to forge into that overgrown tangle, make room to endure it long enough to see a way out.

'And I know,' Anjelina added quickly. 'Boo-hoo, poor little rich girl. And yes, it would be worse if I were crippled or sick or begging for cigarette butts in Calcutta. But I hate it. I *hate* what I look like.' Her gaze lifted to the small mirror in the visor, and she glared at her flawless face with tangible loathing. 'Everyone thinks I have all this value because of who I am –'

'Who are you?'

She glanced at him, confused and rattled, and once again her beauty struck Evan like a revelation. It was unsettling, preternatural, a curse just as she'd said, testing her and everyone around her all the time.

'How many conversations have you had about me?' she asked.

'Since you were busy getting fake-kidnapped and being held hostage? Quite a few.'

'Okay. Fine. Those women in that chicken coop. How many conversations are being had about *them*? Or are they just lost like all those girls in Ciudad Juárez because they're not Aragón Urrea's daughter. And I mean . . .'

'What?'

'Would you be fighting so hard to save me if I weren't his daughter?'

'Yes.'

'Fine. If I had Down syndrome?'

'Yes.'

'If I were . . . I don't know, ugly? Would you *really* help me if I didn't look this way?'

'Yes.'

'Well, great,' she said. 'That makes one of you.'

'Two,' Evan said. 'That makes two of us. If what you said about Reymundo is true.'

She was silent for a long time, and when she spoke, her voice was even throatier than normal. 'It is.'

'Then don't forget that. What he's risking for you. It's not just you now.'

She nodded, tears spilling, and her hands moved to the swell of her belly.

The lead SUV threw on its signal and banked right into the hospital's drop-off area. Evan pulled to the curb, sandwiched between the two SUVs filled with the Dark Man's acolytes.

'And to be fair,' he said, 'the tree trimmer did look a *bit* like you.'

She halted with her hand on the door handle, looking back at him with a surprised expression on her face.

Then she smiled.

A sad smile that quickly faded.

'I've never done this before,' she said.

Evan waited.

'Will . . . will you stay with me? In there?'

Evan hesitated. Found his answer. 'Yes.'

She reached for his hand. Her skin was cool, impossibly soft, the skin of a child. Evan looked away, uncomfortable.

She squeezed his hand once, took a sharp inhale, and climbed out.

41. A Little Pressure

A fussy man with a comb-over, the chief of staff met them in the lobby, shaking hands and offering praise for Raúl Montesco that sounded strained. They filed past the ER – Evan, Anjelina, Jovencito, and three armed men – bulling their way through the other departments. Doctors, nurses, and patients parted like the Red Sea. The remaining six henchmen waited back with the SUVs, an early alarm system for would-be attackers. Without his gun Evan felt naked, and he clocked the passing surroundings for makeshift weapons – metal tray, syringe, clipboard.

The chief of staff apologized for the state of the hospital. 'Lack of funds have made things difficult,' he said in Spanish. 'We've had to make do with what we have, but we cleaned up our *biggest* room – one of the surgical suites – and made sure it has everything needed for an ob-gyn examination of this importance.'

In the lead, Jovencito said nothing, his forearm ushering his jacket aside to show off the polished chrome Desert Eagle .44 at his waist.

Anjelina quickly stepped in to thank the doctor. 'I'm sorry for any inconvenience.'

He waved her off. 'No inconvenience at all. And this' – a gesture to a white-coated woman, handsome and strong of jaw – 'is our finest obstetrician.'

He grinned. She did not. She didn't look a day over thirty, and yet she wore a skunk streak of white in her thick black hair. The name tag on her scrubs read DR ORTEGA.

She said, 'Put your guns away.'

The men hesitated a moment and then complied, Nacho obeying last. Jovencito stepped forward to Ortega. 'The protocol for this visit will be –'

Dr Ortega extended a flat hand, placed her knuckles on the side of Jovencito's arm, and pressed him aside, clearing her sight line to Anjelina and Evan.

'Are you the father?' Ortega asked.

'What?' Evan said. 'No. No, no, no.'

Ortega cast a gaze past her alarmed chief of staff to Jovencito and the other henchmen. 'All you men will wait outside.'

The chief of staff grinned nervously at Jovencito. 'Of course, we're not giving any orders here –'

'That's fine,' Jovencito said, as if Ortega's demand were something he needed to approve.

Ortega extended a hand to Anjelina. 'I'm Maya,' she said as they shook. 'Let's get you taken care of.'

She started to lead Anjelina away, but Anjelina turned back to Evan, 'Wait. Can he come with me?'

Jovencito said, 'Absolutely not.'

Anjelina blanched, shoulders folding inward. She lifted her gaze to find Evan's, a split second of eye contact. He tried to convey something to her without words. Sure enough she straightened back up, squared her shoulders, looked to the doctor.

'I want him with me,' she said, switching from Spanish.

'Then he will be with you,' Ortega replied in perfect English.

She reached past Jovencito, gripped Evan's arm, and steered her charges through the thick metal door into the surgical suite.

As Anjelina changed into a hospital gown, Evan turned

301

his back. Ortega set her up on a padded table with a sheet of paper pulled over it. Stirrups were attached but lowered to the sides.

After a quick initial checkup, Ortega said, 'You wait here. I need to search out an ultrasound cart. We had a slew of gunshot wounds roll into emergency an hour ago, so they pulled all our imaging gear to place central venous catheters and look for bleeding.'

She vanished behind the heavy door, which sealed with an airtight thud.

The suite was cold, all sharp edges and surgical gear, a perfect rectangle.

Anjelina shivered beneath her gown. 'I'm cold.'

Evan realized he was standing five feet away, told himself to move forward, and made his legs work. At her side now, staring down.

Hair pulled back in a ponytail, not a trace of makeup – she looked exceedingly young, not a day older than fourteen. For an instant Evan felt the weight of the awesome responsibility on his shoulders. This child and her child, two lives in his hands.

She took a shaky breath. 'For so long . . .' She trailed off.

Evan waited.

'I feel like I've been stuck in my head and can't come out. You know? I can't make what it feels like inside match the outside world. It's like . . . you 'member osmosis? From bio?'

'Sure.'

'It's like that. This constant *pressure*. And now I've just made a mess of everything. And I don't know how to clean it up. I don't even feel strong enough to find out about this baby I'm responsible for. All alone here, in this room, without Reymundo. And then I go back there to those armed men. To that place. It's all . . . it's all so much.'

She was trembling, on the verge of coming apart.

Evan said, 'Bend your knees, put the soles of your feet on the table, and let your knees knock gently together.'

She looked at him. A rustle of paper as she obeyed.

'Now point your arms straight up at the ceiling – good. And then cross them so you hug yourself. Either arm on top, don't think about it.'

She did.

'How does that feel?'

'Better,' she said. 'Like I'm . . . dunno. Supported.'

'Right. You're supporting yourself.'

'Like, talking to my body?'

'No,' he said. 'Letting your body talk to you. It's smarter than you. It's showing your nervous system that you're okay right now. In this moment. That you're safe.'

Her big eyes looked even bigger. She mouthed, *Thank you*, and then closed them.

For a time she just breathed, the hospital sounds forming a kind of white noise.

When Dr Ortega returned pushing a trolley, Anjelina seemed calmer.

'Got one early,' Ortega said. 'Patient died.' A wink to Anjelina. 'Lucky us.'

As soon as the stirrups came up, Evan backed away, giving them a wide berth, but Anjelina said, 'Will you . . . can you hold my hand?'

Evan gritted his teeth. Moved closer to her. As Ortega snapped on latex gloves, he stood facing the other way, holding Anjelina's hand, his back to the proceedings.

'A little pressure now . . .' the doc said, and Anjelina's hand tensed in Evan's.

He had never been in a situation like this in his life.

Anjelina bucked now and again with discomfort, and then

Evan heard Ortega snap off the gloves and stretch on new ones. The stirrups clanked back down, and Anjelina lowered her legs.

'Everything looks good,' Ortega said. 'No abnormalities, some shortening of the cervix, but that's normal. Should we take a peek at the baby now?'

Holding her breath, Anjelina gave a nod. Her palm was sweaty in Evan's, the seal tight. He risked a glance back as Ortega readied the conductive gel, warming it in her palm as she reached for the transducer.

Back to Anjelina. Sweat sparkling at her hairline, face drawn with emotion.

'Okay,' Ortega said behind Evan. 'Looking good. See, that's the head there, and – oh, an ear – and that – that's the heartbeat.'

Tears were streaming down Anjelina's temples, dotting the paper.

'You can look, you know,' Anjelina told Evan in that smooth, low voice. 'It's just my belly and a monitor.'

He turned cautiously. The lower part of her abdomen was exposed, the transducer gliding across it through translucent gel. The monitor, swung to face Anjelina, showed a shifting charcoal cone of blobby shadows. Her fingers, still interlaced with his, tightened. The moment was elevated out of normal life somehow, imbued with a surreal glow that bordered on celestial. It was like being inside a Renaissance painting.

'We can't always tell the gender at twelve weeks,' Ortega said. 'Depends on the angle of the genital tubercle, but – *Oh*. There it is. Do you want to know?'

A male heir was what the Dark Man desired. A baby boy would make him more likely to be lenient to Anjelina and his own son. A baby boy would add a tactical advantage to the mission, and gaining tactical advantage was all Evan cared about.

And yet if Ortega confirmed the gender, the chief of staff would no doubt inform Montesco's men. If it was a girl, Anjelina's plight would worsen. It would be better not to know than to risk the wrong outcome, and yet he couldn't bring himself to object. It seemed profane to interfere with this moment.

Anjelina hesitated. Tears kept streaming down the sides of her face. Wiping her nose, she nodded a few times quickly, like a little kid. 'Yeah.'

Dr Ortega set down the transducer and did something Evan had thought her incapable of. She gave Anjelina a soft, warm smile. Everything about her had transformed, all that steely confidence turned soft, maternal.

Evan braced himself.

Ortega said, 'You're having a girl.'

He felt the answer in his spine, the shuddering backstep after a landed punch. Anjelina held a loose hand over her face and began to sob, and he understood that the news had hit her just as hard.

Then she curled forward, still sobbing, and said in a hoarse whisper, 'I never thought it could be so beautiful,' and Evan understood that he understood nothing at all.

He stood stiffly and held her hand, and Ortega rested a loving hand on her leg. Then the phone at the doctor's hip vibrated. She glanced at a text and said, 'They need me in the ER. I'll give you a moment alone and be back to check you out.'

'The gender,' Evan said. 'Can we keep it between us?'

Hesitating on her way out, Ortega glanced at the ultrasound unit. 'I can't alter medical files. But I don't have to volunteer anything.'

The door thunked shut behind her. They heard her muffled exchange with Jovencito demanding to know when they could leave, and then silence reasserted itself.

Anjelina smiled through her tears.

'Listen,' Evan said, pressing buttons on the computer to try to erase the imaging. 'We have to tell Montesco it's a boy.'

'Wait – I don't understand –'

'Montesco only cares about a boy. You're just an incubator to him.'

'But I'm having a girl. I saw her.'

He tugged at the cords connected to the monitor. 'Keep your voice down.'

'Everything's different now,' she said, squirming upright. 'A baby girl. I saw her. She's real.' She was still crying, just tears, no sobbing. 'X, you have to get me and Reymundo away from him. You have to get us out of there.'

He sensed it before he heard it, the click of the door opening.

He turned to see Jovencito in the room, staring at them, revelation writ large upon his face.

Jovencito grabbed for his gun.

42. The Fist of God

Evan kicked the trolley, which scooted across the floor, ramming into Jovencito's knees as he raised the Desert Eagle .44. The first shot shattered the computer, conveniently obliterating Anjelina's medical files. The second trailed close enough to Evan's right cheek that he felt the heat from the round as he charged.

Shoulder into Jovencito's solar plexus, driving him up into the door to slam it shut, knock the wind out of him, and maybe crack a floating rib.

The pistol skittered off, disappearing beneath a cabinet. As Evan and the *sicario* tumbled away, Evan slapped the lever lock on the door an instant before one of the henchmen hit the other side. Jovencito grabbed Evan around the midsection and hurled him across the nearest counter. He shattered through glass jars holding swabs and cotton balls, plowing into the far wall.

Wedged at the end of the counter, he felt something pinch into his hip.

A defibrillator.

Lucky day.

He swatted the bright orange button to charge it, the electronic whine increasing in intensity, not loud enough to drown out Anjelina's cries from the bed. Jovencito snatched up a graduated syringe rolling on the countertop and came at Evan.

Evan caught the base of Jovencito's hand, stopping the needle tip inches from his eye, and smashed Jovencito's fist into the wall. The syringe shattered inside Jovencito's palm, and he howled. He opened his fist, his palm studded with shards, and drew it back to swipe across Evan's face. Evan kicked him off just in time, heel to his chest to knock him over.

Evan rolled off the counter, bringing a rainfall of wreckage with him and catching a Dutch-angle glance at a panicky Anjelina yanking on her clothes. The defibrillator slid off the counter after him, knocking his shoulder and falling to the tile between him and Jovencito.

Charged and ready, it emitted a steady tone.

They lunged for it at the same time.

They grabbed it from opposite sides and tumbled apart again, Evan coming away with the paddles, Jovencito with the toaster-size base. They stared at each other, connected by two thick spiral cords suited to old-fashioned telephones. Both parts of the unit had their own set of controls.

Evan lunged forward to crash the paddles onto either side of Jovencito's head, but Jovencito caught his forearms, keeping them barely at bay. Evan reared back, ready to shove them forward, but Jovencito kicked the base, discharging it. A spark crackled between the paddles, spending the charge an instant before Evan got them to Jovencito's face.

Straining, nose to nose, sprawled out on the floor, kicking for purchase among the shards of glass. The henchmen's pounding at the solid door was joined by the shouts of doctors.

Sweat popping on his face, Jovencito found time to smile at Evan before flinging him into a cabinet beneath the window.

Younger and stronger indeed.

Behind Jovencito, Anjelina detached one of the metal stirrups from the exam table, but Evan shook his head at

her – the last thing he needed was a pregnant woman entering the fray.

Rolling onto his side, Jovencito smacked the button on the
defib base to charge again. Evan fumbled open the cabinet
door behind him, implements clattering down over his
shoulder.

Scalpels.

He snatched one up.

Jovencito got a foot beneath him in a low crouch and dove
at Evan with the paddles, his body stretched horizontal a few
feet above the floor.

Evan brought his fist around in time for Jovencito to
impale himself on the scalpel. But Jovencito had aimed well
at Evan's exposed flesh, one paddle shoved into the side of
Evan's neck, the other high on his biceps beneath a hiked-up
sleeve.

Jovencito's thumb clamped down over the orange button.

The shock was unlike anything Evan had felt.

A massive blow going straight through him, like the fist of
God driving a clean channel through his torso. The force
knocked him across the floor, racking him into the wall, his
entire left side seized up, muscles contracted excruciatingly.
An acrid reek of burned flesh, a black wisp curling past the
edge of his eye, the skin sizzling at the side of his neck as if
someone had pressed an iron into it.

He couldn't breathe, couldn't move, his lungs locked up.

Jovencito was on his knees, staring down.

The scalpel had embedded itself in his side at the base of
his torso, likely between the eighth and ninth ribs, right
through the intersection of the tattooed pendant cross. Too
low for the heart, too shallow to puncture a lung. The cutting
edge had gone in only an inch or so, the handle dangling out
like a dart sunk poorly into a corkboard. He stared down at

it in disbelief, his injured hand hovering over it. Too stunned to yank it out.

Evan needed the intermission himself. He opened a channel of air, a screeching sip of oxygen working through the contorted muscles of his left side, and then he managed to heave himself forward on the floor to kick the bottom of Jovencito's hand. The glass-crusted palm flew up, smacking into Jovencito's right eye, and he bellowed, finding his feet. For an instant he swayed above Evan and then tumbled backward, his shoulders crashing against the base of the wall across the suite.

They lay there panting, recovering strength. Aside from their heaving chests, they barely moved, but their eyes remained locked on each other. Jovencito's right socket was lost beneath a wash of blood, a glittering crimson eye patch. The scorched flesh of Evan's neck stung, and his elbows simmered from tile burn. The room stank, a haze of rubbing alcohol, conductive gel, and blood hanging in the air.

More commotion from outside the door. A shout and then a round cracked off the sturdy surgical door, followed by the whine of a ricochet.

Evan tried to unkink his left side, but the muscles weren't listening, fibers and tendons kneading tighter. On the plus side, he was getting some air into his lungs and his right arm mostly worked.

Anjelina had backed behind the exam table, wielding the metal stirrup before her like a baseball bat. She'd managed to pull on her jeans, and her shirt was half on, her belly exposed.

Using his legs and the muscles of his right side, Evan rolled himself up into a sitting position. Across the room Jovencito did the same. Like boxers trying to find their feet, they moved to all fours, straining to stand.

They crawled toward each other. Jovencito stood first,

kicking out Evan's arm. Evan's chest slapped the floor. With his right hand, he reached into the mound of scalpels next to him, miraculously not catching an edge. Jovencito stooped, picking up the base unit of the defibrillator and hoisting it overhead, readying to bring it down on Evan's skull.

Anjelina hurled the stirrup, but it flew wide over Jovencito's shoulder, spinning end over end before crashing into the wall.

Giving Evan the split-second opening he needed to jab a scalpel through the bottom of Jovencito's calf.

Jovencito grunted, dropping the unit, which glanced off his cheek as it fell, knocking him down. Evan pressed the advantage, dragging himself atop Jovencito and pounding his face with his right fist. No hapkido, no muay thai, no shotokan – just whaling away with what little he had left. That scalpel still drooped from between Jovencito's ribs, out of reach, and Evan didn't dare stop swinging to go for it.

Jovencito managed a throat strike, Evan reeling away from the pressure, choking, the younger man atop him now, fingers digging for his eyes. Evan bucked, and they slammed over into a skein of glass shards, smearing a confusion of blood on the floor beneath them. Jovencito's Kyocera phone had spilled out of his pocket and gotten smashed to pieces in the fray.

Jovencito punched Evan's left ribs once, twice, the already contracted muscles screaming. Evan moved with the next blow, Jovencito tumbling, Evan on top of him once more, fastening his hands around his throat, choking him out.

Losing oxygen, Jovencito slapped at Evan's face, weaker, weaker, but Evan's left hand was cramping, a line of fire intensifying down that whole flank. The knotting came up from his rib cage, claiming his shoulder, his biceps, forearm. Jovencito was purpling, fatiguing.

But so was Evan.

His left hand was aflame, cramped into uselessness, and he had to let go, fingers clawing. He collapsed onto Jovencito, the men lying spent, chest to chest, face to face. Jovencito coughed himself back to life as Evan tried to shake feeling back into his left side.

Jovencito slid his forearm beneath Evan's throat, grabbed Evan's hair, and ripped his head forward and down. Grinding Evan's windpipe into the hard edge of his ulna, cutting off oxygen. Evan could feel the younger man's breath on the top of his head.

He could sense Anjelina in his peripheral vision, terrified, gathering her nerve to come forward. Given what Jovencito had overheard, Evan had to gain the upper hand and get her out of here or Montesco would slice her to pieces.

No air in or out. Jovencito overpowering him, cinching off his breath.

Evan's vision tunneled, crowding in at the edges. Face on fire.

If he died, she'd die.

It seemed headed that way.

Evan groped for anything on the floor but came up empty. His vision compressing, a shrinking point of light. Their bodies were too close for Evan to get at Jovencito's groin, his stomach. His right hand slid up Jovencito's side, grasping for anything.

Struck metal.

The protruding scalpel.

With the last of his strength, Evan fastened his hand around it and drove it inward. Jovencito screamed, an ungodly high wail. Evan dug it farther inward, then upward, felt a lung pop. Jovencito let go of the choke hold, flinging them onto their sides, grabbing Evan's wrist with both his hands to stop the scalpel's progress. Evan's fist, wrapped around the end of the scalpel, froze in place, trapped in the push-pull.

Willing life into his clawed left hand, Evan forced it open into an insensate slab of flesh and drew it back. For a moment his flattened palm hovered high over the union of their three hands.

Then he hammered it down, striking the butt of his own fist, driving the scalpel into Jovencito. The point slid up and through the thoracic cage. Jovencito arched back onto heels and shoulders as if struck by lightning and shuddered violently with equine vigor. Evan's muscles gave out with fatigue, and he slumped down on Jovencito's body. His cheek rested on the *sicario*'s chest, vibrating with each labored thump of the dying heart. Evan's head rose and fell with Jovencito's last heaving breaths. The sound of the heartbeat against Evan's ear grew slower, slower, slower. A last whistle leaked through Jovencito's teeth as he deflated, and then his head rolled up and sideways.

Evan lay on the body in exhausted stillness.

Then he drew himself up. There was a horrible screech, and it took a moment for him to realize it had escaped his own mouth.

Anjelina stared at him, lips agape, then rushed to him and caught him as he stumbled.

'The window,' he said. 'Need to break the window and go.'

'No,' she said. 'We can't.'

'We have to go. We can get out. I can protect you.'

'He'll kill him. He'll kill Reymundo.'

'It doesn't matter –'

'We can't,' she said. 'I can't. I won't.'

The horde at the door banged away, the reinforced metal thundering in its frame.

Her shirt was still stuck up above her belly, the slope of

brown skin protruding. He could barely breathe, the left half of his torso in full spasm from his armpit to his waist. His left hand was still cramped beyond comprehension, and he straightened the fingers, flexing it, pins and needles creeping beneath the skin.

'Please,' she said. 'I don't know what I'd do without him.'

She took Evan's trembling hand and placed it on her belly.

Her skin, so smooth, so warm. And then the faintest pulse of movement beneath.

He looked up into her face.

Limped across to the door.

And unlocked it.

43. A Special Relationship with Pain

Before Evan could cross the threshold, he was greeted with a faceful of muzzles – .44s and MP7s rammed at his head like a bouquet of microphones from a clamoring press.

'Get El Moreno on the phone!' he barked. 'Now!'

Nacho jabbed the MP7 at his chin. 'Who the fuck do you think –'

Evan swatted the barrel aside. 'I found the mole. Call him *now*.'

'Where's Jovencito?' another of Montesco's men shouted out.

'You guys are a slow study,' Evan said, shouldering through them, keeping Anjelina at his back. There was a throng of onlookers – doctors, nurses, the chief of staff, and a smattering of patients.

Some of the men moved into the surgical suite, exclamations and swear words ringing out. The remaining men hesitated but didn't lower their guns. They stayed shoulder to shoulder, blocking Evan's way out.

The chief of staff rubbed his hands nervously. 'Perhaps you could resume this conversation out –'

'No one's going anywhere,' Nacho said.

'We have to move,' Evan said. 'If Jovencito knew we were here, there's probably a team of Gulf Cartel assassins en route already.'

The men exchanged glances. With Jovencito gone, they weren't sure who to listen to.

Grimacing against the pain, Evan started forward, but

Nacho stepped in front of him. 'I've known Jovencito for years. Why the fuck would we believe you?' He raised the slung MP7 once more, aiming at Evan's chest. 'Step away from the girl.'

The others stirred, encircling Evan and Anjelina. He couldn't push the ruse any further. It was hard for him to project strength when half his body was barely functioning. He'd hit a dead end and was in no condition to fight his way out.

A feminine voice broke through the periphery. 'I heard him.'

They pivoted to face Dr Ortega.

'The *sicario*,' she said. 'When I came out to get the ultrasound cart. He was up the hall there.' She pointed to a brief hall leading to the bathrooms. 'I heard him calling in the location here to someone. His back turned, voice low. I remember thinking it was odd he was telling someone you were all here when it was made clear to us to keep this visit confidential.'

Montesco's men shifted on their feet. Studied Evan. Ortega's lie had set them on edge, injecting the right amount of doubt at the right time. Suddenly their eyes looked wider, their expressions worried. What reason would a doctor have to cover for Evan?

And yet the muzzle of Nacho's MP7 stayed where it was, aimed at Evan's heart.

One of the henchmen shouldered to the front, lowering a phone from his ashen face. 'The forest lab's been raided,' he said. 'Burned to the ground.'

Wordless agitation circled the men.

A freighted pause.

And then the MP7 lowered. Evan let out his breath slowly through clenched teeth.

Nacho turned, rushing for the exit. 'Let's go.'

Evan limped after them, Anjelina looping an arm around his waist to hold him upright. As they passed by, Dr Ortega gave the faintest dip of a parting nod.

The chauffeur drove Nacho, Evan, and Anjelina back to the estate, Evan doing his best to breathe through his seized-up left side. In the backseat he and Anjelina stared out opposite windows, not a word exchanged. His neck burned. Hands sore from the failed strangulation. His chest tight and pinched as from a tension pneumothorax, of which he'd had three, including one he'd had to self-puncture with a bicycle-pump needle in a mechanic shop outside Ankara.

In the passenger seat, Nacho made a series of calls but was unable to reach Montesco, who was evidently some-where dealing with the aftermath of the assault on the forest lab. From this end of Nacho's conversations, Evan gleaned that the lab had been taken down by a DEA–Policía Federal Ministerial joint raid. Which meant that Aragón had deliv-ered on his promise to forward intel about the Kontact supply chain to the authorities. The pieces were there for Evan to stitch this all together into a narrative he could sell to Montesco, but the pain was intense enough to prevent him from figuring it out now.

He'd have to unstick his body first.

And in the meantime keep respirating.

Back at the estate, Darling Boy greeted them at the front door, twirling his combat knife around the back of his hand and catching it again like a baton. Given the look of unmiti-gated hatred he leveled at Evan, it was clear that news of Jovencito's demise had reached the grounds. It would be up to the Dark Man to decide whether to believe Evan or not.

Reymundo rushed into the foyer and embraced Anjelina. 'You're okay!'

'Yes,' she said. 'Thanks to him.'

Reymundo took in Evan – ripped clothes, bloodstains, painfully contorted posture – and said, 'Thank you.'

Two simple words, but there was a universe of gratitude behind them.

Evan gave a nod.

When Reymundo helped Anjelina off to her room, Darling Boy moved to stop him. 'I'll take her.'

'She's bearing El Moreno's grandson,' Evan said. 'You'd best let her do what she wants.'

Darling Boy's lips twisted in disdain. But he didn't object. He stuck out an arm, letting the couple lead the way, and then followed them tightly. Anjelina was smart enough not to look back at Evan.

Wobbling on his feet, Evan took a moment to set his balance. The left side of his torso was locked up badly enough that he had trouble walking. His foot dragged as he passed down the narrow hallways, guards watching him impassively, grenade pouches at their belts.

He barely made it to his bedroom suite. Heeled the door shut behind him. Stood on the lush carpet. Breathed the still, private air.

Now – finally – he allowed the pain all the way in. It came in a rush, robbing his breath, the entire side of his body stitched up from hip to shoulder, knotted with charley-horse intensity.

Certain people – victims, athletes, the terminally ill – find a special relationship with pain. Evan had been taught by Jack Johns and subject-matter experts how to understand it intimately. Some injuries have to be identified early. Others ignored. There are those that can be put off for a while. And the ones that announce in real time that you will carry them to the end of your days.

This was none of them.

An excruciating but nonpermanent impairment, brought on by a vicious beating and a thousand volts passed through the major muscle groups of half his torso.

He did not have time to let it heal slowly, to coax the muscles into relaxing over the course of a few days.

Locating the thermostat, he clicked the heat to high, the vents firing immediately overhead. He searched for an appropriately heavy book on the shelves, found a Spanish translation of *Crime and Punishment*, jacketless and upside down. Nice and sturdy, the size of a yoga block. As he plucked it out, he noticed his torn knuckles, Jovencito's dried blood speckling the back of his hand.

He lowered himself to the carpet, groaning as his weight tugged him down the last few inches. For a moment he lay flat on his back, gathering his nerve. Then he planted his feet and lifted his hips, sliding the book beneath his sacrum. Grimacing, he lowered his pelvis again.

The Supported Bridge was the best position for him to check the infrastructure of his spine, assess what was going on and what he needed to do. Right now he couldn't do anything except breathe.

If he could slow the breath down, that would tell his body it was safe. Time after time the pain objected but time after time he rerouted it to a different corner of his mind. Despite a stubborn hitch at the bottom of his exhalations, he made headway. He held his breath for a ten count to reset his nervous system again, and when he exhaled, the air moved smoothly all the way out.

Removing the block, lowering his hips, he gave himself a thirty-second reward of stillness. Rolling to his stomach caused more pain than seemed humanly bearable, a cattle-prod jolt up to his brain. The heat of Nuevo Leon, augmented by the

HVAC unit, felt infernal. Perspiration sprang up in beads on his arms, drained off his flanks.

Facedown, toes touching, heels falling to the sides, palms stacked beneath his forehead.

He told himself that this pain was nothing more than the space between needing to release and actually releasing. He'd been trained to close that gap a millimeter at a time.

Right now his training didn't mean a fucking thing.

Right now the pain needed to have its say.

He let it. There was no choice. For a time it ravaged him.

He kept trying for the breath and finally found a version of it that wasn't so ragged as to be unrecognizable.

Loosening. Loosening. Loosening.

Pressing his right cheek to the carpet, he cactused his arms and slid his left knee up beside him, keeping the inner seam of the leg pressed flat to the floor.

Half Frog Pose.

Like a chalk outline prone on the floor.

He was making noises he didn't recognize. Panting, spent.

But now he was here.

This was the pose he needed to loosen his left side. As he was taught years ago, he visualized each bundle of fibrous tissue, picturing each tendon and ligament so he could breathe into them and restore them to laxity.

He started with the superficial layers. The tightened muscle resisted, resisted, and finally yielded, a sensation like interlaced fingers pulling slowly apart.

Then he moved to the deeper layers, opening them up slowly, one at a time.

Sweat dripped onto his lashes; he blinked it away. He was panting, his mouth cotton. He tried to relax everything – toes, jaws, the space between his eyes.

Detaching muscle from fascia, bone from ligament, letting them sag weightlessly, his body nothing more than a sack of skin and fluid. He let his bones settle to the bottom and held the pose for five minutes, seven, felt a hip flexor roll across the iliac crest and pop over the bone, a tug he felt all the way up in his ear canal.

He was sobbing soundlessly, and it wasn't grief, it was the pain shuddering through the channel of his body as it exited, striking ancient chords.

— backhanded by the Mystery Man, laid out on a handball court at the age of twelve —

— fished out of a pool during drownproofing training in his early teens, lungs filled with water —

— writhing in shards of broken glass in a lampshade shop in Gaza, twisting beneath a Syrian rebel, his hands aching around the handles of a garrote —

He was in all ages of himself all at once, the pain compounding through his muscle memory like an echo, a Russian nesting doll, a hall of mirrors. When the pains past and present aligned, they reached an unsustainable altitude, knocking him clear out of his body.

Jack was there, squinting his baseball-catcher squint, arms folded, staring down at him. He looked unimpressed, but that was just Jack's face.

We don't rise to the level of our aspirations, Jack said. *We fall to the level of our training.*

Through gritted teeth, Evan forced out words. *Who's that?*

I think Archilochus. Greek poet.

He the fox-and-hedgehog guy?

The very one. Jack eyed him. *You look like a monkey trying to hump a football.*

The pain's pretty good.

We have to heal ourselves. Every day. Or else we're just dying.

Helpful, Evan grunted. *You just show up to lend the moral support of ancient thinkers?*

Modern ones, too.

What you got in that category?

Jack pondered a moment. *What we resist pursues us. What we accept transforms us.*

Who said that?

Aren't you listening, son? That almost-smile, the one that crinkled his eyes at the edges. *I just did.*

Evan came back into himself. He had perspective on the pain, could see it for what it was, even feel gratitude for how it was trying to protect him. His hip opened wider. His heart melted into the carpet. It was like he was hugging the floor and it was hugging him back. He felt good, strong.

Sliding himself up to all fours, he took *balasana,* a knees-together version of Child's Pose, third eye to the earth, arms stretched behind him, palms facing up. Puddled over the curled stack of his body as if he'd been poured into the shape. Thighs pressing into his chest, his back bowed, spread wide beneath the painted heaven above.

The muscles slackened around his vertebrae, a freeing sensation like pulling a shoelace through the eyelets of his spine. Loose on the bone, braised meat ready to slough free.

He drew in a diaphragmatic breath that filled his entire body.

And released it with a single sharp exhalation.

As his body sank, it folded vertically around the center line of his thighs and spine, and his back cracked all the way from sacrum to shoulders.

He stood up.

Fresh blood rushed into the points of compression. No pain anywhere, just a soft, lovely ache that reminded him he was alive.

He shook out his neck, let his hands snap back and forth on his wrists. Everything realigned. He was ready, his sixth sense humming to life again.

His gaze tracked to the door a moment before it opened.

El Moreno entered.

44. What I Do

Before Montesco could enter the room, Evan said, 'Congratulations.'

Montesco halted, his hair jumbled across his eyes. He stank of body odor and cigarette smoke, his skin shiny with sweat. From the look of it, he'd had a longer day than Evan had. He mopped at his forehead but did not comment on the roasting room temperature.

'My *sicario* is dead,' he said. 'And the *federal a la verga* took out my biggest production facility. So what are you congratulating me about?'

'You're having a boy.'

At this the Dark Man paused, rolled his lips over his teeth, released them with a popping sound.

'Your name will continue on,' Evan said, 'well after the noise of any given day.'

'That's why Reymundo is with her now? Without my approval?'

'You can do whatever you want,' Evan said. 'But that baby needs to grow healthy and strong. He will need his father there just as Reymundo needed you.'

Montesco took this in for a moment solemnly, weighing it in his mind. Then he padded across the carpet, snapped off the thermostat, and sat on the bed, pulling the sheets out of alignment. 'Jovencito. Talk.'

'He placed a call in the hallway, then came in, pulled his pistol to shoot the girl. I did what I do.'

At this, Montesco grinned a wolfish grin.

'The Gulf Cartel doesn't just want you dead,' Evan said. 'They want your lineage snuffed out.'

Montesco looked haggard, dark skin sagging beneath his eyes. 'Darling Boy found irregularities in the bank accounts of three of my men here.'

'Payments from the Gulf Cartel?'

'That was unclear.'

'What did you do?'

'Gave them to the lion.'

Evan said, 'Oh.'

From two *sicarios* and forty-one men to one *sicario* and thirty-eight men.

Progress.

The more Evan could manipulate Montesco into killing his own men, the fewer Evan would have to contend with on his way out.

'There might be more,' Evan said. 'Sleep with your door locked, gun under the pillow. Only your most trusted men at your side. Have Darling Boy keep prying into every employee. If Jovencito was a snake in the grass, that means anyone else could be, too.'

Montesco rubbed his eyes, screamed, '*Fuck!*' into his palm as loudly as he could, the cords of his neck standing out. His voice was hoarse, desiccated. 'This is my paradise. If I can't relax here, where can I?'

'I'll get this taken care of for you,' Evan said.

'How?'

'Jovencito's phone shattered in our fight, but I have a colleague who can trace any call after the fact.'

'It's a piece-of-shit Kyocera. We prepay so there's no call history, no nothing.'

'She is a technological wizard.'

'She?'

'A woman,' Evan said. 'But competent.'

A man like El Moreno would not be able to imagine how competent a sixteen-year-old girl like Joey Morales could be.

Montesco nodded.

'She's already tracked it to a number with a 909 area code,' Evan lied. 'San Bernardino.'

Montesco said, 'The third shooter.'

'That's right. As we speak, she's charting the cell-phone towers it last pinged.'

'So you can triangulate location?'

'Advanced forward link trilateration,' Evan said. Joey would have been proud.

Montesco frowned, impressed. 'Find him. Put him in the ground.'

'That is what I plan to do. But . . .'

'What?'

'It's nothing.'

'Speak.'

'Just something I noticed Jovencito doing before we left this morning.'

'What?'

'He was eyeing the sewer grates,' Evan said. 'And I noticed his vehicle slowed as we passed certain storm drains heading out to the freeway.'

Montesco's face tightened. 'Those aren't all storm drains. Those are –'

'Disguised hatches for your escape tunnels,' Evan said. 'I think he was –'

'Charting them. To help plan a raid –'

'– an inside man, like they had in San Bernardino,' Evan said.

'I will have my men check all routes and tunnels in and out of here.'

'How can you know who to trust?'

Montesco rose, paced a tight circle. He opened his mouth again, head shaking, teeth bared, as if he were screaming. But he made no noise. The effect was unsettling.

Evan waited.

At last those wide eyes lifted to him through the curtain of fallen hair arcing from that severe widow's peak. 'What do I do, then?'

'There's specific technology I want to use to scan the escape tunnels. Countermeasures I'd like to get in place. I'm talking the real shit they use in Gaza, not knockoff toy-soldier garbage from Mexico City.'

'Fine.' Montesco said. 'How much?'

'One more of those should do.' Evan jerked a chin at the rolling suitcase on the luggage rack, packed with a hundred grand. 'My procurement guy is in South Texas. I'll drive there to put in an order, then fly to LA to take care of business.'

'You'll have your pick of my vehicles.'

'No,' Evan said. 'Not with the Gulf Cartel waiting out there. Going in one of your cars is too conspicuous. I saw a Hertz at the edge of the city. Have one of your men drop me there. I'll handle the rest of my arrangements.'

'Fine. When will you leave?'

'As soon as I've showered off Jovencito's blood.'

At this, Montesco smiled that wide, loose smile. 'You and me, we are *carnales*!'

He offered Evan a hand to clasp and yanked him in for a one-arm embrace. The stench coming off him was powerful, but Evan, covered with dried sweat and blood, wasn't one to talk.

As they pulled apart, Evan said, 'Can I have my gun now?'

Montesco considered this a moment. 'I thought you might

ask.' He reached into the back of his waistband. Held out the ARES 1911 to Evan. As Evan took it, the muzzle swept across Montesco's chest for a moment. Short-term temptation. Long-term disaster.

He knew his pistol like it was a part of his body. He felt its heft and understood right away.

Pretended to check and notice for the first time.

'No bullets,' he said.

Montesco tapped Evan's temple a few times, hard enough that his fingernail pinched the skin. 'You just said I can't know who to trust.' He reached out and took the gun back. 'I trust you, Caballo Oscuro, because you are like me. This is also why I *don't* trust you. You see?'

'Fair enough.'

'Bring me the head of the third shooter. Then we will see about allowing you a weapon under my roof.'

He slapped Evan not so gently on the cheek and withdrew.

The sun was setting as Evan stepped out onto the portico. He wheeled a hard-shelled carry-on suitcase with each hand, the most valuable luggage he'd possessed in some time.

The chauffeur named Raudel waited in one of the SUVs. Spotting Evan, he hopped out and loaded the suitcases into the cargo hold, then held the rear door for Evan.

He climbed in. Gazed across at the jailed row of human beings, another commodity waiting to be shipped out. Soulful eyes, gaunt cheeks, bruised arms from rough handling. They had a few more days of captivity before being moved along the assembly line. At the next stop, they'd be treated like product, like possessions, like meat. Used once all the way through or thousands of times until they wore out. He had to wrap this mission up before the shipping date that would consign them to an unknown fate.

As the chauffeur walked around the SUV, a voice called out from the blind spot. 'Hold on!'

A form flashed past the tinted window, and then Reymundo got into the driver's seat. 'Mind if I drive you?'

Evan shrugged.

Raudel tapped the driver's window with a knuckle, and Reymundo rolled it down.

The chauffeur took Evan's measure. He was a squat, barrel-chested man with a manicured beard. Even from here his breath smelled of chewing tobacco. He spoke in heavily accented English. 'I don't think you should be alone with this *gabacho*.'

'I'll keep an eye out.' Reymundo drove off, leaving the chauffeur standing in the quartz stones, head tilted, looking befuddled.

Evan called up the white-noise app on his phone, placed it on his thigh.

Reymundo took note, his eyes flashing in the rearview.

'*Gabacho*,' Evan repeated. 'He's one of Darling Boy's buddies?'

'Most of them are,' Reymundo said. 'My father has relied on Darling Boy for many years.'

'Why are you driving me?'

'I wanted to tell you . . .' Reymundo hesitated. 'I'm grateful. To you. For what you are doing for Anjelina. She told me about the hospital. Not just that you protected her. But that . . . you comforted her. I haven't –' His voice wavered, and he paused to regain his composure. 'I haven't been able to. Protect her. Not like I should.'

'How about the other women? In the chicken coop?'

Reymundo's voice came low, like a little boy's. 'I haven't been able to protect them either.'

For a time they drove in silence.

Wind howled through the rock walls, an ungodly sound,

the force strong enough to blow the SUV around on the road. At last they spit out onto the valley, the highway stretching ahead like an arrow pointing to the broken city of Guaridón. The air-conditioning blew cool and steady against Evan's face. He tasted stale cigar smoke seeping up through the leather upholstery. Everything the Dark Man touched carried his scent.

'For as long as I can remember,' Reymundo said, 'I prayed to God to take him away. Not kill him but just . . . take him away. My hands sweat every time he walks into the room. My heart rate jumps when I hear his voice. Even when he's not there, I hear it thundering in my head. To fear the person who is supposed to protect you most, the person who brought you into the world –' His voice was rising, but he caught himself. 'Now I no longer pray to God to take him away. I pray to God that he will die.'

'If I can figure out how to give you a fresh start, are you ready to do anything you need to do to protect Anjelina?'

'Yes.'

'Even if that means leaving and never coming back.'

'*Especially* if it means that. But . . .' The tires rolled across the gritty asphalt, and then the SUV bounced off the exit, burrowing beneath an overpass, the cavernous space crammed with homeless encampments. 'What if I screw this up? She loves me now. But she's giving everything up. *Everything.*'

'You are, too,' Evan said.

'What if she decides it wasn't worth it? That *I'm* not worth it?'

'Make it worth it. Every day.'

'How do I do that?'

'Pay attention.'

'To what?'

'Everything.'

The city was desolate, decrepit high-rises, few cars on the street, sporadic packs of roving boys. They stopped at a red light, the Hertz rental place waiting across the intersection. Chain-link and barbed wire protected the collection of shabby vehicles. Evan would refuse the first two they offered in case El Moreno had made arrangements to bug them, and then he would chose the ugliest vehicle on the lot.

An elderly blind man stood at the sidewalk, tapping his walking stick along the edge of the curb. He tentatively stepped down into the crosswalk, brown polyester pants tugging up at the ankles to show black socks and strips of dry, cracked skin.

'No one ever taught me,' Reymundo said. 'How to be a good man. I grew up with killers and whores.'

When the light changed, he didn't roll off the line, though there was plenty of time for him to clear the intersection. Instead he waited for the old man.

In slow motion the elderly man tapped along in front of them, feeling his way with the walking stick, avoiding a pot-hole and then a spill of shattered glass. He wore dark shades, his skin sun-burnished, the color of walnut. Evan couldn't help but think of Belicia, all those wrong turns that led to her sight being robbed. And how she and Aragón, despite all their suffering or because of it, seemed to have discovered deeper places within themselves.

Evan leaned forward, pointing past Reymundo's shoulder at the blind man. 'What's he doing?'

Reymundo watched a moment. 'Seeing where to walk?'

'No. Seeing where he *shouldn't* walk.'

From the other side of the crosswalk, the blind man turned his face back to them, doffed an imaginary hat, and kept on his instinctive way.

'That's where to start,' Evan said. 'Sometimes that's all we have.'

45. Up in Smoke

After two days inside the torture palace, a lethal brawl in a surgical suite, and the three-and-a-half hour drive back to Eden, Evan was in no mood for security theater.

Special Ed and Kiki, manning the front gate of Aragón's compound with a few PMCs, alerted as Evan pulled up in an overheated Chevrolet Matiz. He'd hidden the suitcases of cash in the spare-tire compartment, crossing the border tensely but without incident.

Slinging their AR-15s, the two men ambled up on either side of the cramped hatchback. 'Ah, look who came crawling home,' said Eduardo. 'Thanks to you, *Patrón* is burning more product at the northeast end of the compound. Day and night he destroys his business. *Un chingo de lana*, up in smoke. Wait here while we –'

Evan said, 'Open the gate.'

Something in his face made clear he needed to see Aragón immediately.

The men stared at him a moment, and then Kiki lifted a radio to his face and mumbled into it. The gate retracted behind the concrete-block wall, and Evan accelerated into the compound. A few shouts behind him as the two lieutenants hopped into a Jeep to follow.

The sky was a confusion of dark and light, the fallen sun throwing a cold gray glow from below the horizon, illuminating the firmament. After the tacky extravagance of Montesco's estate, Aragón's land seemed downright homey – dirt and generators and a normal suburban residence plopped down in the center.

As Evan blazed to the house, a number of other vehicles came visible, raising trails of dust in the gloaming. They vectored toward him from the perimeter, spokes of a wheel converging.

Clearly the alarm had been raised – the Nowhere Man returning with news of the imperiled daughter – and all the manpower of the compound was assembling for the update.

Evan reached the front of the house, the other vehicles irising in on him, and parked by the driveway. A Jeep careened up, Aragón hopping out while it was still moving, nearly stumbling as he ran for Evan.

'Where is she? Is she alive?' Aragón's shirt was unbuttoned at the top, showing off the sunburned skin of his chest.

'She's alive,' Evan said. 'But there's more. And you're not going to like it.'

Aragón stormed to Evan even as the other vehicles slanted into place, headlights skewering them, the front of the house. Men unpacked, doors slamming, breath huffing in the semidarkness. Across the manicured front lawn, the door clicked open, La Tía visible behind the screen. The air carried a tinge of acrid smoke, probably from whatever haul Aragón was incinerating at the periphery.

Aragón charged as if to barrel straight through Evan, but he halted just in time, chest heaving. 'What? What is it? *Tell me where she is!*'

'She is with Reymundo, El Moreno's son. She went there by choice. She is being held captive now. And . . .'

Aragón looked confused, the meaty flanges of his nose flaring. That thick shock of black hair looked grayer, though it had been less than seventy-two hours since Evan had seen him.

'What?' Aragón snarled. '*What?*'

'She's pregnant.'

Aragón staggered as if shot, one hand clamped to the spot where his shoulder met chest. The screen door banged, and then La Tía drifted across the lawn, nightgown fluttering about her ankles, not walking toward them so much as gliding.

Aragón's voice came low now, little more than a growl. 'What did you say? What the *fuck* did you just say?'

'Anjelina is pregnant. With Reymundo's child.'

'No. *No!*' Fury cut with disbelief, even a hint of pleading. 'It's not true.'

Headlights stabbed Evan's eyes, but he did not look away.

Aragón's gaze was feral, murderous. Baring his teeth, he doubled over as if heaving, and a bellow escaped him, more a roar than a yell. His cheeks trembled.

The others had gathered around them in a loose circle, giving them space. Special Ed and Kiki were a half step in front but frozen in their boots, locked to the ground, stunned by the sight of their boss in this state.

Aragón straightened back up. 'She lied to me? She *staged* this? That ungrateful –' His face looked to be tearing itself apart. 'With them? The Leones? El Moreno's son? She has his bastard seed in her belly?' He flung a hand toward the rise of black smoke to the northeast. 'For *her* I'm burning down my kingdom?'

'For your daughter, yes.'

Aragón thundered at him, teeth clenched, veins popping in his neck, 'This is worse than if she was dead.'

'You don't mean that.'

'Don't you dare tell me what I mean right now.'

'Your daughter –'

'She can be anything she wants to be. *Anything.* Except this.'

'You'd rather she were dead?'

'Yes. *Yes.* I'd rather my daughter was dead than a fucking *whore.*'

Evan cuffed him.

Openhanded but hard, a thunderclap to Aragón's left cheek. It caught him off guard, toppling him. He landed on one knee, head lowered, hair shielding his eyes. His shoulders heaved with his breath.

For a moment there was no sound save Aragón's labored breathing. The men around them were paralyzed, in absolute shock. For once Special Ed and Kiki held their tongues. Their eyes were shiny, and beneath the facial hair and acne scars and cover-up and rawboned glares of killers Evan could see the boys they had been, and for a single bright moment none of them were killers and cartel leaders and private military contractors and ex–government assassins but just men beneath an open sky enacting an ancient ritual they could comprehend but scarcely understand.

Eduardo reached for his pistol and started to step forward, but Kiki caught his eye and gave him a slight shake of the head. This was not for them.

Aragón rose with dignity, wiped his mouth.

He walked quietly out of the ring of men. They parted, and he passed his aunt, standing barefoot in the grass.

He opened the door, closed it gently behind him, and the night was still.

46. Another Arrogant Gringo *Pendejo*

La Tía stood glowering at Evan, her nightgown rippling around her in the breeze. Then she turned and followed Aragón inside. The instant the door closed, the sound of their shouting carried outside. Rapid-fire Spanish, too fast for Evan to understand.

The others looked at him, unsure what to do.

After a few minutes, the door hinged open. La Tía skewered Evan with a glare. 'Get in here.'

Not a request.

He went.

Slack-jawed and stupefied, the men parted for him as well. The house smelled of onion and cilantro, a pot simmering on the stove. Aragón was pacing around the ground floor like a raging bull, heat emanating off him. Muttering low to himself, sweeping his shiny black curls off his forehead again and again.

La Tía's arms were crossed, head drawn back. Somehow, miraculously, she was wearing makeup. With her nut-brown skin and white hair, she was as imposing a figure as any Evan had encountered.

'You disrespect my *sobrino*,' she said. 'On his land. In front of his men.'

'He disrespects himself.'

'You know nothing of our family. Nothing of our culture. Another arrogant gringo *pendejo*, sticking your nose into something you scarcely understand.'

'I understand that right now his image of his daughter is more important to him than she is.'

In the kitchen Aragón cursed and swept his arm, knocking the cast-iron pot off the burner, caldo de res splattering the wall. He slammed the heels of his hands onto the counter, shoulders pinching up into his neck, a pained guttural noise escaping him.

'His daughter – my granddaughter – has standards to live up to. A family name. This decision she made, it's unconscionable. Those people, the Leones, are *animales*. And she chose to go to them. To be unsafe. To have relations before marriage. And above all the *lying*. To us. Putting lives at risk. Inviting them here, into Eden, to raid our very own community –'

'I don't disagree.'

'And yet you *dare* to lay hands on her father?' La Tía came at Evan, jabbing a manicured finger. 'He has every right put you six feet in the earth! He should –'

'*Stop!*'

A low feminine voice from the top of the stairs, clear as glass, sharp as a scalpel.

La Tía halted.

Belicia stood on the landing, toplit by a recessed overhead light. Despite the hour she was fully dressed. Evan imagined her up there hearing the commotion, pulling on her jeans, buttoning her blouse, brushing her hair by feel alone. Her bearing was erect, shoulders pulled back and down, the picture-perfect posture of a gymnast or a drill sergeant.

She reached for the railing, her fingers wavering over the wood before her palm cupped the top. She descended. In the full light, she was radiant.

Reaching the bottom of the stairs, she halted, hand on the newel post. Her ghostly eyes took the measure of the room. She turned to La Tía, her angle only barely wrong. 'Enough.'

La Tía said, 'If you'd heard the tone this man took with –'

'I heard *everything*,' Belicia said.

337

'Then you have to know –'

'I don't *have* to know anything. This is between me and my husband.' Those sightless eyes turned to Evan, and he could have sworn she saw him as well as anyone ever had, if not better. 'And the Nowhere Man.'

La Tía's mouth pursed, etched lines contracting. Then she dipped her chin deferentially and walked past Belicia and up the stairs. All this time, in violation of the First Commandment, Evan had assumed that La Tía was the materfamilias. He'd assumed wrong.

Belicia drifted into the living room and sat in the leather armchair Aragón had commanded a few nights before. She nodded at the couch, and Evan crossed the small room and sat. Aragón stayed in the kitchen, out of sight, his fuming palpable.

'Aragón,' she said quietly. And then, a touch louder, '*Mi vida.*'

Aragón flew into sight. 'Don't you dare try to talk me into accepting this. That child – *your* daughter – she had everything. *Everything.* She lived a perfect life!'

In the face of Aragón's fury, Belicia's calm demeanor was even more pronounced. 'Behind these gates.'

'She had everything she could possibly want. Every freedom in the world. Every luxury. Wake up in the morning in a soft bed. Turn on a tap and fresh water pours out. Come downstairs, drink coffee with beans picked where? Kenya? The shaded *pinche* slopes of Guatemala? Shipped here. To our house. Our normal fancy house.' Aragón paced before her on the carpet, reminding Evan of Montesco's caged lion. 'How many bars of soap do we have under the sink? How many boxes of pasta in the pantry? You don't know, do you? Neither do I. Because we don't have to. Because we are living the *actual* dream.'

'Those are things,' Belicia said soothingly, as if to a child.

'Okay. What were her responsibilities? Her only job to better herself with school. To learn. To paint . . . or . . . or to play piano. To flourish. To be loved. No, not just loved – *adored*. Adored by us.'

'It's not about –'

'Her chores? What – she took out the trash once a week just so we could think of something for her to do!' Aragón was shouting at his wife, Evan to the side, forgotten. 'Think of the slums of Neza-Chalco-Izta, forty-five minutes by car from where you grew up. Eighty thousand people per square kilometer. Disease, starvation, drugs. No fresh water. Seven-year-old children raising their younger siblings. Dirt floors, living in sheds, cages no bigger than dog kennels.'

Belicia said, 'Walk to school both ways in the snow –'

'Don't you dare patronize me right now. At this moment –'

'Words, words, words,' Belicia said. 'And talk. So much talk and not about anything that matters. That's what men do, yes?'

'I am warning you, Belicia . . .' Aragón's voice trembled with rage, and in the set of his features Evan could see the fearsome man who'd built a worldwide criminal enterprise.

But Belicia continued, undeterred, 'Aragón, *mi vida*, if you are half the man you tell everyone you are, you would close your mouth and listen to what you *don't* know.'

But he blew right past her, resuming his tirade. 'She could travel anywhere! Pick a man she loved. How many people, how many *girls* in the history of the world have been allowed such freedom? It was perfect here. She had *paradise*.'

Evan said, 'Maybe that's why she did it.'

Aragón stared at him, his mouth literally agape.

'I grew up like you,' Evan said. 'We ground our way out. Maybe she had nowhere to grind. To learn about herself. The world. Maybe this is what she had to do to find her way to herself.'

'You don't even know her.'

'Maybe not. But I've met her. And I've met Reymundo –'

'Don't you speak that fucking name under my roof –'

'– and he's a decent kid. Which says a lot, given where he came from.'

'You're not a father. If you were, you'd understand that you have to be merciless in this world to be good.'

'You think I don't know about being merciless?' Evan said quietly.

Aragón's hands, clenched loosely at his sides, swayed. He stared at Evan, stooped, one shoulder higher, his complexion ruddy. He looked punch-drunk, unmoored.

'You also have to know when to be kind,' Belicia said to Aragón. 'It's the hardest thing a man can ever learn, and most of them never do.'

Aragón swung his head to his wife. Some of the heat had bled out of him, but his tone was still bitter. 'What would you have me do?'

'Everything you need to know, you know already,' Belicia said. 'It just comes down to if you're going to listen.'

'I *am* listening, Belicia.'

'No,' she said. 'You are shouting so you don't have to.'

Aragón's eyes were flared, lots of white, his face flushed as if he'd just finished a sprint. He looked on the verge of losing control, but his words came softly now, even gently. 'Tell me, then,' he said. 'What do you want me to understand?'

'You love that child more than anything on this earth,' Belicia said. 'Including me.'

His face quavered.

'And she has broken your heart,' she continued. 'A father's love for a daughter. How strong is it? What's she worth to you? Not as a thing to preserve but as your daughter? Our Anjelina? Beyond it all? Beneath her foolish choices and our reputation and what she has risked so blindly and callously? Do you love her down to the marrow?'

His mouth bunched. He moved his head very faintly. Up, down.

Somehow Belicia noted this.

'Then should God grant us the blessing of being with our girl again, the only thing to say to her is what you just said to me.' Belicia paused, wet her lips. ' "What do you want me to understand?" '

Aragón exhaled, truly exhaled, for what seemed the first time since Evan had entered the house. His muscles came loose, shoulders melting away from his ears, neck untensing. A landslide of movement, and yet he had barely budged.

And then he was sobbing. Great, wet, gasping sobs, shuddering his frame.

Evan had the sudden sense that he was observing something intimate, something he was not meant to see, and yet neither husband nor wife seemed embarrassed by his presence, and they did not ask him to leave.

Hand over his eyes, Aragón staggered forward like a blind bear.

'I know, *mi vida*.' Belicia held out her arms. 'I know.'

He fell to his knees before her, collapsing into her, clutching around her midsection, face buried in her stomach.

And he wept.

47. Far from Fucking Okay

Aragón's Jeep Wrangler blazed across the craggy terrain of the compound, the sash of the passenger seat belt locking across Evan's torso. Evan found something soothing in the rough drive, bouncing him along across the earth, rocking him soporifically. Aragón presided over the wheel with a confidence just shy of reckless. They'd endured the drive thus far in silence.

They passed between burning pyres, black smoke wafting through the open cabin. It looked like the aftermath of a battle, which in a sense it was. Hundreds of millions of dollars of drugs aflame, an empire in ruin. It remained to be seen what would rise from the ashes.

Twenty minutes prior Evan had retreated upstairs for a shower and a change of clothes, leaving Aragón and Belicia to regroup. When he'd returned, bags packed and ready to go, the energy between the couple was different. Softer, more vulnerable, like flesh freshly healed.

'You hit like a girl,' Aragón finally said.

Evan smirked. 'That was a slap. If I'd punched you, you'd still be lying in your front yard.'

'Between my aunt and my wife, it's like getting pecked to death by ducks,' Aragón said.

'Sounds like you got where you needed to get.'

'With Belicia, yes. She is like a divining rod for bullshit. The best women are. And what can we say in the face of that? "I'm sorry that my deficiencies have caused you pain"? "I'm grateful that the pain you were willing to endure led me to a greater awareness for myself"?' Aragón laughed, shook his head. 'That is the awful, beautiful, sacrificial power of love. We sharpen ourselves against those we love in order to cut ourselves open and see what's inside. Sometimes I wonder if wisdom is nothing more than shortening the time before you realize how ignorant you are about something.'

They rocked up a rise, the Wrangler jogging severely, the plain of the east end of the compound coming into view. It boasted a private runway with a Cirrus Vision Jet. At a hair under $2 million, it was the cheapest private jet, but it sure as hell beat commercial and allowed Evan to skip subjecting $200,000 of carry-on to a security check.

'Humility,' Evan said.

'Yes. And the thing about humility is, you never *have* it. You have to earn it every day. And every single time you embody it, you're tempted away from it. Just take a *little more* credit. Feel a *little bit* superior. Angle that light you're shining a *tiny bit* more on yourself and a *tiny bit* less on the truth you're searching for.'

'You're okay with Anjelina?' Evan asked.

'No,' Aragón said. 'I am far from fucking okay. But I am connected with her again. In my heart.'

'If I can manage to bring her here?' Evan said. 'If I can convince her to come, you'll let her make her own choices?'

'No,' Aragón said. 'But Belicia will convince me, and I will reluctantly listen.'

'And Reymundo?'

Aragón's jaw set. 'Get them here. And I won't castrate him. That's as far as I'm willing to go right now.'

'No castration,' Evan said. 'I'll see what I can do.'

'How are you going to get her out?'

'I'm not sure yet,' Evan said. 'But I need a wide array of weaponry and top-shelf gear.'

'I can get you whatever you need here.'

'No,' Evan said. 'Even you can't do that.'

They drove parallel to the runway now, the ground at last smooth and flat beneath the rugged tires.

'I can't take a run at Montesco's estate,' Evan said. 'Not directly. I'll need to get back inside and see about getting her out. *Them.* Getting them out. I'll have to get them clear of the area, and then I'll need someone standing by for extraction.'

'You'll have my best men.'

A team of trained private military contractors should be sufficient if Evan could escape the estate and surrounding area. The dangerous part would be starting at the heart of Montesco's realm and fighting his way out.

'I'll send you coordinates once I'm close,' Evan said.

Aragón skidded to a halt, the river of dust from their wake mingling with smoke, blowing past the windows, the landscape turned apocalyptic.

Evan started to climb out, but Aragón rested a hand on his leg, halting him.

'As she grew up . . .' Aragón hesitated, cleared his throat. 'I loved that child so much, like an *ache* . . .' It was odd to see him so hesitant, working out his words in advance. 'I got so afraid for what the world might do to her that I pushed her toward the very thing I feared most. I didn't realize it. But now I do. My part in her asinine, self-destructive decisions. And for me to get here, for me to *see*, she needed to break me the way she did. It's all so . . . *jodido*.'

'You can't see unless you let go of everything you think you know,' Evan said.

'Maybe that's all faith is,' Aragon said. 'Whatever you tell yourself to not be controlling.'

Evan climbed out and headed for the plane.

'Hey!'

He turned back.

Aragón rested his elbow on the ledge of the windowsill, looking across the V of his elbow. 'Bring my daughter home to me.'

He drove off before Evan could reply.

The dedicated pilot waited at the top of the rolling set of steps, framed by the clamshell door next to the fuselage. 'Welcome aboard, Mr Nowhere Man.'

Evan ducked to climb aboard. 'No flight plan, nothing in the logbook, fake tail numbers only.'

'As discussed.' The pilot eased into the cockpit, clicking a few of the overhead switches. 'Where to?'

Evan settled into the bolstered executive seat in the front row. 'I need to visit an old friend in Vegas.'

48. One Unsanctioned Individual

When Evan rambled up to the ostensible auto-repair shop at the edge of a desolate desert road on the outskirts of Vegas, he was greeted with the sound of gunfire.

That was generally the sound around here, though Evan had never shown up at six in the morning before.

He parked his third rental car of the week in front of the low-slung building and climbed out. Aragón's pilot was on standby back at the Henderson Executive Airport; Evan knew to show up here alone. Wheeling his carry-ons on either side of him, he picked his way through the engine blocks, tires, and car bodies that formed an automotive garden of sorts in the scrubby brush that passed for a front yard. The gunfire was coming from the rear, so he moved past the heavy metal door, dodging the sight lines of the surveillance cameras and easing along the side of the building.

Behind the auto-repair shop façade, there were no lifts or oil pans or vehicles requiring new brake pads. Instead there were crates of mortars and select-fires. Specialized drill presses, lathes, mills, Dremels, welders, CNC machines, and threading dies to make customized weaponry. And all stripes of ammunition, from armor-piercing to wad-cutters. It was an old-fashioned armorer's lair, part lab, part dungeon, where one of Evan's most trusted contacts developed ghost weapons for numerous sanctioned black-ops groups and for one unsanctioned individual known by code and letter.

As Evan neared the corner, he caught a whiff of cigarette smoke, then heard a few more snaps of gunfire, the sound of shattering glass, and a three-pack-a-day voice singing surprisingly on key, '"Stand, Navy, out to sea, fight our battle cry! We'll never change our course, so vicious foe steer shy-y-y-y!"'

Tommy Stojack reclined in a retro aluminum lawn chair with fraying multicolored straps sun-faded to varying shades of bleached yellow. Roaring the navy's march song, he used what looked like a ray gun from a 1950s science-fiction movie to fire at a half dozen empty Jack Daniel's bottles lined on a flat rock about fifteen yards away.

'Roll out the TNT, anchors aweigh!'

Six bottles of the Tennessee sour mash had already met their maker, reduced to puddles of glass. A nearly empty bottle rested at Tommy's side, and he picked it up, snugging it beneath his bulbous nose to lips framed with a biker's horseshoe mustache. The movement brought Evan into his peripheral vision, and Tommy lowered the bottle, grinning wetly.

'Tommy,' Evan said. 'Got started early this morning?'

'It ain't early, brother. It's just past late.' When Tommy spoke, the Camel Wide bobbed in his mouth as if stapled to his lower lip.

'Been a while.'

'Yeah, well, time flies when you're in a coma.'

Evan drew nearer. 'Is that a . . . Borchardt C-93?'

'Look at you, knowing a thing or two. Not bad for a mouth-breathing trigger puller.' Tommy raised the pistol to the incipient sunlight, admiring it. 'First commercially successful nine-mil semiauto, saw light of day in 1893. Every last one hand-built and hand-fitted. Rough as a corncob, but hell, if you know what you're doing, you can make it go bang. Took me all day to refurb this pea-shooter for a fancy-pants collector who needs every piece in his collection to be

347

functional 'cuz: Rich People. That's why I figured me and Mr Daniel here would have a celebration. Suck down a coupla bottles of loudmouth and see what shakes loose.'

Visibility was low, daybreak threatening, but Tommy lifted the bizarre gun, sighted, and knocked off the next bottle. The two-piece arm of the toggle lock flexed on the recoil, flinging an empty cartridge from the breech. The pistol – and ammo – were not made for accuracy, but no one had told Tommy Stojack that.

'Been shooting all night?' Evan asked.

'Yup. Had a lady drop by in the wee hours, needed a tire changed, found me out here. Poor gal looked like she'd stumbled in on Caligula in the boudoir.'

'It would be shocking, finding a Roman emperor in an eighteenth-century French bedroom.'

'Don't annoy me with your book learning.'

'What'd you do?'

'Changed her damn tire. I ain't gonna leave no damsel in distress.'

Evan lowered himself into the rusting lawn chair beside Tommy. The webbing had frayed, vinyl points poking into him like needles. Tommy slung the bottle Evan's way, brown liquid sloshing inside. 'Want a nip?'

'No thanks.'

'Lemme guess. Nothing but that fancy fruity vodka can touch your pristine lips.'

'Yup. Fancy fruity vodka.'

'What is it you drink again?'

'I'm tired of talking about alcohol this week.'

'Ain't that a first.' Tommy sucked another lungful of smoke, shot it out through the gap in his front teeth, and then spit tobacco juice between his boots. He had a nicotine patch on his neck, two on his arm, and one on the back of his shooting hand. His other hand, the left, was missing a finger – or more precisely half a finger – one of many arcane injuries he'd accrued sometime in his early spec-ops days.

After Evan's penthouse had blown up, he'd stayed with Tommy for a few nights as they arranged the early stages of the rebuild. They'd been the oddest of odd couples, the worst of roommates. Tommy washed dishes only before using them, stored clean laundry in the dryer, and used the bathtub for making moonshine. By the third night, Evan was sleeping outside, where at least the dirt was where it was supposed to be. By the fourth his OCD drove him to a hotel on the Strip.

'How's sugarbritches doing?' Tommy said. 'That girl. Frankie?'

Tommy knew her name. He was immensely fond of Joey but refused to admit it.

'Joey,' Evan said. 'She wants to go on a road trip. By herself.'

'Dangerous world out there.'

'That's what I'm trying to tell her.'

'I mean, dangerous world for everyone else if a girl like her gets turned loose. Gimme a heads-up if that one makes it out in the wild.' Tommy smirked. 'I'll retreat to my bomb shelter.' He raised the gun once more and knocked off the next bottle. 'So I assume you didn't swing by for parental advice or whatever the hell you'd call it.'

'No.'

'Drove down from LA?'

'Private jet.'

'Whose?'

'Cartel guy.'

'Oh,' Tommy said. 'Mission?'

'To knock off a different cartel guy.'

'You are one complicated former whatever-the-fuck.'

'I contain multitudes.'

'What's the drill?'

'Gear for an exfil. I'm undercover. With the different cartel guy.'

'Which cartel?'

'Leones.'

'Undercover in the Leones?' Tommy whistled. 'Could you be more eager to punch yourself in the dick?'

'After this mission I'm swearing off self-dick-punching.'

'Tell me some about this Mongolian clusterfornication you've got yourself up into.'

Evan sketched the details of the mission, leaving out particulars.

When he finished, Tommy scowled, mustache bristling. 'I hate those cartel sadists with their thug armies and private castles. All flash and bling and crybully cruelty. Uday Hussein gold-plated toilets, holding their chrome-plated guns sideways like kids in one-a them rap videos.'

'A rap video, huh?'

'You know what I mean. So yeah, I'll help you give that motherfucker a habanero enema.'

'That's touching in a racist kind of way.'

'What do you need?'

'Tunnel security. The good shit.'

Tommy looked offended. 'I only deal in the good shit. This look like a Radio Shack?'

'No. It looks like a junkyard for disused Radio Shack gear.'

'Well, hell. You want a pretty face, talk to an LA waiter.'

Tommy aimed and squeezed, and another Jack Daniel's bit the dust. An alertness had returned to his hound-dog eyes. Over the years Evan had learned that no matter how much

350

Tommy drank, he was always one serious conversation away from sober.

'Now,' Tommy said. 'I got me some microsurveillance tech outta Haifa. Waterproof, high-res, impossible to spot, lens the size a' the head of a pin. Hide 'em in a real pebble, hollowed out. Salesguy paraded out a sample at Shot Show, buried one in a real quarter, sliced in half and put back together. The camera was George Washington's eye. Dude was so excited to show it off he shoulda been tripod-mounted.'

'Vivid imagery.'

'We aim to please. I also got fusion sensors with traditional IR night vision and thermal, both technologies in the same tube. Cool thing about those puppies is they can scan a pitch-black area with zero ambient IR, let you see inside the devil's asshole. Small, too – four inches by an inch and a half.'

'Weight?'

'Real light. About the same as one and a half loaded 1911 magazines.' Tommy measured most items in munition units.

'Okay. But all that stuff? It's a ploy. For what I really need to smuggle in.'

'Which is?'

Evan pulled a crumpled cocktail napkin from a cargo pocket. On the flight in, he'd jotted down his wish list and then taken a quick nap.

'I need these delivered in a utility van to this address.' Evan tapped the napkin, where he'd written the location of the Hertz rental lot in Guaridón. 'Stored beneath a false bottom in the cargo hold. All the tunnel tech goes above on full display. They're just props.'

Tommy reviewed the list of weaponry, tugging at his mustache, a devious smile edging his lips. '*Now* you're lighting candles in my church.'

'Van's gotta be lifted, but not so much to be noticeable. Oversize tires will be less obvious than giant shock absorbers.'

'When do you need to get your dickskinners on all this gear?'

'Tomorrow noon.'

Tommy laughed. He finger-scooped the wedge of tobacco from his lower lip and flung it into the dirt. 'That's a hard no fucking way. I can't lasso all that gear, custom up the van, and have it waiting in the dead center of Cartelsville in' – he shot his wrist clear of a nonexistent cuff, glanced at a nonexistent watch – 'thirty hours.'

'I'll give you until end of day.'

'Another five whole hours? You're the picture of charity.' Tommy cocked his head, chewed a lip, considering. 'Friday five o'clock, Guaridón. That's a big ask on top of a big ask. How you gonna pay for it?'

'I'm not.' Evan nodded at the two carry-ons. 'He is.'

Tommy sucked down another half inch of cigarette and flicked it into the sand. 'Making a man pay for his own execution. Tell ya what, I'll make that cargo van black, match the color of your heart.'

'Thanks, Tommy.'

'Hell, there's a pregnant broad riding on it. Who am I to stand in the way of your redemption story?'

Evan let that one go.

'Can you trust him?' Tommy asked. 'Her old man? The first cartel guy?'

'Not really a cartel guy,' Evan said. 'More like an unconventional businessman.'

'Well, doesn't that sound like a load of shit.' Tommy shrugged. 'Answers the question, though.'

'He's not all the way right,' Evan said. 'But he's right in the right ways.'

Tommy nodded soberly. 'Ain't that all of us. Tuned to different frequencies. This one's gotta have two-point-three drinks a night to get right, and that one's gonna heist an armored car 'cuz he needs to learn or die from the punishment. *He* works a hundred twenty hours a week on the stock exchange, *she* takes meds, pumps out crumbsnatchers, and waits for that five-o'clock chardonnay. Whether we shoot up or fuck up, we're all in the same bathtub. But it's nice now and again when you find someone hums the same tune as you and rows the same direction.' He hoisted the bottle and tipped it to Evan in a toast. 'That's the only shelter in this wondrous, nasty world. The only thing that matters. Everything else is just wainscoting.'

Evan made a noise of affirmation in his throat.

Tommy offered him the gun. 'Wanna take a shot?'

'I'm good.'

'Look at that. There. See that sun coming up? Is there anything makes your heart ache more than a desert sunrise?'

Evan took in the sight. Glorious purples and oranges shaded with pastels. The kinds of hues he forgot nature could make until he remembered that nature made everything. It called to mind Peter's crayon colors, Atomic Tangerine and Wild Blue Wonder, all the everything. Which led to thoughts of Mia and her neurosurgery consult, mere hours away. Another outcome that could turn a family's world upside down in a hot second.

So much beauty out there. And so much pain.

The two men soaked it in, each with his private thoughts.

'Man,' Tommy said, 'what I'd give to be sitting here with a chunky round-faced brunette with bangs right now instead of your skinny ass.'

'Skinny? And here I've been doing power squats and everything.'

Tommy admired the slender barrel of the pistol, that cerebellum bulge of the recoil spring housing. 'Know what "sin" means? I mean, the root or etymology or whateverthefuck?'

Evan thought back to his lessons with Jack in the study, flickering orange light from the fireplace, smell of peat wafting off Jack's old-fashioned glass. 'It's Greek, isn't it? *Hamartia.*'

'That's the one. From *hamartanō*. Now, why would a knuckle-dragger like me know a ten-dollar word like that?'

'Because it's an archery term.'

'That's right.' Tommy smiled big. 'Means, "to miss the mark." That's what we do when we sin. We miss the mark. And I been thinking out here alone these past few nights, just me and the mosquitoes, that maybe that's why I do what I do all these years. Why I became a marksman. To aim right. Aim true. And maybe that's why *you* do what *you* do. These bleeding-heart missions of yours. Trying to hit the mark. Trying to get one goddamned thing right for once. It may all be FUBAR'd out there, but a bullet? A bullet flies straight if you treat it right. And with all the mess and mayhem in this goddamned world, even you, Orphan X, can fly straight once in a blood moon.'

It was the first time Tommy had ever used Evan's code name. They'd always dodged direct questions about their respective pasts, Tommy allowing Evan the fiction that he didn't know – *really* know – who he was. But something about the early-morning light and the sour mash allowed a loosening of the screws, a sense that what was spoken here, in the pale blue glow of real Vegas, would stay in Vegas.

Tommy brought the Borchardt up and squeezed off three quick shots, all of them bull's-eyes. He eyed the last bottle standing, then let his gaze lift to the horizon.

Then he tapped the barrel against Evan's forearm. 'When's

the last time you held history in your hands? Come on. Give it a go.'

Evan took the Borchardt C-93 and lined the iron sights at the lonely bottle of Jack. He eased out an exhale. Waited for the space between heartbeats. Fired.

And missed.

Tommy took another glug from the bottle, patted Evan's knee. 'Maybe next time instead of power squats, young Padawan, you should get your damn eyes checked.'

49. Blech

Evan sat on the floor with his back to door 12B of Castle Heights. He didn't know how long a neurosurgeon's consultation should take, but Mia's appointment was at ten and it was already past one o'clock. A long time in a neurosurgeon's office didn't make for optimism.

He was drifting off when the elevator dinged and a cacophony of voices spilled out. Here came the family, lumbering toward him, Mia's face tight and stoic, Peter glazed, Wally red-eyed from crying, and Janet looking meek and defeated.

Evan popped to his feet as they descended on him.

Mia moved past him, fumbled her keys into the dead bolt. 'I thought you were out of the country.'

She scarcely looked at him, but he could tell she wasn't upset with him; she was barely holding it together.

'I'm back.'

The door opened, and Peter bounded into his room and slammed the door behind him.

They'd all sort of tumbled into the condo, and the adults now stood awkwardly around the wooden kitchen table, Mia leaning on a chair back as if for support, arms locked.

Wally and Janet looked stricken.

Janet said, 'It'll all be okay, Mia –'

'Janet? No. Okay? Just . . . no.' Mia was shaking her head.

Wally scratched his nose, looking down. 'We . . . uh, should give you and Peter some space. Rest up, and uh, uh . . .' His voice was wavering.

'Is there anything we can do?' Janet pleaded. 'Give us something to do.'

'You don't need to do anything, sweetie,' Mia said.

Janet's lips were trembling. 'Just – please – tell me something to do.'

'Okay,' Mia said. 'After the surgery everyone from the office is gonna be overly helpful and bring too much food by, and I don't want Peter eating a bunch of frozen *casseroles*.' She emphasized the noun like it was a curse word. 'Okay? I want him to eat healthy. And not all leftovers, you know? When Roger and I got married, we drove to Niagara Falls for a kind of ironic throwback honeymoon, and his mom sent us off with a Honey Baked ham. I've always thought that's the definition of eternity: two people and a ham. So if you can make sure he's eating well, that will give me one less thing to worry about. Okay?'

Janet bunched a fist over her mouth, nodded rapidly.

Wally looked on the verge of collapse. 'I really think we should give you some space, sis.'

'Okay, Wally. I'd like that.' They embraced, and Wally sobbed into her shoulder a minute and said, 'Sorry.'

'It's okay.'

'Sorry.'

'It's okay.'

'Sorry.'

'Enough.'

Mia pulled back and managed a tremulous smile, and then Wally and Janet were gone and it was just Evan and Mia in the sudden silence of the condo.

Emotions were still swirling in the air, tangible enough to grab. Grief and fear, thick like a scent. Evan did what he often did, throwing up a filter, compressing the situation into boundaries that could be contended with, a set of challenges to be confronted. He needed facts and figures, and from them he would determine a battle plan.

He said, 'I'm going to assume the news wasn't good.'

'That is a fair assessment.' Mia took a breath, held it. Big exhale that puffed out her cheeks. 'Could be worse, though.'

Evan said, 'Diagnosis?'

'Cavernous hemangioma. A bleed. It's not so much *what* it is as *where* it is. Dead center of the corpus callosum, millimeters from the fornices, which is the memory center.'

She seemed relieved to be talking facts. Evan knew it, too, the comfort of hard numbers, of staring a threat in the teeth unblinkingly.

'Requires a craniotomy,' she said. 'Cut a hatch in the skull and drill right down through my brain.'

'Prognosis?'

'Fifteen percent or so I die on the table. Thirty I suffer permanent short-term memory loss. Like: In two years I'll wake up every morning and still think Peter's nine. And in ten years. And twenty. Maybe even every hour, every fifteen minutes, I'll have to rediscover his real age and then figure out how to catch up to it. Not to mention what *he'll* have to figure out. So I'd prefer the fifteen percent to the thirty actually, but I don't get to choose.' Her eyebrows hoisted, a there-you-have-it punctuation. 'So yeah. It sucks.'

'Like ham and casserole.'

A hint of a smile. 'Like ham and casserole.'

'Date?'

'Monday. My mom had heart stuff, so I take a baby aspirin a day. I stopped today because: anticoagulant. They can't wait for it to clear my bloodstream entirely – too pressing – but wanted to give it at least four days. Assuming I don't get all gorked out by then. Are you . . . ?'

'What?'

She bit her lower lip, rolled it between her teeth. 'I don't know if you're . . . out of the country again. I think it might be good for Peter if . . . Shit, I don't know.'

'I will try to be back.'

'You'll try to be back.'

'Yes.'

'What you're into. It's life-or-death?'

'It is.'

'Right. Right. It always is.'

'But so is this.'

'Yes,' she said. 'So is this.'

She kept her hands clenched on the chair back, the table between them, like she was walling herself off from him, the world. A tilt of her chin toward Peter's closed door. 'Would you like to see him?'

He had to be back in Guaridón, but it was clear she needed him here. What was more important? A pregnant young woman in the hands of the Leones? Or a terrified single mother and her nine-year-old boy? This was the kind of math he did not do. How was he supposed to balance these scales? He reached for the Seventh Commandment for guidance: *One mission at a time.*

Evan said, 'No.'

She stared at him. 'Okay.' She started to say something else, hesitated, caught herself.

There was a fragility in the air between them, as if they were both aware that they were embarking on the type of conversation that was outside the purview of their relationship. And that they'd have to tread lightly in case they broke something that couldn't be put back together.

'Here we go.' Mia took a deep breath. 'All the things I like you for aren't the things you think I like you for.'

'My matinee-idol looks?'

Another near smile. 'No. And not your two-percent body fat, which is nice sometimes but mostly annoying – like, eat a cheeseburger. The thing is, I know what you're made of. I know what you're capable of. I've caught a glimpse of it. But you have no idea what *I'm* capable of. And I am going to get through this alive. For Peter.'

'I believe you.'

'*But.* All my rah-rah, go-me, I'm-gonna-beat-this-thing energy? I can't afford to indulge it when it comes to Peter. So I have to steel myself to make sure I get through while making plans for that little boy' – the first quiver in her voice – 'in the event that I don't. Do you understand?'

'Perfectly.'

'Right. You're good at this because it involves danger and menace.'

'Yes,' he said. 'I am.'

'Wally and Janet get custody of Peter if . . . ya know. You've met my brother. He has a great heart and I love him to the bone. But he's a dipshit.'

' "Dipshit" might be harsh.'

' "Dipshit" is charitable. And I'm worried Wally might not have everything Peter needs.'

'I have money,' Evan said. 'I will make sure Peter *never* ends up in a foster home.'

The words came out in a burst, with an intensity he scarcely recognized as something he possessed.

Mia was staring at him, surprised and – it seemed – moved. She knew nothing of his past, and he realized he'd just opened a window into the core of himself.

'I have money, Evan,' she said gently. 'It's not about money.'

'Okay.' He was trying to recover, backpedaling within himself. 'What . . . what's it about, then?'

'You're a . . . hmm. A gentleman. And there aren't a lot of places young boys can look and see gentlemen these days.'

'I'm not a gentleman.'

'You prove my point. And. I'd like you to be there for Peter. Emotionally.'

The sound went out. For a moment Evan only heard white noise and the *thump-thump-thump* of his heart. He knew that words were required, but they were out of reach. He had no idea what he was feeling or how to direct those sensations into sentences.

Mia watched him with patience. And what looked like kindness.

'You have to raise a kid to have trust that the world will treat him fairly,' she said. 'Then maybe he'll have enough trust to get through when it doesn't. And I don't want . . .' She tilted her head back, eyes pulling to the ceiling, holding the brimming tears in. 'I don't want him to ever need comfort and not find it.'

'That's not what I do,' Evan said.

'What?'

'Comfort.'

'You do. More than you think.'

'This is too big a responsibility for you to risk being wrong.'

'I'm taking that risk,' she said. 'I'm playing the odds as is, letting them, ya know, cut my head open.'

'If I promise to do something,' he said. 'I do it. Every time. I don't know that I can do this. So I can't promise it.'

'I'm not asking for a promise. I'm laying my potentially last wish on you and leaving it up to your sense of duty. Which means you at least have to try.'

'How does someone *try* something like that?'

She thought about it. 'A lot of people have good intentions but the wrong words. And you can fight them on the wrong

361

words all day without seeing through to their intentions. Like you. If I just paid attention to your words, I never would've let you into my bedroom. And my . . . shit, I guess my heart. *Blech.*' She stuck out her tongue. 'I'm shockingly not good at this.' Another breath. 'But what I mean is, with kids, with Peter, he has the wrong words sometimes. What he says he needs. What he thinks he wants. You have to see beneath that. To what his intentions are. Because that boy?' Another quiver. 'He's got the purest intentions of anyone I know.'

Evan nodded.

She said, 'And . . .'

'And?'

'When there's a kid around, you have to try to be the best version of yourself. Me. But you, too, now.'

'Of myself?'

'Yes. Like, you suck at asking for help. I can't be mad at you for that. But I sure want to be sometimes. And . . . I don't want Peter to grow up like that. Not asking for help. Don't put that on him. He's a boy. He'll get that enough. I want him to be . . . healthier.' She wasn't crying, but there was a deep sadness in her words and great respect for Evan as well in her stating boldly what needed to be boldly stated. 'I want him to be better than you.'

Evan said, 'Me, too.'

She nodded. 'Don't hug me, please. A hug would wreck me right now.' She glanced to Peter's closed bedroom door. 'I need to go talk with him. And then just *be* with him. As much as I can.'

'I understand.'

Evan started out, hesitated. Looked back at her. 'I'll do everything I can to be here for your surgery.'

She summoned a sad smile that crinkled the edges of her eyes. 'Thank you, Mr Danger.'

She started toward Peter's room.

Pausing halfway out the front door, Evan watched her walk across the living room. She set her hand on the doorknob, head lowered. Paused. Two seconds. Three. Four. Her hunched shoulders rose as she took a deep breath. Settled back lower than they'd been.

He watched her enter her son's room, then eased out of her condo.

Halfway down the hall, the door to the trash room was ajar. The soporific voice of Hugh Walters echoed inside the walls. '– need to ensure that the chute width is up to code, as specified in section eighty-two of the NFPA's waste- and linen-handling systems.'

At the sound of the HOA president's voice, Evan clenched his teeth hard enough to engender an ache in his molars.

Assessing the open-door threat, he made a threshold evaluation, moving to a tactical stride. Light on his Original S.W.A.T. boots, he hugged the near wall to minimize exposure. He zipped by silently, padding to the elevator, finger extended to punch the up button, when –

'Mr Smoak!'

Evan stared at the elevator doors. Freedom, mere inches away.

He turned to see Hugh striding toward him, clipboard in hand.

There was nothing in the world Evan wanted to see less right now than Hugh Walters with a clipboard.

Farther down the hall, a repairman stared after Hugh with exhausted dismay before withdrawing his turtle head into the trash room.

Hugh closed in on Evan like a self-guided missile. 'I'm glad I caught you, Mr Smoak. I feel that you and I got off on the wrong foot and never really found . . . well, I suppose the *right* foot.'

'I don't actually have any issues I need to –'

'The thing is, here at Castle Heights the buck stops with me. When the trash chute is two inches too narrow. When there's a cricket infestation in the garage. When there are service-animal provisions that must be updated.'

'About that, I don't really require a –'

'And . . . well, this really isn't very kind to say, but sometimes I get quite frustrated with our fellow tenants.'

'I can't imagine what that's like.'

'I know I'm considered a bit of a hard-ass around these parts.' A self-satisfied chuckle. 'But every time I'm tempted to judge someone for wanting environmentally friendly coffee filters in the lobby or asking to replace our perfectly suitable social-room chairs or having goddamned allergies' – Hugh paused, breathing hard, his face shiny, eyes huge behind the Coke-bottle lenses – 'I stop and ask myself, I wonder what they're feeling that I'm not? I wonder what vulnerabilities or worries they're dealing with that I know nothing about?'

Hugh tapped the clipboard against his thigh, a show of emotional agitation. He was pushing himself here, getting out of his comfort zone. Evan couldn't help but have a shred of admiration for that.

Hugh continued, 'And . . . well, I want to tell you that I've waived the preregistration requirements for service animals. Because . . . well, I guess what I'm saying is, I don't know what worries you might have that I don't know about, Mr Smoak.'

Evan stared at him, dumbfounded. 'I appreciate that.'

Hugh tipped his head in a nod. Evan saw him for the first time as an actual person rather than a self-created caricature.

Hugh had always seemed one of those people who'd decided on a persona early in life and worn it so long and so rigidly that he'd forgotten he was anything else. But now Evan found himself wondering at Hugh's inner life. What did he think about before he fell asleep at night? Did he need his clipboards and regulations the way Evan needed his missions and Comandments, because they gave him a sense of order, of purpose?

'I know I'm not as interesting as some of the folks who live here,' Hugh said. 'You probably feel that way, too.'

Evan matched his confiding look.

'But . . . well, I'm *reliable*,' Hugh said. 'And reliability might be considered . . . *unsexy* out there these days. But when someone is struggling with their allergies or anxiety, when they've lost faith that the rules will hold, that they can count on what to expect from the world, that they'll be dealt a fair hand . . . I guess what I'm saying is that when they've lost *trust*, I want to be the one who can restore that for them.' He lowered his eyes and nodded a few times, as if only now agreeing with what he'd just said. 'Do you understand?'

For the first time, Evan dropped any pretense of his cover. He felt like himself, his true self, answering an honest question with an honest answer. 'I do.'

Hugh offered his hand.

Evan shook it.

50. Human Eye Juice

Inside the Vault, Evan parked himself behind his sheet-metal desk and called up the OLED screens covering the walls. Various windows had been left open, providing a history of Joey's latest searches. Countless crime reports, articles, and internal DEA documents on Raúl Montesco. Even more on the tentacles of the Leones operation. And a number of failed inquiries for Jacob Baridon.

Evan's biological father.

Joey had continued looking into this even after their altercation. Despite the fact that he didn't want to pursue finding out more about his father, he took a moment to think beneath her words to her intentions and was momentarily undone.

He called up an encrypted videotelephony app that she had installed for him – her fingerprints were all over his life – and dialed her.

After two rings the screens wallpapering the front wall rendered her life-size before him.

In her pod of a hacking station. Camo pants. Bare feet up by the keyboard. Sleeveless tank top showing off the defined muscles of her arms.

No smile.

On the circular ledge of the desk encompassing her were various keyboards, a number of speed-hacking cubes, a Big Gulp, and a half-eaten hot dog with an excess of mustard.

She crossed her arms. Glared at him.

'Hear that?' she said.

'What?'

'That's the sound of me not talking to you.'

'I apologized.'

'Yes. You did. Now, if you'll excuse me, I'd like to get back to enjoying what little freedom my overlord allows.'

'Is there a version where we ...'

'Where we *what*?'

'I don't know. Talk this out?'

'You? Talk something out emotionally?' She stiffened up and gave him Robot Arms and Robot Voice, one of her many preferred means of impersonating him. 'Me am Orphan X. Me want to have conversation about feeling states of living organism. But me Cylon programming is not enabled to compute human eye juice.'

'What's a Cylon?'

Robot Voice continued, 'I lack knowledge of all things pop cultural. This is another infuriating trait that makes me feel superior to my human counterparts.'

'*Josephine.*'

At the sound of his voice, Dog the dog padded over into Joey's workstation and stuck his snout up into the frame. His big tail was wagging, audibly thwacking the curve of desk behind him.

Joey scratched his scruff, her voice softening. 'Who's a sweet boy? You want a bite?'

She offered him the remaining half of her hot dog, which he scarfed down.

'You know,' Evan said, 'you don't have to feed him *every time* you eat.'

She pinned him with a bruised expression. 'See? That's so *you*. Not thinking about it from his perspective.'

'The dog's perspective?'

'*Yes!* Think how friggin' pissed you'd be if someone ate all kinds of food in front of you and you had to eat the same

367

canned crap over and over. Like, you have no opposable thumbs and can't get, like, your *own* food for yourself 'cuz you've been taken out of nature into a world of opposable-thumb privilege. And this selfish a-hole buys whatever she wants and opens it up with, like, her superior digits, and it smells all delicious, and she can't even spare a scrap? Oh – and by the way, you *bred* me to be, like, super loving and loyal, I mean, I'm *literally* evolutionarily designed to *have to* be nice to you, like, it's *in my DNA* to not kill you and take your food, but hey, tough shit and just sit there and watch me eat, 'cuz, screw you, right? You want to raise a dog with dignity. Not just to *obey*. See, that's what you still don't get, X. Sometimes you have to take care of people the way *they* want to be taken care of.'

'Dogs.'

'Huh?'

'You mean *dogs*. Sometimes you have to take care of *dogs* the way they want to be taken care of.'

'That's what I *said*.'

Click.

Once again he was alone in the Vault, but Joey's hostile absence made alone feel lonelier. Just him and the history of her digital meanderings, including a search for the father he'd never known and didn't care to know. He thought again of his half brother out there, whom he still hadn't reconnected with since the last mission. And his half brother's daughter. Which would make her Evan's . . . what? His niece?

I have a niece, he thought.

He'd never met her in person. He had a not-really-significant-other heading into a life-threatening surgery. Her nine-year-old son whom he not-really mentored. Aragón and Belicia Urrea who were not-really friends. Their daughter, not-really a client. And Joey, his not-really niece-person who *was* really angry with him.

It wasn't hard to see that he was the common denominator of all this not-really-ness.

He looked to the side of his mouse pad where Vera II used to sit. Her vacancy was disconcerting. He shoved back from the desk and walked pointedly to the kitchen, doing his best to ignore the Velcro wall and the mirrored globe dangling overhead. He'd deal with them later.

No signs of life yet from the living wall, but Vera III was there on the island in the glass salad bowl where he'd left her. She lay on her side, roots splayed, bereft of pebbles to take hold of.

He straightened her up to restore for her a bit of dignity. Fed her an ice cube.

To meet Tommy's shipment, he had to be at the Hertz office in Guaridón by tomorrow at 5:00 P.M. Aragón's pilot would meet him at the Santa Monica Airport at oh-dark-hundred, which would give him plenty of time to get back to Eden and from there across the border in the rented Chevrolet Matiz.

That gave him one night at home.

Instinctively, his gaze moved to the freezer room. Joey'd had the armored sunscreen shades installed, though they were drawn up beneath their inset housing, leaving a breathtaking view of Los Angeles at night. The city lights shone through the armored glass and the panes of the freezer room, silhouetting the bottles of vodka with their sultry curves.

But with everything going on here, in Eden, in Guaridón, he had to stay sharp.

Back to the master suite, averting his eyes once more so as not to let in the Velcro rise to his side and the disco ball above.

Out of his clothes, into the shower. He used Dr Bronner's Magic Soap to scour his body, the peppermint variety that made his skin tingle. Back to the bedroom, into a pair of boxer briefs, up onto the floating mattress.

Wait. His bed.

He stared down past the edge of the levitating slab of metal at the floor three feet below. Neodymium rare-earth magnets and steel cables created a push-pull effect that held his bed suspended in thin air. He'd climbed right onto the hovering unit without noticing that it had been restored.

Another task accomplished by Joey in a wholly implausible time frame. Everywhere he looked, it seemed he was being confronted with evidence of her competence and self-sufficiency.

But still. An unchaperoned road trip.

No way.

He had one night to sleep before his return to the baking heat of Guaridón with its caged victims and human-eating lions and men unshackled from the laws of civilization.

In a few hours' time, he'd start his journey into the heart of darkness. Already he'd rehearsed the exfiltration in his mind's eye dozens of times, making adjustments, running iterations, each wrong turn or hesitation leading to a bullet in the head, his skin flayed from his body, the air choked from his lungs in a concrete-filled oil drum. Every last scenario ended in death.

His death. Anjelina's death. Reymundo's. The unborn baby's.

Every last scenario.

Except one.

To pull this off, Evan couldn't merely be excellent.

He'd have to be perfect.

He had to find the place within himself where he ceased to exist, where he yielded to instinct and muscle memory and neural pathways, where'd he'd run the mission so many times that it was rote, grounded not in thinking but in habit, where he could slow it down to a snail's pace or manage it on fast forward, where he could conduct it blind or see it through despite a fatal injury.

The Second Commandment: *How you do anything is how you do everything.*

He veiled his eyes, not quite open, not quite closed, until the world turned to a gauzy fog of half-light. It took a solid ten minutes for him to find his breath properly, to feel where it expanded the floor of his stomach, his ribs, until it rose up to press out the space beneath his clavicles. In the single inhalation filling his body, there were more air molecules than there were grains of sand on every beach on earth. A miracle and a wonder in every mundane instant. Just a man suspended twenty-one stories above the ground and three feet above that, breathing in until he became the air and the air became him, until he was merely a respiring organism in the whole of the universe, which itself was fire and gas and blackness pricked by points of light, the entire weightless mass expanding and contracting like the walls of his own lungs.

He narrowed his focus to the hazy band of the Milky Way.

Zoomed in on the solar system.

Flew past the sun, Mercury, Venus, to the blue mossy ball tinged with white.

Zeroed in on North America.

Vectored to the West Coast.

The hanging chad of California.

Closed in on the southern half of the state.

Los Angeles flying up at him.

Down, down into West LA.

The Wilshire Corridor.

Through the roof of Castle Heights.

His penthouse.

The walls of the master bedroom.

The four corners of his mattress.

His body, all of it, the shape and sound and feel of 30 trillion cells structured and harmonized, breathed into life by the air moving through them.

He was here and there.

He was omnipresent and impalpable.

Everywhere and nowhere.

The Nowhere Man.

And he was ready for the horrors that tomorrow promised to hold.

51. Professional Courtesy

At 4:57 P.M., Evan picked up the cargo van, black as promised, from the curb adjacent to Hertz. A homeless guy stinking of tequila lay slumped against the oversize front tire, tattered cowboy hat pulled over his eyes.

Evan roused him, a gentle tap of his boot against the guy's sandaled foot.

Before the soft kick connected, the guy rolled onto his feet with surprising grace and stared at Evan with clear brown eyes. 'Tommy said to tell you, "Don't miss the mark,"' he said, then dropped a single car key into Evan's palm and shuffled away.

Evan climbed into the cargo hold, which was grubby, a few oil spills, grime at the seams, an amoeba of hardened chewing gum on the floor in the corner. He took a moment to change into the clothes he'd requested. They looked like what he'd worn for the bulk of the mission, facial-recognition-thwarting pattern on the button-up, tactically discreet cargo pants with streamlined inner pockets. A number of Pelican crates held the surveillance gear he'd ordered.

But the clothes and the security equipment weren't what mattered.

What mattered was what was hidden beneath the false bottom of the cargo hold.

Forty-five minutes later, he pulled beneath the giant carved monkeys of the grand archway. The chicken coop looked empty, each cell showing only a band of late-day sunlight near the bars, the invisible inhabitants pulled back into the shade like overheated zoo animals. He double-checked the position of the decoy sewer grates and storm drains along the driveway and gardens as he had those leading into the estate, then noted the positions of the guards.

Sure enough his favorite *sicario* was waiting at the portico, arms crossed.

Evan edged off the driveway and parked half over a disused flower bed. Rolling down the passenger window, he caught a waft of jasmine and could hear rats scurrying in the gardens, awaiting their next feast.

'The hell kind of parking job is this, *gabacho*?' Darling Boy asked, approaching.

'Lotta valuable gear in here,' Evan said, climbing out. 'I don't want one of you idiots clipping the van on your way in.'

'Don't move.' Darling Boy stopped Evan with a spread hand, spun him around less gently than was warranted, and frisked him from the ankles up, groping at his crotch with brisk, pragmatic intent. '*Jefe* is smart enough to forbid you having weapons in the house.'

Evan turned around, holding his arms wide. 'He made that clear to me.'

'Well, *I'm* making it clear, too. Open the back.'

Evan unlocked the rear door, and Darling Boy climbed up and in. He examined the interior carefully, his sunken eyes picking across every crack and fissure, his foot tapping beside the blackened disk of gum. Then he opened and studied the gear in every last Pelican case. Finally he climbed through to the front and searched the seats, the glove box, the center console.

He wormed back out to where Evan leaned against the side of the van, face tilted to the sun, soaking in some vitamin D. 'Find anything interesting?'

'Not yet,' Darling Boy said, and headed into the mansion.

Evan locked up the van and entered.

The lean, jittery guard named Nacho greeted Evan in the foyer with a lowered MP7 and a hot glare.

'*Jefe* wants to see you,' Nacho said. 'In his bedroom.'

Evan started back.

'You should know,' Nacho called after him, 'that you are hated here.' He had hungry, sullen features, gold-framed sunglasses pushed up into his glossy hair. Hand loose at his belt, thumb tucked behind the grenade pouch. And those fucking teeth, like a mole rat's. 'You've been whispering poison in *Jefe*'s ear. Making him paranoid. About us. But he should not be paranoid about us. He should be paranoid about you.'

'Ah,' Evan said. 'One of Darling Boy's men.'

'Darling Boy has been with *Jefe* for seventeen years. Darling Boy recruited most of us. We are *all* Darling Boy's men. And we will wait for you to stumble.'

'Careful that you don't get hurt first,' Evan said. 'While you're waiting.'

He padded down the corridor, passing the first set of spiraling stairs and ascending the second. Montesco's suite was at the end of the corridor, double doors thrown wide, the sounds of vigorous sex issuing out.

Evan stood in the doorway. A giant picture window overlooked the pool and cabana. The bed was enormous, two king-size mattresses set side by side, the furniture modern and overly sleek, lacquered woods and shiny chrome fittings.

Montesco was entangled with five or so women, a confusing, squirming mass of limbs and flesh. Evan tried to do the math in his head and failed.

A burly guard stood against the far wall, hand gripping opposite wrist by his waist, classic bodyguard position. His MP7 was slung, his eyes averted, expression impassive.

Evan cleared his throat.

Montesco's head popped up from the scrum. It took some effort for him to extricate himself, and then he shooed the women out. They gathered their clothes on the way, brushing past Evan. Their cheeks were flushed, but their manner was bored, businesslike, a construction crew leaving for lunch break. The guard didn't move. He might as well have been painted on the wall.

Montesco came at Evan, glistening and naked, his left nostril powdered with white, tattooed lion gazing out from his inner arm. 'Did you find the third shooter?'

'No. But I have a lead on him. My associate is still working to track him down. In the meantime I wanted to get back here to safe the estate.'

'I told you to bring me his head.' Montesco slid a flat hand beneath his nose, wiping the excess. The room smelled of sweat and sex. 'I want him dead.'

'And he will be. I'm prioritizing your safety.'

'You have the gear you promised?'

'I do.'

'Has Darling Boy checked it all?'

'Proctologically.'

At this the Dark Man cracked a smile. 'You told me to trust no one. I am taking your advice seriously. I may like you, Caballo Oscuro, but you are still new to me. And my men, they are not taking to you.'

'It's not my job to be liked.' It took some effort for Evan not to acknowledge Montesco's nakedness. 'It's my job to protect you, even against your own men. Like Jovencito.'

'What do you need of me now?'

'I want to check the escape tunnels and hatches for hostile surveillance gear and explosives. Vehicles, too – I want to sweep them, make sure that there are no tracking devices or explosives. Then I want to install additional security measures.'

Montesco nodded a few times rapidly, rooting in the heap of pillows on the floor and blessedly coming up with a bathrobe. Yanking open a drawer on the Hollywood Regency mirrored nightstand, he withdrew a lighter and a crack cigarette. 'Darling Boy will oversee you.'

Evan felt his body heat tick up a half degree. The first hitch in the plan he'd mentally rehearsed a few hundred times.

'We don't like each other,' Evan said. 'Obviously. It's close-quarters work. I move fast, I move efficiently, and I move alone.'

Montesco swung his head around, freshly lit stick between his lips. 'I don't give a fuck what you want. This is how it will go. Tomorrow morning you can start.' That too-wide mouth stretched into an off-kilter smile. 'Try'n relax for once. Take a woman to your suite. Take two.'

'I'm good,' Evan said. 'I want to interview the girl again. See if she remembers anything about Jovencito she didn't mention before. Maybe she saw something I didn't. Could help lead to the third shooter.'

Montesco held an inhale as he spoke, the words an airless screech. 'You said you were closing in on the third shooter.'

'I'd like to close in quicker.' Evan hesitated, for the first time unsure of his status here.

Montesco's bloodshot eyes moved to his guard. The burly man returned the look, a flicker of shared suspicion.

'It's fine,' Evan said. 'I'm tired anyway. I'm happy to deal with it when I get back to LA.'

'No.' Montesco smiled, let the smoke leak through his teeth. 'If you can squeeze more information out of her, do it.'

As Evan withdrew, his sense of unease intensified. His absence had left room for Darling Boy to sow distrust, for paranoia to swell. He could only hope he had enough time before the wave broke. He'd be watched every step of the way now, a feeling compounded by how the guards watched him as he headed to Anjelina's room.

Darling Boy sat in the chair outside her door, using his combat knife to shave the fingernail of his pinkie into a point. He spoke without looking up. 'She is sleeping.'

'Then I'll wake her,' Evan said, barging in.

Anjelina shot up in the sheets with a yelp, startled by his entrance.

'Shut up,' he said loudly as the door swung closed behind him. 'I have a few more questions for you.'

The door sealed, and he thumbed on his white-noise app and eased to her side. 'Listen to me carefully,' he said quietly. 'Do not leave this room for any reason until I come for you. Do not give anyone an excuse to get upset. Anything asked of you, obey. No complaining, no conflicts, no throwing off sparks. Tension is mounting, and until I can initiate extraction, I need you to stay as removed from Montesco's mind as possible.'

She crossed her arms atop the bulge of her belly. 'What tension?'

'I don't have time to explain. I just need you to listen. Understand?'

'Okay, okay.' She planted her feet on the mattress, pulled her thighs up against her belly. 'Did you see my father?'

'Yes.'

'What did he say?'

'He won't kill Reymundo.'

'What else did he say?'

'I don't have time to explain.'

'Did *Mamá* talk to him?'

'Yes.'

'Did he listen?'

'Yes.'

There were tears in her eyes instantly. 'Then everything will be okay.'

'I need to know that Reymundo won't get in the way of anything I need to do here.'

'What do you need to do?'

The question surprised him. Despite what she had been through, what she had seen, she was still an innocent. 'Kill everyone,' he said.

She blinked at him. 'Why would you do that?'

'Because it's the only way I can get you out. And it's the only way you won't be looking over your shoulder for the rest of your life. I'll ask you again. Will Montesco's son try to interfere?'

She shook her head. 'I don't think so.'

'Talk to him. Make sure. This is the last you'll see of me. Before it's time.'

He started out.

'Wait,' she said in a whispered rush.

He halted, picturing Darling Boy outside, that shared look between El Moreno and his guard in the bedroom. Evan's impatience intensified, a simmer in his stomach. 'What?'

'My *papá*, I didn't want to disappoint him.'

Evan said, 'I don't care.'

'The pressure of it,' she said. 'In his eyes I was perfect. I tried to be for so long. And then I just couldn't.'

He understood that she was terrified, but he couldn't bring himself to empathize with her.

'The more I did right, the more proud of me he was,' she said. 'And the more I could disappoint him.'

'This is something that can be dealt with later.'

'I know,' she said, in a diminutive voice that sounded much younger than her eighteen years. 'But I had to say it before

I went home.' Her enormous brown eyes pulled to him. 'I needed someone to hear it.'

'I heard it,' Evan said. 'Now, stay in the room.'

Before going to sleep, Evan emerged from his bedroom and walked the mansion at night. Guards watching him with glittering eyes, cologne and cigarette smoke wafting off them. The place was desolate, abandoned, just the armed men there in every room like staging props, as unnatural as the rest of the decor.

He took a pass through the front yard, breathing the scent of night-blooming jasmine. The guards at the front gate kept him in view, shadowing him from afar. He gauged the distance from the front door to the van, from the van to the gates, from the gates to the limestone formations beyond, and he wondered if his planning had been sufficient. The margin for error was zero.

He'd drifted close enough to the chicken coop to see someone's breath huffing out from between the cell bars. He moved closer. The captives were asleep, save for a young lady in her twenties with ratty hair and a pronounced nose. She hacked a few times, an unforgiving, dry cough, and then glared out at him with discerning eyes.

'You should be ashamed of yourself,' she said in passable English. 'You have a mother, sisters, a daughter maybe. You see us. But you pretend you don't. All those pretty girls come and go in the big house. And you keep us out here like cattle. Voiceless, faceless, nameless.'

Behind her, her cellmates slumbered. Buckets on the floor, filthy plates crusted with residue. Slots in the bottoms of the doors sized for trays to be passed through. Body odor and human waste, a barnyard reek.

Evan stared at her through the bars. 'What *is* your name?'

'Aurora,' she said.

He dipped his head in acknowledgment.

'God is watching you,' she said. 'Everything you have done. Everything you will do.'

Evan thought, *I hope not*, and walked back inside.

The foyer guard rose as he passed. He drifted through the kitchen under the watchful eyes of two more men positioned at the bar in the adjoining conversation pit. The knives were missing from the wooden block, put away since Evan had left. Interesting.

He walked past the antique steel safe, his 1911 and Strider knife held captive inside along with a collection of other visitors' phones and weapons. Grabbing a bottled water from the refrigerator, he headed back through the ground floor. Behind him in the dark house, boots scuffed floorboards, doors opened and closed, the men tracking him as he made his quiet rounds under the guise of a nighttime stroll. A surfeit of lights illuminated the yard. Through the windows he confirmed guard positions, tallied the manpower, noted familiar gaits and postures and faces.

His running count showed one *sicario* and thirty-eight men, and nothing he saw now indicated an update was in order.

The morning would hold a lot of killing.

As he walked down a tight hallway, he spotted the rustic oak door of the study. It was ajar, its rounded top casting a skewed tombstone shadow across the tile floor. A bluish glow emanated through the threshold.

Evan moved to the doorway and froze.

A spa-like blue from the aquarium glass irradiated the dark walls and bookshelves, the rolling ladder and imposing mahogany desk. But none of the furnishings held Evan's attention.

The figure floating inside the tank did.

Slow-motion twists, like a synchronized swimmer who'd lost his partner. Bare-chested, tattered pants, claw marks pronounced across the back of the torso from a leonine mauling. Half the head gnawed off. One leg missing at the knee, an arm ending in ribboned streamers of flesh. In the bisected jaw, a row of exposed molars glimmered like pearls. Hunks of flesh taken from the right flank, the left buttock, the meat of the thigh. Bubbles clung to what remained of the nose, the eyelashes, the spaces between the remaining toes.

Venustiano. The tree trimmer.

Evan sensed movement in his peripheral vision. Way down at the ends of the hall, figures moved into view, faces barely lit.

Darling Boy to the left.

Nacho to the right.

Darling Boy smiled at him. Even from this distance, his teeth looked like stumps inserted at random into his caving gums. 'We figured this *mono* needed to be taught a lesson more than Romeo did. I convinced *Jefe* not to wait till the end of the month.'

Evan shrugged. 'You don't have patience for the long-term plan.'

'What long-term plan is that?'

Evan looked back at the corpse spinning slowly in the ethereal light, sea-changed and gruesomely bewitching with pallid skin and purpled viscera. Faint whiff of chlorine and formaldehyde. The study itself was like a theater set, all those unread books, the empty blotter, the disused Montblanc. To men like El Moreno and Darling Boy, little in this world was authentic. Other humans weren't real. Their suffering wasn't real. The families they left behind weren't real.

Evan pulled back, walking toward Nacho, but turned right down the next corridor, leaving the men momentarily behind.

A dark stone corridor, thick with the scent of animal musk.

He heard it then, a low ticking growl.

No, not a growl. A contented snore.

Floor-to-ceiling bars set in the stone near the end, light falling through, broken into slats.

He neared.

Sure enough the king slumbered, lying on his side, spine pressed to the cold rock of the rear wall. Muzzle stained from the day's feast. Massive paws like spiked boxing gloves, twitching with a remembered pursuit.

Evan put his shoulder blades to the wall opposite and slid down to sit on the floor.

The lion hoisted his massive head and regarded him, orange-brown eyes burning bright. He curled his top lip and tasted the air, tasted Evan's scent, the ridiculous brown pom-pom at the end of his tail shushing across the floor. The tuft was used for balance and to lead other lions through the long grass. Spined tongue sharp enough to slough the skin off your hand with a few licks. Incisors spaced to slide between the vertebrae of prey and sever the spine surgically.

Everything by design, cruel and majestic.

The lion didn't care about lost daughters and damaged sons. Didn't know how to engage in small talk or what to bring to a dinner party. Didn't understand how to talk to a frustrated sixteen-year-old hacker, a woman on the verge of a life-ending surgery, a nine-year-old boy terrified of being left motherless.

He was built for one thing and one thing only.

They shared the air for a time. The mansion was so quiet it could almost be mistaken for peaceful.

Finally Evan rose, one knee cracking. The lion's head lifted to track his movement. They regarded each other through the bars with something approaching professional courtesy. Evan gave him a nod.

'You and me, pal,' he said, and headed out.

52. Scared of Him All the Way Down

Evan was awakened by screaming. Tumbling out of bed already dressed, banging into the stupid floor vase as he yanked on his boots. Laces untied, stumbling to the door.

El Moreno bellowing somewhere in the mansion. And then the sound of a gunshot, amplified inside interior walls.

Evan sprinted down the hall toward the commotion, heart pounding. The guards were standing by the chairs, heads cocked like dogs alerting to a threat. As Evan passed them, they sprang into action, following his lead.

Evan was weaponless, running into the unknown.

Another gunshot.

Montesco was juiced up on crack and cocaine. Had he just ended the mission with a bullet to Anjelina's head?

Evan flew down the floating spiral stairs, clearing the final twist to see that it wasn't Anjelina at the end of the gun. It was Reymundo.

On his knees in the sunken conversation pit by the bar, cheeks smashed in the grip of his father's hand. Montesco placed the gun parallel to his son's temple. 'Tell me!'

'Papá, I swear –'

Bang.

Reymundo fell over, clutching his ear. Another hole opened up on the couch cushion behind him, tufted white foam appearing next to the other ruptures, a trio of eyeballs. Darling Boy stood down in the pit with them, the heel of his hand resting on the pommel of his sheathed knife. A few other guards rimmed the top of the space, looking on awkwardly, other men running toward the sound of gunfire, pouring into the mansion from all directions.

'What the fuck is this?' Now El Moreno was shaking something in his son's face. 'What do you need an untraceable phone for?'

'It was to call Anjelina. Before you knew about us. I swear –'

'Why did Darling Boy find this beneath your mattress now? *Why?*'

'I forgot about it. I –'

'Did you set me up in San Bernardino?' Montesco shouted, saliva flying from his lips. 'Were you working with Jovencito? Did you know who the shooters were?'

The gun now in his son's mouth. 'Nuh. Nuh nuh nuh –'

Barrel to the temple. 'What are these fucking numbers? Why were you calling America?'

'I was calling –'

Bang!

This shot, close enough to nick the edge of Reymundo's ear. He clamped a hand over the side of his head, trickles of blood forking around his index finger.

'We are searching for traitors under my roof, and we find *this*? From *you*? I don't care if you're my blood. I will kill you. Understand? I will end you.'

The situation was redlining and Evan's position fraught, his cover one false move from being blown. And he had to do something fast before Reymundo's gray matter wound up spattered all over the couches.

Evan stepped down into the conversation pit and opened his mouth to speak when a voice from behind him shouted, '*Stop!*'

He could not bring himself to believe it. Not even when he turned and saw her racing down the spiral staircase, bare feet fluttering, Nacho tearing along the catwalk above in pursuit.

386

Anjelina clutched her stomach with one hand, her hair swept back, cheeks aflame. In her stubbornness and outrage, Evan saw an echo of her father, the fervor that would get her killed.

The one order he'd given her. After everything he'd put on hold and put at risk. After all the blood and sweat the past two weeks had brought. After the meticulous planning, risks taken, injuries accrued, dangers outstanding. She'd had one task and one task only: stay in her room until he could save her.

And despite everything at stake, she'd been unable to listen. At the worst possible time, she'd barreled into the powder keg, sparks flying.

His anger strained toward the breaking point, found alignment with his cover, true emotion undergirding his fictitious role. A lifetime spent holding back that fury, channeling it into calm action, but now he felt it bucking at the reins, his grip starting to slip.

She reached the bottom of the stairs, Nacho at her heels. Guards were already moving to intercept her when Evan blew his top.

He arrowed at her, leading with a diamond tip of cold rage. 'God*damn it*, girl.'

She stopped flat-footed, recoiling from the sight of him, confused terror flashing in her eyes.

She was scared of him all the way down. She had every reason to be.

'I told you to stay in your *fucking* room.'

He drew back his hand to strike her. Beneath his boiling temper, he sensed the terrible alignment of interests, felt the dark streak within himself that was thinner but no less deep than Aragón's or El Moreno's, the fathomless malevolence no one on the planet was above or beyond.

'*Wait!*'

Evan stopped his hand back by his ear, freezing the windup.

El Moreno walked over to him, his expression resembling surprise; Evan's overreaction had jarred Montesco out of his own frenzy. 'Calm down, Caballo Oscuro. Calm down.'

Evan felt the spell break, felt the rage he'd summoned drain out of him. The ploy had worked. He lowered his hand to his side.

Montesco moved to him. 'Funny, I know. *Me* telling *you* to calm down. But you can't hurt this *vaca*. She holds my future here.'

Montesco peeled up Anjelina's shirt. Trembling, she let him. He placed his hand on her bare stomach. Her face was contorted with disgust, anger yielding to shame. So many guards in the room, all of them looking on, spellbound. Nothing she could do but allow him to touch this most intimate part of her.

'Since my son is a traitorous *culero*,' Montesco said, rubbing her skin, 'the boy in her belly is all I have left.'

'Let me see the phone.' Evan held out his hand.

Montesco looked at Darling Boy, then placed the throwaway in Evan's hand.

Evan thumbed up the call history. Several dozen listings.

'These are all to one number,' Evan said.

'With an *American* area code,' Darling Boy said.

Evan thumbed redial.

A two-second delay.

Followed shortly by a spectral ringing in the room, the sound echoing metallically. The guards looked up, around, at one another.

Evan stared at the rusting old-fashioned safe.

Montesco's jaw clenched. He walked over. Spun the dial.

Removed an iPhone in a pink rubber case with ANJELINA spelled out on the back in gold-studded stickers. The phone rang once more and then made a woeful dying noise as it lost charge.

Darling Boy lowered his eyes, hands limp at his sides. Humiliated before his beloved overlord and the others. The full manpower of the estate had been drawn inside, all thirty-eight men.

A tactical disaster begotten by narcissism.

Montesco demanded the attention of everyone around him every waking minute; his mood set the tempo of the entire estate. All eyes had been on him as he'd fumed and bellowed and fired his weapon into the couch cushions.

He'd been too coddled too long to learn one of the key lessons imparted to Evan in his training.

You can either be the center of attention or pay attention.

You can't do both.

The mood had shattered, and Evan wasn't about to let someone else set the new tempo. He pressed his advantage, spinning as he addressed Montesco's men. 'Why are you all here? Who's watching the front gate? The rear perimeter? Who's guarding your posts around the house? Or did you forget we still have Gulf Cartel assassins out there gunning for *Jefe*? Go. *Go!*'

They dispersed.

Evan looked at Anjelina. 'Get back in your room. Clean up your boyfriend. Both of you stay there. I'll deal with you both after I finish my job in the morning.'

As he headed back to his bedroom, he slapped the disposable phone into Darling Boy's hand. 'Excellent work,' he said.

53. Filthy Boy

Evan spent the morning pretending to check Montesco's fleet of SUVs for digital transmitters and explosives. Darling Boy sat in a lawn chair beneath the portico with Raudel, sipping lemonade as Evan moved back and forth to the van, hauling undercarriage mirrors and RF wireless signal-detector wands. Every time he emerged from the cargo hold with a new piece of gear, Darling Boy made him bring it over to him to inspect.

For extra fun Darling Boy would ask the chauffeur's approval. 'That look okay to you, Raudel?'

'*Yo no sé*,' Raudel would reply with a smile, biting off a fresh plug of tobacco and spitting a brown stream across the toes of Evan's boots. 'Let me see it again.'

On the sixth round, Darling Boy finally seemed to tire of the power play and waved Evan off. 'Hurry up and finish. You haven't even started on the tunnels yet.'

Evan kept on his examination, assessing every inch of the SUVs. As he worked the undercarriage mirror on the third and last one, he heard a ragged cough from the chicken coop, repeating like a sickly leitmotif. After a time he stormed over to the bars.

'Shut the hell up!' he shouted.

Aurora recoiled from the bars, stumbling back into her cellmates, who caught her, murmuring in Spanish. Passing the wooden pillar with the skeleton key, he hurled the undercarriage mirror against the wall.

'How am I supposed to work with you hacking over here?'

he shouted, banging the bars. 'Knock it off. You have plenty of water!'

Back on the porch, he could hear Darling Boy and Raudel chuckling. 'He's got a bad temper, this *gabacho*.'

Evan leaned on the bars, lowered his voice. 'The mirror snaps off – *don't look right now*. The arm will reach the key. Wait until later.'

Aurora eyed the undercarriage mirror with its extendable arm, barely within reach through the slot in the barred cell door. 'How will I know when to do it?'

'You'll know.'

He made a show of spitting on the ground at her feet and returned to the van as Darling Boy and Raudel applauded him. Climbing into the cargo hold, Evan used his heel to crack the dried blob of gum on the floor.

It hid a small flush-mount ring pull.

Which he fished up out of its housing and used to lift a hidden hatch door, revealing the storage cabinets beneath.

The small items he needed for this phase were waiting right on top. He pocketed them surreptitiously, eased the hatch closed, and moved a Pelican case to cover the eyelet.

Back to the SUVs.

With his scanners and wands, he had every excuse to climb through the interiors, search the undercarriages, check the steering columns.

He finished his work there. Returned to the van and loaded the fusion sensors, microsurveillance tech, and basic tools into a black duffel.

Dusting his hands, he approached the portico, already counting his steps from the van. *Thirty, thirty-five.*

Darling Boy rose. 'Put the bag down. There.'

Evan obeyed.

Crouching, Darling Boy searched every last item, holding

each one up to the light, turning them this way and that, examining them for anything untoward. Then he patted Evan down once more. Raudel watched with satisfaction, blowing Evan a kiss.

But there was nothing hidden on Evan's person or in the gear.

'Inside,' Darling Boy said, leading the way. 'Tunnels next. But I will watch your ass like a hawk.'

Evan followed him into the house, still counting.

Forty-five, fifty.

Montesco was waiting on his feet in the study, arms crossed in front of the aquarium tank, spine straight, as if expecting someone to come in and paint his oil portrait. Before him the grand desk with its blank blotter, fancy fountain pen, and white residue from three snorted lines. In the bluish water behind him, what remained of Venustiano spun listlessly.

Nacho sat on the black leather couch, cradling a Glock 19 and trying to fit his lips over his teeth.

'Are my vehicles clean?' Montesco's eyes were puffy and dark, the rest of his face pallid with drug toxicity.

'Yes,' Evan said, entering just as his step count neared three hundred. 'I scanned them stem to stern. No explosives, no digital transmitters, no listening devices.' He chinned at the duffel bag slung over his shoulder. 'I'm ready to move to the escape routes. Where do I access them?'

'*It*,' Montesco said. 'There is just one, and it runs straight from here.'

He kicked aside the saddle-leather wing chair behind the desk. It slid to the wall, nearly toppling. He snapped his fingers, and Darling Boy peeled up the frosted-PVC chair mat to reveal a circular wooden scuttle-hole cover in the floor. It had an inset metal ring not unlike the one installed in Evan's van, which lifted to reveal iron rungs descending into the earth below.

Evan said, 'After you.'

But Darling Boy just smiled. 'I'll wait for you here,' he said. 'Have fun.'

Montesco rubbed the heel of his hand into his eye and trudged out. 'I'll be in my room. Don't wake me till it's done.'

Evan took hold of the rungs and lowered himself, the duffel tugging at his shoulder. No more than three feet in diameter, the hole bored right through the foundation and into the sweating soil.

As he eased down through the floor, Darling Boy's boot slid forward and caught him beneath the chin. A tilt of the toe cranked Evan's head upward. 'You come back here every hour, understand? Exactly sixty minutes.'

Evan jerked his head away. 'I understand.'

'If you don't, I'll come looking for you.'

Darling Boy stepped away.

The light of the aquarium played over Evan's face as he descended, the corpse's intact foot twisting as if pirouetting. It was the last thing he saw before semidarkness swallowed him.

Twenty feet down to the dirt bottom where he was greeted by a naked light switch mounted on a crooked two-by-four. He clicked it, a string of Christmas lights pegged to the walls at intervals illuminating the long, dark way.

He peered up to see Darling Boy and Nacho staring down the hatch at him.

He couldn't imagine two less palatable faces.

Something soft brushed at his ankles, a rat scuttling for cover. A deep inhale brought the scent of mud and musk. The cramped walls forced him to walk in a half stoop.

He started his step count over from zero.

The tunnel was long and bare. It seemed to vector beneath the house, an endless trek through patchy darkness. Now and then roots curtained down from the low ceiling, dragging across his shoulders like limp hands. His RoamZone showed no signal, as he'd anticipated. He was disconnected from everything down here in the underworld, able to prepare and scheme.

Fifty-five. Sixty.

It was a good quarter mile to the first ladder up. A blade of light leaking through the hatch above brought visible a slice of the subterranean tunnel. He dumped the duffel at the base, sending a sheet of rats squealing and scurrying. Then he removed an electric torque screwdriver with flathead and Phillips attachments and kept going.

He resumed his count, his boots mashing through mounds of rat droppings.

Hundred seventy-five. Hundred eighty.

Another ladder led to a hatch he hadn't noted from above, likely somewhere near the portico.

He passed two hundred, wondering how much his count was thrown off by his stooped gait. Was he overcompensating or undercompensating?

When he crossed three hundred, he started to worry. Had he miscalculated? Or was Montesco lying about there only being one escape tunnel?

Three hundred twenty-five. Three hundred thirty.

And there, finally, another set of vertical rungs hammered into a concrete throat ascending to ground level.

His heart quickening, he scaled the ladder. The hatch at the top opened with a simple thick slide bolt. It gave with a rusty thud, the lid lifting up to let in a spill of daylight.

The lid rose to a forty-five-degree angle and stopped, striking the undercarriage of the van.

Giving him just enough room to access the hinges of the lid. Flathead screws, three per hinge.

Wedged in the vertical concrete tube, clinging to a rung with one hand, he had barely enough leverage to get the screwdriver into position. A trickle of dirt from the flower bed ran into his eyes. His hand cramped. For a moment it seemed he'd be unable to make the angle work, but finally the first hinge screw extracted, clearing the housing and tumbling past his cheek to the soft ground below. The next came easier.

His technique evolved enough to make the second hinge give way quicker, but he had virtually no angle on the third. Goosenecking his hand, he tried to worm the flathead into position but needed another half inch clearance.

No go.

With his right heel dug into a rung and the sole of his left boot braced on the opposing wall, he tried again. He was perspiring, his grip slick. If he slipped, he'd wind up with a twisted ankle or a broken leg, and he could afford neither. He shoved the lid harder up against the undercarriage of the van, but there was no more give.

Was it possible he'd come this far to be undone by a half inch?

Removing the flathead insert bit, he set it between his lips, but as he did so, the screwdriver unit slipped through his palm. He lunged for it, missed, his grip faltering, boot fighting for purchase on the far wall. His right heel gave, bumped painfully down another rung, and then skipped into open air. He tumbled two feet in near free fall before exploding outward in a show of panicked centrifugal force, jamming himself in place at a painful angle – metal bar dug into his shoulders, both feet hammered into the wall opposite.

Somehow, miraculously, he'd held on to the bit between his lips.

He reset himself on the rungs, scrabbled back up to the top. Pinching the bit in his bare fingers, he inserted the flathead into the screw slot.

He twisted. Nothing. He tried again, knuckles straining, hand knotting all the way through the palm. Still no give.

A half fucking inch.

His forearm was burning now, one thigh getting in on the action, his body tired of spidering him in place while he worked. At last the screw loosed a quarter turn, not much but enough to give a bit of air around the head. He dug his fingernails in place around it and twisted until his skin frayed.

At last the screw popped loose.

He paused, panting, sweat dripping down his face. He armed it off, succeeded in smearing mud across his brow.

Same process for the second screw, but more painful given the shredding beneath his nails. He got it halfway free, cursed with irritation, then hammered his fist against the wood near the flap of the hinge, knocking the entire lid loose.

For several seconds he froze, listening for footsteps on the quartz gravel. Hearing none, he lowered the lid nearly flat to the dirt and slid it aside.

Now he had a straight view up to the bottom of the van.

And to the trapdoor he'd instructed Tommy to make near the fuel filter between the right frame rail ahead of the rear axle.

Four latches undid the trapdoor.

Now he had access to the hidden compartments beneath the cargo hold of the van. It would take a lot of heavy hauling for him to get the gear out and position it where needed. Time was short, and Darling Boy was waiting.

Gripping the edges of the trapdoor, Evan hoisted his head up into the hold and took stock.

For the first time in a long time, he allowed himself an exhale.

Two hours and forty minutes later, Evan was on the verge of completing his last underground trek. He was drenched in sweat from running back at intervals to Darling Boy in the study. Every time he emerged, Nacho would shove him over the desk and pat him down from head to toe while Darling Boy looked on with predatory delight. Then Evan would crawl back into the earth and sprint to make up time for the shadow operation he was running in place of the one he'd disclosed.

The terminus of the tunnel was two and a quarter miles from the estate. A dead sprint humping gear would give him barely enough time to get there and back in time for his next hourly check in with Darling Boy.

Rats skittered out from beneath Evan's boots as he ran, shouldering the black duffel he'd emptied out to make room for the actual gear he was using. The moist walls muffled their squealing, the sounds absorbed in the belly of the earth. Sporadic lengths of Christmas lights had shorted out, leaving him to run through pitch-black stretches. His boots heavied with mud; his clothes clung to him.

The last outlet was a fake storm drain with a wheel on the underside resembling a dog handle on a submarine door. Dumping the duffel at the base of the ladder, Evan retrieved a loaded ARES 1911 and scaled the rungs with it in his teeth. It was a longer climb up, almost double the height of the others. Gauging from the walls, bored through solid stone, Evan assumed he'd made it out past the limestone formations to the carved rock before the highway. In the event of a raid on the estate, this was far enough from the mansion for Montesco to pop free and escape.

Reaching the top, Evan spun the wheel to unlock the lugs and then stashed the ARES beneath the curved metal handle for safekeeping. He pushed the cover up, starting to emerge, when a boot set down, filling his visual field.

A moment later a stream of tobacco landed in the dirt right next to his cheek.

He looked up into the face of Raudel, his favorite chauffeur.

Raudel pulled the fake storm drain cover upright, easing behind it so he faced Evan over the top. If he let it fall, it would strike Evan in the face, sending him tumbling forty feet to the bottom. Raudel pretended to let his grip slide, grabbing it just before it hit Evan.

He laughed as Evan cringed. 'Whoops.'

If Raudel leaned forward a few inches, he'd see the pistol wedged on the underside of the lid. In fact, his fingertips were touching the aluminum slide.

Setting an arm on the dirt, Evan had to contort his head to see the chauffeur over the top of the raised hatch. His view was limited, but he could see that he'd emerged on a rocky bluff overlooking the dirt road to the estate. And he made out a truck of some kind stashed beneath camo netting in the bushes at the edge of the clearing.

Montesco's getaway vehicle.

With a driver standing by at all times.

'Filthy boy,' Raudel said.

Evan could feel it. Dirt crammed beneath his nails, in the creases of his eyelids, the cracks of his knuckles.

'What are you doing way out here?' Raudel asked.

Evan's extracurricular shenanigans had left him with scant time to get back to Darling Boy in the study. Two and a quarter miles in nineteen minutes wasn't undoable, but any further delays and he'd be pushing it. The last thing he needed right now was an altercation.

'Safing the tunnels.' Foolishly, Evan had left all the equipment he was supposed to be installing a mile back where he'd emptied the duffel bag. 'Fusion sensors with night vision and thermal, microsurveillance pin-cameras.'

'Microsurveillance.' Raudel spit again. 'Sounds like some white-boy shit. Can I see it?'

'No,' Evan said. 'That's the whole point.'

A drawn-out pause as Raudel squinted down at him. Beneath the wheel handle, the 1911 slid a bit, threatening to drop. Evan wondered if Raudel had felt it inch away from his fingertips.

Raudel finally finished his internal translation and laughed. The motion shook the hatch lid slightly, the pistol barely holding on.

If it fell, drawing Raudel's attention, all he'd have to do was let go of the hatch to send Evan plummeting.

'We done?,' Evan said, 'I've got work to do.'

Raudel spit again, the brown juice splattering Evan's arm. Evan had repressed his OCD as best he could in the tunnel, but the tobacco-laced saliva on his skin brought it to the surface.

Raudel blew him another kiss. 'Have fun, *gabacho*.'

He lowered the lid quickly enough to force Evan to scramble down out of its way. When it sealed with an airtight thunk, the ARES shot free. Evan caught it before it fell and secured it back in place. Then he wiped his arm off.

He'd been planning to hide the duffel on the surface, but there was no time for that now; he'd have to haul it up with him on the exfil and deal with Raudel then. Less than optimal.

He checked his watch fob. Seventeen minutes to get back to the study.

He bounced down the rungs as quickly as he could, hitting the earth hard, his boots sinking in rat shit.

Readying himself for the run, he spun around.

Darling Boy was standing there, MP7 aimed at Evan's chest.

He bared those awful yellow teeth, enamel stubs screwed into his suppurating gums. 'Surprise.'

54. Gun to a Knife Fight

Evan faced Darling Boy in the tunnel, both of them stooped to accommodate the low roof. The arch of it seemed to crowd down over Evan's shoulders. Darling Boy was five feet away, too far for Evan to make a grab for the weapon.

'I promised I would catch up to you, *gabacho*,' Darling Boy said.

A few rats darted past him tentatively, scaling the curved wall.

'But you made a fatal mistake,' Evan said.

Darling Boy grinned that terrible grin once more. '*I* made a mistake? I'm the one with the MP7.'

'Right. You brought a gun to a knife fight.'

'I don't think that's how the saying goes.'

'Fire that weapon and find out,' Evan said. 'This tunnel is minimally reinforced. You release a burst of rounds in here, you'll be buried alive.'

Darling Boy licked his lips, a nervous tell. 'Even so. You don't have a knife.'

'No,' Evan said. 'But you do.'

He charged.

Darling Boy dropped the MP7 and grabbed for the fixed-blade combat knife sheathed on his belt.

But there were two problems he hadn't accounted for.

The sling on the MP7.

And the retaining strap on the leather knife sheath.

Both designed to secure the weapons on him.

But in this case they secured him to the weapons.

401

The submachine gun tangled at his waist, his hand fumbling at the strap.

Evan hit him in a high tackle, knocking him over, the MP7 flying up between them, smacking Darling Boy's jaw. Rolling through the mud, swinging and clubbing, Evan got in a few blows, grabbing for the knife at Darling Boy's waist, thumb digging at the metal snap.

It popped free, Evan raking the blade up at Darling Boy's throat, getting a solid nick before a tumbling kick to the gut sent him flying up the tunnel.

Evan landed on all fours, knees sunk in the mud, his fist still gripping the knife.

Five feet away, partly visible in the Christmas lights, Darling Boy clutched at his throat. A trickle of blood dribbled down his Adam's apple. It was bad, but not enough to kill him anytime soon.

He lowered his hands and tried to say something, but all that came out was a hoarse rush of air. His larynx had been punctured.

Darling Boy reached for his boot and came up with a straight razor, which he opened with a practiced flick of his wrist.

Evan rose.

They faced each other over their respective blades.

Darling Boy lunged first.

Evan dodged the thrust, bringing the combat knife around to slash at the distal biceps tendon at the elbow.

Darling Boy tried to scream, but with his damaged throat it was little more than a rasp. His forearm would be going numb now, his grip useless. He looked down impotently as the weight of the straight razor peeled his fingers apart and it started to tumble.

He caught it with his left hand.

Wielding it unsurely now, panicked eyes reading Evan in the darkness.

Another feint, but Evan rolled beneath the edge, blade angled to slide straight across the back of Darling Boy's ankle just above the throat of the boot where the Achilles tendon inserted into the calf.

An airy moan as Darling Boy stumbled, catching himself against the muddy wall, ripping a string of Christmas lights free. The MP7 bobbled about his waist now, and he nearly tripped as he high-stepped out of it.

He staggered upright, and he and Evan faced each other once more, their second do-si-do in the tight dirt walls.

A strand of the lights remained stubbornly on, casting low illumination across the muddy ground. Behind Darling Boy dozens of red dots peered from the darkness.

Rat eyes.

Sensing their presence, Darling Boy put his shoulders to the wall, trying to keep Evan in sight as he glanced behind him.

Another soundless moan of terror.

Before he could reorient himself, Evan flashed past him once more, drawing the point of the combat knife across Darling Boy's left forearm, opening up a bone-deep gash.

Darling Boy hissed, his breath pungent in the trapped air, the straight razor falling to the mud. He collapsed to grab it, digging frantically, his useless hands flapping at the ends of his arms. As Evan approached, Darling Boy lashed out with his functional leg, a heel kick to Evan's groin.

Evan twisted aside and parried with the knife, swiping at Darling Boy's leg, cutting through his pants behind the knee. A wet snap as the lateral hamstring tendon gave way. That left the *sicario* with no functional limbs. Darling Boy curled into a loose fetal position, gurgling into the dirt.

One of the rats darted forward and nipped at his nose. Limbless, he jerked his face to scare it away, and it retreated.

Eyes bulging, Darling Boy looked up at Evan. He tried to speak but couldn't make words.

Around him in the darkness came scurrying noises. Barely audible high-pitched chirping, calls and responses. Shadows gathered on the floor just beyond Evan's vision.

He took a step back.

Darling Boy stared at him with pleading eyes, his jaws sawing on air. Using his chin, he tried to roll himself over. Trapped in this tunnel beneath the earth, stuck in the walls of his own body, voiceless. Much like the women he'd helped lock in the chicken coop.

Evan took another step back, letting the *sicario* fade into darkness.

In the faint glow of the remaining lights, he sensed a flurry of motion and a wheezing that couldn't rise into words. Both sounds quickened to a fevered pitch, the bloodlust excitement of a feeding frenzy.

Evan heard it echoing up the tunnel after him as he started the long sprint back.

55. Down

Nacho was waiting right where Evan expected him at the top of the scuttle hole in the study, peering down over the barrel of his MP7.

Evan blinked up at him. 'Can I come up?'

'Where's Darling Boy?'

'Helping me finish with the pin cameras,' Evan said. 'We just positioned them around the last hatch, so I have to grab an iPad from the van to test the connection. I think we might need a booster, since the signal sucks down there.'

He grabbed the lower rungs to start up but Nacho said, 'Don't fucking move.'

Nacho fished out a phone, dialed a number, waited. 'Straight to voice mail.'

'I told you. Shitty signal.'

'I don't believe you.'

'You're welcome to come down.'

'He didn't say he would help you.'

'This part requires two men.'

'Hang on.' Nacho placed another call.

Evan waited twenty feet down, soaked in sweat and mud, breathing the dampness. A few moments later, he heard a fleet of footsteps above.

'Show me your hands,' Nacho said. 'Okay. Come up slowly. Slower! Up. Up.'

As Evan emerged, Nacho grabbed him by the shirt collar and flung him up against the desk. He hit it hard enough that the blotter skidded beneath the heels of his hands. There were three other men in the study, all toting MP7s, all aimed at him.

Nacho frisked him toe to head and then head to toe. Found nothing on him.

'Get your iPad. Move it.'

He gave Evan a shove toward the door, and Evan hustled out, leaving muddy heel prints.

In every hallway and room, the guards watched him pass, raising their phones to their faces, communicating his progress each step of the way.

In the corridor before the foyer, he hustled up the winding stairs to the second floor.

The guard at the top blocked his path. 'What are you doing?'

'Need to check signal up here. See if it'll reach the second floor. *Jefe* will need reception in his bedroom.'

The guard protected his weapons and the grenade pouch as Evan slid past him in the narrow hall, heading for Anjelina's room.

Through a security door into the final hallway. The Montblanc fountain pen Evan had liberated from the desk blotter while being frisked rested comfortingly against the inside of his wrist beneath the cuff.

His one-man raid on the Leones headquarters in San Bernardino had started with a pencil.

The exfil from Montesco's estate would begin with a pen.

All the complexities Evan had been forging through this mission – fathers and daughters and mothers and babies and birthrights and betrayal – he froze in place, like bugs in amber. Stacked them to the side. Now was the time for action. For moving forward.

For the Ten Commandments and the clarity they brought.

A plug of a guard sat on the chair outside Anjelina's closed door, Glock 19 resting on his knee. At the sight of Evan, he found his feet.

Without slowing or speeding up, Evan closed on him, letting the pen slide down his sleeve into his palm. A quick twist of thumb and forefinger and the cap came off, bounced at his feet.

Confused, the guard stared at the cap pattering on the floor. As he looked up, Evan sank the fountain pen's tip into his left ear canal, punching it with his palm to sink the metal shaft deeper. He stripped the Glock from the guard's hand as he lowered his body silently to the floor.

In through the door.

Anjelina and Reymundo stared at him unblinkingly.

He was covered with grime, the floor behind him wet from the guard's emptied bladder. The heavy fabric of Evan's clothes – heavier than usual – was saturated with mud and sweat, tugging at his shoulders.

He dropped the blood-tipped pen, the Glock 19 in his left hand, aimed at the floor.

The Tenth Commandment, *Never let an innocent die*, and its variant, *Never let an innocent kill*, demanded that he keep them both out of the fray.

'Follow me,' he said in a low voice, snatching a pillow off the bed. 'Follow everything I do. We have to be quiet. Until we don't.'

Anjelina stared out the window into the front yard. Already guards were running confusedly back and forth, barking into their phones. A half sentence reached them, snatched away by the wind: '– *y dónde está Darling Boy?*'

Evan said, '*Now*,' snapping them from their trance.

They stayed at his back, Anjelina gasping as they stepped across the puddle around the fallen guard. Evan's boots moving up the corridor were sticky, making a moist sound as the soles peeled up. The security measures of the mansion – narrow halls, small doorways, tight staircases – were designed to deter intrusion.

Now Evan could turn every last one of them to his advantage.

Through the security door, the next guard moving toward them on alert, phone at his face, gun gripped loosely in his other hand.

Evan wrapped his fingers over the slide of the Glock, a set of makeshift polymer knuckles, and struck him in the nose with the magazine baseplate. Straddled him on the floor, muzzle to pillow, pillow over face, muffled gunshot to the head. The smell of burned powder mixed with singed down stuffing.

Barely breaking stride to the spiral stairs, Reymundo and Anjelina breathing heavily at his back. Across the cramped landing, the security door to the facing hall flung open. Montesco reared up behind two guards desperately trying to halt, his eyes showing white. They locked on Evan.

A suspended instant as recognition dawned – El Moreno spotting his son and Anjelina at Evan's back, the depth of treachery hitting him. His expression twisted with outrage.

Evan brought the Glock up, but by the time he fired, the guards had heaved Montesco back, slamming the door, the rounds ricocheting off metal, making Evan's ears ring.

Before they could regroup, he had to get his charges to the ground floor. His shouted command – '*Go, go, go!* –' spurred them to action as he leapt onto the stairs, taking the lead.

Skittering down, boots moving almost too fast for purchase. The foyer guard came visible, charging into the fray, MP7 at the ready.

Whipping through the last curve of the stairs, Evan shot him twice in the chest, once in the face for good measure.

The man jellied as Evan spun down onto the tile, catching the submachine gun and stripping it from the man as he collapsed out of the rifle sling.

Evan got off a three-round burst at the front door to give the outside guards something to think about, then glanced back at the stairs. Anjelina and Reymundo cowered several steps up. The security door above, leading to Montesco's wing, was still shut, but not for long.

Evan said, 'Move.'

Vectoring toward the kitchen, incoming rounds already clipping the threshold. Evan sliced the pie, leading with the muzzle, ripping bullets through the chests of the two guards in the conversation pit. They jerked back onto the cushions, bodies dancing, weapons dropping.

Five down, thirty-three to go.

And the Dark Man himself.

Evan had taken splinters in the side of his neck from the frayed doorjamb. He noted the burn, gauged it nonessential, turned down the volume of the pain.

Pounding footsteps, shouts from above, outside.

Evan hadn't slowed. He cut straight through the sunken pit, grabbing grenades and spare magazines from the dead men's pouches, another battlefield pickup as he headed to the rear of the mansion.

Pulling pins, bouncing the frag grenades ahead of him through the intersecting back hallways. A wall-shuddering explosion, two more guards eating shrapnel, the overpressure sending one flying up to strike the low ceiling.

Confused sounds upstairs, yelling for El Moreno, shouted orders. Evan glanced back, caught Reymundo staring wide-eyed at the damage, Grabbing the young man by the sleeve, Evan yanked him forward, Anjelina tripping to keep up.

'Stay on my back.'

Montesco's men hadn't counted on a raid starting from within. The very architecture of the mansion prevented their mustering a mass response. Every hall was a fatal funnel, every door sized to accommodate one man at a time. Excellent safeguards if that one man weren't Evan.

And for the moment Evan had a second advantage. They had to wait for target acquisition so they wouldn't fire at their colleagues or the *Jefe* himself, whereas Evan could kill anyone who crossed his sights. But soon enough they'd figure out his location and close in with numbers; he had to get below-ground as quickly as possible.

Anjelina stumbled along, eyes glazed with shock. Reymundo was breathing hard enough to hyperventilate. Shouldering to the wall before the next corridor, Evan used one arm to press them flat beside him.

Then he came around the next corner, MP7 raised. Down at the end, a trio of frozen men stared at him – *burst, burst* – the manpower count dropping to twenty-eight. Hot brass bounced off the wall and stuck to his neck, a quick sting and then the smell of his own skin burning. He swept the scalding metal off, the wounds already cauterized.

Barreling toward the study now, MP7 tight against his chest, muzzle pointed forty-five degrees off his right foot, the couple at his back.

Nacho's voice issued through the doorway, a desperate cell-phone query: '– *es Jefe en camino al túnel?*'

Evan turned to Reymundo and Anjelina, finger across his lips. Easing forward, heel to toe, heel to toe, the noise of his approach covered by sounds of screaming throughout the mansion.

Next to the threshold, he raised the MP7 to his shoulder, barrel horizontal, then rolled past the doorway, sending a steady stream of rounds across the rear wall.

The aquarium glass gave way with a whoosh, a tonnage of water sheeting through the study, smashing the desk and couches to the walls and knocking the men off their feet. It roiled through the room, sloshing through the doorway, nearly sweeping Anjelina and Reymundo down the hall.

Once the initial torrent slowed, Evan spun back through the doorway from the far side. One of the guards lay face-down in the pooled water, floating beside the wing chair, his skull staved in at the temple from a collision with the over-turned desk.

Another pulled his head up, gasping and choking. Evan shot him through the neck and then waded in, stock seated at his shoulder, sighting down the top of the MP7. The third man had racked up against the wall, face studded with slivers of glass. Evan hit his torso with a three-round burst.

The tree trimmer's waterlogged corpse bucked and flopped in the far corner. Evan stared at it curiously until Nacho rolled out from beneath and heaved himself to his feet, sputtering and yelling. He'd lost his weapons in the deluge. Nacho panted, mouth agape, teeth protruding. His eyes were weary, resigned.

The desk drifted past, sliding on a skein of water, an MP7 tangled on the corner. Nacho lunged for it, and Evan shot him through the chest. Nacho tumbled back to sit on the ledge of the aquarium, splayed awkwardly as if balanced on a swing, legs dangling. His bottom lip turned down, wet and fat. His foot jiggled twice. His eyes had depth in them, and then they did not.

Evan pivoted back to the open door.

Anjelina and Reymundo stared inside with crazed expressions.

'What do we do now?' Anjelina cried. 'Where do we go?'

The scuttle hatch was open, water draining through the hole. Evan pointed. 'Down.'

56. Front Toward Enemy

The rungs were slick and moist, and the damp hole stank of decaying flesh from the tank water. Evan sent Anjelina and Reymundo first and slid down after them. When he struck dirt, his boots sank to the ankles.

He shouldered past them into the lead, sprinting, mud flying up and splattering their clothes. A length of Christmas lights shorted out at his side, a dying fizzle illuminating a fleet of confused rats as they fled or tried to burrow into the walls. Aquarium stench mingled with silt and rat feces, gumming his soles.

As Evan and the couple ran through the tunnel, muffled shouts reached them through the earth above. He'd embedded fusion sensors in the muddy walls and pin cameras at intervals along the ground, a mesh Wi-Fi signal that transmitted to his RoamZone.

At a quarter mile, they passed the first ladder, their breath amplified in surround sound off the walls. Another eternity passed before the second hatch flew by overhead. The quality of noise shifted behind them, distorted voices rumbling. Some of the guards had entered the tunnel.

Anjelina tripped, went down with a yelp, found her footing, and kept on. Reymundo lagged back with her as Evan sprinted ahead. They had to reach the terminus before Montesco's men or they'd be trapped.

For a moment Evan was worried he'd somehow overrun the third escape hatch but finally spotted a rise of rungs glinting in the semidarkness. He leapt onto them and scurried up the claustrophobic chute, popping his head out like a groundhog. His position beneath the van's undercarriage gave him a good vantage onto the driveway and portico.

A dozen guards stirring around on the quartz rock like penned livestock. Montesco appeared at the door, screaming orders. '*Muevan sus culos! Hay que chingarlos de los dos lados!*'

Evan's gaze moved to the chicken coop. Aurora stood in the cell, hands wrapped around the bars, the skeleton key pegged on the pillar just out of reach. To the side near the slot in the door, the extendable undercarriage mirror waited. Even from this distance, Evan saw her eyes move to it.

'They're coming for us!' Anjelina screamed up from the base of the rungs. 'What's going on?'

'They're trying to beat us to the end of the tunnel,' Evan called down.

'It's too far!' Reymundo cried. 'We can't outrun the SUVs.'

In the thin slice Evan's view afforded him, he watched the men pile into the three waiting SUVs, four to a vehicle.

Montesco sprinted for the rear SUV when the first two started up.

And detonated with a thunderous blast. Flashes of violent orange from the fuel tanks, black billowing smoke rocketing skyward.

The blast knocked Montesco back onto his ass on the portico.

He held an arm against the heat, screaming at the remaining men. 'Stop! Stop!'

When Evan had been ostensibly checking the SUVs for bugs earlier, he'd wired encrypted transmitters to the fuse boxes at the side of the steering columns. Each chirper linked to a microchip receiver/kicker on the quarter-size patch of C4 he'd adhered to the inside of the gas tank's flap.

Eight more pieces off the chessboard brought the man-power count to twenty.

The four survivors spilled out of the intact SUV, regrouping with Montesco at the porch.

'*Trae los camiones de combate!*' Montesco screamed. '*Ahora!*'

Combat trucks.

The words hit Evan's bloodstream like adrenaline.

He didn't know about the trucks. If Montesco's crew commanded a second fleet and drove to the extraction point before Evan and the couple reached it, they'd be dead in the ground.

Dirt trickled past Evan, the escape hatch starting to crumble from the explosion's aftermath. The rung beneath his left hand gave way, one side rattling free of its concrete base.

He swung one-handed, toes digging until they locked on the lower rungs.

Then he half slid, half fell the rest of the way, nearly striking Reymundo as he tumbled the last ten feet. Landing on shins and knees, left hand bent backward beneath the wrist, mouth full of dirt.

Silt trickled from the curved ceiling. A sheet of wall dribbled down in front of them, a partial cave-in.

Evan spit, rose. 'We need to hurry.'

They scrambled over the loose dirt, the sounds of approaching men growing closer. Behind them a burst of fire strobed the throat of the tunnel, the starburst muzzle flare a quarter mile back.

The earth creaked and groaned, a supporting two-by-four fraying and then giving way with a wet snap.

More shouted voices, the men screaming at one another not to shoot.

Evan led the way, swiping sweat and grime from his eyes. He had his phone out, the feed up, counting bodies as they flashed by the surveillance cameras behind them.

Five men in the tunnel.

Wait – more forms strobed past the first pin camera. At a dead sprint, Evan counted the additional shadows – *one, two, three* – before his shoulder nicked the wall and almost sent him tumbling. He shoved the phone into a cargo pocket and picked up the pace.

The men seemed to be gaining, but Evan focused only on the run ahead. If he could reach the final escape hatch before Montesco's vehicle convoy, they still had a shot.

It seemed an eternity, the tunnel telescoping before them, ever receding as if in a nightmare.

But at last he spotted what was left of Darling Boy, rags and gleaming bones. Evan hurdled the body and reached the last set of rungs. The heavy duffel bag waited at the base where he'd left it.

When he glanced back over Reymundo and Anjelina's shoulders, he could see shadows thrown around the bend just behind them.

He reached for the duffel with both hands, grimaced against the pain in his left hand. He'd sprained the wrist badly in the fall.

'I can't carry the duffel up,' he told Reymundo. 'I need you to take it.'

Reymundo shouldered it, staggering under its weight. 'I have to climb with this?'

'Yes.'

Anjelina pulled close, and Evan grabbed her with his good hand, yanking her tight to him. *'Don't. Step. There.'*

She looked down at the convex green-gray plastic case peeking out from where Evan had embedded it earlier at the base of the muddy dead end. Three words embossed in all caps: FRONT TOWARD ENEMY.

She eased out a breath, minded where she stood.

Evan scaled the rungs, using his good hand and the elbow of his left arm. Anjelina climbed at his heels, Reymundo bringing up the rear, grunting with every movement.

Halfway up, boring through stone walls, Evan peered down.

Flashlight beams played across the hole below, jerking back and forth as the guards neared.

He quickened his pace, crabbing his way up with one hand and an elbow. Mouth gone dry, bitter taste in his throat, pain screaming in his wrist. Up, up, up the rabbit hole.

He reached the base of the hatch, the ARES 1911 wedged beneath the circular handle where he'd left it. His shooting hand was compromised, so he freed the gun with his right hand. Even in the wrong hand, it felt like home.

Below Reymundo was barely holding on, the weight of the duffel pulling on him. The shouted voices from the tunnel grew closer yet, the flashlight glow intensifying. They were down to seconds.

Evan leaned past Anjelina and whispered hoarsely to Reymundo, 'When I knock, shout up. Pretend you're one of the guards.'

Wedging his left elbow into the top rung, Evan curled his fist around the pistol grip and pounded the bottom of the fake storm drain three times.

His voice strained beyond recognition from exertion, Reymundo shouted up, '*Somos nosotros! Apúrate! Abre la chingada escotilla!*'

The hatch cracked, the cover peeling up.

A clear view of Raudel peering down, backlit by a beautiful blue sky.

Evan shot him through the chin.

He tumbled back, Evan taking the weight of the hatch lid with his shoulders. He heaved upward, flinging the cover open. Flipping onto his knees, he hoisted Anjelina up, ripping her free of the rungs. She kicked in the open air, one shoe spiraling down. He flung her to safety. She rolled a few times on the rocky bluff, stopping herself at the edge of the sheer drop leading to the dirt road below.

Reymundo and the overburdened duffel clogged most of the chute, but in the gaps around him Evan saw faces appear way down at the bottom. Guards staring up, trying to determine who and what they were seeing.

Reymundo was three rungs down, just out of reach. The duffel strained on his shoulder. Evan lowered flat to his stomach, reaching for it. Reymundo's fingers slipped on the rungs. He grimaced and tightened his grip.

The bag was straining on Reymundo's shoulder, the strap starting to pull through the buckle. Reymundo's face was red, his neck shot through with veins. Below, the men were shouting, arguing among themselves. One of the guards started up.

Evan slid forward on his stomach, the bag still out of reach.

'I got you.' That deep feminine voice from behind him, suddenly cool and collected. He felt Anjelina grab his belt with both hands, letting him dip his torso farther into the hole. He caught the strap just as it was on the verge of unthreading from the buckle and hurled the weighty bag up onto level ground.

Reymundo scrabbled up the last rungs, heaving himself out onto the baking dirt as a volley of bullets erupted in his wake.

Sprawled flat on his back, Evan swung around on the pivot of his hip and kicked the hatch shut.

Thumbed up his RoamZone and the grainy surveillance feed from the pin cameras.

Seven guards clustered at the base of the chute. One on the rungs.

Evan switched apps to bring up the red virtual button that would detonate the mine below. The Vietnam-era claymore that Tommy had acquired for him would spray hundreds of steel ball bearings in a sixty-degree arc, fanning out to a hundred meters and aerating the minimally reinforced walls.

Evan pressed his thumbprint to the screen.

A deep rumble, and the earth heaved beneath them as if suppressing a cough. The hatch lid blew straight up, flying high and then bouncing off the stone a good thirty feet away.

At their side a trough opened up in the earth, tumbling inward, rock and dirt churning in a straight line as if run through with an invisible plow. The destruction snaked back in the direction of the estate, not a full cave-in but an implosion of silt and rock disrupting the limestone formations adjacent to the road below.

Eleven men left.

And Montesco.

Reymundo coughed out a single note of relief. Anjelina tipped her forehead into her hands. A moment of silence.

And then the roar of engines in the distance.

Zooming into view around the sweeping turn leading to the estate, five pickup trucks beelined toward them along the strip of intact dirt road. Three klicks away, maybe a bit more.

Reymundo let out a low groan.

Anjelina's voice came weak and warbling. 'Oh, no.'

Toyota HiLux four-by-fours. Fat posts welded to the beds. Pintle mounts with general-purpose machine guns, likely Fabrique Nationale M240 Bravos.

Montesco stood in the back of the last one, wind riffling his crazy hair.

He'd brought the war machines.

57. The Killing Alley

Evan scrambled to the duffel bag, unzipped it, and took out the big gun.

The .50-cal Barrett was a recoil-operated, antimatériel semiautomatic. Tommy had outfitted it with a muzzle brake to redirect propellant gases to counter recoil and unwanted muzzle rise. A few spare magazines for Evan's ARES lay in the duffel, along with a scattering of ten-round box mags, steel coated with Cerakote. Evan had specified that they be loaded with armor-piercing rounds sufficient to get him through conventional reinforced windshields. And that every fifth round should be a green tracer so he could adjust his aim once vehicles entered the choke point of the rock walls a half mile away. The tenth and final round was a red tracer that would signal a magazine change.

What Evan hadn't accounted for was a fleet of Toyota pickups outfitted like an ISIS brigade.

They were closing distance fast, nearing the killing alley. He was out of time.

Shoving spare pistol magazines into his cargo pockets and hauling an armload of box mags, he lay on his belly at the edge of the cliff, setting down the black plug of the monopod to stabilize the weapon. The dominoes had ticked over one at a time, charting the course from a fountain pen to the large-caliber rifle before him. For better or worse, he'd reached the end of the run.

His sprained left wrist wouldn't be able to take the recoil, so he'd have to shoot right-handed. He made the adjustments, finding his position, the sun-baked earth cooking through his shirt, warming his belly. One motion to flip open the rear and front scope covers, tug the bolt back, and let it fly forward to chamber the first round.

Box mags at his side, cheek to the barrel, eye to the Leupold scope, he adjusted the illuminated reticle so that it was faintly visible against the rock walls.

Anjelina and Reymundo waited behind him. 'How can we help?' she asked.

'Stay down, plug your ears,' Evan said. 'And don't talk.'

He watched the grille of the lead pickup, magnified to 8x. It weaved to dodge a cracked strip of road from the collapsed tunnel. The other vehicles followed its lead, a sidewinder undulating.

The convoy entered the funnel, high rock walls crowding in on either side. Evan had a clear angle down on the first windshield, the trucks driving nearly straight at him. Easing out a breath, attuning to his heartbeat, holding, holding, holding.

He wanted all five trucks in the constriction before he opened up.

Safety off, slack out of the trigger, waiting for the stillness between heartbeats, for all five trucks to slot within the walls of stone.

And then they were.

He opened up, grouping the rounds into the lead windshield, recoil rippling through his bones. The bullet-resistant glass spiderwebbed and then gave way, the driver disappearing in a haze of pink mist.

The pickup veered right, clipped the stone wall, then swerved back, somersaulting. The guard manning the machine gun in the bed rag-dolled onto the road, crushed beneath the axle of the following truck. The second Toyota impaled itself on a limestone abutment, hurling the driver through the windshield, his body weight ripping the bullet-resistant shield from the frame.

A pileup, trucks skidding and crashing, men scrambling from the wreckage.

Anjelina cried out.

Without moving his head, Evan said, 'Don't look.'

He picked off the men spilling out of the vehicles – a head losing its dome, a chest giving way, an arm severed at the shoulder flying free.

He was in the zone, his muscles remembering the rhythm of the semiautomatic Barrett.

Press trigger, recoil jabbing back like a sparring partner in the ring.

Inhale.

Let the muzzle settle.

Exhale long and smooth, press trigger once more.

His shots were four to five seconds apart, each round finding flesh or a vulnerable part of a truck. There was no cover inside the sheer rock walls.

The Barrett was getting warm, sending slight heat mirages through his scope.

A tracer round came next, Evan pulling his cheek off the stock, watching it fly all the way to target, a brilliant green trail. He made a microadjustment, zeroing in on the gas tank of the second truck, the rifle bucking against his shoulder.

The round hit, the explosion amplified in the stone chasm. Everyone from the first two pickups was wiped out. The third tumbled end over end from the blast, flinging the men free.

One wore a suit of flame. Running sporadically, fire licking up his torso, rising off his shoulders. Evan tried to put him down but missed, and then he ran into a rocky ledge and fell still.

The fourth pickup was boxed in, smoldering trucks in front of it, Montesco's pickup pinning it in from behind. The men were petrified, looking up the steep walls, trying to source the ambush. The driver hopped out to make a break, and Evan shot him through the kidney and scapula. He landed with a skid, plowing up a wake of dust. Evan hit the passenger through the open side window, then snapped a round through the chest of the guard manning the mounted machine gun on the bed. He flew back as if clotheslined, bouncing off the reinforced windshield of Montesco's truck.

Through the scope Evan followed his movement. The reticle landed on Montesco in the bed of the last truck, standing firm behind the mounted Fabrique Nationale M240 Bravo.

And aiming directly at Evan.

Evan flung himself to the side an instant before the cliff edge exploded, the rocky lip turned to shrapnel. The Barrett flew up, cartwheeling end over end through the air.

Tracer rounds worked both ways, in this case giving up Evan's position. At the rear of the convoy, Montesco had been offset enough from the line of fire to backtrack the pyrotechnic flare to Evan's sniper perch.

The incoming rounds didn't cease, 650 per minute chewing the bluff to pieces, sending Evan rolling backward on the ground away from the edge. Blood ran into his eyes; a chip of stone had split his right brow, a stinging surface pain.

Anjelina and Reymundo cowered behind the storm-drain hatch, Raudel's body splayed at their side.

'What now?' Anjelina shouted.

Evan pulled himself toward them with his forearms, chinning at Montesco's getaway vehicle beneath the camo netting. Finally he was out of the machine gun's sight line, but that didn't stop the 7.62x51 NATO rounds from peppering the bluff relentlessly behind him.

He found his feet, risked a peek over the edge.

Montesco's driver backed up, nosed forward, four-wheeling his way over corpses and wreckage, lurching the pickup through the choke point.

The last two men alive.

Coming for them.

Evan ripped the camo netting off the vehicle.

A Ford F-150, just like Evan's. Big tires, good clearance.

Maybe he and Montesco were *carnales* after all.

Evan slid behind the wheel, the familiar leather seat fitting him like a glove.

Anjelina dove into the back, Reymundo hopping into the passenger seat. Evan called up Google Earth on his Roam-Zone, brought up the holographic display, and then flipped the phone to stick against the windshield just below his eyes.

It projected a 3-D rendering of the rocky bluffs, the limestone formations, the dirt road below.

Swiping at the blood streaming from his forehead, he punched the gas, rocking them out from the stand of brush, eyeing the virtual map to find a path off the stone rise to the highway below.

He heard a ripping of fabric, and then a strip of cloth whipped around his forehead, cinched tight in the back as Anjelina knotted it, a makeshift bandanna to stanch the bleeding.

The truck rocked violently down the treacherous slope, threatening to capsize. A limestone outcropping gouged the passenger side, snapping off the mirror. A dead tree branch screeched along the roof.

He fumbled his ARES out and into the cup holder, then

grabbed the wheel with both hands, his injured wrist screaming. He fought the Ford down the rocky face, blazing his
way to level ground. The treacherous descent reached nearly
30 percent – too much for even a truck as fine as the F-150 –
and they joggled down the uneven slope, banging the earth
at the bottom with the bumper. The truck shuddered forward, bulldozing up a spray of dirt, and then the mud-terrain
tires found purchase, leveling them out.

Too much momentum to stop. Evan could barely steer.
On the verge of losing control, he skidded along the edge of
a boulder before the truck found its balance.

He exhaled through clenched teeth, holding steady as the
truck whipped forward, narrowly dodging limestone formations. The dirt road flashed into view ahead between two
rocky rises.

Wrenching the wheel, Evan aimed for the gap.

Reymundo yelled as they skidded sideways onto the dirt
road.

And slammed into the Toyota pickup careening up to
meet them.

Side by side, staring at each other, the driver's eyes flared
wide, Montesco in the bed, legs spread for balance, knuckles
bloodless, gripping the massive machine gun.

Clawing the wheel with his injured left hand, Evan grabbed
the ARES with his right, whipping it to aim across the cabin.
Reymundo jerked back against the headrest.

Evan shot out the passenger window, firing into the
driver's window of the neighboring truck. Three rounds,
four, the bullet-resistant glass holding on. Evan was firing
Black Hills Honey Badgers, machined out of a solid bar of
copper, their noses milled to look like the front of a drill bit.
It was only a matter of time.

Montesco screamed, staggering as the trucks jockeyed. He

set his base once more, bringing the muzzle of the massive FN M240 Bravo around.

If he fired on them from this proximity, he'd turn them into confetti.

Evan shot again and again at the driver's window, aiming for the weakened glass. The last round punched through, the driver's head jerking back, the pickup starting to coast away just as Montesco brought the mounted machine gun to bear.

Evan hit the brakes as Montesco opened up, the rounds strafing the hood of the Ford and then the road ahead of them. The pickup skidded off, the driver lolling lifelessly behind the wheel.

White-knuckling the steering wheel, Evan felt his left hand giving out. He went for a one-handed reload with his right, thumbing the catch, dropping the empty mag. New one from his cargo pocket, end against his thigh, slamming the open mag well of the ARES's grip down on top of it. He dug the rear sight into the steering wheel and pushed forward, cycling the slide and chambering the first round.

The Ford was fishtailing on the road now, so he pumped the brakes. The hood was smoking, the front right tire unspooling from the axle, shedding strips of tread and reeking of burned rubber.

The left front wheel disintegrated also, the truck bucking forward to skid on the axles, throwing up plumes of sparks. Evan slammed into the dash, the ARES skipping from his grip. The truck slid sideways and at long last rocked to a stop.

Groaning, he tugged at his door and fell out onto the scorching road.

Reymundo and Anjelina exited more gracefully, running to his side, pulling him to his feet. Her shirt was torn at the hem from where she'd liberated the strip of fabric to stem his bleeding.

Montesco's pickup had vanished into a cloud of dirt on the verge.

'He crashed,' Anjelina said.

Evan didn't take his eyes from the shifting haze. 'My gun,' he said. 'Where's my gun?'

The dust tornado undulated and respired nightmarishly, like something living. Sure enough the swirling grit took form around the outline of a man.

Montesco emerged. A flap of his scalp had lifted, painting one side of his face red. His left shoulder hung low and looked to be dislocated. The machine gun was back with the truck, no doubt demolished, and he appeared to be unarmed. But despite his injuries, he was moving capably, lips snarled with rage.

Behind Evan, Anjelina said, 'No.'

Her voice was trembling, breaking with emotion, her beauty receded behind a façade of horror, and for a moment Evan misunderstood her fear.

Then he shifted to see Reymundo holding his ARES, aiming with a shaking hand at his father. Evan angled toward Reymundo while holding the Dark Man in his peripheral vision.

The head wound bled like hell, turning El Moreno's face into a mask of crimson. With dust billowing behind him, he looked like he'd crawled out of hell.

Evan's mind raced, the Tenth Commandment on a manic loop.

Evan said, 'Anjelina, get behind the truck.'

She said, 'Reymundo, please –'

'Everyone – just – *quiet*!' Reymundo's features had changed, turning flat, almost lifeless – the blank face of trauma.

Anjelina looked at Evan. He gestured, and she eased back to safety.

He held a hand out to Reymundo, showing him an open palm. 'If you pull that trigger, you can never take it back.'

'I don't want to take it back.' Reymundo's teeth were clenched, his face quivering. 'A lifetime. *My* lifetime. Hour after hour being terrorized by him.'

Thirty yards away the Dark Man halted in the center of the road, glowering at the trio. His bloody lips moved. 'Hour after hour trying to shape you into a man. And look at you. Look at you now. Still a scared and useless little –'

Reymundo's upper lip peeled back, his grip firming.

Evan stepped in front of him. 'Wait, just –'

Reymundo fired into Evan's chest.

58. All the Troubles and Promise of the World

Evan felt the rib break, a snap he sensed all the way down to his feet.

He looked down.

The shirt had bunched around the bullet.

He was clutching the point of impact, left side three inches down from the breast.

Fatal placement.

He felt his knee buckle, but he firmed it, keeping his feet.

From behind the truck, Anjelina was screaming.

Reymundo stared at him in horror, his mouth agape, the ARES dangling loosely in his hand. 'I didn't . . . didn't mean to . . .'

Evan's hand rolled away from his chest.

On the flat of his palm, a flattened .45 Auto slug, still hot, its end mushroomed from impact with the shirt he'd asked Tommy to supply.

Its fabric woven from the same carbon nanotubes used to make flexible body armor.

He'd known it was lab-tested and highly effective against low-caliber rounds.

He'd had no idea it could possibly hurt this much.

Thank God he'd reloaded the ARES with conventional hollow points; one of the Honey Badgers would've bored straight through his torso.

He coughed, felt it through his entire skeleton. Pain was

good. Pain told him he was still alive. No pain was not good. No pain meant he was dead.

The round tumbled from his hand, plinking down into the dirt at his feet. He tried to take a breath, but his intercostals weren't having it.

Reymundo was poleaxed, his expression migrating to sheer wonder, as if he'd just witnessed something from the pages of a comic book.

Evan managed to lift his right hand and strip the gun away before Reymundo could do any more harm with it.

Reymundo's eyes shifted to look over Evan's shoulder, his dark pupils dilating suddenly. Adrenaline dump.

Fear.

Evan dropped him onto the ground, a heel strike to the sternum, then dove at a forty-five-degree angle off the mark. Somersaulting over his shoulder, pain screaming through his rib cage, he felt the wake of a bullet skim up his spine, sensed the heat and the riffle of the slipstream. Heard the second crack as he finished the rotation, second bullet sailing overhead. Landing flat on his back, his head to the threat, aiming the ARES behind him.

The sight picture was upside down.

Montesco holding a Glock 19 in an impressive modified Weaver stance.

He'd fired twice for a double tap, and the slide had kicked back, interfering with his target acquisition. He needed a split-second recalibration to reset, to gauge Evan's new position and low profile, to determine whether Evan had been hit as he appeared to be.

But Montesco didn't have a split second.

As Jack used to say, *The gun runs just as well upside down.*

Evan pressed trigger, stitching the Dark Man from crotch

to throat, six rounds into the torso, the seventh through the bridge of the nose.

Montesco remained on his feet for a moment, standing like a zombie.

Then he toppled.

Evan let his senses flood back in. A sumptuous array of pains. Taste of dirt and blood. The padding of Anjelina's footfalls somewhere behind him and then the sound of her sobbing with relief.

He rolled himself onto his boots with a groan and looked at them, clutching each other there in the road, dirty faces burnished by the midday sun. Where she'd torn her shirt, her belly protruded.

She was holding Reymundo's cheek to her chest and staring up at Evan, and he just looked at them there, a wildly imperfect family of almost three with all the troubles and promise of the world before them.

She must have sensed something in his expression because she said, 'What?'

He rolled his bottom lip between his teeth, spit once to clear the taste of dirt. 'Nothing.'

He started the long walk to the meet point.

A few seconds later, he heard them rise to follow.

59. Homecoming

Evan couldn't believe it when he saw the men screech up in the Jeep Wrangler.

Special Ed and Kiki spilling out from either door, Kiki tripping and nearly rolling onto his rotund belly. They ran to Anjelina.

And embraced her.

They pulled apart, Kiki kissing her hand with avuncular warmth. 'You scared the shit out of your father, *niña*.'

'Outta you, too,' Eduardo said to Kiki. 'Look at you, all crying and shit.'

'I'm not crying. Just got grit in my eye.'

Evan said, 'Aragón promised to send his best men.'

Kiki threw his arms wide. 'Here we are.'

'I'm going to have to talk to him about quality control.'

The men smirked.

Reymundo stepped forward, offering his hand. 'I'm R—'

'Not yet, motherfucker,' Eduardo said, turning to indicate the Jeep. 'You ride in the back.'

Evan hobbled toward the Wrangler, stooped to favor his left side.

'Someone needs to go back to the estate to check on the women,' Anjelina said. 'The captives.'

Special Ed said, 'Once we're closer to the border, we'll call in the *federales*, tell 'em it's safe.'

'And the lion,' Evan said. 'They need to take care of him, too.'

'A lion.' Special Ed shook his head. 'Fucking cartel.'

Eduardo and Kiki rode up front, Evan behind them with Anjelina, Reymundo crammed in the far back. They eased off the shoulder of the highway, aiming north for America.

'We was talking about gaydar,' Eduardo said. 'It's like "gay" crossed with "radar."'

Evan said, 'You don't say.'

'We was playing a driving game. Seeing if Special K here has the gaydar, you know? Looking at people we pass.'

'He is fascinated by this,' Kiki said. 'Perhaps *too* fascinated.'

From the rear, Reymundo peered forward, head swiveling side to side. It seemed the kind of conversation he'd not been privy to. His arm was draped over the seat back, he and Anjelina holding hands.

'And who he thinks is hot, you know,' Eduardo said. 'Turns out it's hard to predict.' He jerked his head to indicate Evan behind him. 'How 'bout *güero cabrón* back here? He your type?'

Kiki turned around to assess Evan, mustache sagging as he frowned thoughtfully. 'Nah,' he said. 'He's just an ordinary guy. Not too handsome.'

Once they crossed the border, Anjelina asked that they stop at a motel so she could clean up before returning home. They were covered with grime, sweat, and blood, the price of two rooms well worth it even if she weren't pregnant and in need of a rest after the day's ordeals.

In the presence of Anjelina, Kiki and Special Ed seemed to have evolved from murderous henchmen to nursemaids, running out to bring them clean clothes. Evan emerged from his room wearing stiff blue Wranglers, rattlesnake boots, a hammered-gold oval belt buckle, and a fitted black-and-gold western shirt with Caballero cuffs and embroidered leather yokes.

The men waited in the parking lot, leaning against the front of the Jeep, stifling laughter.

'*Ése* looks like one of them Village People,' Eduardo said.

Evan scowled and banged on the neighboring room's door. 'Let's get going.'

His ribs ached with every inhalation, his forehead still bled sporadically, his wrist was swollen, and he'd be unable to fish the majority of the splinters from the side of his neck until he got home to his surgical tweezers and a magnifying mirror.

He knocked again, and Reymundo stuck his head out. He was freshly showered, his dark curls wet, and he looked more handsome than he had any right to be in the same outfit that made Evan look like a gigolo or an extra in a third-rate version of *Oklahoma!* 'She wants to see you.'

'Me?'

'Yes.' Reymundo emerged, gave Special Ed and Kiki a wide berth, and climbed into the rear of the Jeep through the trunk.

Evan entered the room.

Anjelina was lying on the bed, soles planted, knees turned inward, arms crossed at her chest in a hug.

Constructive Rest Pose.

She was staring at the ceiling. 'I'm scared.'

Evan said, 'Okay.'

'How can I face everyone? After what I've done? My *papá*?'

'A lot of people have done a lot worse.'

'It doesn't feel that way.'

'It never does.'

'I don't know what I'll do. Who I'll be.'

'Figure out the second and you'll answer the first,' Evan said. 'Then you'll know what you need to apologize for. What you shouldn't apologize for. What responsibilities you should shoulder. And what freedoms you deserve.'

'Do you know all that?' she asked. 'For yourself?'

'No.'

'I can't live there anymore,' she said. 'In Eden.'

Evan said, 'Okay.'

She looked at him, eyes brimming. Then she took note of his outfit and laughed. 'What have they *done* to you?'

The more sullen he looked, the more she laughed, and then finally he looked down shyly, shook his head, and gave her the grin she'd been pushing for.

She eased out of bed cradling her stomach with the shelf of her forearm.

He held the door for her.

They were out in droves.

All the people of Eden, lining the street of the brief downtown, waving and showing off flowers and signs welcoming Anjelina home.

Standing on sidewalks, holding hands and holding babies.

The electronic scoreboard at the high school read RAT-TLERS CELEBRATE ANJELINA URREA'S SAFE RETURN!

Evan had no idea what to make of it. Nothing in his personal history came close to a reference point for an impromptu parade like this.

Throngs of folks in front of the coffee shop, the taquería, hoisting mugs and cups of horchata in toasts. There were Hortensia and Arnulfo, his face mottled purple-yellow with fading bruises. The barbers paused in mid-haircut along with their clients, who stood in rippling plastic capes, heads half shorn, smiling with delight and relief.

The two stoplights, mercifully, were green.

434

Anjelina waved and waved and made tiny exclamations beneath her breath.

She sobbed quietly all the way to her family compound.

Evan remembered arriving at these razor-topped walls for the first time, seven days and a lifetime ago.

Special Ed had called ahead and made arrangements for Evan. Once they dropped Anjelina off at her front step, he'd drive Evan immediately to the airstrip, where Aragón's plane would fly him home.

The PMCs had laid the gate open and formed a neat welcoming formation, the Jeep rolling through their midst with the mock formality of a honeymoon limousine's departure. The men offered a foil to the townsfolk – courteous, professional, and brisk.

The Jeep rumbled across the rough terrain, arrived in front of the suburban house with its white picket fence. Evan felt a pull in his chest, a sense of homecoming, though it was not a homecoming for him or even Anjelina.

Eduardo parked in front of the little gate.

They all got out.

The front door of the house was open. Through the screen door, Evan could make out Aragón's and Belicia's shadowy outlines, waiting for their daughter across the threshold.

Reymundo said, 'I'm gonna wait out here.'

Special Ed said, 'I don't fucking blame you.'

Anjelina stood at the edge of the picture-perfect lawn, gathering herself, hands pressed to her stomach for support or comfort.

She moved through the prop of a white gate, heading down the walk to her childhood house.

Evan sensed the shadows in the foyer shift, Aragón's arm moving across Belicia's shoulders, Belicia curling into his side.

Anjelina got a few steps further. Then hesitated.

She looked back.

Then she was running toward them – no, toward Evan. She threw her arms around his neck, buried her face in his shoulder, and squeezed him hard.

He held her.

It felt natural. He sensed a kind of longing he was unfamiliar with, a desire to stay here in this place, to freeze this moment in time before everything blew open once more into countless complications. She was a child and a soon-to-be mother at the same time, and she held him with a kind of familial need and gratitude that he'd never known outside of Joey.

The screen door creaked open to receive her.

Anjelina tore herself away from Evan and walked to her house.

This time she didn't look back.

While the pilot ran a few last-minute checks on the Cirrus Vision jet, Evan waited outside and breathed the arid South Texas air, tasting mesquite and sage. He'd cuffed his sleeves and untucked the shirt and felt slightly less ridiculous in the cowboy wear.

The pilot called over to him, and Evan started to board when he heard a horn bleating.

Aragón commanding the Jeep, flying toward them.

He hopped out, meeting Evan at the bottom of the unfolded airstair. He set his hands on Evan's shoulders and regarded him. Evan regarded him right back.

Those big, noble features. Thick, dark hair threaded with gray. And his eyes, warm and alive and textured with the things he'd seen and done.

It was incredibly intimate, the act of looking into another man's eyes.

'Señor Nowhere Man,' Aragón said. 'No one measures up to a myth. But you come close.'

'Remember,' Evan said. 'She's not perfect. She's a kid.'

'None of us are perfect,' Aragón said. 'You and I least of all.'

'Can you make it right?'

'I have to.' Aragón extended his hand. 'Until next time.'

Evan stared at his proffered hand. 'Are we . . . ?'

He caught himself, unsure of what he wanted to ask.

'Yes,' Aragón said. 'I will be your friend. And you will be mine.'

He took Evan's hand, pulled him into a one-armed embrace. It made Evan's broken rib sing with pain, but somehow he didn't mind.

They pulled away, Aragón taking him in with a final look. He nodded at the plane. 'Keep the window shades open,' he said. 'Enjoy the view.'

Then he walked away, back to the truck, his family, the many large and small wrongs he had to set right.

Evan boarded the plane alone.

60. The Smashed White Gumdrop

After setting down at the private airport in Santa Monica, Evan walked a mile and a half to where he'd left his own Ford F-150 in the last Westside residential neighborhood that didn't require parking permits.

Grateful for the spare clothes he kept in the truck vaults, he changed out of his mariachi costume. If he showed up to his next stop in that outfit, he'd never hear the end of it.

He did not drive home.

Instead he drove to Westwood.

Found the apartment building, went straight to the second floor, and knocked.

She answered.

Same glum expression. Flannel shirt over her worn Hello Kitty with an AK-47 T-shirt. A slightly more feminine version of the cargo pants he wore.

She scanned him.

He felt a trickle down his cheek and realized that the gash in his forehead had opened up again. His neck was glistening, the embedded shrapnel giving off a silvery burn. He was hunched to the side, protecting the broken rib, his left hand pronated to relieve pressure until he could get the wrist wrapped.

For once she had no ready remark.

Her expression migrated to concern. He read in her face that she understood that his coming home, his coming here, meant that the mission was over.

She stepped back, opening the door.

He hobbled in, bone-tired. Climbing the stairs had cost him a bit.

It took some effort for him to lower himself to sit against the wall next to the dog bed. Sensing the seriousness of the situation, Dog the dog lifted his head, gave him a nuzzle, and then returned to his croissant-shaped slumber.

Joey plopped down in the gamer chair inside her workstation. She felt safe in there, protected.

She faced him through the gap in the circular desk.

He said, 'What do you want me to understand?'

She pulled a Red Vine from the ever-present bucket and chewed off a length, skipping her front teeth and going straight to her molars. Washed it down with Dr Pepper. Flipped her hair over to show off that shaved strip on the right side. The emerald of her eyes, brighter than usual, seemed to be burning.

She said, 'Really?'

'Really.'

She chewed some more. Thought about it. Gathering herself. Then:

'When I went into the system, I had nothing, right? You know that kind of nothing. Like not-one-pair-of-socks-without-a-hole nothing. Like no-soap-for-your-shower nothing. And people – grown-ups mostly, but kids, too – just treated you however. Used you. And this one year, a week after Christmas, someone from a church dropped off a gingerbread house. It was all stale, right? And the kids, we got to choose one piece to break off and eat. But it went by age. And I was the youngest. New in the house, the last stained cot in the corner. And so I chose last. And all that was left was the smashed white gumdrop. And it sucked. It fucking sucked. The one thing we had to look forward to in, like, a *year*, and I got the worst piece. Didn't even have any flavor. And anything else that came up? Like, *ever*? I never picked first. No one ever picked me first. I was never special. I never got to just – *fuck, fuck* – do what *I* wanted to do. Getting pulled out for the Program. Going to Switzerland. Even coming here. All of it. I never chose any of it. And now all I want to do is go on a road trip with my big bad-ass lion-hunting dog, and I am trained in more martial arts than I can name, and rapists – like, like – *they* walk fast and don't turn around when *I'm* behind *them* in an alley, and I'm capable, X. I'm capable. And I'm special. I am. And I want to do this so, so bad, but I can't do it if you'll be mad at me. I'll just feel so awful and guilty but if I stay I'll feel so awful and resentful and I don't know what to do. But I know I can do this if you'll let me. No – if you *happily* let me. I can take care of myself. I'm special, X. I'm *special*, okay? I *am* special. And I'm worth it.'

She finally stopped, rocking forward in her chair, smearing at her cheeks with the heels of her hands.

'You're right,' Evan said.

She looked up distrustfully. Her tiny voice, the one that broke his heart a dozen different ways. 'I am?'

'Yeah,' he said. 'Every single way you're worth it.'

She lowered her face into her palms and wept.

61. Fuck It

Evan stopped at the pet store on his way home. It stank of birds and stagnant fish tanks. He found the section in the back where aquarium pebbles hung on metal prongs, arranged by color.

He picked a packet of soothing cobalt blue.

Got halfway to checkout.

Then went back.

With a sigh he put the packet back and chose rainbow instead.

Riding next to Lorilee on the elevator, Evan tried to straighten up so as not to draw attention to his broken rib. He stayed in the corner, hiding the slivers studding the side of his neck and pretending to scratch his forehead with his functional hand to hide the gash.

Prattling on about a recent failed date, Lorilee stopped with a punctuating exhalation. When Evan didn't inquire, she gave another pained moan, this one slightly louder.

'What?' he finally asked flatly.

'It's just been *so much*,' she said. 'I've been holding a lot of stress in my shoulders.'

Evan said, 'Me, too.'

The penthouse was suffused with the golden hues of Angeleno dusk, which turned every surface gold-plated.

The front door sealed behind him with a weighty thump, the silence wrapping itself around him. No smell of migas, no audience with a *padrino* in the living room, no pregnant young woman requiring care.

No Joey.

His walls of glass didn't look west, but the sunset colored the visible sky, bruised mauve, the color of the underskirts of a Toulouse-Lautrec whore.

Evan walked over to Vera III where she rested on the kitchen island, unmoored in her salad bowl. Pulled the packet of glass pebbles from his pocket and spilled them in around her.

A rainbow array.

All the everything.

He set her upright with great care.

'You and me,' he said.

She looked underwhelmed.

The living wall had sprouted its first signs of life, seedlings pushing out like fine hairs.

That pleased him.

No one had answered his knock at 12B; he assumed that Mia had taken Peter out for one of their evening drives along PCH. Imagining her on the surgeon's table left him with a feeling of helplessness unmatched since childhood. His skills were useless. No amount of planning or sacrifice would make any difference.

It would all come down to fate and the scalpel.

Evan stared at the freezer room and its rows of vodka bottles. All anyone had talked about this whole damn mission was alcohol, and he was sick of it.

He turned away, moving through the great room, padding toward the hall.

Paused in a draft of air-conditioning, the disco ball hanging overhead.

There was a light switch on the wall at his side. He clicked it.

The disco ball spun into motion, throwing jewels every which way, bringing the hard surfaces to life with dizzying motion. At his feet lay the Velcro suits that Joey and Peter had sloughed off.

He studied them for a moment. Then picked up the biggest one, loosened the straps, and donned it.

He felt absurd, more absurd than he had wearing the cowboy getup the Special boys had foisted on him. But he stood there in the puffy suit, glittering lights playing across him.

His rib hurt like hell, and he had a headache, but he decided –

'Fuck it.'

He took a two-step running start and flung himself at the wall sideways in a half flip.

He smacked the wall and stuck. Head lower than his feet, his body like an accent mark.

The pain subsided with a few breaths, and he hung there Velcroed onto the wall, staring out at the dying light of day from an entirely different vantage.

It was glorious.

62. Until

The waiting room at the surgical suite was filled with a dozen weary souls, gray faces and bitten nails. Mia was there, wan and exhausted, along with Peter, Uncle Wally, and Aunt Janet, who had inexplicably brought a picnic basket though it was 6:00 A.M.

Mia looked awful, eyes swollen with sleeplessness, her hair stiff and brittle. In anticipation of the surgery, she'd had to lather her locks with antibacterial shampoo, which had washed the life right out of them.

The small crew had commandeered a corner of the waiting room, Evan sitting among them as if he belonged. Mia had retreated within herself, Peter was listless at Evan's side, Wally barely holding himself together. Janet kept up a stream of perky chatter despite the fact that no one else was participating.

A half hour in, Joey showed up with a gas-station bouquet of flowers. Only a miracle or a tragedy could drag her out of bed this early, and Evan wasn't sure which this would prove to be.

She gave the sunflowers to Mia, wished her the best, said her hellos, then signaled to Evan that she wanted to get going. Joey was jittery; she'd hated hospitals ever since her aunt who was like a mother to her – her maunt – had died when she was young. 'Walk me out?'

Evan nodded.

Before going, Joey crouched before Peter and placed her hands on his knees. Even now Peter perked up; Joey was a source of endless fascination to him.

'I hate hospitals,' he told her. 'My dad was in the hospital before.'

'Hospitals are also where people go to get well,' Joey said.

Peter appeared unconvinced. Joey looked down, bit her lip, searching for words. 'I didn't have much family growing up,' she said quietly, 'unlike you. But I had a maunt who I loved very much. And you know what she used to tell me?'

'What?'

'That I was one of the magical people. And she knew. 'Cuz she always did. And I want to tell you something, Peter. You're one of the magical people, too.'

He brightened, blinking back his delight. Then hugged her around her neck.

Joey started out, Evan at her side down the hall.

Evan said, 'What about me?'

'You?' Joey said. '*Definitely* not one of the magical people.' She made a fist, pressed it into his shoulder, and pushed him off balance. Then she grinned.

She'd bought a new truck, the Ford P758, which looked like Evan's F-150 if someone had put it through the dryer and shrunk it down. The back was loaded up, passenger window down. Dog the dog's big head stuck out, tongue lolling, big smile.

Evan halted. 'You're leaving straight from here?'

'Yup.'

'Still don't know where you're going?'

'Nope.'

They stared at each other awkwardly.

'Welp,' she said. 'Bye.'

'Bye.'

He started away.

'Wait.'

He turned.

'Okay, *fine*,' she said. 'I'll let you give me *one piece* of advice.'

'I didn't ask.'

'Yeah, but you know you want to.'

He considered. 'When you come into a situation, don't want anything. Don't want approval. Don't want to scare people. Don't want anyone to like you. Don't need to prove anything to them or make them angry. Then you can see what's really happening.'

She scooped her hair behind her ears, nodded nervously, then nodded again. 'Okay, right. And if I need you, I can always call 1-855-2-NOWHERE.'

Evan said, 'It's not a helpline.'

'Shut up,' she said. 'It is for me.'

She was still grinning when she pulled out.

At seven o'clock a nurse arrived to give Mia a five-minute warning before taking her back for prep. She received the news stoically, Evan, Janet, and Peter looking on.

Wally had already hit his limit. 'Listen,' he said after the nurse withdrew. 'It's an eight-hour surgery, and I don't want to wait here. I mean . . .' Tears were running down his face, which he and everyone else pretended to ignore. 'I'll just be in the cafeteria reviewing my cases.'

Peter had stopped talking, smashing his flattened hands together between his knees.

'I understand,' Mia said, planting a kiss on Wally's cheek.

'I'll stay with Peter,' Janet said.

Wally lumbered out, head lowered, shoulders shaking.

Evan squatted before Mia, rested his hands on her knees. She remained deep inside herself, curled on the seat, breathing. After a few minutes, the nurse came up at their side and waited patiently to take Mia back.

Mia looked at Evan. 'Remember what we talked about.'

He said, 'I will.'

'I just have to get on the table. Let them put the needle in my arm.'

'That's it,' Evan said. 'See you on the other side.'

'Janet will call you when it's over.'

He noted that she didn't say that she herself would call when it was over.

The nurse led Mia back. Evan ruffled Peter's hair. And started out.

Halfway down the hall, he heard the pounding of tiny footsteps.

'Evan Smoak!'

He turned around. Peter was standing there, angry little face, fists clenched at his sides.

Evan's throat was dry. He swallowed.

He said, 'Do you need my help?'

Peter's face was fighting with itself. He forced out words. 'A girl in my class, she had cancer. Her hair fell out, and then she left school and she didn't come back again.'

Evan just looked at him.

'I don't want to talk about it,' Peter said.

Evan said, 'Okay.'

'I want to see my mom in there. Before she goes in. And Uncle Wally's all like too sad and doesn't want to cry in front of me. And Aunt Janet talks too much. So . . .'

Evan waited.

'Will you go in with me?'

Evan said, 'Yes.'

They walked back to the waiting room. Janet had buried herself in the picnic basket. She popped up as if emerging from a burrow. 'Oh. I was just going to run down and check on Wally. Ask the nice lady at the desk. She said she'd take you both in.'

Evan went over with Peter and asked the nice lady.

She led them in.

Mia was in a curtained section in pre-op. Already in a gown, her unruly hair pushed back, the surgeon's initials written in Magic Marker on the left side of her forehead at the hairline.

Without hesitating Peter climbed into the hospital bed and curled into her. 'Hi, Mama.'

'Hi, little man.' She stroked his hair. 'Look. It's obvious I'm your biggest fan, right? The thing is, it's not because of how you act or what you do or what your grades are, okay?'

His face was below her chin, and she turned away so he wouldn't see the tears dotting her gown.

'I don't care what you *do*. It's who you *are* that I love, that I'm proud of. And no matter what happens' – a hitch in her voice, but she caught it – 'when you grow up, you don't ever have to be sad that I didn't know how spectacular you turned out. I already do. I already know how amazing you were in high school and in college and how great your girlfriend is – or boyfriend.'

'*Mom*,' Peter said. But he was crying.

'And your job. And your kids. How wonderful they are, too. I know it all already, okay?'

'Okay, Mama.'

'I need you to know that I see you fully. And that means everything you will ever be. I see that, too. All of it.'

She closed her eyes, tears leaking, and kissed the top of his head, breathing in his scent deep.

She let go.

Peter slid off the bed.

Walked back out to the waiting area, Evan trailing him.

Peter hopped up onto a cushioned chair.

Evan sat beside him.

They stared at the electronic board showing patient ID numbers and status.

'How long can we stay?' Peter asked.

'How long do you want to stay?'

'Until,' Peter said.

Evan gave a nod.

On the electronic board, Mia's ID number moved from one column to the next.

Peter's breathing quickened a bit.

Evan reached over, turned his hand palm up, and set it on the armrest between them.

Peter took it.

The Hunt for X

Victoria Donahue-Carr was two-thirds into her morning swim when she sensed the vibration of footsteps along the tile. The indoor pool had been installed in the west terrace in 1933 by Roosevelt so he could exercise his polio-riddled muscles. With its arched ceiling, decadent rows of elevated half-moon windows, and scenic murals of Caribbean sailboats commissioned by JFK, it had an Old World grandeur that helped motivate her morning workouts. Disused since Tricky Dick had drained it to make room for press briefings, it had languished until she'd restored it to its former glory.

One of the many updates to the White House that had required a woman's touch.

She finished breaststroking to the wall, pulled herself up, and snapped off her goggles. She hated to be disturbed here; it always meant bad news.

Her dread intensified when she saw the woman waiting patiently at the end, arms crossed.

Special Agent in Charge Naomi Templeton, the closest thing to a personal liaison Victoria had in the Secret Service.

Templeton wore an ill-fitting suit, her large shoulders barely constrained by the fabric. Her blond hair was cut bluntly as always, a strip-mall haircut that seemed to complement her tough, handsome features. She was one of those women, Victoria had always thought, who was one makeover away from being a jaw-dropper.

'I'm sorry to disturb you, Madam President.'

'No,' Victoria said. 'You're not.'

'I suppose I'm not. It *is* about him.'

'I see.'

'Remember when I briefed you about that massacre at the cartel estate in Guaridón? The one that bore his fingerprints?'

'You mean the one that violated the terms of his pardon?'

'The very one. We've turned up our surveillance efforts. I got an alert from NSA forty-five minutes ago. Facial recognition was scrambled – he seems to have some kind of sartorial camouflage that disguises the nodal points –'

'Did you say *sartorial camouflage*?'

'I'm afraid I did. As I said, we don't have clear facial image, but we hit the cherries on biometric gait recognition for someone entering the Cedars-Sinai Medical Center yesterday.'

'Medical Center? Is he ill?'

'We're unsure what he was there for. We are looking into patient records, hitting the obvious complications.'

'Hmm.' Victoria leaned back, let the water ripple around her, hoping she would find it soothing. 'How sure are you?'

'Ninety-seven point one-four-three percent.'

That was a very Naomi Templeton answer.

'So it's back on, then,' Victoria said. 'The hunt for X.'

Naomi gave a curt nod.

'Very well, then,' Victoria said. 'Take him down.'

She sank back into the water. Stayed under until the watery shape of Naomi Templeton receded. The president kicked off the wall and continued her workout.

Somehow it felt less relaxing than before.

Acknowledgments

It takes a village to raise an assassin.

Michael 'Borski' Borohovski kept Joey ahead of the game (and everyone else) when it came to intrusion engineering.

Philip Eisner was kind enough to lend his narrative elegance and muscle.

Marge and Alfred Hurwitz offered generational wisdom.

Dr Melissa Hurwitz and Dr Bret Nelson were willing to violate their Hippocratic Oaths on Evan's behalf, instructing him on how most effectively to do harm.

Maureen Sugden saw to it that X crossed his t's and dotted his i's in keeping with the Second Commandment.

Kurata Tadashi made sure the Nowhere Man aimed straight and true.

An extra serving of gratitude goes to Luis Alberto Urrea, a national treasure of an author, whose wise words and keen observations helped me approach some of the places and people of this book with the complexity and accuracy they deserved. All mistakes and missteps are mine.

When Orphan X needed help, he called:

– Keith Kahla, Andrew Martin, Sally Richardson, Don Weisberg, Jennifer Enderlin, Alice Pfeifer, Hector DeJean, Paul Hochman, Kelley Ragland, and Martin Quinn of Minotaur Books.

– Rowland White, Louise Moore, Laura Nicol, Ruth

Atkins, Christina Ellicott, Jon Kennedy, and Katie Williams of Michael Joseph/Penguin Group UK.

– Lisa Erbach Vance of the Aaron Priest Agency.

– Caspian Dennis of the Abner Stein Agency.

– Stephen F. Breimer of Bercheen Feldman Breimer Silver & Thompson.

– Dana Kaye, Julia Borcherts, Hailey Dezort, and Nicole Leimbach of Kaye Publicity.

– Simba, Cairo, and Zuma of Rhodesia.

Lastly, I wish to acknowledge Delinah Raya and Natalie Corinne. Without their support, humor, patience, insight, and grace, I would not have navigated through these past four years intact.